Praise for Charlotte Betts:

'A colourful story with a richly-drawn backdrop …
a wonderful debut novel'
Carole Matthews

'Romantic, engaging and hugely satisfying.
This is one of those novels that makes you feel
like you've travelled back in time'
Katie Fforde

'A vivid tale of love in a time of plague and prejudice'
Katherine Webb

'If you are looking for a cracking good story and to be
transported to another age, you really can't beat this'
Deborah Swift

'A thoroughly enjoyable read which will keep you
enthralled until the very last page'
Jean Fullerton

Charlotte Betts began her working life as a fashion designer in London. A career followed in interior design, property management and lettings. Always a bookworm, Charlotte discovered her passion for writing after her three children and two step-children had grown up.

Her debut novel, *The Apothecary's Daughter*, won the YouWriteOn Book of the Year Award in 2010 and the Joan Hessayon Award for New Writers. It was shortlisted for the Best Historical Read at the Festival of Romance in 2011 and won the coveted Romantic Novelists' Association's Historical Romantic Novel RoNA award in 2013. Her second novel, *The Painter's Apprentice*, was also shortlisted for Best Historical Read at the Festival of Romance in 2012 and the RoNA award in 2014. *The Spice Merchant's Wife* won the Festival of Romance's Best Historical Read award in 2013 and was shortlisted for the Romantic Novelists' Association's Historical Romantic Novel RoNA award in 2015.

Charlotte lives with her husband in a cottage in the woods on the Hampshire/Berkshire border.

Visit her website at www.charlottebetts.com and follow her on twitter @CharlotteBetts1

By Charlotte Betts:

The Apothecary's Daughter
The Painter's Apprentice
The Spice Merchant's Wife
The Milliner's Daughter (e only)
The Chateau by the Lake
Christmas at Quill Court (e only)
The House in Quill Court
The Dressmaker's Secret
The Palace of Lost Dreams

The
Palace of
Lost Dreams

Charlotte Betts

piatkus

PIATKUS

First published in Great Britain in 2018 by Piatkus
This paperback edition published in 2018 by Piatkus

1 3 5 7 9 10 8 6 4 2

Copyright © 2018 Charlotte Betts

The moral right of the author has been asserted.

*All characters and events in this publication, other than those
clearly in the public domain, are fictitious and any resemblance
to real persons, living or dead, is purely coincidental.*

A CIP catalogue record for this book
is available from the British Library.

ISBN 978-0-349-41418-8

Printed and bound by CPI Group (UK) Ltd, Croydon, CR0 4YY

Papers used by Piatkus are from well-managed forests
and other responsible sources.

Piatkus
An imprint of
Little, Brown Book Group
Carmelite House
50 Victoria Embankment
London EC4Y 0DZ

An Hachette UK Company
www.hachette.co.uk

www.littlebrown.co.uk

For Howard and Ann

Chapter 1

1774

Hyderabad, India

The dawn chorus, a crescendo of rising chirrups, squawks and whistles, woke Bee as a glimmer of light infiltrated the folds of her mosquito net. Fists clenched, she listened intently for a moment but the sounds of shouting and weeping from behind Mother and Father's bedroom door had stopped. They had quarrelled every day during the past week and the servants had moved about the house like ghosts, their eyes turned to the ground, silently clearing away smashed plates and trying not to flinch as another door slammed.

Bee had attempted to remain unnoticed, too, and secreted herself in her favourite refuge, the massive peepul tree at the end of the garden. She'd been hiding amongst the great whispering leaves with her book when she'd first met Harry. Her eye had been caught by a flashing light coming from the overgrown garden next door. Peering out between the leaves, she saw a dark-haired boy sitting cross-legged on the ground. He was whittling a piece of wood, watched closely by a brown dog. The shiny blade of the knife twisted and turned as the boy worked, catching the sunlight and reflecting it towards her. She'd laughed and he'd looked up. Within moments he'd scrambled through the branches to join her.

Now, lifting a corner of the mosquito net, Bee peeped into the shadowy bedroom and saw that Madhu, her *ayah*, or nursemaid, still lay curled up on her mattress making snuffling sounds as she slept. Bee fumbled for the clothes she'd hidden under her pillow the previous night, along with a handful of *jaggery* purloined from the kitchen. It was impossible to resist and she popped one of the small brown pieces into her mouth, closing her eyes in contentment at the explosion of intense sweetness on her tongue.

Once dressed, she slid out of bed, her bare feet making no noise as she padded across the floor to her brother's bed. Ralph woke when she touched his fair hair and she lost no time in posting a morsel of *jaggery* between his lips to keep him quiet. This was the difficult bit. Ralph was only five, three years younger than herself, and couldn't be relied upon to remember that they were going on an adventure and mustn't wake the servants. Pressing a finger to her lips, she helped him out of bed.

A few minutes later they crept out of the bungalow into the grey dawn. They giggled as they tiptoed past the cook, who snored on his *charpai* on the veranda, and then ran hand-in-hand across the garden. Bee dragged a loose plank in the fence sideways until there was a gap wide enough for them to squeeze through.

Ralph scraped his shoulder on the splintered wood and started to squeal but Bee was too quick for him, pressing her palm over his mouth and shoving him backwards through the gap.

'It's not bleeding,' she whispered, examining the graze, 'and if you make a fuss they'll come for us. Here, have another sweetie.'

Ralph nodded, the welling tears disappearing as if by magic as his cheek bulged around the sugar lump.

Bee took his hand again and led him through the Residency grounds and out of the side gate. 'Harry said he'd wait for us by the river,' she said. 'He had something to do first.' She hoped he hadn't had second thoughts about taking a girl and her little brother with him on his quest.

By the time they reached the river the sky at the horizon was growing lighter.

'Where is he?' asked Ralph.

Bee looked along the river bank, squinting her eyes to see into the distance. An egret stood in the muddy shallows, wreathed in the white mist that coiled above the water but nothing else stirred. She shrugged, disappointed.

The melancholy cry of the call to prayer drifted over from the walled city on the opposite side of the river and Bee watched while the white mosques, palaces and monuments were brushed with gold by the first rays of the rising sun. Chattering monkeys gambolled and chased each other along the walls between the watchtowers.

Bored, Ralph poked a stick into a dark shape caught in the reeds.

Bee reeled back at the sudden sickly stench that filled her nostrils and snatched the stick away from him. 'Leave it!' she said, shuddering with distaste. 'It's a dead dog.'

Further along the bank, the British Residency was silhouetted against the sky, now streaked with a pink as vibrant as Madhu's *dupatta*. Then the egret stretched out its neck, unfolded its wings and lifted itself into the air as a figure loped towards them.

Bee smiled. Harry had come after all, his dog Bandit trotting along at his heels.

'Hello,' he said. 'We'd better hurry.' His face was so darkened by the sun and his *kurta* so crumpled and daubed with dirt, he might have been a native sweeper boy, especially as he spoke in Urdu, one of the many languages and dialects he'd picked up from different *ayahs*.

Just for a moment, Bee hesitated. He didn't offer any apology or excuse for being late. Perhaps Mother was right. She'd called Harry a 'little savage'. But it wasn't his fault if his mother had died and his father was too busy to look after him. Mother said it was a disgrace that the boy was ten years old and still hadn't been sent back to England to be schooled.

'Are you coming or not?' said Harry, frowning.

'Of course we are,' said Bee, following him as he marched off.

'Wait for me!' wailed Ralph, scurrying to keep up.

They hurried along the muddy foreshore of the river, past the pleasure gardens and country houses, until they reached a high wall.

'The Jahanara Mahal,' said Harry.

Bee had seen the palace before but never so close. She tipped back her head and looked up at the dozens of domes, minarets and towers clustered together in tiers, the pink granite walls glowing in the morning sun. 'I've never seen anything so pretty,' she said.

'Pretty?' Harry shook his head in disgust. 'It's a fort built in a good position to stop invaders crossing the river.'

'I still think it's pretty.'

He shrugged. 'I'm going to tell you a secret but you mustn't tell anyone else.'

'We won't.'

'My father's *syce* told me about a diamond called the Rose of Golconda. His father was working here when it was stolen. The palace guard chased and killed one of the thieves but the other got away and they never found the diamond. The thing is, I'm really good at finding things.' Harry's face was taut with determination. 'It must still be here somewhere! My father will be so proud of me if I find it.'

'I'm sure he will,' said Bee.

Harry set off along the perimeter wall until it disappeared into a thicket of vines and tangled thorn bushes. Bandit ran ahead, wagging his tail, and dived into the undergrowth.

Bee grasped Ralph's wrist and followed Harry as he ducked under the prickly branches. She stood up in the dappled shade and saw a low door set into the wall before her. Carved into the wood was a

4

strange creature. It had the fearsome head of a lion plus elephant's tusks, and the sinuous body beneath was that of a serpent. Despite the warmth, she shivered at the sight.

Harry heaved his shoulder against the door. There was a scraping sound and it opened inwards. He turned to his dog. 'Stay, Bandit!' he commanded. 'Come on then, Bee.'

Ralph's hand slid into his sister's when he saw the dark space open up before them. 'I don't like this,' he whispered.

Neither did Bee but she followed their friend, dragging Ralph behind her.

They were in a store room. Light filtered in through a barred window above. Harry opened another door and peered cautiously into a shadowy passageway, before striding off. Several times he stopped to climb onto a stone bench and peer through the *jali* screens set at the top of the walls.

'Look!' he whispered eventually, pulling Bee up to stand beside him.

She pressed her face to the fretwork and the chamber beyond came into view. It was one of the largest rooms she'd ever seen, with columns and arches soaring to the ceiling, all carved with lotus flowers. Every inch of the walls was painted in bright colours and the many alcoves were piled high with scarlet and gold cushions. A movement caught her eye and she saw that a servant, a girl barely older than herself, was scattering rose petals on the floor.

'What can you see?' said Ralph, tugging at Bee's skirt.

The girl started, a handful of crimson petals falling from her fist as she stared at the fretwork screen.

'Shut up, Ralph!' whispered Harry, stepping down from the bench.

They hurried onwards, creeping past the kitchens where already the aroma of wood smoke, *chapattis* and frying onions hung in the air. At last, Harry slid aside a lattice panel and they entered a small room.

Bee caught her breath and leaned closer to see that shimmering pieces of mother-of- pearl were inlaid all over the walls. 'It's beautiful!' she said.

'The Pearl Room,' said Harry. 'My father's *syce* says this might be where the thief was killed. He could have hidden the Rose of Golconda behind a secret panel before the guards caught him.'

Bee shuddered, studying the white marble floor for rusty bloodstains. She was relieved there weren't any.

'The diamond is at least the size of a pigeon's egg and it's pink,' said Harry. 'There's a curse on whoever steals it.'

Bee ran her fingers slowly over the panels, her tongue protruding slightly as she concentrated. She really hoped she'd be the one who found the diamond.

After about fifteen minutes Ralph had grown fidgety and bored.

Harry sighed. 'It's not here, is it?'

'I'm hungry,' whined Ralph.

'We ought to go,' said Bee, 'before we're missed. Mother will be cross if she can't find us.'

'No one will notice if I'm not there,' said Harry. 'I'll stay on.'

Bee folded back the *jali* screen at one of the windows to reveal a small courtyard with a pool and splashing fountain, where pigeons sipped and flapped their wings.

Ralph pushed her aside and stood on tiptoe to see. 'I want to go out,' he said, opening the door.

He kicked off his shoes and paddled in the marble rill edging the courtyard, singing a native song that Madhu had taught him.

The sun was already hot and Bee and Harry sat together on the side of the pool, wriggling their toes in the water. 'Won't you get caught if you stay here?' she asked. 'People will be getting up soon.'

He shrugged. 'I can look into most of the rooms from the service passage before I go in. If anyone finds me, I'll pretend to be a servant.'

Ralph stepped onto the side of the pool beside Bee and jumped into the water with a huge splash. Startled pigeons scattered into the air with a flurry of feathers.

'You beast!' she cried. 'My dress is all wet!'

Harry threw himself into the pool with a great belly-flop, making a tidal wave, and Ralph shrieked in delight. War had been declared. By the time the battle was over all three children were sopping wet and aching with laughter.

Bee wrung the water out of her thick blonde hair and watched the two boys tussling. Harry chased after Ralph, threatening to tickle him, until the little boy hid behind a giant pot filled with cascading flowers.

Harry shook his head vigorously, spraying Bee with drops of water, and gave her a brilliant smile. 'You know what, Bee Marchant,' he said, 'you're not at all bad – for a girl.'

Bee smiled back. The sun was probably freckling her nose but she didn't care. She'd never been so happy and promised herself to remember this day for the rest of her life.

Half an hour later Bee and Ralph slid through the gap in the fence and sauntered through the garden towards the bungalow.

Madhu ran down the veranda steps, her face streaming with tears. 'Where have you been, you wicked children? I thought a tiger had taken you, dragging you over the fence and into the fields.'

'We were in the peepul tree,' said Bee, fingers crossed behind her back.

'Did you not hear me calling you?'

'No. Sorry.'

'The memsahib is asking for you.' Madhu snatched hold of Ralph and roughly brushed dirt off his nightshirt. 'Hurry now!' The sun had steamed the water from their clothes but they were stained with river mud. Alternately kissing and scolding the children, she herded them into the bungalow.

Bee heard Mother's reprimanding tones even before they were

inside. A large trunk stood on the veranda and servants were hurrying back and forth carrying armfuls of clothes.

Madhu pushed the children into the hall and retreated to the safety of the nursery.

'There you are!' said Mother. She frowned at the sight of Ralph. 'Have you been playing in the garden in your night clothes?' She sighed. 'And, Beatrice, your face is filthy. Clearly your *ayah* has been neglecting her duties. Tell her to dress you both in something clean. And then wait in the nursery until I fetch you.'

'Yes, Mother.' Bee knew better than to argue and steered Ralph away. She stopped in the nursery doorway. Their cedar-wood chest was open and clothes and toys lay tumbled upon the floor.

'What's happening?' she asked as Madhu started to undress Ralph.

Sniffing, the *ayah* shook her head. 'You must ask the memsahib.'

Bee scratched crusts of dried mud off her ankles and listened to Mother's footsteps clipping backwards and forwards across the hall. Where was Father? She wanted to hear his booming laugh and for him to snatch her up and kiss her and ask her what his busy little Bee had been up to all day, flitting from one interesting thing to another.

Madhu dragged a clean dress over Bee's head, doing up the buttons with shaking fingers.

'You're hurting me!' said Bee, as the *ayah* jerked a comb through her knotted hair. Madhu never hurt her usually, not even when she'd been naughty.

A crash came from the hall and a high-pitched argument began between two of the servants. Mother's voice rose above the commotion as she railed at them both.

Madhu crouched on the floor and pulled her *dupatta* over her eyes. Ralph whimpered and buried his face in her neck, his thumb in his mouth. Madhu rocked him and sang a lullaby, the soothing rhythm broken only by her hiccoughing sobs.

Something was very wrong. Bee huddled against her nursemaid, waiting for something awful to happen.

She didn't have long to wait.

The door burst open. Mother appeared, her face white with anger. 'Get up at once, children! How many times do I have to tell you not to sit on the floor like the dirty natives?'

'But ...' Bee didn't have time to utter another word before Mother slapped her cheek. The girl gasped in outrage.

Madhu cried out.

Bee clung to her, inhaling her familiar and comforting scent of coconut oil, cardamom and warm skin.

'Don't you ever, *ever* argue with me again,' shrieked Mother, and then burst into noisy tears. 'As if I didn't have enough to contend with, my own children turn against me. Get outside!'

Glancing fearfully at her mistress, Madhu hurriedly shepherded her charges out of the nursery and down the front steps of the bungalow.

A driver waited beside a bullock cart laden with boxes and trunks.

'Quickly now!' said Mother, wiping her reddened eyes. 'We must be gone before your father returns.' She bundled a protesting Ralph into the cart and then snatched hold of Bee's wrist.

'But I don't want to go!' cried the girl, still clinging to her *ayah*.

Mother dragged Bee out of Madhu's arms and thrust her onto the seat next to Ralph. She ignored the driver's offered hand as if it were something diseased and scrambled up into the cart. 'Drive on!' she said, even before she'd sat down.

'Where are we going?' asked Bee.

'Home,' said Mother, as the cart lurched forwards. 'We're going home to England,' she said, 'the place I should never have left.'

'But Hyderabad is our home!' wailed Bee. She gripped the side of the cart and turned to look behind them.

Madhu, her beloved Madhu, wailed and pulled her hair, beating her forehead with her fists. She grew smaller and smaller as the cart jolted away until, at last, she disappeared from sight altogether.

Chapter 2

July 1797

Hampshire

The sound of carriage wheels rolling into the drive aroused me from my nap. Yawning, I eased myself off the chaise-longue, one hand supporting the mound of my stomach. Dr Mason had been very clear that, now I was in my sixth month, I must rest every day. Having a first baby at the advanced age of thirty-one was not something to be undertaken lightly. I stood to one side of the window and peered outside at the carriage. The coachman made me look again since he was dressed in a long white coat with a full skirt. He wore a red turban and his brown face was adorned by a dense black beard and moustaches. He opened the carriage door and a youngish man in a caped riding coat descended, who handed down a lady and a boy.

I hastily smoothed my hair as the doorbell rang and had composed myself by the time Annie opened the drawing-room door.

'There's a Mr and Mrs Clements to see you, ma'am.'

I pursed my lips. I didn't know the name but no doubt they were acquaintances of my husband. 'Please bring some tea and ask Mr Sinclair to join us. I daresay he's in the rose garden, as usual.'

A moment later, the Clementses entered.

'We're so pleased to have found you,' said Mrs Clements with a warm smile. 'Our hopes were quite dashed at first when we called at Holly Cottage and were told that Miss Beatrice Marchant had moved away.'

'But then a maid in one of the neighbouring properties told us that you'd married and moved here to Hill House,' said Mr Clements. 'We understand you are now Mrs Sinclair?'

'Indeed,' I said, glancing at my wedding ring. It still gave me a shock of pleasure to see it since I'd thought for so many years that I would remain a spinster. 'Would you like to take off your coats?' I was curious because the visitors wore heavy outer garments, far too thick for summer.

'Thank you, no,' said Mr Clements. He glanced fondly at the boy, who clutched a brown paper parcel. 'We've just arrived from Calcutta to take young William here to his new school and haven't yet acclimatised to the cold.'

'India! How interesting.' I wracked my brains but couldn't remember ever having heard of the Clementses. 'I apologise but have we met before?'

'Never,' said Mrs Clements, shaking her head. A curl of regrettably red hair escaped from her bonnet.

'I was born and lived in India, as a child,' I said. 'My father was employed by the East India Company and held a post at the Residency in Hyderabad. In fact, my brother works there now.'

'So he mentioned,' said Mr Clements.

'You've met him?'

'Indeed I have. I too am employed by the East India Company,' he said. 'I'll be taking up a new position at the Residency in Hyderabad next year. When your brother discovered I was coming home on leave first, he charged me to bring you a letter and a parcel.'

Charles, a red rosebud pinned to his old tweed coat, ambled into the drawing room then, closely followed by Annie with the tea tray.

I looked at his shoes and hoped he wouldn't drop mud onto the carpet, which had been taken outside and beaten that very morning. 'Allow me to introduce my husband,' I said. 'Charles, this is Mr and Mrs Clements and their son William. They have recently arrived from India, where Mr Clements is soon to take up a new post with the East India Company.'

'Always happy to meet my wife's friends,' said Charles, bowing to the visitors. He lowered himself into a chair and ran a hand through his silver hair. Some twenty-five years older than I, he still cut a fine figure, despite presenting himself in his gardening clothes.

'In fact, we haven't met before but Mr and Mrs Clements have brought me a letter from Ralph,' I said, as I poured the tea. I frowned slightly to see a fingerprint on the polished silver. Mother would never have tolerated that. I'd have to speak to Annie about it later.

Charles turned to Mr Clements. 'And how is the present situation there?'

'The French are causing a great deal of trouble.' He sighed. 'If they're not speedily overthrown they'll shake the British hold on India.'

Charles shook his head. 'Napoleon will never be content until he's taken over the entire world.'

'Not if we can help it,' said Mr Clements, puffing up his chest.

Mrs Clements whispered to her son, who was fidgeting beside her.

I smiled at the boy. 'I expect you'd like a piece of cake, William?'

The boy nodded and proffered the brown paper parcel. 'This is for you,' he said.

Mrs Clements opened her reticule and withdrew a letter. 'Mr Marchant asked us to wait while you read it,' she said, 'in case you wished to respond. Although, in the circumstances ...' She glanced at my swollen stomach and fell silent.

I reached for the letter. 'If you will excuse me?'

'Of course.' She sipped her tea.

I broke the seal and began to read.

My dear Bee,

Thank you for your last missive. I learned with sorrow that Mother had passed away but cannot help thinking it a merciful release for all of us. It has been eleven years since I returned to India but I am well aware that you have devoted your time since then to caring for her single-handed, to the probable detriment of your own happiness. If she had not become an invalid, I daresay you would be married with a brood of little ones by now.

I have some news of my own to impart and hope you will be pleased for me. I consider myself the luckiest of men to have married the sweetest girl alive! When I told her that you are now all alone in the world, she immediately said you must come and live with us. She and her family will welcome you with open arms and hearts. There is plenty of space here for you, either for an extended visit or to live permanently with us.

Mr and Mrs Clements have offered to escort you on their return to India and I have made all the financial arrangements for your journey, so you need not be anxious on that score.

I hope most sincerely that you will come. I wish for nothing more than to have my dear sister close to hand.

Affectionately yours,

Ralph

Postscript: I trust you will like the present. It was made by my wife. She hopes the colour will lift your spirits but, if it is not to your taste, will work another after you have chosen the silks.

I handed the letter to Charles, swallowing the lump in my throat. At least Ralph recognised that I'd made personal sacrifices in order to care for Mother.

'Very decent of your brother,' Charles said after he'd finished reading. 'Shows a proper respect for familial duty.' He patted my wrist. 'Completely unnecessary invitation now, of course.'

And too late, far too late, to rescue me from those lost years. 'It would appear that Ralph hasn't received my latest letter,' I told Mr and Mrs Clements. 'Two months after Mother's passing, I sent another informing him that I am now Mrs Charles Sinclair.'

'I'm sure your brother will be delighted to hear it,' said Mrs Clements.

'Indeed,' said Charles, beaming at Mr Clements, 'you'll be able to tell him that his sister is in my care now and that we expect a happy event before very long.'

'I shall write to Ralph myself,' I said, 'and I must send him a wedding present.'

'We sail from Southampton on the second of September,' said Mrs Clements. 'I'm disappointed not to have your company on the long journey but, since we'll almost pass your door, it would be no trouble to us to call here again on our way to the docks, if you'd like us to convey a letter to Hyderabad?'

'That's very obliging,' I said. 'I can be sure then the letter won't go astray and shall have time to embroider some bed linen for a wedding present.'

William nudged the brown paper parcel towards me and whispered, 'Aren't you going to open it?'

I smiled at the boy. 'Thank you for reminding me.' I untied the string and pulled aside the brown paper, gasping as a sea of rose-pink silk flooded out, spilling over my lap and pooling on the floor. 'Oh!' I breathed. 'Isn't it glorious?'

'It's very fine work in the Indian style,' said Mrs Clements, lifting up a corner of the shawl to examine it more closely. 'My brother-in-law owns a shop in Bond Street selling fancy goods of the highest calibre to ladies of discernment. This is exactly the quality I would expect to find in his establishment.'

I stared in delight at the embroidered peacocks, jasmine flowers and twining tendrils worked around the hem. 'I consider myself an accomplished needlewoman,' I said, 'but this is very special.'

Mr Clements rose to his feet. 'We must be on our way if we're to reach our destination before dark.'

After the Clementses had driven away, Charles returned to his beloved garden.

I draped the shawl around my shoulders. A hint of something spicy, cloves or coriander perhaps, mixed with attar of roses emanated from the silk. It saddened me to think that I would never return to India. All my childhood I'd longed to go back and dreamed sometimes of a fairy-tale palace glowing in the morning sun and of the brilliant smile of a dark-haired boy.

The misery of caring for a cantankerous hypochondriac, however, had eroded my spirit until I'd given up my dreams and simply existed from day to day. Mother had never once thanked me for my endless ministrations, taking pleasure only in finding fault. Eventually, I'd ceased listening to her complaints, fearful that I'd become so bitter I'd poison myself. Drop by drop, my youthful vitality had drained away. Mother had rarely allowed me to leave Holly Cottage, except to go to services at St Biddulph's and, one by one, my friends had married. By the time I was thirty I considered myself doomed to a life of spinsterhood and, without companions, my future was bleak.

Then Mother had begun to grow thin. Her skin turned yellow, except for two bright pink patches on her cheeks. She coughed blood. All her imaginary diseases had somehow become real, and one day she coughed herself into a spasm and died.

After the funeral, I returned alone to Holly Cottage and sat in the immaculately tidy but undeniably chilly parlour. I had no idea how to resume a life I had forgotten or how to forge a new one.

And then, a week later, Charles had called to see me, bringing flowers. He was a widower of the same generation as my parents, with whom I'd sometimes exchanged a few polite words after church. He explained that since his wife had died six months before, he found it hard to manage his household and, worse, was lonely. He wondered if I felt the same. I'd wept at his kind words, the flood-gates opening and allowing the pent-up misery of the previous years to flow. He'd patted my back and, when he asked me to marry him, I said yes.

And now I had the unimaginable joy of a baby to look forward to. Smiling, I rubbed my cheek against the silky shawl and breathed in the fragrance of attar of roses, together with the underlying scent of spices. The combination unlocked a door in my mind and I recalled Madhu taking me to the bazaar when I was a child.

I'd been overwhelmed by the array of exciting goods piled high on the stalls: gleaming copper pans, gold bangles, puppets, bright clothing and embroidered slippers with pointed toes. The strident shouts of the stallholders and the hullabaloo of bartering resounded in my ears as Madhu pulled me through the milling masses. Birds twittered in wooden cages and clouds of tobacco smoke floated up to the vaulted ceiling so far above. A wrinkled old man in a fez rubbed attar of roses on my arm as we passed, imploring us to buy the highest-quality perfume in Hyderabad, no, in all of India, for the cheapest price! Brushing him off like an irritating mosquito, Madhu led me away to see the pyramids of spices in glowing shades of ruby, russet, saffron and ochre. I had thought the bazaar the most wondrous place I'd ever seen.

For years after I arrived in cold, drab England, I'd longed to return to Hyderabad. And now here was Ralph's invitation. I placed one hand on my stomach as the baby stirred inside me, and smiled. If the invitation had come as soon as Mother had passed on, I'd have grasped the chance of an adventure. But now I had a new life. It wasn't perfect but a few months ago I could never have dreamed I might be granted the opportunity to have a husband and a child of my own. I was thankful indeed for my good fortune.

Chapter 3

I sighed as I changed to go to my stepdaughter's house for dinner. Arranging the silk shawl around my shoulders, I frowned critically at my reflection in the looking glass and decided I would do. The rose-pink shawl complemented my honey-coloured hair and gave me the necessary courage to face Alice.

Pretty Alice Babcock was the thorn in my side. Charles' daughter had the same large blue eyes and dark ringlets as her dead mother, whose portrait still hung in the study. I rested my hands on my swollen stomach and wished that Alice and I, both expecting babies, could have been friends. But she wouldn't forgive me for marrying her father and never thought to attach any blame to him for wishing to wed again barely six months after her mama had been placed in the cold ground.

Sighing, I picked up my bonnet, cast an eye over the bedroom to ensure I'd left it tidy before I went downstairs.

'You look delightful, Beatrice!' said Charles, waiting for me in the hall.

It was only a short walk through the village to the Babcocks' charming cottage and I stiffened my spine as we waited for our knock on the front door to be answered. For Charles' sake, I would make every attempt not to rise to Alice's barbed comments, I decided.

The maid, dressed in a soiled apron and with greasy hair falling out of her cap, led us down the narrow passage. Upstairs a child screamed with rage, the shrill sound reverberating through the entire cottage. There were scuffles and giggles above and several small faces peeped through the banister rails at us.

The curtains were half-closed in the parlour and I shuddered at the air of dust and neglect, the stale air. Faded flowers in greening water drooped their heads and shed brown petals onto the console table. I couldn't have borne to live in such a slovenly muddle.

Alice reclined on the sofa with a novel open on her knee. She made no attempt to rise but held out her dimpled arms to her father, who hurried to kiss her.

'How are you keeping, Alice?' I enquired, looking in vain for somewhere to sit that wasn't covered in a jumble of odds and ends. I moved aside an apple core and a crumpled handkerchief and perched on the edge of a wing chair.

'I'm bored,' she said. 'Henry doesn't understand how exceedingly tiring it is for me to keep house and look after four little ones all day while I'm increasing.' She frowned at me and levered herself upright. 'Wherever did you buy that shawl, Beatrice? Since we've been at war with France it's impossible to buy pretty things.' She sank back, sighing, and picked out a candied apricot from a box at her side.

She didn't offer to share them, which might partly explain why she'd grown so plump of late.

'Where's Henry?' asked Charles.

'He'll be here soon, I expect,' said Alice. 'Now that you only work a few days a month in the business, Papa, Henry is rarely at home and I'm left to my own devices much of the time.'

I remembered how hard, a few months ago, Alice had petitioned her father to retire and allow her husband to become managing partner in the wine merchant's business Charles had founded.

'Henry needs to make his own decisions without me breathing over his shoulder,' said my husband. 'Besides, there's plenty for me to do in the garden at Hill House. I can't expect poor old Tom to look after it properly any more.'

'The garden is far too large for you,' said Alice. 'A man of your age, a *grandfather*, should be resting, not taking a new wife who's young enough to be his daughter. And now there's a child coming.' She clicked her tongue in annoyance. 'How will you cope with that?'

Charles laughed. 'Really, Alice, you speak as if I'm in my dotage. I've never felt better and the baby will give me a new lease of life.'

'Well,' she said, pouting, 'it's extremely embarrassing that my father is having another child at the same time as I am.' She sent me an accusing look, as if it were solely my doing.

The front door slammed and my blush went unnoticed as Henry Babcock, brown hair falling foppishly over his eyes, threw open the parlour door. 'Am I late?' he demanded.

'You're always late,' grumbled Alice.

'*Still* on the sofa?' He bent to drop a kiss on her forehead.

'I suppose I'd better see if dinner's ready.' Alice rang the bell and a short while later we all trooped into the small dining room.

The maid, who still hadn't changed her soiled apron, served a watery soup and an overdone leg of mutton. Upstairs, children's feet thundered about, making the chandelier tremble. Dinner was accompanied by a rising crescendo of childish quarrels. I presumed the children had a nurse and wondered if Alice had made any attempt at all to train her servants.

Henry, already on his fourth glass of wine, sighed and threw his napkin on the table. He went into the hall and bellowed upstairs for the children to be quiet.

'This cottage is far too small for us,' said Alice, 'and it will be worse when the new baby comes.' She narrowed her eyes at her father. 'It's ridiculous that the two of you live in such a large house, while we're all cramped into this tiny place.'

'You were happy enough with the cottage when I bought it for you,' said Charles, blotting his mouth with his napkin.

'There were only three of us then,' said Alice. 'Can't we come and live at Hill House with you? There's plenty of space and we could share the cost of the servants.'

I froze, my fork halfway to my mouth.

'Certainly not,' said Charles with a laugh. 'Henry will move you somewhere larger when he expands the business.'

I let out my breath slowly.

'I'm sure Mama wouldn't have minded if we'd all lived together,' wheedled Alice. 'After all, her dowry contributed to the purchase of Hill House.'

'But your mother isn't here now,' said Charles. 'You shall have to wait until I'm in the arms of my Maker to take over the family home.' He laid a hand on my wrist. 'And, of course, I shall make proper provision for you, too, my dear.'

I smiled warmly at him. Although he was a little sedate in his manner, I counted myself extremely fortunate that my husband was such a considerate man.

Sunshine slanted in through the open windows of the freshly painted nursery. I hummed as I folded the tiny pin-tucked nightgowns, smoothing each one perfectly flat and aligning it exactly with the rest of the pile in the lavender-scented chest of drawers. Hugging one of the nightgowns to my chest, I imagined it with a warm little body inside. It was odd to be able to touch the swell of my stomach and feel parts of the baby, a heel or an elbow, but not to know what he, or she, looked like. Charles wanted a boy, of course, but secretly I hoped for a girl.

I touched the wicker cradle, draped with spotted muslin, and set it gently rocking. Charles had gone out specially to purchase it and presented it to me with a hug.

'I don't suppose the babe will care if he sleeps in a drawer,' he'd said, 'but I knew you'd set store by it.'

In that moment I'd felt that it wouldn't be difficult to grow to love my husband.

Closing the windows, I looked down at the garden, where Charles and old Tom were digging manure into the rose bed.

Downstairs in the morning room, I opened my workbox. I'd bought a pair of the best linen sheets and pillowcases available in the draper's shop in Winchester and was embroidering them with a repeating pattern of blue lovebirds for Ralph and his nameless bride. It had touched me that she'd taken so much trouble to make the rose-pink shawl for me. I'd worn it to church and it had drawn a great deal of jealous attention, together with several enquiries as to where I had purchased it.

I threaded my needle and made a stitch. It was only three weeks until the Clementses would return and I must have the sheets and pillowcases finished in time. After a while, my head began to nod and I put down my needle. The baby stretched within me and I laid a hand on my stomach.

'Sleep, little one,' I whispered. The baby stilled and I dozed, too.

I dreamed my baby was crying and, as the cries grew louder, I awoke. Someone was calling my name. Disorientated, I shook my head. It was growing dark already and Charles hadn't had his tea.

The drawing-room door burst open and then Annie stood before me, twisting her hands in her apron.

'Whatever is the matter, Annie?'

'Oh, ma'am! Please to come at once. It's the master...'

A lurch of alarm washed over me. 'What's happened?'

'Old Tom came shouting to the kitchen door. The master fell in the garden and something's not right.'

Outside, I ran to Charles, who lay motionless on the ground. Cook singed feathers under his nose with a lighted taper and Old Tom turned his hat round and around in his gnarled old fingers.

Awkwardly, I sank to my knees and lifted my husband's unresponsive hand. Fear made me shiver. The right side of his poor face looked twisted, as if it were made of wax that had melted. 'Annie, fetch Dr Mason. Hurry!' I coughed and waved away the coiling smoke from the singed feathers.

'The poor man!' Cook wiped away tears.

'He's too heavy for us to move,' I said, my thoughts whirling. 'Cook, fetch some blankets and a pillow! We must keep him warm until the doctor arrives.'

She scurried off as fast as her bulk would allow.

Charles' eyelids flickered and he made a strange sound.

'It's all right, my dear,' I said, stroking his forehead as he looked up at me with frightened grey eyes. But I already knew with cold certainty that it was very far from all right.

'The master was set on finishing before dark,' said Old Tom, his face working in distress, 'even though I said I'd do it on the morrow. He said he had a sudden terrible bad head. And then he groaned and slid to the ground.'

I loosened Charles' neck cloth. 'Is that more comfortable, dear? Help is coming soon.' I squeezed his hand and hoped this was true. What would happen if he didn't recover? Suddenly, it felt as if a great chasm had opened up before me. Dizziness made me close my eyes. My teeth began to chatter and my fingers were icy cold.

Cook returned with an armful of blankets and I covered Charles and placed a pillow under his head. He moaned and I was grateful when Cook draped a blanket around my shoulders, too.

Dusk engulfed us like a shroud and it seemed to be hours before the light of a lantern approached through the dark.

'Now what's all this I hear, Sinclair?' said Dr Mason in a bracing tone. 'Had a bit of a slip?' The doctor held up his lantern and leaned forward to study his patient's face in the pool of light. He lifted Charles' right arm. 'Will you squeeze my hand, sir?' He sighed and placed the unresponsive limb back at my husband's side.

Dr Mason and Old Tom carried Charles between them, staggering slightly since he was a well-made man, and laid him on the day bed in the morning room.

Dr Mason drew me into the hall. 'I'll ask the apothecary to send his boy with some medicine,' he said. 'Unfortunately, your husband has suffered an apoplexy. It's possible he'll recover some movement on his right side and a little of his speech but we'll have to let Nature take her course. He'll need careful nursing.'

I stared at him, too shocked to speak. In my mind, I heard the clang of prison gates slamming shut.

After the doctor had gone, my knees gave way and I sank down on the stairs. The last few months had been so full of hope but now I was condemned to give up my own life, yet again, in order to nurse another. How could I bear it? I buried my face in my hands, my shoulders heaving as I sobbed.

Sometime later, sickened by my selfish thoughts, I took a deep, wavering breath, dried my eyes and went to sit with my husband.

Chapter 4

Within a few days I had become accustomed again to the familiar routine of the sickroom, except that, unlike Mother, this patient never complained. I moved quietly about my duties on leaden feet and made sure that I never wept in front of Charles. It hurt me to see the terror in his eyes and to listen to his guttural grunts as I attended to his personal needs or fed him teaspoons of soup that dribbled from the corners of his mouth.

Alice and her husband came to visit. She shrieked when she saw her father's condition and then turned on me. 'This is your fault, Beatrice,' she said in venomous tones. 'It's your insatiable demands on an old man that have brought him to this.'

'That's not true!' I protested. I began to shake, too exhausted from dozing in a chair at Charles' bedside every night to quarrel with her.

'Steady on, my love!' said Henry, taking hold of Alice's arm.

She pulled herself free. 'Who knows what else Beatrice will do to harm him?'

I exploded at this unjust accusation. 'Your father's sheets are soiled again and he needs to be changed. Perhaps you might care to take on some of the nursing duties yourself, Alice, if you fear for his safety?' A pulse thudded in my head like an iron spike.

Alice stormed out of the sickroom, slamming the door behind her.

Henry squeezed the bridge of his nose. 'I apologise,' he said. 'Naturally, my wife is a little overwrought. She has such delicate sensibilities.'

Delicate sensibilities, my foot! I gritted my teeth to stop myself from making a retort that would only inflame matters further.

In the hall, Alice shouted for Henry to attend her immediately.

'I must go,' he said.

I nodded and went to sit beside Charles. Seeking comfort, I lifted his good hand to my cheek. He responded with a slight squeeze and I laid my head down on his shoulder.

That evening it poured with rain. I listened to it lashing the windowpanes for a long time, too miserable even to read a book. Drawing a rug over my knees, eventually I drifted off. Exhausted, I slept the sleep of the dead.

At first light I awoke and stretched. I drew back the curtains. The rain had ceased, though it had battered Charles' carefully tended roses. The garden was blanketed in grey mist and dewdrops beaded a spider's web stretched across the window. It was beautiful. I savoured the peaceful moment.

Something, the perfect peace perhaps, made me uneasy. The back of my neck began to prickle. I whirled around but everything was still. Too still.

I ran to the bed and touched my husband's forehead. Cold. 'Charles!'

He didn't respond to my panicky cry.

I shook his shoulder. 'Charles!' Nothing. Wrenching back the bedclothes, I pressed my ear to his motionless chest. There was no heartbeat.

Collapsing into the chair with my arms crossed over my chest, I rocked back and forth. As considerate to me in death as he had been in life, my husband had released me from the life sentence of having to nurse him. A flash of joyful relief flooded over me. That shocking realisation reverberated within me as I wept great shuddering sobs of shame and sorrow until there were no more tears left.

I moved through Charles' funeral in a daze. Alice prostrated herself on the ground beside her father's grave and had to be supported out of the churchyard by her husband and Dr Mason.

The funeral party retired to Hill House, where the drawing-room windows and mirrors were draped with black crepe, shutting out the light and rendering the room full of shadows.

Alice held court while reclining on the sofa. The skirts of her new mourning dress were carefully arranged so that the toes of her black kid slippers, adorned with glinting jet beads, were visible. She dabbed her eyes with a black lace-trimmed handkerchief and consumed several glasses of sherry and a variety of cold funeral meats while she extolled her father's virtues.

Attired in the hastily altered dress I had worn after Mother died, I spoke a few words with each guest, even though I knew few of Charles' family and friends.

Dr Mason brought me a glass of Negus. 'You must sit down, Mrs Sinclair,' he said. 'And that's a doctor's order. You're too pale and must conserve your strength for the coming weeks.'

'It's so cruel my husband didn't live long enough to see his child.' I bowed my head over the glass, remembering Charles' delight at the prospect of our baby.

'But it would also have been cruel if he'd had to endure a half-life,' said Dr Mason. 'I shall encourage everyone to go home now and will send you a mild sleeping draught.'

Grateful for his kindness, I watched him move amongst the guests until, one by one, they came to say goodbye.

At last only Alice and Henry remained.

'Would you like any further refreshments before you go?' I asked, hoping they would leave.

Alice ignored me and nodded at her husband. 'I'm waiting for you to tell Beatrice our decision.'

'Ah, yes.' Henry ran a finger around the inside of his neck cloth, as if to loosen it. 'Alice ... that is, we, have visited her father's lawyer to ascertain our financial position.'

'Your position?' I said. 'Even before Charles was laid to rest?'

'My father-in-law left his entire estate to my wife.' Henry's gaze slid away from my face and focused somewhere over my right shoulder. 'Therefore, in law, it now belongs to me. Unfortunately, it appears he failed to add a codicil to his will, to make provision for you.'

Alice's blue eyes gleamed with spite as she awaited my reaction.

I swallowed, waiting for the wave of nausea to settle before I spoke. 'As you well know, your father had every intention of providing for me and I'm sure you will respect his wishes.' But, looking at her expression, I was frighteningly unsure that appealing to my stepdaughter's good nature would serve any useful purpose. 'There is also the matter of my legacy from my mother ...'

'Yes,' said Alice, sitting up abruptly on the sofa, 'which became my father's property upon your marriage.' She smiled triumphantly.

'But that is quite separate! Your father promised to keep it safe for me to draw upon when needed,' I protested. 'It forms no part of his estate.'

'We'll see about that!' said Alice.

I couldn't believe we were even discussing the matter. Surely it wasn't their cruel intention to leave me and my baby with nothing?

'We should not wish to send you away from Hill House a pauper,' said Henry.

Glancing at Alice, I wasn't so sure. I clasped my hands together to still their trembling.

'We shall move into this house shortly,' said Alice. 'However, out of the generosity of our hearts,' she rested a hand against her breast, 'and because my dear father would have wished it, we will allow you to stay. Until other arrangements may be made, anyway.'

I couldn't speak, terror and anger warring for possession of me.

Alice rose to her feet. 'I shall make an inventory now, to be sure everything that belongs here, remains here.'

I gasped at the implied insult.

Henry laid a hand on his wife's arm. 'Is there any need for that?'

'I give you my word that I shall not run off with the silver tea-spoons,' I said, my lips pinched with fury.

'Still, I shall make a brief inspection of the house,' said Alice. 'I must decide what furniture we should bring with us from the cottage.' She swept out into the hall.

Henry shuffled his feet. 'You must understand, Beatrice,' he said, without meeting my eyes, 'Alice was deeply distressed by her mother's death, and when her father remarried so soon afterwards ...'

'I do understand that,' I said, 'but contrary to what Alice believes, I did not seduce Charles into offering for me. And I tried so hard to be a good wife to him ...'

'Come now!' said Henry, awkwardly. 'My wife is a woman of many passions but there is no harm in her.'

'She wishes *me* harm,' I said in bitter tones.

The floorboards creaked overhead.

Incensed at the thought of Alice poking her nose into my personal possessions, I hurried upstairs.

She was in the principal bedroom, running her fingers over the polished mahogany of the chest of drawers.

I clenched my fists behind my back and forced myself to keep my expression impassive as my loathsome stepdaughter rumpled the neatly folded blanket at the end of my bed and inspected the mantelpiece for dust.

'Henry and I will have this room,' she said. 'It's not necessary for you to have the largest now you're on your own, Beatrice. You shall sleep in one of the attic rooms and then we'll all have our privacy.' She tapped her cheek thoughtfully as she turned to look at me. 'I will say one thing for you, you seem to be able to make the servants keep house properly.' She sighed. 'I've never had the knack of it.'

'Perhaps,' said Henry, his brow clearing, 'Beatrice might take charge of the running of the household for us?'

'Exactly what I was thinking,' said Alice.

I shook with anger. So I was to be nothing more than their housekeeper, relegated to the attics?

Alice continued her inspection, leading the way to the nursery. She smiled to see the newly decorated room. 'This is very pretty.'

'I made the curtains and chose the primrose yellow paint,' I said, unable to suppress a glow of pleasure.

Alice nodded. 'My baby will be very happy here.'

'*Your* baby?' I said.

'Of course,' she said, raising her eyebrows at my show of surprise. 'We can't possibly have two babies sharing the same nursery.' She walked towards the landing, talking to me over her shoulder as I followed close behind. 'If one woke up it would wake the other and then they'd always be screaming. No, your baby shall reside in the attics with you. And I'm sure you'll still hear if my baby or one of the other children needs attention in the night.'

I gripped the newel post at the top of the stairs, my growing rage and hatred barely contained. 'So I'm to be your nursemaid as well as your housekeeper?'

'Perhaps,' said Alice, 'you forget your position, Beatrice? You have nothing and it is only our generosity that will keep you and your child fed and off the streets.'

Her gloating smile made the bile rise in my throat. My fingers itched to slap her face, to yank her hair and scratch her cheeks. I knew if I laid a finger on her, I wouldn't be able to stop. I had to escape, to the garden or anywhere else I wouldn't have to be near her. As I turned around abruptly to descend the stairs, my foot caught in the hem of my skirt and I lost my balance. While teetering on the top step for a long, heart-stopping moment, I flailed my arms, desperately attempting to grab the handrail. Then, with a mew of terror, I fell.

I tumbled head-first down the stairs in a flurry of petticoats, crashed against the banisters and banged my forehead. Lying dazed upon the hall floor, I heard screaming above me and then everything went dark.

The pain rose in waves, gripping my belly like the jaws of some terrible beast. My head pounded and every part of me ached.

Someone lifted my shoulders and I sipped cool water.

'So you're awake?'

I opened my eyes, blinking in the candlelight.

Dr Mason's face came into view and he pressed me back against the pillow as I tried to rise. 'Gently! You've had a bad fall, Mrs Sinclair.'

I gasped and clutched my stomach as the pain grew sharper. 'My baby?'

'Well now,' said Dr Mason, 'you've lost a great deal of blood and it looks as if the baby is coming.'

'But it's too soon!'

'The midwife will stay with you and I'll call in on you after I've seen my next patient.'

He turned away and I heard him whispering to the midwife before another contraction came and I couldn't think about anything else.

The midwife wiped my forehead. 'Shouldn't be long now,' she said. She smiled encouragingly, her plain, country face and starched apron reassuring.

The next hour was torture as the midwife urged me on and I

called upon God to help me. There was a growing and irresistible pressure inside me and then a tearing agony. Something warm and wet slipped out between my thighs and the midwife snatched it up in a towel.

Pain-hazed, I pushed myself up on my elbows. 'My baby?' I whispered.

The midwife didn't answer as she rubbed the infant with a towel. After an aeon, she sighed. Taking my hand in both of hers, she said, 'I'm so sorry, my dear, but your son was stillborn.'

It was unseasonably cold for late August as I walked slowly between the ancient yew trees that lined the path to St Biddulph's church. Over the years, countless women grieving for their husbands and babies must have taken the same route but I wondered if any of them had been so consumed by guilt as I was. It was my first day out of bed and I felt as light-headed and hollow as an empty eggshell. Faltering, I leaned against a gravestone to catch my breath and read the moss-covered inscription.

JOHN WALDEN
BELOVED SON OF JAMES WALDEN AND MARY WALDEN
SLAIN BY THE FRENCH IN BATTLE AT SEA
4 MAY 1778 – 1 JUNE 1794

I wondered if the agony of loss had been easier or harder to bear for Mary Walden than it was for me. For sixteen years Mary had watched her son grow towards manhood before Revolutionary France's greed for power had snatched him away from her. At least she had her memories. I had nothing. My son had never breathed, never held out his chubby arms to me or kissed me.

I was early for morning service, unable to face walking down the aisle and feeling the pitying eyes of the congregation turning towards me. Slipping into a pew near the back, I knelt down.

It was impossible for me to pray; I was far too angry with God. He had punished me so terribly for that moment of relief when I'd known I wouldn't be obliged to nurse Charles. And then He had punished me for my anger with Alice, the violent and appalling anger that made me so careless I'd killed my own baby. Screwing my eyes shut, I pictured my son's tiny, perfect face and the mauve colour of his rosebud mouth when I'd cradled his lifeless body against my breast. My chest ached as if I'd been torn open and my heart ripped away.

The shuffling steps of an elderly parishioner interrupted my thoughts and I sat up again, my head bowed. Gradually, the rest of the congregation filed in. There were darting glances and whispered comments but no one came to speak to me. Mother had always made it plain she didn't care for friendly overtures.

Alice and Henry arrived and took a pew near the front. They hadn't spoken to me since I'd lost my son and I'd asked Annie to send them away on the afternoon they called.

The service began. When the others went to take Communion, I remained where I was. Looking up, I saw the altar cloth I'd embroidered the previous year in plum silk and gold thread. It was a beautiful thing, worked to glorify God and to distract me from Mother's caustic comments during our incarceration in the sickroom.

At last the service was over. I filed out with the other parishioners, avoiding those gathering around the vicar, waiting to shake his hand. I wouldn't come to church again; attending simply because it was expected of me only added to my guilt and self-loathing.

At Hill House, I picked at a plate of cold meat and bread and then retired to the drawing room, unable to shake off my desolation and wondering how to face my empty future. Shivering, I wrapped myself in the Indian shawl, not caring that rose pink was totally unsuitable for a woman in mourning. I fingered the silk fringing and let the hint of cloves and attar of roses soothe me.

The bang of the door-knocker echoed through the silent house. A moment later Alice stood in the doorway, with Henry at her side. Had she come to gloat at my misery?

Henry nudged his wife forward. 'Go on!' he whispered.

'I'm sorry for your loss,' she said, folding her hands over her pregnant stomach, 'but at least you won't have a fatherless child to worry about now.'

Fierce hatred made me look away from her pitiless gaze.

Henry cleared his throat. 'We've had further clarification from my father-in-law's lawyer and you'll be pleased to hear that your mother's legacy is to be returned to you. Since it is not a large sum, my wife and I still intend to offer you a place in our home ... that is, Hill House.'

'As your nursery maid and housekeeper?'

'I'm sure that we'll all rub along together very well, now that we've cleared the air,' said Henry, his expression hopeful.

Alice sighed. 'Since you will have to earn your living, you might as well do that at Hill House with us.'

I closed my eyes and swallowed. Alice would never, ever forgive me for marrying her father and had firmly decided I was to blame for his death. I imagined the pain of seeing another child lying in my son's cradle in the nursery upstairs. I pictured years of walking on eggshells, pandering to Alice's whims, of always being the shadowy figure of Poor Aunt Beatrice hovering in the background, picking up the pieces and never belonging. It would be a constant torment to remain at Hill House, forever to be reminded of my guilt and the future I'd lost.

Wrapping myself more tightly in my shawl, I fixed my gaze on the embroidered peacocks. Then a shaft of pale sunlight lit up the drawing room and the embroidery silks shimmered, bringing the peacock rippling to life.

All at once, everything became clear to me. Charles had brought me contentment but that life had gone forever. I must decide how

I wished to live from now on. I wanted new challenges. I wanted to live in a way that made me feel alive, even if that meant taking risks. I wanted an adventure. My heart began to thud. 'I can't stay in England,' I said. 'I've been too unhappy here.'

Alice raised her eyebrows. 'Where will you go, then?'

'I'm going to India,' I said.

The sight of the shock and astonishment on her face almost made me laugh.

Chapter 5

February 1798

Masulipatam, India

I peered out of the porthole and watched the Indian coastline slipping by. The long voyage was nearly at an end and dread gnawed at me again. There was absolutely no going back for me now. Dabbing perspiration from my face, I prayed the air would be fresher up on deck. My personal possessions were already neatly stowed in the travelling trunk and I glanced around to be sure I hadn't left anything behind.

I'd become accustomed to living in the confined space of a cabin though, since I'd had a room of my own for years, it had taken a while to become used to sharing it. Mrs Clements' Indian maid, Neema was allocated the second bunk in the cabin but she was so modest and shy that it was no imposition. Every creaking, swaying inch of the ship was packed with cargo, sailors and troops, leaving limited room for passengers. The Clementses' manservant, Bhupal, had been forced to sleep on deck until he found himself a berth amongst the lascar sailors.

When the Clementses and I had boarded the *Lascelles* the previous September, I'd still been consumed by grief and guilt. My misery was intensified, shortly after setting sail, with a violent bout of seasickness. I felt so wretched I wanted to die. I could only imagine that God was continuing to punish me for my wickedly selfish thoughts when Charles fell ill and that the loss of my husband and baby hadn't been enough to appease Him. Neema had taken pity on me in my distress, ministering to me without complaint. During one particularly stormy night she'd tied me to my bunk while the ship rolled and pitched. She sang the native lullabies of my childhood and her soft voice reminded me of Madhu's and brought me comfort.

When, at last, the sickness left me, I knew that if I was ever to regain my mental equilibrium, I must find a focus for my thoughts other than my own misery. I set to work finishing the embroidered bed linen for Ralph's wedding present. Sewing, however, does not prevent a needlewoman from escaping into her thoughts. The decision to travel to Hyderabad to join my brother had been born out of a desperate desire to escape but I fretted that I'd made a terrible mistake in leaving behind all that was familiar to me.

I had the idea of asking Neema to talk to me in her native Urdu while I sewed. As a child I'd spoken Deccani, a dialect of Urdu, as easily as I used English, but had forgotten much of it after I left India. Now, after five months of conversational practice, the cadences and vocabulary I'd originally learned from Madhu had returned to me.

A tap on the cabin door broke my reverie and I opened the door to see Mrs Clements. Her nose glistened with a sheen of perspiration.

'Are you ready?' she asked. 'Bhupal will come shortly to carry your trunk up on deck before we disembark.'

I nodded and locked my travelling trunk.

Mrs Clements, tearful at leaving little William behind at his new school in England, had been sympathetic to my distress during the voyage but disappointed that I'd turned away from her kindly intentioned questions, unable to discuss my desolation. Mr Clements had remained brusquely cheerful.

'I've spent a year travelling,' said Mrs Clements, 'and I'm heartily sick of it. We can't arrive in Hyderabad too soon for me. Shall we go on deck?' She fanned her face. 'It's so close down here.'

We emerged from the companionway and found Mr Clements, with the wind in his hair, waiting for us in the shade of one of the sails that cracked and billowed above.

I shielded my eyes against the sun and watched barefoot sailors climbing in the ship's rigging. I turned my face into the gusty breeze, the prickle of salty sea spray refreshing on my skin. Leaning against the rail, we watched the land grow closer and closer until I could distinguish trees and a backdrop of hills. I fancied I could already detect the scent of vegetation on the wind.

Half an hour later a pilot ship came to guide us into the port of Masulipatam. Despite my doubts about the wisdom of leaving England for a country I barely knew, a tingle of excitement and curiosity ran through my veins as we docked. The *Lascelles* would be sailing on to Calcutta after taking on fresh water, and only a few passengers, mostly merchants, disembarked with us. There was a cacophony of shouting and a bustle of confusion as sailors hurried hither and thither, furling sails, coiling rope and rolling barrels about the deck. The pungent stench of rotting fish and boiling tar hung in the shimmering heat and turned my stomach.

We had no sooner set foot on the wharf than a mob of dark-skinned men, dressed in little more than ragged lengths of cotton tied around their waists, descended on us like a swarm of bees. Chattering at the tops of their voices, they pulled at our clothing and pushed each other out of the way, vying for our attention. I gripped my reticule anxiously as one of the natives thrust his face so close to mine I could see the yellow tinge in the whites of his eyes and smell the rancid coconut oil in his hair.

37

Bhupal waved his sword hilt, grasped hold of four of the largest men and barked commands at them to carry our luggage.

'I shouldn't have cared to arrive here without your manservant,' I said to Mrs Clements, watching Bhupal fending off the other men with curses and cuffs to the head. His fierce black moustache and beard, combined with his tall stature, made him an imposing figure.

'He didn't want to cross the "black water" to accompany us to England,' said Mrs Clements, 'but he's been with us for four years and I've come to rely on him to make everything comfortable.'

'Is he afraid of the sea?'

Mrs Clements shook her head. 'It's against his religion to cross it, but he has a wife and four children to support and we made it worth his while. He says he can do penance by fasting and the sin will be wiped away.'

Our baggage was retrieved from the deck of the *Lascelles* and the newly hired bearers hoisted it upon their shoulders. We left the wharf in a small procession and walked to the nearby town. We'd become so used to the rolling motion of the ship that our footsteps were unsteady on solid ground.

The sun was hot, despite an onshore breeze, and my black mourning dress soon stuck damply to my back.

'Thank goodness it's still the cool season,' said Mrs Clements, fanning her face.

I was almost expiring from the heat by the time we came to a halt in the shade of a large chenar tree at the edge of the town. Bhupal ordered the bearers to place the luggage in a pile. The Clementses and I sat on the travelling trunks to wait while he went to secure accommodation for us. The bearers hunkered down in the dust nearby.

The sun was lowering itself in the sky by the time Bhupal returned.

'I have found a house for you, sahib,' he said to Mr Clements.

We set off through the town. I looked doubtfully at the run-down houses, the heaps of detritus in the street and pigs rooting about in a foul-smelling stream. 'I don't remember everything being so poor and filthy,' I said to Mr Clements.

'You'll find abject poverty everywhere,' he said, 'but there are the most beautiful forts, temples and palaces, too.'

We passed a tumbledown house where a woman squatted on the dusty earth outside, stirring a cooking pot over a fire. The aroma of spices and onions made my mouth water, though eating food prepared in such dirty conditions would be sure to make me ill.

'A century or so ago,' continued Mr Clements, 'Masulipatam used to be a great trading place. The port was the gateway to the Golconda diamond mines, but now that the East India Company has moved its main administrative and trading centres to Bombay, Madras and Calcutta, Masulipatam has fallen out of favour and into disrepair.'

Bhupal stopped outside a stuccoed house, two storeys high with a shady veranda and a flat roof. Inside, the rooms had lofty ceilings. The matting underfoot was shabby and the walls stained, but I was beyond complaining. I had a room of my own and sank down on the bed with a grateful sigh.

Several exceedingly hot days later, Bhupal had assembled the essentials for the week-long overland trek to Hyderabad: two watchmen armed with curved swords, several bearers, a cook, a buffalo cart for Neema and the luggage, and horses for himself and Mr Clements.

We made an early start and I was alarmed and delighted when I discovered the means by which Mrs Clements and I were to travel along the Old Golconda Road. An elephant waited for us outside the house, gaily decorated in a crimson caparison blanket and with a saffron-painted *howdah* seat perched upon its back. A mahout sat behind its ears.

Mrs Clements eyed the elephant suspiciously and I jumped as the creature unfurled its trunk and blew a gust of warm, damp air into my face. It had small eyes deep-set in folds of leathery skin but also a pair of astonishingly long eyelashes.

The mahout gave a command and the elephant slowly folded to its knees. We ascended by a ladder leaning precariously against the side of the animal and climbed into the *howdah*, while I tried to ignore its richly feral scent.

Mr Clements roared with laughter when his wife squealed as the elephant heaved itself up off its knees again. I gripped one of the carved posts that supported the sunshade, closed my eyes and clung on. A tumble to the ground seemed inevitable and I expected momentarily to be trodden on by the beast's enormous feet, but then we swung fully upright again and set off at a steady pace. The rhythm of the elephant's measured steps was something akin to the motion of the *Lascelles* and before long we began to appreciate our elevated view of the countryside as we marched inexorably onwards. Mr Clements rode beside us on a fine Arab mare with the watchmen at both ends of the procession.

The road was well used and over the following days we passed many travellers and caravanserai heading for, or returning to, Masulipatam. We forded the wide Krishna river and saw men by the banks washing themselves free from dust. I longed to cool my feet, too, even though the water was a muddy brown.

The days fell into a pattern. We arose before dawn each morning to begin our journey before the sun grew unbearably hot. In the heat of midday we dozed in whatever shade we could find, scratching our mosquito bites and dreaming of a proper bed while the pack animals were watered.

We set off again in the late afternoons. Some of the servants would ride on ahead to pitch our tents and we'd arrive to find a pot of spicy stew simmering over the campfire. After supper we sat around the fire with a mug of *chai* before retiring. I lay under suffocating swathes of mosquito netting, listening to the unfamiliar and disturbingly close sounds of creatures in the night. I slept fitfully, dreaming of holding my baby in my arms and waking with my cheeks wet as I relived yet again that terrible moment I teetered at the top of the stairs before falling headlong.

On the final day of our trek I grew increasingly anxious with every plodding step the elephant took. When we stopped to rest on the outskirts of a village, Mrs Clements asked Neema to bring water and towels. A cloud of black flies descended on us as we washed behind a blanket draped over a rope slung between two trees. I longed for the chilly privacy of my old bedroom in Hampshire.

'I refuse to arrive at the Residency looking like a gypsy,' said Mrs Clements. 'First impressions are important.'

'I haven't seen my brother for eleven years,' I said, wincing as I attempted to comb the dust out of my matted hair.

Mrs Clements must have heard the quaver in my voice because she put down her washcloth to look at me. 'I'm sure he'll be very happy to see you.'

Neema proffered a towel to her mistress.

'The thing is, I hardly know him,' I told her. 'I was eight when we left India and Ralph was five. He went to boarding school as soon as we arrived in England so I only saw him in the holidays.' I didn't say that my last memory of him was as a pompous, spotty youth inclined to plumpness. 'When he was sixteen, he joined the East India Company's regiment. He never came home on leave.' Mother's complaining nature had seen to that.

'I suspect it may be more important for you to be on friendly terms with your sister-in-law than with your brother,' said Mrs Clements. 'Men don't usually concern themselves over-much with female relatives.'

'Perhaps not,' I said. It still hurt that my father had never visited me or even written me a letter once Mother had taken us from India. I'd loved Father with his loud voice and jolly manner, and still remembered him throwing me up onto his shoulders and cantering around the garden while I squealed with pleasure. He had patiently taught me to play chess, a pleasure revived when I married Charles. But now Father too was dead, carried off by the cholera, leaving me no chance to ask him why he'd abandoned me so entirely.

A sudden commotion and a series of shouts made us hurry out from behind the curtain to see what was happening.

The elephant, with two of our bearers in the *howdah*, was marching off along the road back towards Masulipatam. Bhupal and the two watchmen were fighting with the cook and the other bearers in the buffalo cart. I gasped when I saw the lid of my travelling trunk was open and my petticoats, stockings and stays had been thrown into the dust.

Mr Clements came running from where he'd been performing his ablutions on the river bank and joined in the fight, wrestling a canvas bag away from one of the bearers.

The cook screamed as Bhupal forced him back against the cart. The tip of Bhupal's sword pierced the man's chest and a few red drops appeared. Sinking to his knees, the cook blubbered and whined for forgiveness, kissing Bhupal's feet.

A few minutes later all the hired servants, except the two watchmen and the driver of the bullock cart, had been seen off at the point of Bhupal's sword, their running feet raising a cloud of dust behind them.

Scarlet-faced with embarrassment, I gathered up my scattered underwear and crammed it back into the trunk without even shaking it free from dust. The robbers had pawed through my most private possessions. This wasn't at all like the India I remembered. Perhaps Mother had been right to hate it so much, after all.

'I suppose it might have been worse,' said Mr Clements, his face grim. 'At least we won't have to pay them for the remainder of the journey,' he said with some satisfaction.

'But how will we travel now, without the elephant?' asked Mrs Clements.

'I doubt there will be any palanquins for hire here,' he said, glancing at the few hovels that constituted the nearby village. 'I'm afraid, my dear, you must ride in the bullock cart.'

'I suppose we must be thankful the thieves didn't run off with that, too,' I said, cramming on my bonnet again and tying the ribbons firmly under my chin. I was coming to the conclusion that, in my haste to escape from Alice and because Ralph had paid for my passage, I had made a rash decision in coming to India. But then, what else could I have done?

Chapter 6

The remainder of the journey wasn't pleasant. There was no sun canopy over the bullock cart and our teeth rattled as we jolted along the pot-holed road. We sat upon the metal trunks, which were blisteringly hot, and the creaking of the wheels set my teeth on edge. I spared a thought for Neema, who had suffered that mode of transport for the entire journey, while Mrs Clements and I had travelled on the elephant, just like *maharanis*.

We left the paddy fields behind and the traffic grew heavier as we lurched through the outlying villages to the city. Mr Clements pointed out the roofs and domes of Hyderabad on the horizon and a flicker of interest lightened my malaise. Camels, elephants, horses, carts and pedestrians travelled alongside us; the ammoniac reek of animal dung pervaded the simmering air. As we approached the city, two-storeyed houses with canopied shops at the lower level lined the road, which was thronged with women in vividly coloured shawls, men in flowing robes, running children and barking dogs.

The tap of hammers rang out from the silversmiths, saddlemakers implored us to look at their wares, women held up ripe mangoes for sale, and lengths of scarlet, orange and saffron silk fluttered in the breeze outside a cloth merchant's stall. A deliciously sweet aroma drifting from a confectioner's drew a crowd from the bustling street. Ahead, straddling the intersection of two busy roads, was a monumental building with a domed minaret at each corner reaching up to the sky.

'The Char Minar!' I exclaimed. 'I remember it from when I was a child. You can see the whole city laid out before you if you climb to the top of the minarets.'

We drove through one of the giant, pointed arches of the Char Minar and a moment later were rattling over the bridge across the river. Mangy dogs roamed in a pack, snarling and fighting over a bone. Lepers begged beside the road and a group of French soldiers made insolent suggestions to Mrs Clements and myself, which we pretended to ignore by staring straight ahead with our noses in the air.

'It's very different from Winchester, isn't it?' I said, assailed by a wave of homesickness.

Mrs Clements gave a wry smile. 'India remains a complete assault on the senses, even though I've spent two years here. I'm told it's more difficult in Hyderabad for European women than it is in Calcutta. There are hardly any British wives here and very few pleasant diversions such as balls and masquerades.'

'I've never been to a ball,' I said, 'so I don't suppose I shall miss that.'

I twisted my fingers in my lap, anticipating the imminent meeting with Ralph. My cheeks burned with the heat, there were mosquito bites on my arms and my clothes and person were coated in dust. I knew I'd grown too thin of late and there were new lines of unhappiness on my face. I was no longer the pretty sister my brother had once looked up to and I feared I would be a disappointment to him.

Mrs Clements dabbed her face with a handkerchief as the buffalo cart drew up outside the Residency gates. 'It would have made a much better impression,' she said, 'if we'd arrived on the elephant instead of all jumbled up with the luggage in a cart.'

Bhupal announced us to the elderly gatekeeper, who slowly pushed open the gates, scattering a troop of monkeys.

Our little procession made its way through the wooded grounds, past the stables and the elegant bungalows that housed the Residency staff. I wondered which of them was Ralph's and hoped it might be our old home with the rustling peepul tree at the end of the garden. I wondered what had happened to Harry and Madhu.

We came to a wide area of cleared ground, swarming with workmen noisily unloading wagonloads of sand and timber.

Mr Clements instructed our driver to stop so that we could take a closer look. 'The British Residency,' he said. 'It's the seat of diplomatic relations between the Resident, James Kirkpatrick, and the court of His Exalted Highness, the Nizam of Hyderabad State. So much depends on maintaining a good relationship with the Nizam. As you can see, Kirkpatrick is building a much grander property here.'

Some of the new walls were already higher than a man and it was clear that, in time, the new Residency would make a strong statement of its occupant's power.

We set off again. As we passed a domed pavilion, I had a fleeting memory of peeping through its windows many years ago to spy on the Residency staff in their dining room.

We drew up outside the existing Residency, a dilapidated two-storey building.

A servant showed us into an ante-room and we were invited into the Resident's office. A little older than myself, he sat with his boots up on the desk and his dark eyebrows drawn together in a forbidding frown.

Mr Clements bowed to him. 'Clements, at your service, sir.'

James Kirkpatrick continued to frown. 'Welcome to Hyderabad,

Clements. Good journey, I hope? You've arrived at what may be an interesting time: the damned Frenchies are up to something again.'

'I look forward to being briefed on the situation, sir. Meanwhile, may I present my wife and also Mrs Sinclair, who travelled with us to join her brother, Ralph Marchant.'

Kirkpatrick removed his feet from the desk and made his bow. 'Welcome to you both.' His warm smile made him look far more approachable. He clapped his hands and a manservant entered the room. 'Take Mr and Mrs Clements to their bungalow and request Marchant to attend me.'

Mrs Clements held out her hands to me. 'We shall meet again very soon, I trust.'

'You must come and dine with us, Mrs Sinclair,' said Mr Clements.

'I thank you both sincerely for your care of me during the journey,' I said.

They followed the servant from the room and all at once I felt very alone.

'I hope you will enjoy your stay here in Hyderabad, Mrs Sinclair,' said Kirkpatrick. 'I know you and your brother lived here when you were children but I don't suppose you remember much of it?'

'I remember how sorry I was to leave,' I said.

Footsteps clattered across the hall, followed by a tap at the door.

Ralph, a much broader, taller Ralph, strode into the room and then stopped in his tracks.

I took a step towards him and he caught his breath.

'Bee?' he said, uncertainly. 'Is it really you?'

'It's been a long time, Ralph.' My brother had always had a sweet tooth but it took me aback to see that he'd grown quite so plump.

Laughing, he caught me up against his chest, knocking my bonnet awry. 'I didn't think you were coming!'

It was abhorrent to me to know that I probably smelled unpleasantly of stale perspiration. 'You've grown a moustache!' I said, once he'd released me.

He laughed again and turned to Kirkpatrick. 'I was only sixteen, sir, when I last saw my sister.'

'Then you will have a great deal to discuss. I give you leave to go home early today.'

'Thank you, sir.'

'It was a pleasure to meet you, Mrs Sinclair,' said the Resident. 'Marchant, we'll take a ride out early tomorrow, say five o'clock in the morning before it grows too hot. I want us to look at the French cantonment on the other side of the river, to see what's afoot there.' He waved a hand in dismissal and began to shuffle papers on his desk.

Ralph guided me from the room and I had to keep glancing at him, trying to align my memories of a pimpled youth with this substantially built man beside me. His fair hair had darkened and his face had taken on a ruddier hue.

'I wasn't expecting you!' he said as we walked down the Residency steps. I noticed he kept looking at me, too. I knew grief had stolen my looks and supposed I was no longer the girl he remembered.

'I hope it's not inconvenient?' I couldn't bear to be a nuisance.

'Of course not! I very much hoped you'd come, but then I received your letter telling me you'd married and assumed you wouldn't take up my invitation. Is your husband here, too?'

'Oh, Ralph ...' I broke off, my face twisting as I fought back tears.

'What is it?'

'There wasn't time to write again so I just came.'

'Tell me what?'

'Charles died. And then ...' I swallowed the lump in my throat. 'And then I lost my baby. I had nowhere to go. Two weeks later I was on the *Lascelles*.'

Ralph came to an abrupt halt. 'Your husband *and* your child?'

'Within the week. My son was stillborn at seven months.'

His face paled. 'I saw your black gown and thought you were

being overly dutiful in still wearing mourning for Mother. My God, Bee, I can't imagine what you've suffered.'

He put his arm around me and it felt strange that my little brother was comforting me for a change.

'We'll talk about it later,' he said. 'You look exhausted but my wife will soon make you comfortable.' He led me to a bench under a tree and bade me sit down. 'Where is your luggage?'

'My trunk is in the Clementses' bullock cart. It's probably at their bungalow by now.'

'Rest here while I make arrangements.' He hurried off across the park.

A mongoose in the bushes chittered angrily at being disturbed. I leaned back against the bench and closed my eyes. The relentless sun painted bright orange stars on the inside of my eyelids. Every muscle ached and I was hot and deathly tired. The bubble of grief in my chest had expanded again, making it hard for me to breathe. All I wanted was to bathe away the dust and then crawl between cool, clean sheets and sleep for a month.

I'm not sure if I dozed but in what seemed like no time at all Ralph was back, riding a grey gelding.

'Your luggage has been sent on,' he said, 'and I've hired a palanquin to take you home.'

Two men were running towards us across the grass carrying something that looked like a sedan chair, except that it had scarlet curtains to the sides instead of a solid body.

'I could have walked to the bungalow,' I said. 'It can't be far.'

Ralph gave me a mischievous smile that suddenly made him look like the little brother I remembered. 'You must conserve your strength.'

The bearers pulled back one of the palanquin's curtains to reveal a pile of gaudy cushions spotted with stains. I hoped they didn't harbour fleas.

Gingerly, I climbed into the contrivance and attempted to make myself comfortable.

The curtain was closed, allowing only red light to filter inside, and the palanquin was lifted up. The bearers set off at a smart pace, making a strange grunting noise to keep the rhythm of their running steps. It was stuffy and hot but, when I pulled the curtain aside, the cloud of dust raised by the bearers' feet made me cough so I let it fall again. I could hear Ralph's horse trotting along beside us.

The journey took longer than I'd expected and I imagined Ralph's bungalow must be one of those in the further reaches of the park. I fell backwards against the cushions as the bearers jogged up a hill, their pace slowing as the incline became steeper.

At last the palanquin was set down and the curtain drawn back.

'Here we are!' said Ralph, as he dismounted.

I scrambled out, rather inelegantly, and shook the dust off my skirt, wishing I were less travel-stained for the first meeting with my new sister-in-law.

A groom came running to take the reins of Ralph's horse.

We stood on a walled terrace overlooking the wide plain of the river. The sun was setting in a haze of turmeric and gold, reflecting off the water like molten copper. White egrets waded amongst the reeds in the shallows.

'How lovely!' I said.

'Do you remember how cross Mother used to be if we paddled in the Musi and came home crusted with mud?' said Ralph.

'Father taught us to fish and never minded if we were dirty.'

Ralph sighed. 'Mother was never happy here.'

'Mother was never happy anywhere,' I said, remembering how she used to reduce the maids to tears and be so sharp-tongued with the neighbours that they rarely called, even when she was ill.

'Look!' said Ralph, turning me around.

Wide steps of pink granite rose up before us, flanked by statues of many-armed goddesses. My gaze followed the steps up to a vast archway in a stone wall, framing a pair of studded gates tall enough for an elephant to pass through. I tipped my head back to see the facade of the building appearing over the wall towering above us. Tier upon tier of arched colonnades, staircases that appeared and disappeared mysteriously, stuccoed balconies and balustraded terraces festooned with vines, and above them all a multitude of domes, ruined towers and minarets, all glowing saffron in the evening sun.

'Ohhh,' I said, letting out my breath in a long sigh. 'The Jahanara Mahal.'

'You remember it?' asked Ralph, his eyes alight with mischief.

'How could I forget? It's a magical place.'

'I remember splashing in the fountain and soaking your dress.' He laughed. 'And then Harry jumped in the pool, too, and we all had a water fight.'

'Harry.' I remembered the boy with dark eyes and the brilliant smile. 'I was so happy that morning,' I murmured.

'Until we went home and Mother spoiled it all. That was the day she took us back to England.'

'I wonder what happened to Madhu?' I said.

Ralph shrugged. 'I looked for her when I first came to Hyderabad but no one knew anything about her.'

I sighed. 'Thank you for bringing me here but it's growing dark. Shouldn't we be going back to your house?'

He threw back his head and laughed. 'But I live here!'

'Most amusing. I'm tired, Ralph, and I'd really like to rest now.'

'And so you shall.' He took my arm and I thought he was going to help me into the palanquin but he guided me firmly towards the steps. 'It's true, you know, I do live here. I have an apartment in the palace.'

I stopped. 'You weren't teasing me?'

He shook his head. 'The palace is a home to several families.'

'I see.'

A pulse of excitement began to beat in my throat. A palace! I had wanted an adventure but the prospect of actually living in a palace, even if only a small part of one, was so impossibly romantic that I couldn't help laughing aloud.

Chapter 7

The granite steps were worn into hollows by the passage of countless feet over many years and I was thankful to lean on Ralph's supporting arm. I was too weary to ask questions. A troop of monkeys gambolled on the steps and I was captivated by the antics of their young.

We arrived on a terrace before the palace walls and a wizened old man in a crumpled tunic appeared and dragged one of the gigantic gates open for us, salaaming as we went through into a courtyard garden.

I caught my breath.

'The Persian word for garden means paradise,' said Ralph.

The spacious courtyard was formed by the palace before us, its secretive windows veiled by delicate stone tracery, and arched colonnades to each side. Scarlet and orange flowers tumbled over the rims of great earthenware pots, the blooms glowing as brightly as embers in the evening sun. A central fountain splashed so gently it barely disturbed the surface of the pool.

'A paradise, indeed,' I said, bending to dip my fingers in the greenish water.

All at once a group of children raced out of one of the colonnades and chased each other through the garden, their high-pitched yells and laughter momentarily shattering the peace. And then they were gone, leaving only whirling dust and the echoes of their cries.

'Noisy little devils!' said Ralph.

The avenue of clipped trees that flanked the path to the palace entrance cast invitingly cool patches of shade. We entered through a series of vaulted arches until we reached a cavernous circular hall with a domed roof. Our footsteps rang out into the silence as we crossed the marble floor and turned into cloisters decorated with bas-reliefs of dancing goddesses.

'Not far now,' said Ralph.

He hurried me through a series of connected rooms, all richly decorated with intricate carvings, mirrors, statues and wall paintings. I was unable to take in every detail and let them all pass by in a blur, while promising myself to explore later.

We climbed several staircases and then came to an ante-room, where a maidservant was lighting lamps. She pulled her *dupatta* over her face when she saw Ralph approaching and waited, eyes downcast.

He spoke with her, too quietly for me to hear, and then she disappeared behind a crimson-curtained doorway.

'My wife is unprepared for your arrival,' said Ralph. 'I expect she'll wish to change.'

'I wish she wouldn't on my account,' I said. 'You can see how travel-stained I am.'

He drew me to a window seat in an alcove. 'You can see Hyderabad from here,' he said.

I peered through the window and saw the city on the other side of the river. Domes and minarets soared above the walls. A pack of dogs roamed along the river bank and a few boats were bound for home. Here and there lights began to glow. I leaned against the stone of the window embrasure, exhaustion enfolding me like a cloak. Outside, a dog began to bark in the gathering darkness.

Ralph drummed his fingers on the windowsill and then delved into his pocket and withdrew two pieces of *jaggery*. I shook my head when he offered one to me.

Then I heard a suppressed giggle and looked up to see the crimson curtain twitch.

Ralph, his cheek bulging, stood up. 'Is that you?' he called. He glanced at me and, just for a moment, I detected a certain nervousness in his expression.

A barefooted girl, swathed in embroidered material so fine it was translucent, appeared from behind the curtain and came to stand before us. Underneath a gauzy veil her black hair was dressed in a thick plait falling to below her waist. Pearls shimmered on her nutbrown brow, a large gold ring decorated her nose and her dark eyes were lined with kohl.

Apparently my new sister-in-law liked her serving maids to be sumptuously attired.

Ralph pulled me forward. 'Bee, I'm delighted to introduce you to my wife, Leela Begum.' He whispered in my ear, 'Begum means Lady.'

Bracelets tinkling, my brother's wife folded her hands together and bent her head in greeting.

My eyes widened but I hoped I had otherwise concealed my shock. It had simply never occurred to me that Ralph's wife might be Indian. I remembered that Englishmen in India often had native wives but Mother had disapproved and rarely mentioned it, except in tones of disgust. She'd have been utterly appalled to know her son had married a native girl.

Ralph's gaze was still fixed intently on my face and a muscle tensed in his jaw.

Really, he might have warned me! Nevertheless, I remembered

Mrs Clements' advice about making a friend of my sister-in-law and it was far too late to change anything now. I pressed my hands together in front of my breast and bowed my head. Then I summoned up my best social smile and said, in halting Urdu, 'How very delighted I am to make your acquaintance.'

The girl laughed and took my hands. 'We are sisters now,' she said, in English, 'and your pleasure is my pleasure.'

She was older than I'd first thought, perhaps seventeen or eighteen.

'You will be tired and hungry after your journey. Would you care to bathe before we eat?'

'I can think of nothing I'd like better,' I said faintly.

'I shall see you again when you are rested, Bee,' said Ralph. He lifted a hand and strode out of the ante-room.

I sensed he was relieved to make his escape but, as the door closed behind him, I felt as if he'd abandoned me.

The curtain was drawn aside. With a soft whisper of silk, half a dozen Indian women flowed gracefully into the ante-room, bracelets clanking and leather slippers tapping the floor. The air became filled with exotic perfumes: patchouli, jasmine and rose.

The ladies surrounded me and I flinched as they stroked my hair and touched my face, chattering all the while like a flock of exotic birds. Although I was slender, I felt plain and ungainly in comparison to their sylphlike figures and colourless against their dusky and perfumed loveliness. They spoke very quickly and I was too tired to understand, adding to my discomfiture.

Leela and her companions led me to an echoing marble room with a large sunken bath in the centre. A procession of handmaids carried in buckets of warm water to fill the bath and then sprinkled it with rose petals. Bronze wall lamps cast a warm and flattering glow as the ladies sat down on cedar-wood benches around the perimeter of the room, gossiping and glancing at me while the maids removed their slippers and massaged their feet.

'You are of great interest to my companions, Bee,' said Leela. 'We rarely see hair the colour of honey.'

Apart from Ralph, no one had called me Bee since I'd left India and I rather liked it. 'Beatrice' reminded me too much of the times in my life I'd been unhappy. Then the back of my neck prickled as if I was sitting in a draught and I turned to see a young woman, taller than the others, standing a little apart and watching me intently.

Leela beckoned to her and she moved towards us with a poise and precision that made me think of a cat bunching its muscles just before it springs at a mouse.

'Bee, this is Lakshmi,' said Leela.

I met the woman's curious gaze. Her eyes were amber, like a tiger's. She wore plainer clothes than the other women, almost masculine in style: a long maroon tunic with matching loose trousers. Her fine complexion was the colour of milky tea. I wondered if she was some kind of superior servant.

'Your brother has spoken of you,' Lakshmi said, speaking in lightly accented English.

'Lakshmi,' said Leela, 'you are tall, like Bee. Will you lend her something to wear until her own clothes are laundered?'

Lakshmi nodded and I watched her walk away, her head high.

A maid carrying a pile of towels approached, pretty despite the smallpox scars to her face, and Leela nodded at her.

The girl untied my ribbons and removed my bonnet, then bent to lift my skirt and roll down my stockings. Unused to a personal lady's maid, I was uncomfortable at such intimacy. She moved behind me as I slipped off my shoes and began to undo the buttons at the back of my dress.

I recoiled. 'I can't undress in front of all these people!'

'Why not?' said Leela, her expression puzzled. 'Allow her to help you take off your dirty clothes. You will feel so much better.'

Scarlet-faced, I stared at my grimy feet while the maid stripped

56

me of my petticoat. I snatched up a towel and wrapped it around me, pushing the maid's hands away while I wriggled out of my stays and shift.

The handmaid smilingly indicated I was to lie face down on a marble bench covered with a white cloth. I clutched the towel tightly against my chest and did.

She poured jasmine-scented oil between her palms and began to massage my shoulders and back. I lay as stiff as a board, tensed against the touch of her hands on my naked skin. Discreetly folding back the towel one section at a time, she kneaded and pummelled me with surprisingly strong fingers that sought out every painful muscle.

Several of the ladies had undressed and sat chatting, in the bath together, completely at their ease. Gradually, since no one apart from the handmaid appeared to be looking at me, I forgot to be so self-conscious. The aches and stiffness in my body were replaced by a delicious languor, as if my very bones were melting. The handmaid released my hair from its pins and massaged my scalp with perfumed oil in firm, slow strokes until every last bit of tension drained away. Almost asleep, I barely opened my eyes when my attendant guided me into the bath and washed my hair and body. Afterwards, I sat on a bench while she patted me dry with a soft towel and then wrapped me in a loose, muslin robe.

'Is that better?'

I opened my eyes to see Leela smiling down at me. I nodded, too drowsy to speak.

'You must sleep now, I think,' she said. 'You are too tired to wait for dinner tonight.'

I was grateful for her understanding. She led me along a dark passageway and through a well-lit sitting room furnished with piles of cushions. I stumbled along another passage until Leela opened the door to a room with a high ceiling and a bed draped with mosquito netting. I looked at it with longing.

'Eat,' said Leela. She sank elegantly to the floor, folding her legs neatly under her enveloping veil.

I sat down beside her with somewhat less grace.

Another maid, Jyoti, darker-skinned than the girl with the small-pox scars, brought a tray of little potato fritters and some sweetmeats, together with a cup of warm milk flavoured with cinnamon and cardamom.

Once I had eaten, Leela offered me a bowl of water and a napkin so that I could wash my fingers. 'You will sleep now,' she said. 'I shall come to see you in the morning.' The door closed gently behind her.

Gratefully, I climbed into the bed.

Children's laughter scattered my dreams. Still half-asleep, I blinked in the light filtering through the mosquito netting. I wasn't yet ready to face the day.

A childish squeal awoke me just as I was drifting back to sleep again. Muzzy-headed, I slipped out of bed and padded barefoot to the window. Unlatching the cobwebbed screen, I squinted against the light and saw a sunny, flower-filled courtyard outside. Three children shrieked with glee as they jumped about in a pool, wet hair plastered to their heads and their brown skin glistening. Giggling, the girl wrung water from her plait as she watched the two boys wrestling together under the fountain.

Still half-asleep, I opened the screen a little wider and the warped timber scraped noisily against the stone sill. The children turned towards the noise and I met the direct gaze of one of the boys. His dark eyes gleamed with humour. I noticed the way his black hair stood up in tufts. He gave me a brilliant smile and all at once I was eight years old again, with wet hair and joy throbbing in my veins.

'Harry?' I whispered.

The girl laughed and ran out of the courtyard, her plait flying out behind her. The two boys raced after her, leaving a trail of wet footprints on the stone flags.

Suddenly the courtyard was silent again except for the fountain splashing softly into the pool.

I shook my head but the ghosts of the past had gone; even their footprints had evaporated in the heat of the sun.

Stumbling back to bed, I burrowed into the pillow and pulled the sheet over my head before sinking into oblivion again.

Chapter 8

I drifted back to consciousness to find sunlight streaming through the shutters and painting geometric patterns on the wall. I lay still for a moment, wondering if the children in the fountain had been a memory or only a dream born of my return to the Jahanara Mahal. Rubbing my eyes, I pushed aside the mosquito netting.

I hadn't looked at the room properly the previous night. There was no furniture other than the bed but I discovered that my trunk had been placed at the end of it. The floor, cool underfoot, was of white marble and the walls painted to resemble panelling in restful shades of chalky green. The ceiling was criss-crossed with dark, carved wooden beams, and the squares formed between them were painted with stylised flowers highlighted in gold.

The door opened and the maid, Jyoti, entered. 'I have brought you clothes, madam.' She opened a door in the panelling leading to a small marble-tiled bathing room where fresh towels and a bowl of warm water scattered with jasmine flowers waited for me.

Jyoti dressed me in a tight, short-sleeved bodice and a pair of trousers, full over the hips and tapered to the ankles. A pin-tucked tunic of white muslin edged with silver braid came next. She twisted my hair into a plait before arranging a gauzy shawl over my head and placing a pair of leather slippers by my feet. The clothes were cool and comfortable, allowing me ease of movement.

There was a knock and Leela peeped at me from around the door. Lakshmi stood behind her. 'May we come in?' Leela asked. She indicated my travelling trunk. 'Since the lock had already been broken, I had my *ayah* take your clothes away to be washed.'

'That was kind of you,' I said.

Lakshmi studied me coolly for a moment. 'You look well in my clothes.'

'I'm still in mourning and it feels strange not to be wearing black.' Strange but also liberating.

'Black is too hot in the heat,' said Leela, 'and white is worn by mourners in India.' She reached out to squeeze my hand. 'You are already sad and there is no need to make it worse by being uncomfortable. You wear no jewellery, so no disrespect is shown to the dead.'

'Even my shoes fit you,' said Lakshmi.

I glanced down at my borrowed leather slippers with their upturned toes. They moulded to my feet as if I'd been wearing them for years. 'They're very comfortable.'

She smiled. 'Then I shall take you to the bazaar and you shall buy some of your own.'

'I'd like that,' I said, pleased by her sudden friendliness.

'Ralph is waiting to see you before he rides back to the Residency,' said Leela. 'He had an early meeting with the Resident but has returned to see you.'

Lakshmi and I followed her through to the ante-room beyond the purdah curtain, where Ralph waited for us.

'Did you sleep well, Bee?' he asked. There was dust on his breeches and riding boots and his hair was windblown, which made him appear younger.

'I certainly did.'

'You look refreshed. We'll have dinner together tonight.' He smiled. 'You've gone native. The local clothes are so much more comfortable in this climate. Since there won't be much in the way of balls and routs given by Europeans, I advise you to adopt the local dress. Every night, on my return from the Residency, I can't tell you how much I look forward to changing out of my formal clothing.'

'I borrowed these from Lakshmi and they're certainly more practical,' I said. I wasn't sure I could adopt local dress permanently, though.

Ralph's eyes softened as he turned to his wife. 'You'll look after my sister, won't you, my dear?'

'I'm hoping Leela will take me on a tour of the palace,' I said.

She shook her head. 'We cannot.'

'Cannot?'

'We must stay in the *zenana*.'

'*Zenana*?'

'The women's quarters.'

'Leela, like most women of good family, observes purdah,' said Ralph. 'She remains behind the purdah, or curtain, within the confines of the *zenana*. You will do the same.'

I stared at him. 'I will not! I couldn't bear to be imprisoned like that.'

'But that way your reputation will be protected and you will never be alone,' said Leela, her expression unhappy.

Horror at the very thought of never being alone made me shudder. 'Ralph, how could you expect such a thing of me?'

'If it's good enough for my wife . . .'

'No! I simply will not be confined indoors.'

He chewed at the end of his moustache. 'There's the *zenana* garden. You'll have new women friends and can gossip all day, if you want to.'

'I don't want to gossip all day! I'm British, not Indian, and this purdah custom doesn't apply to me. You don't expect Mrs Clements to be locked away in her bungalow, do you?'

There was a long silence while I fixed him with a determined glare.

He sighed. 'I can see you're going to be obdurate but I insist you stay within the palace. I don't want you racketing about the countryside unaccompanied; it's not safe.'

'Bee needs to buy more appropriate clothes and shoes,' said Lakshmi, 'but I will accompany her to the bazaar.'

'You don't live in purdah, then?' I asked her.

She shook her head. 'I have special status. I'm quartered in the *zenana* but not confined.'

I was curious as to what she meant by that.

Ralph ran his fingers through his hair. 'Keep a close eye on my sister, will you, Lakshmi? I'm going to be late for my next meeting. I'll see you after dinner tonight, Leela.' He hurried from the room.

'You don't eat dinner with your husband?' I asked.

'Of course not,' said Leela, her tone scandalised.

I sighed. There was a great deal for me to learn about the local customs and habits that had passed me by when I lived in India as a child.

'We shall visit my mother and grandmother now,' she said, 'and then pay our respects to my great-grandmother.'

'The women in your family must be very healthy to be so long-lived,' I said.

'Not all of them,' she said, turning away.

I thought I'd detected sadness in her eyes but then Lakshmi said, 'Afterwards, I shall show you the palace, Bee.'

Her hair was scented with patchouli; it was a perfume I'd always found too heavy as a child. I was slightly uncomfortable with the unnerving way she kept her gaze fixed on me, but didn't wish to rebuff any friendly overtures.

The salon I'd seen the night before looked quite different by day. Rugs in tones of mulberry, plum and wine lay on the marble floor, while mirrors and gorgeously vibrant wall hangings added to the opulence. Columns, painted to look like porphyry, framed three large alcoves. Each had cushioned window seats overlooking a walled garden below.

Leela and Lakshmi slipped off their sandals in the doorway and I followed suit.

Several women and three girls reclined upon plump floor pillows, nibbling sweetmeats. I paused on the threshold and they all stared at me. Suddenly nervous, I was relieved when Leela took my hand and drew me towards a woman sipping a glass of mint tea. '*Ammi*, this is my new sister, Bee,' she said in Urdu. 'Bee, this is my mother, Samira Begum.'

Samira's kohl-rimmed eyes were still as lustrous as her daughter's and her bracelets tinkled musically as she folded her hands together and bowed her head. She was only a little older than myself. Her filmy veil had a deep border of beautiful gold embroidery that caught my eye. 'Welcome to our home, Bee.'

I thanked her and returned the gesture with a smile, thankful that I'd first learned Urdu from Madhu and that Neema had spent so much time on the voyage coaching me. I was far from fluent but hoped to improve.

'And this is my grandmother, Priya Begum,' said Leela.

Priya Begum, her silver hair worn in a plait over her shoulder, reclined against a crimson cushion and inclined her head regally to me.

One by one, Leela introduced me to the other women, mostly cousins or second cousins: Indira, whose front teeth were slightly crossed, Parvati and her daughters, Farah and Esha, then plump Bimla and her daughter, Jasmin. Lastly, Veeda, a young woman with finely arched eyebrows, came forward to greet me.

I recognised some of the faces from the previous night but it was impossible to remember all the unfamiliar names. Nevertheless, we smiled and nodded at each other good-naturedly.

'We are going to visit Great-grandmother,' said Leela.

'She is waiting in her garden to meet the new member of our family,' said Samira Begum.

'Then we had better hurry or risk the consequences,' said Leela.

It surprised me that, through my kinship with Ralph and his marriage to Leela, I might now be considered a part of this Indian family. I tried not to smile at the thought of Mother's horror at such an idea.

Outside, we crossed a courtyard and climbed an ancient stone staircase leading to a terrace overlooking distant hills.

'Great-grandmother's garden,' said Leela.

Jasmine and sweetly scented roses veiled the delicate trellises and arbours. Water trickled along rills and collected in a large pool, reflecting the azure blue of the sky. I stopped to admire the waxy blooms of lotus flowers floating on the surface.

'I shall remain here unless the Begum requires me,' said Lakshmi. She paced over to the terrace wall to look out over the hills.

'Is Lakshmi one of your relatives, too?' I asked Leela.

She shook her head. 'Her family have lived at the Jahanara Mahal for three generations. Her uncle Gopal holds an important position as the palace steward and Lakshmi looks after the *zenana*, but she has become my friend, too.'

A domed pavilion, open at the sides, was situated in the centre of the terrace and Leela led us up shallow steps between the supporting columns. Inside, a canopied daybed had been placed in the shade where it could take advantage of the view.

A handmaid rose from her cushion at the foot of the bed and came to greet us.

'May we visit?' asked Leela.

'The Begum is waiting for you,' said the girl.

'Come,' Leela said to me. 'Great-grandmother doesn't speak English,' she whispered.

We approached the daybed and I saw a tiny old woman in a white and gold veil, propped up against silken cushions. Her skin was as wrinkled and creased as unironed linen but her high cheekbones and heart-shaped face made it possible to see the beauty she had once been. She withdrew from her lips the finely chased silver mouthpiece of the hookah set at her side and looked up at us with a penetrating gaze.

Leela bent to touch the old lady's foot with her right hand, then her own forehead and lastly her heart. 'Great-grandmother,' she said in Urdu, 'I have brought you a visitor.'

'Your husband's sister.' The old lady's voice was high and musical. 'Let me look at her.'

I went a little closer, folded my hands to my forehead and bowed deeply. There was something imperious in her manner that demanded respect. '*Namaste*,' I said.

The Begum struggled to sit upright and the ayah placed another cushion behind her. 'You are known as Bee,' she said. 'What kind of name is that?'

'I was . . .' I struggled to find an Urdu word for 'christened' and failed. 'I was Beatrice but now I prefer to be called Bee.' It would be a fresh start for my new life.

Jahanara Begum narrowed her black eyes and looked at me intently for so long that I began to feel uncomfortable. 'You have been so unhappy you felt the need to change your name?'

I hesitated and then nodded. 'My husband and child died last year.' It would have been useless to lie since this woman seemed to see inside my soul.

Jahanara Begum tapped my wrist with a touch as delicate as a feather. 'Your brother told me you were both born in India. You should not have left but, now that you have returned, you will make a new life here in the Jahanara Mahal.'

'Thank you. I hope so.'

'I see it. The Jahanara Mahal has been waiting for you.'

The old lady spoke with such certainty that I almost believed her.

'You have not seen your brother for some time?'

I shook my head.

Amusement lit the old lady's black eyes. 'I wonder how you will find him? He can be arrogant . . . ' Leela murmured a protest and the Begum silenced her with a glance. 'He has now learned, however, not to tell me what to do. His redeeming feature is that he dotes on my great-granddaughter.'

'Ralph is the only family I have left,' I said, bristling to hear this old lady making unfavourable comments about him.

'But you have us now,' said Leela.

I smiled politely and wondered if it would ever be possible for me to feel fully part of her family. I turned back to Jahanara Begum. 'Were you named after the palace?' I asked.

'Not at all. The palace was named after me.' She drew on the hookah and it bubbled at her side.

'Why was that?'

Slowly she breathed out a stream of smoke. 'I no longer wear bells around my ankles,' she said, 'but a long, long time ago I was a dancer.' She lifted her chin to elongate her neck and raised her hands in the air, fingers curved. Humming gently through her nose, she made a few fluid movements with her arms and head.

Immediately, I pictured her as she had once been, beautiful, lithe and sinuous.

'From the time I was a child I trained as a dancer, like my mother before me,' she said. 'And one day my troupe danced before the Nizam.' She gazed into the distance, looking through the arches towards the hills. 'That was Nizam-ul-Mulk, Asaf Jah, the first Administrator of the Realm. One of the other girls was jealous when she saw the Nizam watching me and she tripped me up.'

'How unkind!' I said.

'I fell at the Nizam's feet,' said Jahanara Begum. 'I was shaking at the disgrace of it and didn't dare to look up, but I took a lotus blossom from my hair and laid it on his foot. He stepped down from his golden throne and lifted me with his own hand, calling for the guard to throw the other dancer out of the palace.'

'At least she received her just reward,' I said.

Jahanara Begum laughed. 'And I received mine. I danced for the Nizam for many years after that. Sometimes he even sought my advice when times were troubled. Later, just before he died, he gave me this palace.' She leaned back against the cushions.

'And your family have lived here ever since?'

She nodded and reached for the hookah again. 'The Jahanara Mahal is everything to me.' Her voice had grown faint. 'It has stood through wars and earthquakes and I ask nothing more than that I shall die in peace here. But I sense trouble is coming again.' She sighed and closed her eyes against the tobacco smoke that clouded the air around her.

Leela patted her hand. 'We have tired you.'

The old lady nodded. 'Visit me again,' she murmured. 'I will pray to the gods that your sadness passes.'

We tiptoed away.

Leela returned to her mother and I walked back across the courtyard to join Lakshmi.

Chapter 9

Setting off at a brisk pace, she guided me along endless passageways and through great echoing spaces where cobweb-festooned chandeliers hung from lavishly decorated ceilings. There were columns and arches highlighted in gold leaf and carved with mythical beasts, mirrored alcoves and numerous double-height doors embellished with intricate brass hinges.

Opening a pair of carved doors some twelve feet high, she led the way into a vast chamber. Sunshine poured in through the domed roof light and floor-length windows. The walls were inlaid with semi-precious stones and I caught my breath when I saw how the entire space danced with reflected sunlight in myriad shades from topaz to ruby.

'This Durbar Hall was used for banquets and councils of war in the old times,' said Lakshmi.

Somewhere nearby children were playing and I could hear the sing-song tones of women chattering.

I ran my hand down one of two parallel cracks in the wall, wide enough to push my fingers into.

'Earth tremor,' said Lakshmi succinctly.

The cracks had caused a section of wall a yard wide to drop down several inches from the ceiling and there were corresponding fissures running across the floor. Looking more closely, I saw many of the inlaid jewels had disappeared from those panels, no doubt falling from their settings when the wall buckled during the earth tremor.

Lakshmi crossed the room to open another door and we passed through into the adjacent room. A great number of people had made themselves a home there and they stared at us, making me uneasy because we'd entered their domain without invitation.

Urns full of water, bags of lentils and cooking vessels were stacked against the water-stained walls. There was a shrine to the elephant-headed god, Lord Ganesh, draped with flower garlands and offerings of rice and fruit. A woman cooked *chapattis* on a brazier on a blackened area of the marble floor and half a dozen children ran about. None of them was the boy I'd seen in the fountain earlier.

'What a lot of people,' I said, tentatively smiling at some of the women.

'Several of the servants and their families have lived in the Jahanara Mahal for generations,' said Lakshmi.

'How many people live in the palace altogether?' I asked.

'I've never counted them. As one dies another is born and so life goes on.'

We set off through the kitchens, where Lakshmi told me banquets had once been prepared for hundreds of people. The maze of domestic offices was home now to more descendants of the original palace retainers. The air was thick with the aroma of garlic and *ghee* and something darker: an underlying stench of rotting vegetables and overflowing drains. Veiled women with kohl-ed eyes peered out of curtained doorways, retreating as we passed.

I glanced through an open door and stopped. The exterior wall of the room beyond had collapsed, leaving it open to the elements. Chickens pecked at the floor. 'What happened here?' I asked.

'The earthquake again,' said Lakshmi. 'This side of the palace, including a section of the fortified surrounding wall, was damaged. Unfortunately, it is dangerous as the stonework continues to fall away. The doors on this side of the corridor should remain locked but the servants will keep using them as a short cut to the village.'

'When did this happen?'

'Over forty years ago. There hasn't been a quake as serious since then.'

We crossed a large central courtyard and went into a cloistered walkway. It had a lavishly decorated ceiling but now the bright paint was cracked and flaking. Then, a tantalisingly spicy aroma wafted towards us. A brown dog with tail curled over its back came out of the shadows and lifted its nose to sniff the air. It appeared I wasn't the only one made hungry by the delicious smell.

Lakshmi hissed at the dog and kicked it out of the way. 'Wretched creature! They come in from the village to steal food.'

The dog slunk away and I noticed that her abdomen was distended with pregnancy.

'My aunt Sangita's home,' said Lakshmi, as we approached an open door. 'Perhaps you would like some refreshment?' She hesitated. 'My grandmother, Usha, lives here, too. I should warn you that she was disfigured in an accident many years ago. It was a bad time for her and often she will not speak.'

I wondered what kind of accident might have had such a devastating effect.

Lakshmi called out and a woman a little older than myself appeared. She was carrying a small girl on her hip, whose eyes were outlined with kohl. Sangita had the same lean and athletic physique as Lakshmi, although she was shorter. She welcomed us with a wide smile as she made her *namaste*. 'You have called at a good time. I've been cooking.'

We entered a large room with a balcony overlooking the river. Colourful embroidered panels almost entirely covered the

71

whitewashed walls and there was a small shrine set up in the corner, draped with garlands of marigolds.

'How are you, *dadi-ma*?' Lakshmi called out.

A heavily veiled woman sat on a cushion on the balcony. She lifted her head and her *dupatta* fell back.

Despite Lakshmi's warning, I caught my breath. Usha's cheek bore a dreadful puckered scar from forehead to chin.

'*Dadi-ma*, this is Bee, Marchant Sahib's sister.'

Usha faced me, her *dupatta* carefully draped again over the damaged side of her face.

I saw that she was in her mid-sixties and, now that I couldn't see her terrible disfigurement, her fine features would once have rendered her attractive. I pressed my hands together before my breast and bowed to her.

Lakshmi pointed to the wall hangings. 'Usha made these, Bee.'

I stepped closer. Each scene was embroidered in exquisite detail, depicting Mughal gardens with musicians and dancing girls, ladies bathing in pools, a horseman riding out with a hawk on his wrist or a banquet where the guests were being entertained by drummers. 'They're outstanding!' I said.

'Aren't they?' Pride shone in Sangita's face. '*Maa-ji* is a clever needlewoman. Please, sit.' She indicated the cushions piled against the wall.

Carefully, I lowered myself to the floor. It would take practice for me to learn to sit as elegantly as Indian women did. I was relieved to note that the rush matting, like the rest of the room, was spotlessly clean.

Usha picked up her stick and limped from the room without a word.

I tried not to let pity show in my eyes when I saw how badly one foot dragged behind her.

Sangita laid a quilted cloth on the floor, together with a tray of filled pancakes and a jug of mango juice.

I bit into one of the crispy pancakes and discovered the potato filling was so spicy my eyes and nose watered. I cooled my burning tongue with the mango juice, noticing that the little girl was eating her pancake with every sign of enjoyment. I supposed spicy food was another thing I was going to have to learn to like.

'Everyone is talking about you, Bee,' said Sangita, as the little girl clambered onto my lap. She was a beautiful child and I envied her mother.

Then a boy and a girl burst into the room, full of excited chatter. A tall man in a grimy turban followed them, with another boy on his shoulders. 'May I come in?' he asked.

Lakshmi looked up and smiled, while Sangita pulled her veil over her head and beckoned him in.

'My father is home again!' said the boy, his face stretched into a brilliant smile.

I stared at him. It was the boy I'd seen playing in the fountain. He was just as I remembered him from all those years ago, but this couldn't be Harry.

The man lifted his son to the ground and ruffled his hair. 'Jai, look, *aunty-ji* has been cooking your favourite *masala dosas* again. I'm hungry enough to eat a camel so you'd better eat before I finish them first.' He turned to look at me, a puzzled expression on his face and then he laughed. 'Well, well! It's my old friend Bee Marchant if I'm not mistaken?'

'In fact,' I said, 'I'm Mrs Sinclair now. Harry Wyndham?'

'Who else?' His teeth were very white against his sun-browned skin.

'Jai looks so like you used to,' I said, 'that, for a moment, I thought I'd slipped back in time.'

Lakshmi moved to make a place for Harry to sit beside her but he continued to study me through squinted eyes. 'You still wear your hair in a plait, then?'

'Only since I arrived at the palace.' I took in his heavy stubble and black moustache, trying to picture the ten-year-old boy I'd known twenty-three years ago. He was still as dirty as I remembered, his shoes and the native clothing he wore stained and dusty. Unfortunately, he carried with him the acrid stink of goats, mixed with stale sweat.

'Ralph mentioned some months ago that you might come here,' he said, 'but he didn't tell me you had a husband.'

'I'm a widow,' I said, feeling Lakshmi's gaze upon me again.

'I'm sorry to hear that.'

Lakshmi poured a beaker of mango juice and held it out to Harry.

He sat beside her and began to wolf down the *dosas*. 'Who would have thought,' he said, 'when we crept illicitly into the Jahanara Mahal to look for the lost Rose of Golconda, that we'd meet again here?'

'*You* came here before to look for the Rose, Bee?' asked Lakshmi.

'It was on the day my mother took me away from India,' I said. 'I was eight years old and Ralph was only five. Mr Wyndham found a way into the palace and spun me a story about looking for a lost diamond.'

'The story of the Rose is true,' mumbled Harry, through a mouthful of *dosa*. 'And really, since we were childhood friends, please call me Harry.' He grinned at me. 'I shall address you as Bee, just like the old days.'

I remained silent, unsure how to deal with a man who took no notice whatsoever of the social niceties.

'Why did your mother take you away?' Lakshmi's cat-like eyes were still focused on me.

I shrugged. 'She didn't like the heat or the food or the insects.' I couldn't say she'd hated the people, too. 'India didn't agree with her constitution.' But then, nothing much *had* agreed with Mother.

Lakshmi rose abruptly to her feet. 'Will we see you at dinner, Harry? Ralph invited Bee and myself to join him tonight.'

He nodded and lifted his hand in a vague farewell but barely looked up from his *dosa* as we left.

Mother had been right. She'd thought Harry Wyndham as a boy a little savage, and, all these years later, his personal hygiene and manners didn't appear to have changed for the better.

Lakshmi led me back towards the *zenana* through a succession of echoing halls, innumerable courtyards and endless corridors until I'd completely lost my bearings.

She saw me looking in dismay at a wall hideously blackened by mould stains. 'Unfortunately, the roof leaks during the monsoons.'

I was relieved when she returned me to my room. If she hadn't appeared to be in such a hurry to leave, I'd have asked her what Harry was doing at the palace. And why did he smell so unpleasantly of goats? But at least I knew now that the boy I'd seen in the fountain was his son and not a spectre from the past.

I kicked off my borrowed shoes and sat down on the bed. An ant dropped from the ceiling onto my lap. I brushed it off with a grimace but then it was followed by another and another. Hastily standing up, I shook out my clothing with a shudder.

Despite the apparent grandeur of the palace it had shocked me to see that the gold leaf was peeling, the marble floors cracked; handrails were missing from staircases, even the stonework was crumbling. Although I'd seen servants busy, to some degree or other, with buckets of water and brooms, a furry coating of ages-old dust lay over the window ledges and fretwork screens everywhere we went.

It saddened me greatly to discover that the reality of the Jahanara Mahal was so tarnished and nothing like my childhood memories of a glittering fairy-tale palace.

Sighing, I began to unpack my trunk. Draping the rose-pink shawl around my shoulders, I stroked its silky folds. Lakshmi was right; black was far too uncomfortable to wear in the sun and the Indian custom of wearing white for mourning was more sensible.

I lifted the parcel of linen sheets from my trunk and ventured out to visit the ladies' sitting room.

Leela came to greet me.

'I've brought a wedding present for you and Ralph,' I said.

She unwrapped the sheets and exclaimed with pleasure at the blue silk lovebirds.

'My travelling companion's maid on the voyage sat beside me while I embroidered them, teaching me to speak Urdu again.'

'Your time was well spent. And this is fine work, Bee.'

'They don't compare with beautiful shawl you made for me.'

'I'm happy you like it,' she said. 'In the *zenana* we all like to sew; it passes the time.'

I glanced at the three girls, all aged somewhere between ten and fourteen, and couldn't imagine what it would be like to live your whole life hidden behind a curtain. I supposed the reward of producing something beautiful would be some compensation for the boredom of being cooped up with the same people, day after day.

The women, whose unfamiliar names I was embarrassed to have forgotten, crowded around to examine the sheets and inspect the neatness of my work. Some of them fetched sewing of their own for me to look at. In no time we were chattering away about different techniques and stitches, but I was humiliated when they laughed at my mistakes with the language and frequently corrected me. I resolved to practise hard and improve.

After the work had been put away, Leela and I sat in one of the alcoves overlooking the walled garden below.

'I met an old childhood friend when I was visiting Lakshmi's aunt,' I said. 'Harry Wyndham. Why is he here?'

She looked at me in surprise. 'He lives here. He is my brother-in-law.'

'Your brother-in-law?' It was my turn to show astonishment.

Leela nodded. 'He was married to my elder sister, Noor.'

'So Jai is your nephew?'

76

She nodded. 'Noor died eight years ago, giving birth to him, just a year after my father died from a fever.'

That explained her sadness when I'd commented on how long-lived her family were.

'I was too young then to care for my sister's baby,' she continued, 'but Sangita has brought up Jai with her own three children. Harry was so often away with the army when Jai was small that he needed a foster mother for him.'

'Is Harry still in the army?'

Leela laughed. 'It's hard to know what Harry does. He comes and goes all the time, but he pays Sangita well to look after Jai.' She hesitated. 'There was a time ...'

'Yes?' I prompted.

She shrugged. 'There was a time I thought he'd marry Lakshmi, to provide a mother for his son.'

I recalled now the way that Lakshmi had looked at Harry and wondered if she still nursed hopes of marrying him. Changing the subject, I asked, 'Don't you ever long to leave the *zenana*, Leela?'

She moved her head from side to side. 'When I was growing up, I wondered what it was like outside.' She whispered, 'Don't tell my mother but sometimes I used to creep out before dawn. I explored the palace and climbed to the top of the highest towers to look upon the city.'

'But you don't do that now?'

'The world outside the *zenana* is a dangerous place and I have everything I need to be happy here. With the women of my family beside me, I am never lonely. They are all like my sisters.' She took my hand and pulled me to my feet. 'I want to show you something.'

She led me through a curtained doorway onto a balcony screened with fine bamboo blinds.

'If it's dark in here,' she said, 'and the dining room below is well lit, we can see through the blinds without being seen ourselves. We can hear the conversations between the men and their guests. There is a passage to a ladies' balcony in the Durbar Hall, too, though no banquets have taken place there for years now. So, you see, the ladies of the *zenana* always keep up with all the latest news.'

'Don't the men mind you spying on them?'

'We aren't spying!' Leela's expression was indignant. 'It's important to know what is happening in the world.'

'So you're happy living here?'

'Why wouldn't I be? And, like the other married women, I have my own room where my husband can visit me. Perhaps ...' Leela bit her lip and looked at her jewelled anklet. 'Perhaps there will be children. What more could I want?'

'Indeed. What more could any woman want?' I echoed, my heart contracting in sorrow.

Chapter 10

I spent the rest of the afternoon with Leela and then retreated to my room before Ralph returned from the Residency. My previous life had been very quiet and I found the women's continual friendly questions tiring.

Lakshmi tapped on my door as the sun was setting. She wore shades of lime green and gold that emphasised the green flecks in her amber eyes. I wondered if she'd dressed to please Harry. 'Ralph has returned,' she said.

We left the *zenana* through the crimson curtain and I hurried behind as she strode through dimly lit rooms. At the top of a staircase, I paused before a hideous stone statue displayed in a niche.

'Kali,' said Lakshmi.

The four-armed goddess had beetling brows and her scarlet tongue stuck out. Shuddering, I broke into a trot to catch up with my guide.

We continued, up and down steps and through archways, until finally we stopped before a pair of carved doors, flanked to either side by menservants in long white tunics, crimson turbans and cummerbunds. They threw open the doors and male laughter flooded into the shadowy ante-room. Another manservant ushered us into the dining room.

There were no chairs but two Indian men sat on floor cushions around a low, square table dimly illuminated by a chandelier. One rose and came towards me with arms outstretched. I took an uncertain step back.

'Bee?' he said.

'Ralph! I didn't recognise you in the half-light.' He was dressed in a turban, flowing tunic and white trousers.

'Come and sit beside me,' said the other man with a grin.

Despite his brown skin, he wasn't Indian, either.

'I understand you've already met Harry Wyndham,' said Ralph.

'It was a most unexpected surprise,' I said.

'Good evening, Harry,' said Lakshmi. She sat down opposite him with feline grace and regarded him lazily from under her eyelashes.

Harry, wearing clean clothes, had shaved since I saw him earlier and smelled pleasantly of sandalwood rather than goat.

Ralph laughed. 'A lot of water has flowed under the bridge since the three of us were last together at the Jahanara Mahal.'

'Indeed it has,' said Harry. 'For a start, you aren't a whining little boy hanging onto your sister's skirts any more.'

'Be fair!' protested Ralph. 'I was only five years old.'

'Harry always had a dirty face in those days,' I said, 'but at least he's wearing a clean shirt for once.'

'Entirely in your honour, my lady,' he said, raising a mocking eyebrow.

I looked away. Young Harry had grown into an uncommonly good-looking man, even if his manners still left a great deal to be desired.

'That was all in the past,' said Lakshmi, looking bored, 'long before Leela and I were born.'

Her dismissive comment made me acutely conscious of my age. I wondered why she was dining with us. She'd said she had 'special

80

status'. Perhaps that was bestowed upon her by her aunt's role as Jai's foster mother?

Servants brought us water to rinse our fingertips before presenting a platter of rice and earthenware bowls of vegetable stew, *dhal*, grilled and spiced chicken with fresh green herbs and chutneys, together with a pile of *chapattis*. There were no spoons or forks and I was daunted to discover I was expected to eat with my fingers. Although I knew this was the usual fashion amongst Indians, Mother had never allowed her children to eat in this way.

'What did you do with yourself today, Bee?' asked Ralph.

'I met Jahanara Begum this morning.'

'A lady of great character, don't you agree?'

'There's something almost regal about her.' I didn't mention I'd felt as if she'd stripped my soul bare when she looked at me. 'Then Lakshmi took me on a tour of the palace, and as you know I met Mr Wyndham ...'

Harry glanced at me and raised an eyebrow in amusement.

'I met Harry and Jai when we visited Sangita,' I continued. 'And then I spent the afternoon with Leela.'

Ralph turned to Harry. 'Poor Leela was shocked this morning when my self-opinionated and fiery big sister refused to confine herself to the *zenana*.'

Harry laughed.

'I'm neither self-opinionated nor fiery,' I protested.

'You were, shall we say, always a very *spirited* girl,' said Ralph. 'I remember you being brave enough to argue with Mother and being shut in the coal-hole on more than a few occasions.'

Perhaps I had been that girl, once upon a time, but Mother had finally worn my spirit down.

'Aren't you hungry?' asked Lakshmi, neatly rolling up a small ball of rice and popping it in her mouth.

'It looks delicious,' I said, wondering how to avoid making my fingers a greasy mess. I took a *chapatti* and broke off a small piece.

Swiftly, Lakshmi pressed her hand down on my left wrist and held it there. 'It is very bad manners here to use both hands to eat,' she whispered. 'Use your right hand only.'

My cheeks burning, I pulled my hand free and rested it in my lap.

She turned away to join in with Harry and Ralph's animated conversation.

I envied her easy manner with the men and stared at my plate, wondering miserably how to eat my dinner without further disgracing myself. I studied the walls, decorated with vivid scenes of turbaned men on elephants out on a tiger hunt. The flickering lamplight gave the impression that the tigers in the long grass were moving, readying themselves to pounce.

'The Resident and I rode around the French cantonment this morning,' Ralph was saying.

Lakshmi leaned forward. 'Did you discover anything new?'

'There were too many of their armed scouts for that but it looks as though the French force continues to increase.'

'General Raymond still has the Nizam in his pocket,' said Harry.

'Who is General Raymond?' I asked, attempting to be part of the discussion.

'The commander of the French army in Hyderabad,' said Ralph. 'He's very well regarded by the Nizam since he quashed an uprising here a couple of years ago.'

'The Nizam rewarded him with an immense estate beside the fort at Golconda,' Lakshmi told me. 'It yields fifty thousand rupees a year.' She sighed. 'Imagine having that kind of wealth!'

My stomach rumbled and I coughed to hide the sound.

'It's quite simple,' Harry murmured in my ear. 'Watch.' He gathered up a small ball of rice with the tips of his fingers and dipped it in the dhal, then deftly flicked the rice ball into his mouth with his thumb.

I copied his movements as closely as I could but a few grains of rice escaped and fell to my lap.

'Not bad for a first attempt,' he whispered.

Perhaps he was more chivalrous than I had at first thought.

'Always happy to come to the rescue of a damsel in distress.' He flashed me an impudent grin.

I managed most of my dinner without dropping it, all the while listening to the discussion. The food was highly spiced and I hoped it wouldn't give me indigestion. Once I'd finished I waited, tongue burning and lips tingling, for a lull in the conversation before catching Ralph's eye.

'Would you explain to me the situation with the French?' I asked. 'Napoleon is at war with almost the whole of Europe but I'm not clear why the French are in India.'

'They're doing their damnedest to shake the power of the British East India Company,' he retorted. 'If the French influence isn't overthrown, we'll be expelled from India and lose our trade routes. That would have devastating consequences for Britain.'

'Hyderabad and the Deccan area,' said Harry, 'is a vitally important foothold. The Nizam trusts General Raymond and that might be his downfall. What's to prevent Raymond using his men in a *coup d'état* against him? The Nizam would be left extremely vulnerable to another invasion from Scindia, his old Marathan adversary.'

I noticed that Lakshmi's gaze never left Harry's face.

'And then there is Tipu Sultan, known as the Tiger of Mysore,' said Ralph. He saw my blank expression. 'It's common knowledge now that Tipu is in communication with Napoleon Bonaparte and has already invited him to "liberate" India by driving out the British. If Raymond combined his forces with those in the service of Scindia and Tipu Sultan, then I doubt we'd have the strength to maintain the British position in India.'

'I see,' I said, slowly. 'So, are you telling me that war with the French in India is inevitable?'

Ralph sighed. 'I hope not. James Kirkpatrick is well liked by Old Nizzy and is making sterling diplomatic efforts to persuade him to rid himself of the French, but it's a hard road.'

Lakshmi gave me a sideways look. 'Does this talk of war make you nervous, Bee?'

'Would it affect us at the Jahanara Mahal?'

Lakshmi studied a tray of sweetmeats, selected a particularly delectable sample and presented it to Harry with a smile. 'There have been wars in Hyderabad before,' she said, 'but the palace is still standing.'

'Apart from the walls that fell down in an earthquake,' I said.

'There are always tremors.'

'I'm surprised the damage has never been repaired.' I waved away a mosquito that whined infuriatingly around my head.

'It has,' said Lakshmi, 'but as the last stone was put in place, there was another tremor. The wall collapsed again and a man died.'

'How dreadful!' I nibbled a honey-soaked confection while I thought about the worrying prospect of war. 'The French cantonment is only on the other side of the Musi river, isn't it?'

Lakshmi nodded.

'And where is the British camp?'

'A short ride north of the Residency.'

'So the Jahanara Mahal is in a good strategic position for the French on this side of the river?'

Harry gave me a keen glance. 'You're thinking like a soldier, Bee.'

The prospect of being invaded by the French alarmed me. 'What can we do to safeguard the palace?'

'The Jahanara Mahal was built as a defensive fort over two hundred years ago,' said Harry.

'So don't you worry yourself about security,' said my brother, with a condescending smile. He sucked his sticky fingers as he polished off his third sweetmeat.

'But if three children could let themselves in and wander about without being apprehended some twenty-three years ago and now the palace inhabitants have free access to the village through a hole in the wall, it's hardly secure, is it?' I pressed him.

'Don't concern yourself,' said Ralph, in tones that were meant to soothe but that had quite the opposite effect. 'The Jahanara Mahal can easily be made secure.'

His condescending tone wouldn't allow me to let it go. 'It would be far more sensible to implement such precautions before any threat presents itself, don't you think?'

Ralph's mouth tightened in annoyance. 'As I said, Bee, whatever is necessary will be done. In fact, the wall was made secure again with a stout timber fence recently but the villagers kept stealing it, bit by bit, for their fires.'

'Then it must be rebuilt in stone,' I said. Annoyed, I pinched the life out of a mosquito that was feeding on my forearm.

Lakshmi shook her head. 'No one in the palace will rebuild the outer wall for fear of angering the gods and causing another earthquake.'

I'd opened my mouth to comment that no one could believe such nonsense, when I noticed the gleam of amusement in Harry's eyes. I bit my tongue, unwilling to give him the satisfaction of seeing me start a full-scale argument with Lakshmi and my brother.

In the uncomfortable silence that ensued, I detected a whisper. Glancing up, I saw the bamboo blinds on the balcony move. It appeared that the ladies of the *zenana* were listening.

Harry rinsed and dried his fingers. 'Ralph, shall I call for the hookah? There's nothing like sharing a pipe to soothe away the irritations of the day.'

I gave him a searching look, unsure if he meant that I was the irritation, but he only smiled blandly back at me. 'Perhaps you will excuse me if I retire?' I said, rising to my feet.

'Of course,' replied Ralph, his voice coldly polite.

'I'm still fatigued by my travels and everything is so strange and new.' So far, nothing about India was at all how I remembered it. Dejected, I was beginning to wonder if Mother's dislike of the place had been justified.

'Will you find your way?' asked Lakshmi.

'I'm sure I shall.' All I wanted was to be alone. 'Good night.'

'Pleasant dreams, Bee,' said Harry.

The menservants threw open the ante-room doors and salaamed as I swept off down the corridor.

I hadn't come all the way to India expecting to find myself in the middle of a potential battleground. It appeared to me that the French had the upper hand and there wasn't a great deal the British could do about it. My thoughts churned with disquiet as I hurried through the dimly lit rooms and passageways.

Suddenly unsure of the way, I halted. Retracing my steps, I took another direction, following the flickering light of small lamps set on wall sconces. At the top of a staircase I recognised the disturbing statue of Kali and descended to a galleried landing. There were no lamps but silvery moonlight filtered through the carved window screens.

Lost in uneasy thought, it took me a while to register the sound of footsteps following me. I turned and the footsteps stopped.

Apprehensive, I called out, 'Hello?'

Silence.

I stopped holding my breath, assuming I must have heard the echo of my own feet, and walked on through the murky gloom.

A moment later, the footfalls began again.

Pressing my back to the wall, I froze, the nape of my neck prickling.

The footsteps ceased.

I strained my ears, listening to the silence. Peering into the blackness, I remained still, my heart thumping.

Then I heard a softly exhaled breath. Something stirred in the dark and an indistinct shape began to advance.

Fear gripped me with sharp talons and all reason fled. I let out a mew of terror and ran. Panic-stricken, I raced through shadowy rooms and along passageways, my sandals skidding on the marble and my only thought to escape. The Jahanara Mahal pressed in on me, sucking the air from my lungs, whispering and reaching out at me from the menacing dark.

At last, my legs would carry me no further. Sobbing, I stumbled against a wall and sank down to the floor. I wrapped my arms around my head and squeezed my eyes shut. Silence settled around me like a blanket. Shaking so hard that my teeth chattered, I concentrated on slowing my ragged breaths.

Some considerable time later, I still trembled, although the overwhelming terror had lessened. My fear of walking alone through the looming shadows was far greater than my desire to find my way back to the *zenana*. I remained unmoving, sitting with my back pressed to the wall.

Chapter 11

I awoke with the dawn. Pearly light backlit the window screens and the place that had so terrified me in the darkness was revealed to be a high-ceilinged chamber painted in tones of soft pink and apricot. Curled up on the granite floor, I stretched out my cramped limbs and rubbed away pins and needles.

I was ashamed of my overwrought imagination of the previous night. Opening the shutters to look outside, I discovered that I was at the front of the building. Mist rose from the ground and all was still. After such unreasoning terror, I determined to explore the palace, making a careful note of landmarks, so I shouldn't lose myself again. My plan was to find the main entrance and make my explorations from there.

I walked through a series of rooms connected by ogee archways. A maid busily sweeping the floor looked up curiously as I hurried past. In the daylight, I recognised some of the rooms and eventually came to the circular hall. There were no walls, only endless columns holding up the domed roof and vistas of other halls and chambers beyond. As I pondered which direction to take, booted footsteps clipped across the black-and-white marble and Ralph, again dressed in European clothing, strode towards me.

'You're up early!' he said. 'Are you in a better mood this morning?'

I ignored his last comment. 'I'm exploring.'

He nodded. 'You might care to climb the towers and look at the views.'

I fell into step beside him and was about to say that Leela had mentioned she used to visit them but realised I might be telling tales. 'Which way?'

'Up the front staircase and turn right. Then find the tower stairs and just keep climbing!'

I hurried along beside him until we reached the palace entrance.

'I'll see you this evening when I return from the Residency,' he said, waving to me as he ran down the steps.

Turning around, I made for the wide staircase across the hall and climbed up to the first floor. Running footsteps advanced along a passageway. Jai waved at me and I was struck again by how like his father he was. 'I'm lost,' I said. 'Would you show me how to find the tower?'

'Which one?'

'Any one. I want to see them all.'

He grinned and trotted back the way he'd come.

I followed until he pulled back a tattered curtain, revealing a winding staircase.

'Come,' he said. 'You can see the town from this tower.'

The stone staircase was so narrow my elbows touched the walls to either side, and so steep I swiftly became out of breath. I peered out of an arrow slit window and saw the sun glinting on the Musi as it flowed into the distance.

At the top of the staircase was a small room with a domed roof, lined with mirror mosaics. We stepped out onto a balcony and it made me dizzy to see the rocky hillside so far below. Birds of prey circled slowly around the tower, drifting on the rising air. The minarets of the Char Minar punctuated the skyline amongst the domes of the city on the other side of the bridge. A few small boats were already out on the river and the morning sunlight reflected as brightly off the water as if it were a mirror.

'It's so beautiful,' I said, unable to express fully the passion for my new home that had struck me like a thunderbolt.

Jai leaned over the balcony and I snatched hold of his tunic, frightened he'd fall. 'There's Lakshmi,' he said.

Cautiously, I leaned out and saw a figure on horseback trotting through the palace gates and on towards the side of the palace. I wondered where she'd been so early in the morning.

'Let's go and see her,' said Jai, pulling himself free from my grasp. 'Catch me if you can!'

He darted down the stairs and I hurtled after him, arriving breathless and laughing at the foot of the tower as if we were both children. We clattered down another staircase and soon we were outside.

A brown dog ran up to us, tail wagging, and I saw it was the same animal that had been loitering near Sangita's front door.

'Hello, Swati,' said Jai. He reached into the waistband of his trousers and took out half a *chapatti*.

'Is she yours?' I asked as he fed the dog.

He shook his head. 'She doesn't belong to anyone. Sangita-Aunty thinks Swati will go mad in the sun and bite us. She throws buckets of water at her to make her go away.'

I took a hasty step back but the dog wasn't foaming at the mouth or exhibiting any signs of rabies. 'Swati's going to have puppies,' I observed.

'That's why I keep feeding her.' Jai gave the dog the last piece of *chapatti* and then crooned to her while he fondled her ears.

Swati closed her eyes in bliss, leaning against his skinny knees.

I hoped she didn't have fleas.

By the time we arrived at the stable yard, Lakshmi had dismounted and was watching while a *syce* rubbed down her horse.

The yard was surrounded by numerous, mostly empty, loose boxes. Weeds grew in the cracks and part of the stable wall had collapsed.

'Lakshmi!' shouted Jai, waving his arms to attract her attention.

The chestnut mare took a startled step sideways.

'Careful, Jai!' warned Lakshmi. 'Make yourself useful and fetch Aurora some water.'

He picked up a bucket and hurried away to the water trough.

'You were out early this morning,' I said.

Lakshmi's skin glowed from her exercise. She wore the maroon tunic again with a wide leather belt and her hair was confined in a turban pinned with a large sapphire above her eyebrows. The outfit, combined with her athletic physique, gave her a strangely masculine air, despite her fine features. 'I like a gallop before the sun grows too hot. It's a wonderful way to start the day.' She brushed red dust off her trousers.

Tentatively, I stroked the mare's velvety nose, inhaling her warm scent. 'Could you teach me?'

Lakshmi looked me up and down. 'I don't see why not. There aren't many horses in the stables these days but you could ride Mumtaz. She's the *zenana* pony and very safe.'

'I'd like that.'

'Come here tomorrow morning then.'

Jai staggered back to us with the bucket of water.

She ruffled his dark hair. 'Do you want to come and watch me practise?'

He nodded eagerly and gave his father's smile again.

Lakshmi turned to me. 'Come with us, if you like.' She walked away without waiting for my response.

Jai and I followed her through the gardens. A pair of peacocks strutted along a gravel path, pecking in the overgrown flowerbeds in the shade of the crumbling perimeter wall. From the grounds, it was easier to see the destruction caused by the earthquake. A large part of the rear of the palace had collapsed and tiers of terraces and unsupported balconies hung crookedly over the rubble. Cracks extended out from the epicentre of the damage and some of the windows had slipped sideways. Vines as thick as cobras snaked over the fallen masonry and insinuated their way into the crevices.

Beyond the gardens lay a field of scrubby grass and bare earth.

'The *maidan*,' said Jai. 'When the palace was a fort, the soldiers used to drill here.'

A herd of goats grazing on the weeds stared at us with their clever yellow eyes, watching us closely until we came to a massively solid wall.

Lakshmi opened a teak door carved with elephants, trunks entwined to form an arch. We entered a compound containing a substantial single-storey building that had a dozen or so roof domes with a corresponding number of tall ogee arches to the front wall.

'The *pilkhana*,' said Lakshmi. 'These are the stables where the fort's war elephants were kept.'

'They had spikes fitted to their tusks,' said Jai, his eyes round at the thought, 'and they bellowed when they charged at the enemy's cavalry.'

'And there would have been archers or javelin-throwers mounted upon the elephants' backs,' said Lakshmi.

'How terrifying!' I pictured a row of elephants emerging from the early-morning mist trumpeting and waving their trunks aloft as they charged inexorably towards a mass of soldiers and terrified horses with nowhere to run. 'But there are no elephants here now?'

Lakshmi shook her head. 'Jahanara Begum had four elephants when she came to the palace but that was fifty years ago.'

'Jahanara Begum said they ate too much,' said Jai.

'What a shame!'

'Times change but I make good use of the *pilkhana* yard,' said Lakshmi. 'Jai, will you fetch the target and set it up?'

The boy ran into the building and Lakshmi followed him.

A moment later they returned, Jai dragging a large piece of board behind him. He turned it around and leaned it against the wall. The board was painted with concentric circles, each in a different colour.

Lakshmi carried a bow over her arm and was buckling on to her back a quiver of scarlet velvet adorned with gold braid. 'I train daily,' she said. 'Some days I practise sword fighting with my aunt.'

'Sword fighting?' I looked at her, bewildered. 'With your aunt?'

'Both my parents died from cholera when I was twelve,' she said, 'and I came to the palace to live with Sangita-Aunty. It was unlikely I would ever find a husband because I had no dowry. So she trained me to follow her former profession.'

I couldn't imagine which profession required a woman to be proficient at archery or sword skills.

Lakshmi laughed. 'Don't look so puzzled! It goes back to when Asaf Jah gave the palace to Jahanara Begum. He guessed he hadn't long to live and wanted her and her daughter Priya Begum, then only fourteen, to be secure. He sent them away from Aurangabad to Hyderabad with the Rose of Golconda ...'

'The lost diamond?'

'Just so,' said Lakshmi. 'The Rose was to provide for them for the rest of their lives.'

It surprised me that a Nizam should give a mere dancer, however graceful, such costly gifts. I could only assume that Priya Begum was his natural daughter but I couldn't ask Lakshmi about that. 'So how did they manage after the Rose was stolen?'

She shrugged. 'Jahanara Begum sold her other jewels. As I was saying, they travelled to Hyderabad in covered *howdahs* and bullock carts with a retinue of twenty-five servants, sixteen horses, four elephants, a eunuch and six members of the Nizam's harem guard. The guard, of course, were all women since no men, apart from the eunuch, were allowed in the *zenana*.'

'Female guards?' I was astonished.

'Soldiers, trained in the art of war and to protect the honour and the lives of the ladies of his *zenana* unto the death. As instructed by the Nizam, the guards transferred their loyalty to the Begum and her family.' Lakshmi ran her fingers along the curve of the bow. 'This is made from strips of buffalo horn and is one of the weapons the guards brought with them. You see, I am one of the descendants of those guards.'

I understood now why she carried an almost masculine air of authority. 'I had no idea that there could be female soldiers.' I smiled to myself at the thought of the astonishment on the faces of the ladies of St Biddulph's sewing circle at such an idea.

Lakshmi lifted her chin. 'They train and fight as hard as any man.'

Looking at the way she moved, as if always poised for action, I didn't doubt her. 'So are there other members of the guard, beside you and Sangita?'

She shook her head. 'I am the only one now. Before me, Sangita worked alone for three years. Serving female guards must be unmarried and Jahanara Begum pensions them off when they reach thirty years of age. When I arrived here, Sangita had fallen in love with Gopal, the palace steward who is now her husband. He didn't want to wait until she was thirty to marry her. Sangita saw her opportunity and asked Jahanara Begum's permission to train me to take her place.'

'What happened to the other guards?'

Lakshmi shrugged. 'My grandmother, Usha, you have met. Most of the other original members of the women's guard have died but two, now a great age, remain in the palace. Some, like Sangita, left to be married. My mother, Nadeen, was Sangita's elder sister and she also trained to be a guard before ...'

'Before?'

'Before she fell in love with a visitor to the palace and gave up everything for him. My grandmother cursed her and said she had bad blood.' Reaching over her shoulder, Lakshmi took a reed arrow from the quiver, fitted it to her bow and aimed. The tendons bunched in her slender wrist and then the arrow whistled past my ear, straight to the centre of the target.

Jai let out a cheer.

'Well done!' I was curious. 'Is a women's guard really necessary to protect the *zenana*?'

Lakshmi took another bow from the quiver. 'I keep my ear to the ground, listening for trouble,' she said. 'I control the security of the palace and sleep in the ante-room to the Begum's bedroom. Should the need arise, I will die defending her.' She took aim, loosed the arrow and the tip buried itself in the target immediately adjacent to the first one.

'I'm impressed.'

She withdrew a jewelled dagger from her belt. 'All the guards were issued one of these, each with a different-coloured jewel.' She ran her finger over the sapphires glinting on the hilt that matched her turban pin. Sliding the dagger back into its sheath, she said, 'I am proficient in horsemanship, hand-to-hand fighting and shooting.' She set another arrow in her bow, aimed, and watched impassively as it found the centre of the target.

I stared at the arrow, still quivering beside the others.

'I could sever a man's head with one slash of my sword if I wished.'

Three other arrows followed in quick succession, each hitting their target, the sixth splitting the first down its full length. Her lips curved in a smile.

Jai yelled in delight and I wondered if she'd put on such a demonstration of her expertise to impress me. 'The Begum need have no fear while you are beside her,' I said. 'I'm full of admiration for your skills.'

'Learning these skills, and keeping them honed, takes a great deal of discipline. When I came to the palace I needed a channel for my anger and unhappiness. Hard training provided me with that.'

'Your anger and unhappiness?'

'My father never ceased mourning the loss of my elder sister, a girl I never knew. All through my childhood, he continually related tales of her great intelligence and beauty. I tried hard, so hard, to be as clever and pretty as she had been.'

Lakshmi's full mouth trembled and I pitied her, picturing her as a little girl striving endlessly to please her father.

'Eventually I believed I'd earned a special place in his heart,' she said, 'but after my parents died I learned Father, despite his loving words, had betrayed me.' Her lips tightened. 'There was no money and the dowry he had promised me did not exist. At twelve years old I was left to fend for myself in a cruel world.'

My father had abandoned me, too, so perhaps we were not so different after all. 'I'm so sorry.'

Her face was a mask, her emotions unreadable. 'I do not need your sympathy. I have forged a new life for myself. But I see in you my own earlier sorrow and disappointment. What outlet will *you* find for your anger and unhappiness, Bee Sinclair? Or will you let them destroy you?'

I stared at her, not caring if she sensed my sudden hostility at her intrusive questioning. There was a flicker of amusement in her eyes and I dropped my gaze.

'Well?'

'I don't know,' I said. 'I don't *know*.'

'Then I suggest you think about it.' She strode towards the target to collect the arrows while Jai skipped along beside her.

I disliked her for her observation but she was right, of course. Unless I found a new purpose in life I would drown in the well of my own misery.

Chapter 12

The conversation with Lakshmi had unsettled me. I continued my explorations for a while before returning to the *zenana*. Tentatively, I joined the ladies in the sitting room and breakfasted with them on tea, apricots and mangoes.

Afterwards, Leela took from her workbag a shawl of shimmering peacock blue silk. I watched her nimble fingers as she plied her needle and my own itched to start a new piece of work.

'The ladies in England would love this,' I said, thinking of Alice's acquisitive comments about my rose-pink shawl.

'Tell me about England,' said Leela.

The three younger girls, sensing a story, came to sit beside us, as graceful as young gazelles.

'It's hard to know where to begin. England is much colder than India and it rains a great deal.'

'Even more than here in the monsoon season?'

'It's a different kind of rain from what I remember of the monsoons.' I frowned while I thought how to describe it. 'Sometimes it's so fine you can't see it and at others it might be cold and spiteful, like needles in your face.'

The girls laughed.

'Tell us more,' said Leela. 'Tell me the things Ralph wouldn't notice, like the fashions women wear, how they style their hair and how they amuse themselves.'

The rest of the women pulled their cushions up beside us, some bringing their embroidery to work on while they listened.

An hour later I finished my stories, my spirits restored a little by my receptive audience. Their intense interest in me was heady and quite different from the sharp questioning of the members of St Biddulph's sewing circle.

I left the ladies' sitting room and found my way to Jahanara Begum's terrace garden, where her handmaid came to greet me.

'May I visit the Begum?'

The girl bowed her head. 'She is already waiting for you.'

We went into an airy room with a white marble colonnade allowing glimpses of the ante-rooms beyond. A frieze of shimmering mother-of-pearl fragments made the ceiling and walls glimmer with reflected light.

Jahanara Begum, resplendent in a purple and gold shawl, reposed on a high-backed gilt chair, set upon a dais. The arms of the chair were carved to resemble crouching tigers and her fingers curled over the creatures' heads.

The Begum's lips curved in a smile when she saw me staring at her throne.

'Impressive, isn't it?' she said.

I pressed my hands together and made my *namaste*. 'Extremely.' I eyed the tiger-skin rug on the marble floor, complete with head. Fangs bared, the mouth was open in a snarl and the glassy eyes appeared to regard me with contempt.

She waved a hand and the handmaid hurried forward with a scarlet-cushioned stool and placed it before the throne.

Avoiding the tiger, I stepped onto the dais and perched on the footstool.

'You are thinking that I imagine myself to be a *rani*?' she said.

I wasn't sure how to answer, since that was exactly what I was thinking, but then I saw the glint of humour in her black eyes. 'It seems entirely fitting,' I said, seeking the right words, 'that you sit on a throne, since you are the indisputed queen of this palace.'

She gave a bark of laughter. 'I may have been so once, and I use every means possible to cling to my authority, but the simple truth is that my old knees make it too painful for me to sit on the floor these days.' She spoke slowly, with gestures, to help me understand. 'This throne was made for the Durbar Hall more than a hundred years ago. The palace carpenter added wheels to it so nowadays I can sit at my ease wherever I like.' She leaned closer to me. 'Now, tell me, how have you passed the time since you arrived?'

'I've been exploring,' I said, 'and talking to the ladies in the *zenana*. This morning Jai took me to the top of a tower to see the view over the city.'

'Harry's boy?' Jahanara Begum smiled. 'My great-great-grandson has his father's courage and his poor mother's charm. And what else have you seen?'

'Lakshmi practising her archery in the *pilkhana*. She's very skilled.'

'And disciplined,' said Jahanara Begum. She sighed. 'She is lit from within by an energy that must be expended or it will consume her. She was a troubled girl when she came here and I knew at once that she would never be happy in the *zenana*. The women there are too gentle and compliant to keep her amused.' She regarded me through narrowed eyes. 'I think you have that same energy within you.'

'I'm not so sure about that. Though I understand why she doesn't want to spend her life confined behind the walls of the *zenana*.'

'If you are born to it there is comfort in the company of women.'

'Do you often venture out of your quarters?'

'Often enough to see what is happening.' She called for her

handmaid to bring the hookah and, once it was bubbling away at her side, offered me the mouthpiece.

Reluctantly, I took it from her, not wishing to give offence, and tentatively drew a mouthful of tobacco vapour. I wished I hadn't. As I coughed convulsively, Jahanara Begum's amused glance shifted over my shoulder and her face lit up.

Harry Wyndham stood at the foot of the dais. 'Will you receive another visitor today, Jahanara Begum?'

She beckoned him forward and he bent to touch her foot.

He gave me one of his devastating smiles as he did and I sat up straighter and attempted to stop coughing. 'Good morning, Bee. So you managed to find your way to your room without any difficulty last night? I wasn't sure whether to offer to guide you or if that might have alarmed you even more than the prospect of losing your way.'

My cheeks grew hotter. 'I managed perfectly well, thank you.' At least he didn't mention my first, never to be repeated, brush with a hookah.

'Don't tease her, Harry,' said Jahanara, leaning over to pinch his cheek. 'What mischief have you been up to since I saw you last?'

He shrugged. 'Oh, this and that. I may have to leave the palace for a few days.'

Jahanara looked at him intently as she handed him the hookah mouthpiece. 'Again? You have only recently returned.'

'Nothing escapes your attention, does it? There's a stallion for sale at Golconda. I thought I might go and take a look at him.'

'And I suppose it's possible that while you are there you will take a ride around Raymond's estate?'

Harry drew slowly on the hookah and tobacco smoke curled around him. 'I suppose I might. Simply to spy out the land, as it were. Raymond is currently at court, charming the Nizam again.'

'Take care, Harry! You are looking for trouble if you poke a stick into a hornets' nest.'

'I shall be as inconspicuous as a panther on a moonless night.'

Jahanara turned to me. 'I hope he is less inconspicuous than he was when I found him some years ago, prowling around my palace without an invitation.'

'The Begum caught me red-handed,' said Harry. There was laughter in his voice. 'Jahanara Begum, did you know that Bee once broke into this palace, too?'

The old lady looked at me, her eyebrows raised.

Heat flooded my face again. 'I was eight years old,' I said, 'and Harry brought me here to search for the lost Rose of Golconda.'

A shadow passed over her face. 'I share his desire to find the Rose. If he'd lived, my benefactor would have been deeply disappointed to know I failed to keep it safe.'

She spoke in low tones and I missed some of the meaning. Seeing my confusion, Harry translated for me.

I frowned while I tried to remember the story. 'It was a servant who stole the diamond, wasn't it?'

'One of my guards betrayed me.' Jahanara gripped the tigers' heads on the throne's armrests so tightly her knuckles turned white. 'Of all my guards, Padma was the one I trusted most.'

Harry turned to me and spoke in English again. 'Padma had become involved with Natesh, the palace's senior steward at the time. They schemed together to steal the Rose.'

'I still find it hard to believe,' said Jahanara Begum. 'Another of my guards, Usha ...'

'Lakshmi's grandmother?' I asked.

She nodded. 'Usha grew suspicious when she saw Padma and Natesh frequently whispering together,' she said. 'Then the day came when there was an earthquake and the whole palace shook. People screamed and ran outside. Usha saw Padma hurrying away from my quarters and realised my jewel chest had been forced open. She followed Padma and caught her in the act of handing the diamond to Natesh.'

101

'There was a vicious fight,' said Harry. 'At the end of it, Usha was hideously injured, Padma was dead and Natesh had run away with the diamond.'

'Usha was distraught,' said Jahanara. 'Not only was she devastated that Padma was a traitor but she felt she had failed in her duty to safeguard the Rose. Usha may have mostly recovered from her physical injuries but her mind has never been the same again.'

'To this day, no one has heard any news of the diamond,' said Harry. 'I suspect it must have been cut into smaller stones so that it didn't attract attention when it was sold.'

Jahanara Begum closed her eyes. 'I set a curse on Natesh and anyone else who keeps the Rose from me, its rightful owner. The theft was shocking enough then but, now that I have sold the most valuable of my jewels to pay the servants' wages, I have little left. The palace is falling down around us.' She cupped her hands over her face. 'So many people depend on me.'

Suddenly the old lady appeared very frail. I glanced at Harry and his expression showed concern for her, too.

'Perhaps the palace could be repaired?' I said. 'So many people live here, surely some of them have the necessary skills?'

'Such quantities of building materials are too expensive,' said Jahanara. She twisted her fingers together, obviously distressed.

'Perhaps we should allow her to rest now?' I whispered to Harry.

He stood up. 'We have overtired you, Jahanara Begum.'

'It is not you who have made me weary,' she said, fretfully. 'I worry about so many things. The palace is falling apart and I can no longer support its inhabitants. The Nizam is in a weakened position. I do not trust the French and I do not trust the British East India Company.' She gave a long and wavering sigh. 'Where will it all end?'

Harry and I left quietly, leaving Jahanara Begum's handmaid to tend to her.

We walked in silence through the garden, pausing to look over the wall at the countryside.

'Harry,' I said, 'why doesn't Jahanara Begum trust the British East India Company?'

In the bright sunlight I saw the worry lines traced around his eyes. 'What concerns her is that they might use their strength to annex the valuable Deccan plateau for themselves.'

'But surely the French are the real threat to stability here?'

He rested his hands on the stone wall and watched a drift of smoke rising from the hillside. 'My mother was French, you know.'

'She was?' I was surprised to hear that.

'My father rescued her after the Siege of Pondicherry,' said Harry. 'All I remember of her was a cloud of black hair and her soft voice when she spoke to me in her language.' He sighed. 'Perhaps it's as well that she died young. It was hard for her to be happy, ostracised as she was by my father's friends and knowing their marriage hampered his career.'

'Doesn't being half-French place you in an awkward position now?'

He shrugged. 'Strangely, it's been a great help. The East India Company finds it useful that I speak French fluently, as well as the various Indian dialects I learned from my *ayahs*.' Grinning, he told me, 'It's surprising what information you can discover, sharing a drink around the fire in a French camp.'

'But aren't your loyalties ever divided?'

'I never knew any of my French relatives and feel no affinity with France.' He scowled. 'Napoleon's desire to dominate the world angers me. I shall fight him to the death. I've spent most of my life in India, apart from those miserable years at school in England. India is my home. I love everything about this country,' he said, his voice low and full of passion, 'the stark contrasts and the maddening inconsistencies, the extraordinary superstitions, the intense heat and the diverse cultures and religions. Most of all, I love the people.'

I studied his strong profile, noting the way his jaw clenched and unclenched as he spoke. This was another side of him I was seeing, quite different from his usual teasing manner. I wanted to touch his hand and promise him that everything would be all right.

'My father loved it too,' I said. I squinted into the sun and recalled sitting on Father's knee, while he told me wonderful stories of strange gods disguised as animals and the valour of Indian princes. 'He often told me how much there was to learn from the different cultures here.'

'He was right,' said Harry. 'But I sense change in the air.' The acrid scent of wood smoke drifted towards us, heavier now. 'And I fear, very much, what might happen to India as a result.'

Chapter 13

Lakshmi was waiting for me in the stables the following morning. 'Come and meet Mumtaz,' she said.

On the other side of the yard, a *scyce* was busy tightening the girth on a plump piebald pony.

'You will ride astride, as I do,' Lakshmi instructed. 'We have no side saddles here for European women.'

Mother would have been horrified at the very idea of me sitting astride a pony but that made me all the more determined to proceed. Mumtaz suffered my tentative pat and looked at me with limpid dark eyes fringed with stubby white eyelashes.

A few minutes later, Lakshmi showed me how to mount the creature and hold the reins. I perched on its wide back, wondering how I would manage to maintain my seat.

'Don't look so scared!' said Lakshmi.

I stopped frowning and straightened my spine, unwilling to let her see my nervousness.

'Chin up and hands down! Meld with the pony, become one with her so that she feels your confidence and knows you are her mistress.'

That was easier said than done but I made an effort to loosen my desperate grip on the reins.

'We'll go to the *maidan* and see how you do.'

Mumtaz lurched forward and I clutched at the rough hair of her mane as Lakshmi led her out of the yard on a long rein.

Two hours later I'd had enough. Lakshmi had shouted endless instructions at me and my thighs ached from clinging to the pony's back. Nevertheless, I felt a sense of achievement that I'd managed to walk and then trot around the *maidan* without falling off.

Returning to the stable yard, I slithered down from the saddle and found to my chagrin that my knees trembled.

Lakshmi laughed. 'Don't worry, you'll become used to it. Your seat is good and you didn't do too badly for a first attempt. Now you must watch and see how the *syce* removes the saddle and rubs the pony down.'

'I'd no idea there was so much to learn,' I said, stroking Mumtaz's nose.

'Tomorrow we'll try without the leading rein.'

I ached too much to think about another lesson just then and there was something else troubling me. 'Lakshmi, I need more clothes,' I said. 'My English skirts are entirely unsuitable for horse riding.' I glanced down at my borrowed clothing, now smelling distinctly of the stable. 'And I must have these laundered and returned to you.'

She nodded. 'After my archery practice, we shall go to the bazaar.'

Once Mumtaz had been returned to her stable, I wandered through the echoing spaces of the palace on my way to the *zenana*. I blundered into the room adjacent to the Durbar Hall where some of the servants and their families lived. Discomfited, I drew back as conversation ceased and a number of faces turned towards me.

Then a small child, barely walking and dressed only in a ragged vest, came tottering over. He tripped and fell, bursting into noisy cries. I lifted him up and rubbed his knees, crooning at him until he rewarded me with a smile.

The child's mother, little more than a girl, hurried to take him from me. Smiling, she beckoned for me to follow her. Not knowing how to refuse without giving offence, I obeyed. She led me behind a tattered curtain and indicated that I was to sit on the quilted floor cloth. The little boy scrambled onto my knee and pushed a thumb in his mouth.

His mother busied herself making tea and I noticed with a pang that she was expecting another baby. I sipped the tea awkwardly while the child grew heavy in my arms. The family's meagre possessions were ranged on a makeshift shelf; earthenware bowls containing a little flour, a few ounces of lentils, and a handful of herbs. A small shrine consisting of a crudely painted picture of Lord Krishna, incense sticks and a brass bell had been set up in one corner.

By the time I'd finished my tea, the child was fast asleep. Unable to move without waking him, I sat quietly while his mother mended her husband's torn *dhoti* with small, neat stitches. She told me her name was Hemanti and her son was Talin. Her husband had been one of the palace gardeners.

'But now,' she said, fear in her eyes, 'there is no more paid work for him and he has gone away to seek employment. I have never lived anywhere else but in the Jahanara Mahal.'

I leaned back against the damp-stained wall, reflecting that a few months ago I could never have imagined I'd be sitting on the floor of an Indian family's home, consisting of little more than a curtained alcove. It was all very far away from my genteel life in a Hampshire village.

I stroked the boy's satiny cheek and closed my eyes for a moment, imagining it was the warm body of my own lost child sleeping in my arms. At last Talin stirred and whimpered for his mother. I handed him back to her and rose awkwardly to my feet.

'You are always welcome to our home,' Hemanti said with quiet dignity, 'even if there is no tea left to share.' She buried her face in Talin's hair, her eyes suddenly bright with tears.

It troubled me to speculate what might happen to her small family. I promised to visit again and returned to the *zenana* to change for my visit to the bazaar with Lakshmi.

Jyoti giggled as she helped me into my shift and short stays, clearly bemused as to why I wished to wear such garments. I slipped on my mourning dress, the sleeves buttoned tightly to the wrist and neck. Releasing my hair from its plait, I dressed it in my usual chignon with a few loose curls to the front. All the while Jyoti watched with undisguised interest.

As I walked along the corridor to the ladies' sitting room, I reflected how much more ease of movement I'd enjoyed in native dress.

The ladies were interested to see me in European clothes again and gathered around to examine the button fastenings and to touch my chignon.

'Lakshmi has been teaching me to ride this morning,' I said. 'She's going to take me to the bazaar to help me buy suitable clothes to wear here.'

'If you are going to the bazaar, will you bring me some needles?' asked Leela.

Indira, one of Samira Begum's cousins, waved her *dupatta* at me to attract my attention. 'I need some attar of roses! The best kind, from the Turk who has a stall at the back of the bazaar.'

A few moments later I had a dozen commissions.

I drank a refreshing mint and lemon sherbet with the ladies and then Lakshmi arrived. Although dressed in colourful, feminine clothes again, her watchful expression and her height set her apart from the other occupants of the *zenana*.

'Shall we go?' she said.

I pulled on my straw bonnet and followed her.

We went down the front steps of the palace to the terrace overlooking the river. I stopped for a moment to watch two baby monkeys playing chase.

Smiling, I said, 'Aren't they delightful? Look at their little pink ears!'

'They're savage,' said Lakshmi.

'Surely you exaggerate?' I'd barely said the words when a larger monkey made a run towards us, yellow fangs bared.

Lakshmi pulled me back. 'She thinks you are threatening her young.'

The sun was almost overhead and heat prickled my back and shoulders under my black dress. I regretted forgetting my parasol.

As we walked beside the river the air became full of choking smoke and I saw a small crowd standing around a bonfire.

'A funeral pyre,' said Lakshmi.

Sickened, I covered my nose against the smell.

'The British try to stop it,' she said, 'but often widows still throw themselves on the fire to burn with their husbands.'

'That's barbaric!'

Lakshmi shrugged. 'What life does a widow have after her husband is dead?'

We walked on in silence.

When we were crossing the bridge, a leper called out to me with hoarse cries until I dropped a few coins into his begging bowl. When I moved on again, I couldn't see Lakshmi. A cow lay down in the middle of the bridge, causing an obstruction to the passing traffic, but no one disturbed it. I glanced about me and frowned when I finally glimpsed Lakshmi talking animatedly to a French soldier. The bridge was crowded with carts and a seething mass of pedestrians and I lost sight of her again. I dodged through the throng, narrowly avoiding having my toes crushed by a bullock cart. When I reached her I was out of breath.

'I thought I'd lost you!' I said. 'Was that a French soldier I saw you talking to?'

Irritation flickered across her face. 'You know what soldiers are like.'

'Not really,' I said.

'There are so many in Hyderabad and they pester any female they meet.' She turned on her heel and set off again.

The bazaar was just as I remembered it. My ears rang with the raucous cries of the vendors, the twittering of caged birds and the shrill gossip of women. A fog of tobacco smoke mingled with the greasy vapour from the charcoal braziers drifted up to the vaulted ceiling. On the air was a pungent aroma of onions frying in *ghee*, patchouli and rotting vegetables. Fascinated, I stopped to watch a snake charmer playing his pipe while a hooded cobra appeared out of a basket and swayed from side to side.

Lakshmi pulled me away, elbowing us through the heaving throng until we came to a stall displaying folded lengths of cotton and silk. 'Don't say anything,' she said. 'I shall choose what you need.'

I opened my mouth to insist I was perfectly capable of making my own choices.

'Don't argue,' Lakshmi said, an adversarial glint in her eye. 'He will cheat a European woman.'

She began a conversation with the stallholder. He began to unfold different lengths of cloth, smoothing them flat with plump fingers, all the while keeping up a rapid monologue of sales patter. Lakshmi shook her head and made as if to turn away. Sighing, he took out from beneath the counter an armful of pieces of fine muslin. Picking through the soft material, Lakshmi withdrew a length that pleased her.

I stepped forward to look but she frowned at me so fiercely I shrank back.

She proceeded to enter into a voluble argument with the stallholder, who pressed a fist to his heart and raised his eyes to the heavens, proclaiming that his children would starve if he accepted such an insultingly low offer.

At last the deal was done and, in apparent good humour, he finally folded up several lengths of cloth into a neat parcel and tied it with string.

'I have made some very good bargains,' said Lakshmi with a satisfied smile after we had walked away.

The entire exercise was repeated at several other stalls, including a shoemaker's, and then she haggled for the small purchases required by the ladies of the *zenana*.

While I was waiting, I was disturbed to see several groups of French soldiers wandering around the bazaar, looking at the stalls and eating *biryani* off banana leaves. Now I'd noted them, I caught glimpses of their blue uniforms everywhere.

There was a light touch on my arm and I spun around, afraid it was a pick-pocket.

'Mrs Sinclair! I thought it was you.' Mrs Clements stood before me with a wide smile on her freckled face. 'Allow me to introduce Mrs Ure.'

A stout lady stood beside Mrs Clements. She was stuffed into a too-tight dress, her moon face glistening in the heat. Bhupal, the Clementses' manservant, waited a few paces behind them with an armful of packages.

'Mrs Ure, this is Mrs Sinclair, my travelling companion on our recent voyage to India.' Mrs Clements turned to me. 'Mrs Ure is the wife of the Residency's doctor.'

We made the usual pleasantries while I pitied Mrs Ure, who clearly found the heat intolerable.

'Surely you aren't here on your own, Mrs Sinclair?' asked Mrs Clements.

'Oh, no!' I waved towards Lakshmi, deep in conversation with a stallholder.

'You've brought your maid?' Mrs Clements pressed a hand to her chest. 'What a relief! I'd have been worried to see you alone in such a place as this.'

It was too complicated to disabuse her of the notion that Lakshmi was my maid.

She leaned towards me and whispered, 'Have you seen all the

French soldiers? I hope to goodness they won't murder us in our beds.'

'I hope so too,' I murmured. 'Have you settled in comfortably?'

'Hyderabad is certainly different from Calcutta,' she said. 'I feel the lack of female company and was sorry to find you won't be living in the Residency grounds. Promise me you'll come for tea one afternoon?'

'I'd like that,' I said.

She smiled. 'Then, if you will excuse us, I must continue my search for a pair of embroidered evening slippers. Mr Clements and I have been invited to dine with the Resident.'

We said our goodbyes and the two ladies drifted away.

As Lakshmi and I wandered from stall to stall, I saw her examining some amber-coloured glass bangles. I bought four and presented them to her. 'Thank you for your help today,' I said.

'You bought these for me?' Her face lit up and in that moment I saw how she might have looked as a child, before her character was tarnished by resentment.

With our arms full of purchases, we left the bazaar and walked back over the bridge.

'The other women's clothes are too small for you to use as a pattern,' said Lakshmi. 'Keep mine for now, or we will send for a tailor to make up your material, if you wish.'

'I shall sew them myself,' I said.

'I chose the length of russet cotton to make trousers for riding. They won't show the dust.'

'Thank you for bargaining so well on my behalf.' Laughing, I said, 'That first stallholder met his match in you.'

'I've heard Faisal Mahmoud's tales of woe about starving children before,' she told me. 'Sometimes his wife helps him on the stall and she is always laden with gold bracelets. His children don't go hungry.'

I thought about Hemanti and little Talin. Despite living in a palace, I wouldn't be at all surprised if they went hungry sometimes. Jahanara Begum had been distressed by her inability to continue to support the household and it occurred to me that, if something wasn't done soon, the future of the palace and all those who lived there, myself included, would be very uncertain.

We arrived at the Jahanara Mahal and I was relieved to see the monkeys had disappeared from the steps.

'I've very much enjoyed our shopping expedition,' I said, as Lakshmi handed me the parcels she carried.

She turned the glass bangles around on her wrist. 'So have I.' She sounded surprised. 'But next time,' her eyes gleamed with sudden amusement, 'let me do all the bargaining. You paid far too much for these.'

'I wanted to give you a present,' I said, 'and, to me, they were worth their price to see your smile.' The amusement faded from her eyes then and I wondered uncomfortably if I had presumed too soon on our fragile friendship.

'Sunrise, tomorrow morning,' she said. 'Mumtaz and I will be waiting at the stables for you.' Without waiting for my reply, she walked off down the corridor.

In my room, I slipped on my new tan leather sandals and wriggled my toes, enjoying the coolness and sense of freedom. Gathering up my workbox and some of the packages, I went to the *zenana*.

The ladies crowded around me to claim their purchases and to examine mine. I presented them with a tray of *halwa* and *jalebi* fried in *ghee* and dripping with honey syrup and, from their squeals of pleasure, guessed my gift was a success.

After we'd finished the sticky treats, I laid the russet brown material flat on the floor. Using Lakshmi's trousers as a pattern, I cut out my new riding attire. I tacked the pieces together and slipped them on under my dress.

The three girls laughed to see me in half-European, half-Indian garb and crowded closer to watch.

'Leela,' I called, 'will you tell me if they fit properly at the back?'

She put down her embroidery and tweaked a seam straight. 'They are too loose at the waist but you can gather them tighter with the drawstring.'

Leela's mother and grandmother, Samira Begum and Priya Begum, came to offer their advice, too.

The remainder of the afternoon passed in quiet companionship, chatting while we sewed.

I whispered to Leela when I couldn't remember the ladies' names and she patiently reminded me. Parvati played a *veena*, a musical instrument resembling a lute, while Veeda sang a pensive ballad of unrequited love. The girls giggled and oiled each other's hair before plaiting it and tying the ends with yellow silk.

Later, when I returned to my room, I reflected again on the pleasure to be found in the camaraderie of female friends. Although I'd spent most of my life cooped up with Mother, there had never been the close bond between us that I saw between these women in their small and enclosed world.

It was as I put my half-completed sewing away that I had the idea. I pulled open the window screen and rested my elbows on the sill as I turned it over in my mind. It was a scheme that made good use of the resources available in the palace and might make a significant difference to its future. Undoubtedly there would be difficulties but if I could overcome them ...

Chapter 14

It was early evening when Jyoti tapped on my door to tell me Ralph had returned from the Residency and hoped I would join him for tea in the pavilion.

My new sandals slapped against the floor as I strolled through the palace and it amused me that my footsteps now sounded exactly like those of the ladies of the *zenana*. Mother would have found it abhorrent that I'd 'gone native', which only added a spring to my step because now I no longer had to worry about her censure.

A low sun shone through the grimy windows of the Durbar Hall, filling it with an amber glow and sparking fiery glints from the inset jewels. Although so shabby, the Jahanara Mahal still had the ability to catch me by surprise with its beauty. I left the Durbar Hall through the garden doors and waved to Hemanti, sitting on the adjacent veranda, picking through rice. Several of the other women squatting beside her waved back, too, and a handful of ragged children surrounded me and skipped along at my heels.

I hadn't yet explored the grounds properly but I spied the roof of a pavilion behind the walls of the enclosed garden. Pushing open a gate, I shooed the children away and paused to take in the scene.

The garden was laid out in the formal Mughal fashion, with canals and a rectangular pool to reflect the sky. The pavilion surmounted a raised hillock and the straight paths were lined with trees that were once clipped but now sadly grown out of shape. Everywhere was a delicious profusion of perfumed flowers. My footsteps crunched along the gravel path, alerting a dozen monkeys sitting on the pavilion roof.

I stopped and we eyed each other warily until Ralph came down to greet me.

'It still gives me a shock to see you with a moustache,' I said, as he kissed my cheek.

He smiled. 'I'm no longer your little brother.' Taking my arm, he led me to a *charpai* heaped with cushions. A tray of refreshments had been set on a low table before the couch.

He poured me a glass of mint tea. 'How are you settling in?'

The view from the pavilion was framed by a purple honeysuckle trailing from the roof. I sipped my tea for a moment while I considered how to reply. 'I'd forgotten how overwhelming and surprising this country can be,' I said. 'I was so happy here as a child, but then there were all those miserable years spent living with Mother while I yearned to come back. I hated the cold grey place I had to learn to call home. I missed Madhu and Father and everything that was familiar. Then you were sent away to school.' I glanced up at him. 'You were little more than a baby and I worried so for you.'

'I hated school but it wasn't much fun when I came home for the holidays, either.' Ralph's expression was grim. 'Still, it taught me to be self-reliant.'

'What I used to miss most,' I said, 'was the freedom we had in India. Do you remember how we'd hide in the peepul tree all day and make dens in the garden, or sit and watch the cook while he made us *idlis* for breakfast?'

Ralph smiled. 'He always said he made the best *idlis* in all of India, as "white as the moon and as fluffy as cotton balls".'

I lifted my head to catch the scent of jasmine on the evening breeze. 'On the journey here from Masulipatam some men stole our elephant and tried to make off with my trunk. It shocked me that such a thing would happen in the country I'd remembered as being perfect. And travelling was so hot and dirty! There are starving people living in little more than hovels and hideously maimed lepers begging on street corners.'

'There's always been poverty in India.'

'I didn't notice it as a child. You've had more time to grow used to it. Now, I must learn to love this new India.'

'A fresh start for you,' he said, 'after all your troubles. I was very sorry to hear about your husband and child.'

'Until Charles came along, I thought I'd missed my chance of having a family of my own. It seemed like a miracle when he proposed to me after Mother died. And then, when I knew I was expecting, my happiness seemed complete.' My voice broke and I squeezed my eyes shut.

'Perhaps you will find new joy here.' My brother spoke with no real conviction.

'I'm under no illusions, Ralph. I'm past my prime and won't have the opportunity to marry again. I shall, however, endeavour to be useful. I hope that, in due course, I will become a good aunt to your children.'

He chewed at the ends of his moustache. 'Are you very shocked that I married Leela?' He looked at me with appeal in his eyes.

'I was at first,' I said. 'But she's delightful. I'll admit your choice surprised me since you were always such a phlegmatic and conventional boy.'

'A cover for my insecurity.' Ralph's lips twitched. 'Mother would have been *appalled* if she'd known. It's cowardly of me, I know, but I'm so thankful I'll never have to tell her.'

I shuddered, imagining the scene.

'You know, it's not at all unusual for Englishmen to marry the local women or else to keep one as a *bibi*. A concubine,' he said, seeing my puzzled expression. 'The few European women out here have come to accompany their husbands. Besides ...' He chewed at his moustache again. 'European women always seem so *difficult*. You remember what Mother was like.'

'How could I forget?' I said, a touch of vinegar in my voice. 'I was the one who had to live with her all those years, pandering to her whims with never an iota of gratitude in return. At least you avoided that.'

Ralph hunched his shoulders and glanced at me sideways. 'I'm sorry if you're angry because I wasn't there to share the burden. I didn't have any choice, you know. I'm not a natural soldier and didn't much like serving in the East India Company's army. Father said it was necessary so as to build my career.'

I sighed. At least Father had taken some interest in Ralph, even though he'd forgotten about me.

My brother's expression softened. 'Leela is not only beautiful,' he said, 'but as gentle as a little bird. All she wants is to please me. You can't imagine how much I love her. When I talk about my work, she listens so intently and makes intelligent suggestions that help me to see the way forward. And I owe all this happiness to Harry.'

'To Harry?'

'Leela told you he was married to her sister Noor?'

I nodded.

'It was through Harry that my marriage was arranged. He said that if I was half as content with Leela as he'd been with Noor, then I'd think I'd gone to heaven. And I do.'

'I'm pleased you're happy.' It was true but, selfishly, it made my heart ache all the more for my own losses.

Ralph patted my hand.

Silently, we watched the setting sun paint the sky with streaks of saffron and indigo while we sipped our tea.

'Did you see much of Father after you finished school and returned to India?'

Ralph shrugged. 'We met once or twice in Calcutta. He died long before I was stationed in Hyderabad. It was awkward meeting him. I was so young when we left India that I barely remembered him.'

'I missed him terribly.'

'It's in the past now, Bee. You must look ahead.'

He was right, of course, but it was easy for him to say that, enjoying newfound happiness with Leela.

'Tell me what else has surprised you about India,' he said.

I made an effort to swallow my unhappiness. He really had no idea of all I'd suffered. 'When I left Hampshire I imagined my new home would be in a bungalow in the Residency grounds,' I said. 'I could never have imagined I'd live in a palace. Especially this particular one.'

'Surely you like the palace better than a bungalow?'

'Of course I do! But, Ralph, what's going to happen to it? Some parts are derelict and Jahanara Begum tells me that she's no longer able to maintain it.'

He hunched his shoulders defensively. 'Harry and I do what we can to assist financially. Noor and Leela's father died years ago. The few remaining men in the family are too old to supply much of an income. That's why Jahanara Begum allowed Harry and me to marry Noor and Leela. We didn't ask for a dowry.'

'Neither of you can earn enough for the upkeep of a palace!' I said. 'I can't bear to think of how Jahanara's family and the servants are going to manage in the future. Some of them have lived here for generations.'

Ralph rubbed his temples. 'That keeps me awake at night, too.'

'And the palace is our home now,' I said. 'We can't ignore the problem.'

The corners of his mouth turned up in a rueful smile. 'That's exactly what does happen in India. If a problem is too large to solve, you simply pretend it's not happening.'

'But we *have* to do something about it.'

He shrugged. 'What *can* we do? Apart from find the lost Rose of Golconda.' He smiled at the joke.

The moment had come. 'Ralph, I've had an idea.'

'What kind of an idea?'

'I haven't considered it in depth yet. There are so many people living in the palace: Jahanara Begum's extended family, her servants and their families, friends who came to stay and never went home...'

'The hangers-on will soon disappear once there's no money forthcoming.' Ralph's expression was gloomy in the fading light. 'I expect I'll have to stump up a few rupees to keep a handful of servants. The Begum and the ladies of the *zenana* haven't been bred to do menial work like washing, cooking and cleaning.'

'No,' I said, 'but they can all sew. Even the wives of some of the servants can sew.' I pictured Hemanti mending her husband's *dhoti* with neat little stitches.

'What use is that, apart from for mending clothes and turning the sheets sides-to-middle?'

'When Leela sent me the shawl she'd made, it was much admired. I'm sure there's a market for shawls like that and other richly embroidered articles in England, and perhaps here, too.' I stood up and paced about, warming to my theme. 'Supposing the servant women were trained by the ladies of the *zenana* to make these things?' The more I thought about the idea, the more excited I became. 'I could advise on what styles and colours suit the English market. Since the Revolutionary Wars there are no ladies' fancy goods available from Paris, unless they're smuggled, and I'm sure Indian ornamental items would sell like hot cakes.'

'A pretty idea, Bee, but totally impractical.'

'Why is it?'

He laughed. 'You're a woman and none of the women in the palace, not even you, has any knowledge of business, for a start. No woman is capable of running a successful business; females simply don't have the head for it. It's all very well sewing a few fripperies, but what then? Would you stuff them in your trunk and take them back to Hampshire?'

'We could ...'

'And how would you sell them when you arrived? Or perhaps you intend to take a stall in the bazaar here to hawk the goods?'

I rested my hands on my hips and stood up to face him. 'Why not?'

Ralph's smirk of amusement disappeared. 'Bee, don't be ridiculous! I absolutely forbid it.'

'You have no right to forbid me to do anything!'

'Of course I have. You're under my care and protection.'

Half a dozen monkeys, no doubt curious about the disturbance, swung down from the pavilion roof and sat on their haunches on the pavilion steps, watching us.

'Do you have a better suggestion, Ralph?' I said. 'Or would you prefer to live in a rotting ghost of a palace where women and children huddle in the corners, dying of starvation?' Anger made me shrewish. 'What will become of Leela if she has to leave the *zenana* and go into the world to find menial work, so she can support her mother and grandmother?'

'That's a preposterous suggestion! I'd never allow that to happen. Of course I can provide for them. And you needn't think I'll allow my own wife to become swept up in your hare-brained schemes.' Ralph ran his hands over his hair in agitation. 'Why is it that English women can't find it in themselves to be compliant and gentle like Indian women are? You're as prickly as a burr in my breeches, Bee.' He took a deep breath. 'Now let's forget all this nonsense. I'm going in for dinner with the rest of the men before it grows completely dark.' He pushed himself to his feet and, without waiting for me, stumped off through the darkening garden.

I sat down again, gripping the edge of the bench as hard as if it were my brother's throat, while I forced my breathing to steady. Ralph had become complacent over the years, with an unjustified sense of his own male superiority. He thought I'd grown prickly but, even worse, as I'd harangued him I'd been shocked to hear an echo of Mother's hectoring tone in my own voice. Was it possible that others perceived me to be as pernickety and acid-tongued as she had been?

The monkeys inched closer, staring at me through narrowed eyes. The largest male reared up on his hind legs and bared his fangs.

Suddenly afraid, I called out, 'Ralph?' But he'd gone.

There was a blur of brown fur and two monkeys leaped into the pavilion.

I froze. To my horror the rest of them had commandeered the steps, blocking my escape.

The large male jumped onto the tea tray, knocking over the glasses with a crash. The rest of the group sprang into the pavilion and joined him in pawing over the contents of the tray.

I snatched my chance and raced down the steps.

Chapter 15

I took my dinner in the *zenana* that evening, unwilling to face Ralph again. Still seething with resentment after our quarrel and the fright of coming face to face with marauding monkeys, I was too irritated to sleep. I paced around in the courtyard outside my room until almost dawn, trying to catch a cooling night breeze. I knew Ralph was right regarding my lack of knowledge about the world of commerce but his low opinion of me only served to spur me on to do something to help the inhabitants of the Jahanara Mahal.

In the morning, after my riding lesson, I joined the ladies for breakfast. Leela and her mother, Samira Begum, sat beside me, chattering between themselves when they saw I wasn't in a talkative mood. Still tired, I yawned over my sewing while my thoughts churned.

One of the handmaids came to whisper to Samira Begum that Parwar un-nisa Begum had come to visit. This had a galvanising effect on all the ladies, who hurried to the windows. Outside I saw that two palanquins, richly decorated with scarlet silk, gilded wood and plumes of white feathers, had been set down in the *zenana* garden by liveried bearers. A substantial man, carrying a wicked-looking curved sword at his waist and wearing a gold turban, was assisting a heavily veiled personage to rise from the palanquin's sumptuous cushions. Four handmaids fluttered about nearby. Clearly Parwar un-nisa Begum was a person of considerable importance.

'Who is this lady?' I asked Priya Begum.

'Parwar un-nisa Begum lives at the Chowmahalla Palace in the *zenana* of His Exalted Highness, the Nizam of Hyderabad State.'

'But why has she come here?' I asked.

'She is my second cousin,' said Priya Begum, 'on my father's side and comes to visit us now and again. She is an aunt by marriage to one of His Exalted Highness's wives' sisters so she is very influential.'

Not a little confused by this complicated relationship, I watched in amazement as the ladies and their handmaids scurried around fetching toe-rings, gold bracelets and embroidered shawls, hastily replaiting hair and applying additional kohl to their eyes.

Lakshmi arrived in her guard's uniform, slightly out of breath and armed with her sword and dagger. She waited by the sitting-room door to allow admittance to the visitors.

By the time Parwar un-nisa Begum was announced, the ladies were all gracefully reposing upon their silken cushions, eyes bright and cheeks flushed.

Priya Begum went to welcome the visitor, who was still accompanied by her handmaids and the big man in the gold turban.

'What's he doing in here?' I whispered to Leela. 'Don't the ladies mind?'

She giggled and pressed a finger to her lips. 'It's perfectly acceptable,' she whispered back. 'He's a eunuch.'

I caught my breath and studied him covertly. There was nothing to indicate he wasn't a normal man, except perhaps that he was very plump and his face was rounded and smooth with no moustache.

He made sure Parwar un-nisa Begum was seated comfortably on the largest floor cushion with her handmaids at her side and then retreated to stand with his arms folded and his back to the wall.

Our visitor folded back her filmy veil to reveal her face. Beyond middle years, her looks were unexceptional except for her lively and intelligent expression, but she was magnificently dressed in shimmering coral silk with a border of gold beadwork and heavily decked in gold and diamond jewellery. 'How delightful to see you all again!' she said. 'Though I fear the Jahanara Mahal has deteriorated a little more each time I visit.'

Priya Begum's welcoming smile froze and she glanced at Samira Begum, whose nostrils had flared.

Parwar un-nisa Begum smiled serenely. 'How the little girls have grown!'

Farah, Esha and Jasmin were pushed forward by their mothers to pay their respects.

'And who is this?' Parwar un-nisa Begum's gaze fell upon me.

I approached to make my *namaste*, trying not to sneeze at the overpoweringly musky perfume she wore.

'This is Bee Sinclair, my husband's sister,' said Leela.

'How interesting! Let me see your hair.'

I allowed my *dupatta* to slide down to my shoulders.

'Come!' She patted the cushion beside her and I sat down. Before I knew what she intended, she'd loosened my ribbon and was running her fingers through my hair.

'Remarkable,' she said. 'It's very fine, like gold embroidery silk.' She inspected one of my tresses more closely. 'Is it natural? There's no grey even though you are past the first bloom of youth.'

'Perfectly natural,' I said. 'My brother's hair is the same colour.'

Leela nodded her head in agreement.

The handmaids carried in trays of rose-scented sherbet and honeyed sweetmeats and I was relieved that I was no longer the centre of attention.

'Tell us all your news,' said Samira Begum. 'What is happening in the Nizam's *zenana*?'

'We have a swing,' said Parwar un-nisa Begum. 'It's the latest fashion and has been hung from the neem tree in the garden. There is nothing more agreeable than the gentle motion backwards and forwards and it allows the breeze to cool the face.' Laughing, she said, 'The ladies squabble all the time over whose turn it is to use it next.'

'And what news have you of the Nizam and the outside world?' asked Bimla, greedily licking honey syrup off her plump fingers. 'We heard our old adversaries are building their forces. Do you think there will be another war?'

The ladies leaned forward to listen.

Parwar un-nisa Begum shrugged her narrow shoulders. 'The Nizam has men in each village, fort and city in his territory and spies in every nobleman's palace. There would be warning of any invasion by either Scindia or Tipu Sultan.'

'But if Napoleon joins forces with them,' I said, 'will the Nizam's army then be large enough to defeat his enemies?'

Parwar un-nisa Begum frowned at me. 'What do you know of matters such as this?'

'Nothing at all,' I said hastily.

'The Nizam trusts General Raymond.'

I leaned closer to murmur in Leela's ear. 'I thought the British weren't so sure Raymond wouldn't betray him?'

Our visitor gave me a penetrating glance. 'The Nizam has tangible evidence of the support of French troops while Mr Kirkpatrick has offered only sweet words on behalf of the British. He has so far failed to make any absolute commitment to defend Hyderabad against our enemies.'

Discomfited, I lowered my gaze and was relieved when Samira Begum distracted Parwar un-nisa Begum by offering her the tray of sweetmeats.

The Begum took her time making her selection. 'One of the

female domestics in the Nizam's own *zenana* was discovered passing on information to a palace sweeper,' she said. 'The following day no sign of either of them remained, except for a bloodstain in the dust.'

The women gasped.

'There have always been spies,' said Priya Begum, 'although in a *zenana* it's usually for the purpose of hearing jealous tittle-tattle between two wives as they vie for their husband's attentions and their sons' futures.'

Parwar un-nisa Begum sighed. 'It is indeed most wearisome to witness His Exalted Highness's First Wife, Bakshi Begum, and his Second Wife, Tinat un-Nissa Begum, smiling at each other while their honeyed words drip with poison.'

'It is our good fortune that this *zenana* is quite different,' said Leela, 'since Jahanara Begum has never allowed any of the husbands of her female relatives to have more than one wife. In my own case,' she glanced up through her eyelashes, 'my husband says I am the only wife he desires. Besides, it is not the British way. In Britain there are no *zenanas*.'

Parvati Begum, Leela's cousin, shook her head. 'How uncomfortable it would be to live without female company and in such a way that any man might dishonour you with his gaze.'

The other women murmured in assent and I wondered if any of them had any idea of the threat posed to their way of life if Jahanara Begum could no longer provide financial support for them.

'I must return to the Chowmahalla Palace,' said Parwar un-nisa Begum eventually, rising to her feet with a jangle of bracelets. 'It has been most pleasant to spend time in your company and I hope some of you will come to visit me.' She inclined her head graciously at Samira Begum. 'You may accompany me to my palanquin.'

Samira Begum beckoned to Lakshmi. The eunuch silently moved away from his post by the wall and the small retinue set off for the *zenana* garden.

After they had left, the women discussed the visit at great length, reminding each other of all the details and full of lively interest about the Nizam's network of informers. I was uncomfortable that the British weren't universally perceived to be in a position of particular favour with the Nizam and decided to remove myself from the *zenana* to allow the ladies to talk freely.

I made my way to Jahanara Begum's quarters. A few moments later I was sitting on the footstool beside her throne, trying to avoid the glassy stare of the tiger-skin rug.

'Have you come to tell me about Parwar un-nisa Begum?' she asked.

I smiled. 'Nothing escapes your notice, does it?'

'I hope not. She didn't come to visit me, though.' Jahanara Begum sniffed. 'No doubt she thinks I'm too old to bother with, but I remember her when she was no more than a skinny girl with a head full of nonsense. Now it's stuffed full of her own importance.' She looked down at me. 'So why have you come?'

I bit my lip, not sure how to start or if she might be insulted.

'Well?'

'Parwar un-nisa Begum mentioned that the Jahanara Mahal appears more neglected each time she visits.'

Jahanara Begum exhaled sharply. 'She did, did she? And what business is it of hers?'

'None at all,' I said, 'but unfortunately she's right. The Jahanara Mahal is beautiful but it's fallen into disrepair. If something isn't done, it will become nothing more than a romantic ruin.'

'Do you think I don't know that?' she said, her voice harsh with emotion. She closed her eyes as if it were too painful to hear me talk of this. 'I'm too old and tired now to make it right.'

The uncertainty of the situation gnawed at me. I'd left my old life behind, intending to make a fresh start in India, but the opportunity might crumble away, just like the palace. 'When we met last time,' I said, 'you mentioned how concerned you were that there were no funds left to maintain the palace or to pay the servants.'

She closed her eyes. Tears seeped from beneath the lids.

Doggedly, I continued speaking. 'It's worrying for all those who live here, from yourself down to the lowliest sweeper. As a newcomer, perhaps I see the situation more clearly.'

She lifted her hand and I took this as a signal to continue.

'I've had an idea that might help, though I should tell you my brother doesn't support me.'

'What is it you suggest?'

Her eyes were still closed.

'There are many women living here in the palace,' I said. 'There are the ladies of the *zenana*, of course, but also the wives and daughters of the menservants.'

'Too many of them to count. Some are very old and all are looking to me to provide for them.'

'The embroidered shawls, quilted floor cloths and wall hangings that the women of the *zenana* make are exquisite.'

'I have always encouraged the ladies to sew.' The Begum opened her eyes and looked at me, her mouth curled in a half-smile. 'It keeps them out of mischief if they have less time to gossip themselves into discontentment.'

'I wondered if the ladies might teach the palace women to refine their skills. You see, if they could *all* learn to make these beautiful shawls, embroidered slippers, handkerchiefs, reticules ...'

'Reticules?' Jahanara Begum frowned.

'It's a small bag European women carry with them. They like to take a handkerchief, a few coins, a comb or some smelling salts with them when they go out.'

'How curious!'

'They like embroidered or decorated reticules. As I was saying, if the women could make items like these, perhaps they could be sold to the European market? I believe British women would pay high prices for them and, if we could make enough, it might be possible to bring in a useful income for the palace.'

Jahanara Begum gripped the armrests of her throne. 'Your brother doesn't like the idea?'

My gaze rested on the tiger-skin rug and I tucked my feet more closely under the footstool, out of reach of the snarling fangs. 'Ralph doesn't believe it's possible for women to understand business. He says they don't have the head for it.' I clenched my fists in my lap, fury rising in me again at the memory.

'Of course they don't,' said Jahanara Begum.

I gritted my teeth. I couldn't help this obstinate old woman if she wouldn't even listen to what I had to say.

'Of course women don't have the inclination to start a business,' continued Jahanara Begum. 'Men make sure that women don't understand how business is done and exclude them from the places where business transactions take place. Men like biddable wives who will make their lives comfortable and who demonstrate their belief that their husbands are all-powerful.'

'Perhaps Indian wives are more compliant than English wives,' I said, thinking of Mother.

'Men are taught from their earliest days that they are important. Girls, on the other hand, are led to believe they are useless unless they are beautiful and also good wives and mothers. That is the pinnacle of their achievements.' She sighed. 'Are you strong enough to defy convention, *beti*? The venture you suggest is an interesting one but the outcome would be most uncertain.'

'I know,' I said, 'but I would like your permission to talk to the ladies and explore the suggestion further. Unless they wish to participate, there is nothing to be done.'

'In my experience,' said Jahanara, 'a woman is capable of anything, if only she believes in herself.' She reached out her hand to me.

I gathered it gently between my palms, her tiny, crooked fingers as fragile as a bird's bones.

'Do you believe in yourself?' she asked. 'Lakshmi does now but it wasn't always so. Her life did not take the course she expected but she has forged another life, a stronger life, out of her unhappiness. But you, Bee Sinclair, what will you do?'

My thoughts raced. Could I throw off the shackles of my bitterness and sorrow, build a new life for myself and, at the same time, secure the wellbeing of the inhabitants of the Jahanara Mahal? There would be a great deal of opposition, not least from Ralph, and even if the women agreed to make the items, I had no idea where or how to sell them. The very thought of the struggles ahead made me feel exhausted.

'Well?' asked Jahanara Begum, her frail fingers squeezing mine before she let them go.

'I may not succeed,' I said slowly, 'but if I don't try, I suspect I shall always regret it. Besides, as things are, I see no other hope for those who call the palace home.'

Jahanara Begum nodded. 'My heart nearly fails me but I shall speak to the ladies.' She massaged her temples. 'Allow me a few days. They may be more receptive to your suggestion once they know the truth about their position.' She let out her breath in a long sigh. 'I have tried to protect them from the realities of life, but the time has come to tell them how very close we are to the brink of disaster.'

As I left Jahanara Begum's quarters, the responsibility of what I had taken on weighed heavily upon me. But, at the same time, the excitement of encountering a new challenge fizzed and bubbled somewhere under my breastbone. Perhaps this venture would fill the void in my aching heart.

Chapter 16

Over the following two weeks, whilst I was waiting for Jahanara Begum to summon the courage to speak to the ladies, I went to the stables early every morning to meet Lakshmi, glad to have a diversion from my tumultuous thoughts about the new enterprise. I'd finished making the tunic and trousers for my riding lessons and Lakshmi showed me how to wind a turban around my hair to keep off the dust. She was a hard taskmaster but I was determined not to give up, no matter how sore my muscles became.

Lakshmi sometimes arrived after me, trotting into the yard on her chestnut mare after taking a dawn ride over the country-side. She made no comment or apologies, merely checking that Mumtaz's girth straps were correctly adjusted before I mounted the pony.

I no longer needed the leading rein and, when Lakshmi cantered around the *maidan* one morning, I was confident enough to encourage Mumtaz to follow her. It took a moment for me to settle into the pony's gait but then we raced over the grass so fast I was breathless with terror and exhilaration. The landscape flashed by and the sound of thudding hoof beats filled my ears. I didn't want to stop but after a while Mumtaz's fat little legs had had enough and she slowed and finally came to a halt, her flanks heaving.

I slid down from the saddle with shaking knees.

'Morning!' called a voice behind me.

Harry came trotting towards me, mounted upon a black horse.

I caught my breath at the unexpected jolt of delight that ran through me when I saw him.

He dismounted with easy grace and allowed his horse to graze. 'You looked as if you were enjoying yourself.' His clothes were encrusted with dust again and his jaw shadowed with stubble that gave him a rakish air.

'Oh, I was!' My turban had slipped sideways and I pulled it off, releasing my hair. I shook my curls free and ran my fingers through them in an attempt to restore order. 'It wasn't very elegant,' I said, 'but it was my first canter and I managed to stay on. I never knew that riding was such hard work or so much fun.'

Harry gave me a lazy smile and reached out his thumb to brush away a fleck of mud from my glowing face, which made my cheeks glow even pinker. There was a warmth in his eyes when he looked at me that made my heart flutter.

'You're learning fast,' he said, 'and it won't be long before you need a more challenging steed.' He cast an appraising look up and down my figure. 'Really, you're too tall for Mumtaz.'

'I'm not sure Lakshmi thinks I'm doing that well,' I said, flustered by his disturbing presence.

Harry smiled as his gaze focused on Lakshmi who came cantering across the *maidan*. 'She always was a perfectionist.'

'She's strict,' I said, 'but I'm grateful to her for taking the time to teach me. I can't wait to be good enough to go for a gallop over the countryside instead of trotting round and around the *maidan*.'

Lakshmi pulled up beside us, eyes flashing with annoyance. 'Did I tell you that you were ready to canter, Bee?'

'No,' I said, 'but Mumtaz was happy to follow you and I didn't fall off.'

'Nevertheless, I didn't give you permission.'

'Bee isn't a recruit in the women's guard,' said Harry mildly.

'If I'm going to teach her to ride properly, she must follow my instructions,' said Lakshmi, fixing me with a gimlet glare.

I hesitated but then nodded my head. 'Yes, Lakshmi.'

'Take Mumtaz back to the stable and give her a good rub down before she catches a chill.' She clicked her tongue and walked her horse away.

Chastened, I gathered up Mumtaz's reins.

'We'll find you a more suitable mount soon,' said Harry, 'and I'll take you for that gallop, if you like.'

I couldn't hide my delighted smile. 'I'd love that.'

'Come on then. We'd better get you back to the stables before Lakshmi puts you on a charge.'

Sometime later the horses had all been groomed, watered and turned out into the small field behind the yard and the three of us set off towards the palace. The sun was hot already and I was thirsty.

'Where have you been the last few days, Harry?' asked Lakshmi.

'Looking at a stallion over near Golconda.'

'Will you buy him?'

He shook his head. 'Too much show and not enough grit.'

I wondered if he had in fact been trespassing on General Raymond's estate, as Jahanara Begum had suggested. 'Jai will be pleased to have you back,' I said.

Harry's smile lit his eyes. 'I thought I might take him camping for a day or two.'

'I'm sure he'd love that.'

As we passed the Durbar Hall, I heard a child's tearful protests and saw that Hemanti was on the veranda bathing Talin in a bucket of water. Several other children were running around and women

134

chatted as they chopped vegetables. I waved and Hemanti waved back as she restrained the struggling child.

We entered the palace and when we reached the circular hall, Harry said, 'I'm going to find out what Jai is up to. I'll see you both later.' He smiled at Lakshmi, the expression in his dark eyes teasing. 'Don't be too hard on your pupil.' He clapped a hand on my shoulder. 'Bee's riding is coming along splendidly and I shall take her out myself, soon.'

The heat of his hand burned through my tunic. He might be out of place in a Hampshire drawing room but he really was extremely handsome. There was no denying, I felt a powerful and growing attraction to him.

Lakshmi watched him intently as he loped away.

She turned towards me, her face expressionless. 'Don't be misled by his friendly manner, Bee. He will never forget his wife.'

'Indeed, why should he?' Briskly, I walked on again so she wouldn't see the guilty flush rising up my neck. 'Ralph told me how much he loved Noor.'

'She was much more beautiful than Leela,' said Lakshmi.

'Then it's hard to imagine how very lovely she must have been.' Jealousy stung me. It made me speak sharply.

'You have never seen such lustrous eyes and she sang more sweetly than a nightingale.'

I didn't want to hear any more about Harry's beloved wife. 'Her death was a tragedy for Harry but it's worse for Jai, never to have known his mother.'

'No one will ever replace Noor.' Lakshmi glanced sideways at me. 'Not even if they were young and beautiful.'

We continued walking side by side in silence and I wasn't sure if she was warning me not to have my heart broken or if Harry had already broken hers.

When we arrived in the *zenana*, the ladies were excitedly unpacking a wooden box that had been delivered to them from Parwar un-nisa Begum.

Priya Begum, as the senior lady present, lifted off the lid. Young Jasmin pulled out an armful of packing straw and then a long piece of rope.

They glanced at each other, perplexed, while the ladies twittered around them like a flock of birds.

Parvati Begum thrust her hand beneath the remaining straw and extracted another piece of rope. She tugged, pulling out a great length until it was coiled like a snake on the floor. At the end was a flat piece of wood painted with flowers and adorned with fat, silken tassels.

'It's a swing!' I said.

The girls squealed with joy and clapped their hands.

'Lakshmi, will you arrange for it to be hung from the old mango tree at the top of the avenue?' said Priya Begum.

Lakshmi went in search of a servant to carry out the work.

The ladies peered out of the windows, watching from behind their veils while two menservants shinned up the mango tree with the ropes draped over their shoulders.

A flock of parakeets, disturbed by the intrusion, flew out of the tree in a flutter of lime green.

Before long the swing was suspended from the thickest branch. Once the menservants had left, the ladies jostled each other in their hurry to go into the garden.

Esha, the youngest of the three girls, was chosen to try it first and sat gingerly on the seat, gripping the ropes.

'Push backwards with your feet,' I said. I pulled the swing back until her toes were off the ground and then pushed her forward.

She gasped, and then laughed, as she learned how to propel herself to and fro.

The ladies clapped and begged to try the new plaything for themselves.

Smiling, I left them to their innocent pleasure, though I looked forward to taking a turn myself in the cool of the evening.

I returned inside to fetch my sewing and a notebook, then strolled through the grounds towards the walled garden. Escaping from the relentless sun, I sat in the pavilion, sketching ideas for embellished reticules and beaded coin purses. After I'd run out of inspiration, I unwrapped my sewing. Leela had given me a scrap of peacock blue silk and I'd embroidered it with lotus flowers, stitched it into a self-lined reticule, and now only needed to hem the top and make a channel for the drawstring.

The air was still and full of drowsy heat; the only sound came from a bee, lazily drifting from flower to flower. My needle grew still and I leaned my head back against a sun-warmed pillar.

I awoke some time later. I'd dreamed I was having an important conversation with Mrs Clements. Still befuddled with sleep, I was trying to remember what we'd been talking about when I heard quick footsteps trotting along the gravel path.

Jai was at the other end of the garden, where the wall was obscured by untidy shrubs. He carried a bundle of white cloth in his arms and the dog, Swati, was close by his heels. Jai stopped, looked furtively over his shoulder and then slid behind a trellis almost buried under climbing passion flowers.

I watched for a while but he didn't reappear. Curious, I went to investigate.

'Jai?' I called.

The garden was still tranquil, undisturbed except for the trill of a bird on a nearby branch.

Easing myself behind the trelliswork, I found myself in a narrow gap between the passion flowers and a wooden outbuilding collapsing under the weight of overgrown vines. There was no sign of Jai or Swati so I forced my way through the lush vegetation until I came to the end of the outbuilding, where the space opened out into a small yard. The door of the shed hung crookedly off its hinges and I peered into the shadowy interior.

Jai was hunkered down, facing the wall. Swati lay on the ground while the boy fed her titbits from his pocket.

'Jai?' I said.

He leaped to his feet, fear on his face.

'What's the matter?' The closer I approached, the more agitated he became.

'You can't take Swati!' He ran towards me, head down as if to butt me in the stomach.

I caught him and held him firmly at arm's length while he squirmed in my grip. 'I'm not taking her anywhere. Now keep still!' At last he stopped wriggling. 'Tell me what has upset you so.'

'Sangita-Aunty said . . . ' His face turned bright red as he fought back tears.

'Is Swati hurt?' Gently, I moved him aside to look at the dog and gasped. 'Oh! Aren't they adorable?' Four tan-coloured puppies nuzzled at Swati's side.

'Sangita-Aunty found her making a nest and she shouted at her and beat her with a broom until she went out of the palace gates. She said there are too many dogs and they bring disease.' He rubbed his eyes.

'Jai,' I held him by his shoulders, 'Sangita-Aunty is only trying to keep you safe. Some dogs can be very dangerous.'

'But Swati isn't!'

'She probably has fleas, though.'

'I ran after her and found her having her puppies amongst the reeds, right at the edge of the river,' said Jai. 'She didn't know that the water sometimes comes higher and her pups could have drowned. I wrapped them up and brought them back here. You won't tell Sangita-Aunty, will you?' His dark eyes beseeched me.

I glanced at the puppies and my resolve softened. 'No,' I said, 'but when they're old enough to survive on their own, you must take them out of the palace grounds. If you don't, they'll breed here and the palace will soon be unpleasantly overrun with packs of wild dogs, and that might be dangerous for us all. Will you promise me to let them go when they're weaned?'

Jai nodded his head vigorously.

I glanced at Swati, who was giving one of the puppies a thorough wash. 'Meanwhile, I'll save some scraps for her. You must find out what we can do to rid her of fleas and worms. I'll pay for any medicine she needs and you can help me to treat her.'

Jai flung his arms around my waist and hugged me. 'Thank you, *aunty-ji*, thank you!'

I hugged him back, unexpectedly moved.

Chapter 17

The following morning, Lakshmi and I walked back to the palace together after my riding lesson.

'You have made good progress today, Bee,' she said.

I glanced at her, surprised. A compliment from her was rare and unexpected.

'I thought you might be difficult to teach,' she continued, 'since you started riding lessons so late in life, but it appears you have enough humility to learn.'

'I'm enjoying the lessons,' I said.

Lakshmi smiled. 'Didn't I say you must find an outlet for your anger and bitterness?' Her encouragement, combined with my enthusiasm for the new venture, made me want to share my idea with her. 'As far as finding an outlet for my energies goes, riding is healthy exercise, but I've been thinking of another way to make myself useful.'

'How do you intend to do that?'

'I'm waiting for Jahanara Begum to talk to the ladies of the *zenana* first before I can tell you.'

'She asked me to escort her on a visit to the ladies this morning,' Lakshmi said.

My stomach gave a little somersault at the prospect of soon finding out whether the ladies would greet my plan with approval.

Lakshmi went to see Jahanara Begum and I took a few scraps of bread and vegetables to Swati before returning to my room to change.

An hour later I carried my notebook, the finished reticule and the rose-pink shawl to the *zenana* sitting room. I didn't have long to wait before Lakshmi arrived with Jahanara Begum, accompanied by her handmaids. She sat, straight-backed, in her wheeled throne, dressed richly in lapis lazuli silk trimmed with gold brocade.

The ladies whispered amongst themselves until Lakshmi clapped her hands for attention. 'Jahanara Begum wishes to speak to you.'

Bracelets jingled as the ladies and I pulled our floor cushions into a semi-circle. Lakshmi remained standing at ease beside Jahanara Begum, one hand resting on the hilt of her curved sword.

The Begum waited impassively until the rustling and murmuring died down. Once the room was silent she took a shuddering breath. 'I have come to see you today because it is my painful duty to inform you that your safe and comfortable existence in the Jahanara Mahal's *zenana* may be about to change.'

Lakshmi's posture was suddenly alert.

The ladies whispered to each other until the Begum raised her hand. 'You all know the story of the stolen diamond, the Rose of Golconda?'

Several of the ladies nodded their heads.

'Even after all these years,' she said, 'the theft of the Rose by a woman I thought was my friend, a trusted member of my *zenana* guard whose solemn duty it was to protect me, still has the power to cause me the greatest desolation.' She bowed her head and Priya Begum rose to her feet and hurried to her mother's side.

After a moment Jahanara Begum patted her daughter's arm and motioned her to sit with the other ladies. 'Asaf Jah was generous,' she said. 'He provided me with jewels, servants, livestock and household goods in addition to the precious Rose. When I first came to the Jahanara Mahal I was confident our future, and that of my family and retinue, was secure forever. The Rose was the means to support all my dreams. But then it was stolen from me. Since that time I have sold my other jewels, the gold and silver plate, the elephants and my fine Arab horses, to support us all. Little remains of my former wealth and, though you rarely leave the *zenana*, you will know that the palace is crumbling.' She lowered her head. 'There has been so much change and now, for me, the Jahanara Mahal is the Palace of Lost Dreams.'

Tentatively, Leela raised a hand to catch her great-grandmother's attention. 'You said that our safe existence in the *zenana* may be about to change? What is going to happen to us?'

'I cannot continue to pay the servants,' said Jahanara Begum. 'Soon there will be no one to cook your meals, to fetch your bath-water, to empty the latrines or to help you dress.'

The women looked at each other, perplexed.

'The monsoon season will soon be here,' the Begum continued. 'Each year the rains cause more damage. The cost of the materials required to repair the palace is no longer within my means.'

'We can catch the rainwater in buckets,' said Esha.

Jahanara Begum smiled briefly at the youngest member of the *zenana*. 'We have been catching the leaks in buckets for years, but the roof timbers are so rotten that parts of the palace are unsafe. I don't know how long we can all remain here.' She caught her breath on a sob. 'It may be necessary to sell the Jahanara Mahal.'

The ladies rose to their feet and began to talk rapidly in a rising crescendo until the room reverberated with the hubbub.

Lakshmi stepped forward and clapped her hands. 'Silence!'

The ladies subsided.

'It may not be possible,' said Jahanara Begum, 'to find anyone to buy the palace who can afford to effect the necessary repairs but, if there is a suitable buyer, we will be forced to leave.'

The ladies began to wail, beating their chests with their fists.

Lakshmi shouted for quiet again.

'In this case,' said Jahanara Begum, 'those of you who have husbands, fathers or brothers may find lodgings outside the palace. Sadly, you will lose the company of the women who have grown up with you in the *zenana*.'

'But we would be so lonely!' cried Veeda, reaching out to Indira.

'It's impossible to imagine living somewhere else,' wailed Jasmin. She fell into her mother's plump arms and Bimla began to weep.

'Some of you have husbands,' said Jahanara Begum, 'who contribute to the household, and some of you are widows with a little money put away, but there isn't enough to provide dowries for the girls or to save us, or the great number of servants and their dependants who live in the palace, from losing our home.'

Stunned, the ladies fell silent. Some wept silently into their veils. Girls clung to their mothers.

'But there is one course of action,' said Jahanara Begum, 'that might give us a chance of avoiding this frightening fate.'

Parvati, arms tightly wound around her daughters, called out, 'Please, tell us what it is!'

'As you know,' said Jahanara Begum, 'Bee Sinclair has recently joined our family.' She held out her hand to me and I rose from my cushion. 'She has made a suggestion. The idea surprised me but I have considered it carefully and I want you to do the same.' Gently, she pushed me forward. 'Tell them what you said.'

The ladies turned their tear-stained faces towards me. Suddenly the magnitude of the task overwhelmed me. Jahanara Begum was clutching at straws in the hope I could save the palace but Ralph was right: I had no experience in business.

The Begum squeezed my hand. 'Bee?' Her voice was no more than a thread.

I'd rehearsed what I was going to say, asking Leela to translate some words so that I wouldn't falter or make too many mistakes. My mouth was dry as dust but I took a deep breath and began. 'Last year,' I said, 'my husband died. Then I miscarried my baby ...' My voice quavered and I swallowed while I composed myself. 'My brother wrote to me to say he had married and that Leela,' I smiled at her, 'had suggested I come to live with them.'

'Of course I would welcome my husband's sister,' said the girl.

'I snatched at the chance of leaving my sadness behind and caught the next boat to India. You may imagine my surprise and delight on discovering the Jahanara Mahal was to be my new home.'

Some of the ladies nodded in agreement.

'I knew of the Jahanara Mahal from the time when I lived in Hyderabad as a child. I thought then that it was a magical place. After I returned to England, I used to dream of coming back here.'

'It was your karma,' said Parvati's sister, Indira.

'Perhaps it was,' I said, 'and now that I am here and the palace is my home, I'm not going to let go of that dream without a fight. You see, I have learned something very important since I've been living amongst you all. Something that I didn't know before. Do you know what that might be?'

The ladies looked at each other and shook their heads, then Esha held up her hand. 'You are learning to speak like us now.'

'At first you said things that were funny mistakes,' said Farah. She giggled and clapped a hand over her own mouth.

'I still make mistakes but you are all very patient and have helped me to improve.' I paused while I looked at them, one by one. 'The most important lesson I've learned since I returned to India is this. It is that women are strong.'

Bimla and Indira nodded in agreement.

'You have taught me that, on her own, a woman is weak but together we are strong. We offer each other kindness, friendship and support. I want us to use that strength in working together to save our home, the Jahanara Mahal. Shall I tell you how I think we might do that?'

'Yes! Yes!'

I shook out the silken folds of the rose-pink shawl and draped it around my shoulders. 'Leela made this beautiful shawl for me.' I pirouetted so that the tasselled fringe flew out. 'I wore it in England and it was much admired. So much so that it has given me an idea. You all like to sew and the evidence of that is all around you in the form of wall hangings, quilted floor cloths and the embroidered borders to your veils. Your work, with its exotic designs and complexity, is very special.'

'British women like Indian shawls?' asked Veeda.

'Indian shawls sold there are usually of inferior quality. Ones as beautiful as this would be much sought after.' My enthusiasm returned in a rush and I was swept along by it. 'And there are other Indian embroidered articles that I believe would be popular too.' I held up the peacock blue reticule embroidered with lotus flowers. 'Here is an example that I've made. My suggestion is this: if we work together we could make high-quality embroidered articles for the English market.'

'Sell them in England?' Priya Begum's brow creased doubtfully as she considered this. 'But we can't go there.'

'If you agree with my suggestion, I will write to shopkeepers in London, those who have superior establishments selling only the highest-quality goods.'

'It will take a long time for a letter to reach England,' said Priya Begum. 'And then we must wait for an answer.'

I nodded. 'But we can use that time to make the first shawls.'

Leela raised her hand. 'There are only a few of us and we would have to make a great many shawls to earn enough to save the palace.'

'So we must think on a grand scale,' I said, 'and that necessitates changes.'

'What kind of changes?' asked Bimla, suspicion written across her face.

'We alone cannot make enough goods. What I suggest is this. We must enlarge the *zenana*.'

The women looked at each other, perplexed.

'We need to incorporate more rooms into the *zenana*,' I said, 'because we'll need many of the palace women to join us.'

A hush fell over the room as the women glanced at each other and one or two went into a huddle and began to whisper.

'Surely you don't intend us to work alongside serving women?' Bimla sounded horrified.

'The servants can no longer be paid. Some will leave to find work elsewhere,' I said, 'but those who remain must earn their keep. If they wish to retain the roof over their heads, albeit a leaky one,' I smiled at my little joke, 'then they will have to work.'

The ladies began all speaking at once until their shrill chatter and shocked exclamations made Jahanara Begum tug at Lakshmi's sleeve.

She stamped her foot on the floor until the ladies, except for Bimla, finally became quiet.

'We will not work beside these low-caste women,' said Bimla, bristling with outrage.

I was confused as to why she was objecting. 'But some of the female servants already attend you in the *zenana*.'

'You are a stranger here and do not understand our ways.' She rudely turned her back and began to talk rapidly to the ladies, her enraged tone rising to a crescendo.

I'd learned that palace servants each had their own particular tasks allied to their caste and that they refused absolutely to deviate from these, but it appeared I had seriously underestimated the effect upon the ladies of the *zenana* of ignoring the caste system.

'I apologise if I have offended you by my ignorance,' I shouted. I waited, hastily adapting my plans, until I had the ladies' full attention again. 'Perhaps it would be acceptable to you if the women had their own workroom somewhere else in the palace?'

One or two of the ladies nodded and then Leela raised a hand to catch my attention. 'Surely the women servants don't all have the skill necessary for fine embroidery?'

'We'll give them a sewing test to discover which ones show aptitude for it,' I said. 'Those that have simple sewing skills may be trained to stitch together the embroidered pieces of the items. Others, with some tuition, may learn to embroider to a good standard. The remainder of the women will package the goods or cook and clean in exchange for being allowed to stay at the palace.'

Bimla shook her fist at me, rigid with anger. 'I'm not going to be contaminated by working on cloth tainted by an untouchable sweeper's wife!'

Jahanara Begum pointed a finger at her. 'No one will remain at the Jahanara Mahal if they are not prepared to do whatever is necessary. If you do not wish to stay here, Bimla, you and your good-for-nothing husband are free to leave at any time.'

Bimla pressed a hand to her mouth and sank down onto her cushion.

Indira began to cry, blotting her tears with her veil.

Hoping to relieve the tension, I held up my notebook. 'I've sketched some ideas for the items we could make. Some are small projects, such as coin purses, while others, like the shawls, will take more time but will command a much higher price. Perhaps you would like to see?'

None of the women moved and the smile froze on my face.

Jahanara Begum clenched her fists.

Then Leela stepped forward.

Esha slipped out of her mother's arms. 'I can sew. May I see, too?'

I sat on the floor again, my heart thumping. Leela and Esha sat beside me and I opened my notebook. 'These are reticules,' I said. 'Very popular in England. They can be made from netting, silk or velvet and decorated with beads or embroidery. There's a simple drawstring closure and the bag is carried by a cord slipped over the forearm.' I showed Leela the sample I'd made.

'These wouldn't take long,' she said.

'If the experienced embroiderers do the fancy work,' I explained, 'then afterwards the less skilled can sew the pieces together and make the drawstring.'

One by one, as Leela and I discussed embroidered scarves, slippers, waistcoats, parasols and purses, the other ladies crept towards us to peer over my shoulder, look at the sketches and ask questions, until finally it was only Bimla who stubbornly kept her distance.

Jahanara Begum beckoned to her. She reluctantly rose and went to stand before the Begum. 'It is a great pity,' said Jahanara Begum, 'that your considerable skill as a needlewoman is never seen outside the walls of the *zenana*.'

Bimla's double chin trembled and she wiped her eyes with her veil. 'I don't want to leave the palace!'

'I don't want you, my cousin's daughter, to leave either,' said Jahanara Begum. She rested her hand on Bimla's head. 'You are part of my family, *beti*, even if I believe your husband is lazy. If you decide to contribute your efforts to saving the palace, you will work in seclusion here in the *zenana*. Any item you embroider would be handed on to the sewing women to be finished. You will not need to touch it again and there would be no risk of you becoming contaminated or being forced to associate with women of low caste.'

Bimla heaved a sigh. 'Then, if my husband allows it, I shall help.'

'Oh, he'll agree,' said Jahanara Begum, 'he won't want to be turned out of the palace to look for work.' As Bimla kissed her hand, the Begum caught my eye and gave a small, self-satisfied nod.

Chapter 18

The following afternoon, I prepared to dress appropriately before I took up the invitation to join Mrs Clements for tea. Since the day was so hot, it was with great reluctance that I drew on my stays, but I compromised between decency and comfort by lacing them only loosely. Jyoti buttoned me into a dove grey mourning dress I'd brought with me from England and I slipped off my Indian sandals and crammed my feet into closed shoes.

As I came out of the main entrance into blinding sunshine, the simmering heat made me catch my breath. My parasol was not enough to protect me. I was grateful for the shade of the clipped trees flanking the path of the courtyard garden. Lingering for a moment, I dipped my handkerchief into the fountain pool and blotted the back of my neck to cool it.

The old gatekeeper, asleep on the ground, awoke with a start when I called to him. He scratched his matted white locks and adjusted his *dhoti* before slowly, very slowly, unlocking one of the great studded doors and heaving it open. Outside, heat radiated from the stone and the weeds growing between the cracks were scorched brown.

Dabbing my cheeks with the damp handkerchief, I set off towards the river path to the Residency. It was one of those searingly hot days when all sound is muffled and the air feels thick. Even the birds had fallen silent, as if it was too fatiguing to sing.

I hadn't gone far when I heard the sound of hoof beats cantering along the path behind me. I waited in the shade of a neem tree to allow the gentleman riding a black horse to pass me by but he came to a halt and I saw, with some surprise, that it was Harry.

I called out to him. 'You're in a hurry!'

'I saw you leaving the palace,' he said. 'What are you doing out here all on your own?'

'I'm going to the Residency to pay a call on Mrs Clements.' Perspiration prickled my back and I hoped my face wasn't unbecomingly flushed.

'It's madness to walk in this heat. And you shouldn't have come alone.'

'I don't remember it being dangerous when we played on the river bank as children,' I said, 'even if it is a bit more overgrown now.'

His lips twitched but he still frowned. 'That's as maybe but I shouldn't care for you to be frightened by a wild dog or a beggar. Or a French soldier, come to that.'

'Are they worse than British soldiers?'

He hesitated. 'In my opinion they can be insolent to women. As it happens, I'm on my way to the Residency myself.' He dismounted and walked by my side, the horse's reins looped over his arm.

'I've not seen you in European clothes before,' I said.

'And do I pass muster? I'm meeting James Kirkpatrick.'

'I hardly recognised you,' I replied. It was true. Harry's usual vagabond appearance had been replaced by that of an elegant English gentleman wearing a cutaway coat and tight leather riding breeches to the top of his polished boots. His linen was crisply white and he carried a sword at his hip.

He grinned, teeth flashing against his tanned skin.

I dropped my gaze and concentrated on where I placed my feet. 'Am I delaying you?' I asked. 'You were in such a hurry.'

His expression sobered as he took my arm. 'Half an hour ago one of my men came in all haste to bring me news – information that I must convey immediately to Kirkpatrick.'

'Oh?' I looked at him enquiringly to take my mind off the warmth of his arm under my hand and the hint of sandalwood emanating enticingly from his skin.

He sighed. 'It'll be old news by tonight but I'd rather you didn't discuss it with Mrs Clements until I've spoken to Kirkpatrick.'

'I promise to be discreet.'

'Then I can tell you that General Raymond is dead.'

'The French Commander?'

Harry nodded. 'He was only forty-three. It appears he may have taken some slow-acting poison.'

We moved on again while I considered the implications of this news. 'I suppose, since General Raymond held such influence over the Nizam, his death is extremely convenient for the British?'

'It may be,' said Harry, 'though much depends on the choice of Raymond's successor.'

A twig from an overhanging branch snatched at my parasol, twirling it around in my hand. Harry had just mentioned 'one of my men' so I gathered that, whatever position it was he held within the East India Company, it must be a post of some responsibility.

'Sometimes it's better to deal with the devil you know,' said Harry. He draped his horse's reins over the saddle and drew his sword to hack at the overgrown vegetation obscuring the path. 'At least Kirkpatrick may have a better opportunity now of persuading Old Nizzy to get rid of his French force. But, of course, the British East India Company must then commit to supply enough troops to support him in his efforts to fight off Marathi invaders.'

Trees overhung the path and reeds obscured the river from view so that it felt as if we had entered a leafy tunnel. At least the temperature here was a little cooler. I furled my parasol. 'And will the British East India Company be prepared to make that commitment?' I asked.

'There isn't any choice if we don't wish to lose our hold on India.' He slashed at another clump of greenery, while the black horse nibbled at the grass behind us.

'Perhaps the question ought to be, what right do the British have, any more than the French, to keep a hold on India?' I turned my ankle in a deep rut in the dried mud. I stumbled, clutching at a branch in the vain hope I could save myself from an ignominious descent to the ground.

Harry caught me before I fell, holding me tightly against him. 'Indeed,' he said, 'but India is so divided that perhaps what it needs is to be unified under one rule. And I would far rather the British took on that role than the French, who intend to dominate the world.'

Still pinned to his chest, I remained silent, too flustered to speak.

He looked down at me and frowned, as if he hadn't known I was there. 'Are you all right?'

'Perfectly,' I said.

Slowly, he tipped up my chin with his forefinger and studied my face.

I held my breath. Sunlight streaming through the trees overhead dappled the firm lines of his jaw. For one long, heart-stopping moment I thought he was going to kiss me but then his horse ambled towards us and pushed his head over Harry's shoulder.

'Zephyr!' Harry laughed and released me, turning to run his hand down the horse's nose.

Covered in confusion, I hurried off along the path, hoping he hadn't seen either my great disappointment or my flaming cheeks. There was light ahead at the end of the green tunnel and I could hear voices singing and a regular slapping sound.

A wall of heat hit me again immediately I emerged into the sunlight. The river was wider here, with stony shallows, and a number of washermen and women lifted wet clothes above their shoulders and slammed them down on the rocks. Row upon row of drying clothes and linen were draped over ropes and bushes. Some of the women paused in their labours to stare at me.

I opened up my parasol and by the time Harry reached me, with Zephyr in tow, I had almost regained my composure. 'Is this where the washing is sent from the Jahanara Mahal?' I asked.

He looked at me with a blank expression. 'I suppose it must be.'

'And there's the Residency, just around the bend of the river,' I chattered.

'Yes, it hasn't moved in years,' said Harry, a gleam of amusement in his eyes.

I refused to look at him and focused on putting one foot carefully in front of the other on the uneven ground, giving myself time to think of something to say. 'I expect Jai was pleased to see you when you returned?'

'He was, although . . .'

'Although?'

'I imagined he'd jump at the chance for us to ride into the country and camp out together for a night or two.'

'That would be a fine adventure for a boy.'

Harry shook his head, disappointed. 'He seemed most unhappy about the prospect of such a jaunt.' He shrugged. 'Perhaps when he's a little older.'

Before too long we reached the Residency, where I asked the gatekeeper to direct me to the Clementses' bungalow.

'Thank you for escorting me, Harry,' I said, as we walked along the carriage drive.

'It was my pleasure. Unfortunately, I don't know how long I might be with the Resident. Will you ask Mrs Clements to call for a palanquin to carry you back to the palace? I shouldn't care to think of you walking alone along the river path.'

I nodded, disappointed but also relieved that he wouldn't be able to escort me himself.

The carriageway divided and I took the left hand turning towards the Clementses' bungalow while Harry made for the stables along the right-hand path.

Mrs Clements was delighted to receive me, though horrified to hear I'd walked. 'And where is your maid?' she said.

I smiled to myself as I imagined Lakshmi's reaction if she'd heard that. 'It's not far,' I said, 'and I had an escort but I wonder if you might arrange for me to hire a palanquin for the return journey?'

'I should think so, indeed! But you must have nearly expired in this roasting heat, my dear.'

Mrs Clements instructed her steward to order a palanquin and then I was ensconced in a comfortable armchair with a glass of lemonade. The reed blinds had been lowered to shut out the sun and dampened to cool the breeze through the open window. A boy sat on the floor in a corner pulling rhythmically on a rope that made the *punkah* fan overhead move back and forth, gently stirring the air and cooling my overheated face.

'I heard you're residing in a palace?' said Mrs Clements. 'How intriguing! Do tell me about it.'

'It was a great surprise to me,' I said. 'The family of my brother's wife has lived in the Jahanara Mahal for four generations.'

Mrs Clements' eyes opened wide. 'Don't tell me your brother's bride is Indian? My dear, how awful for you! Whatever can he have been thinking of to choose a native wife?'

'Leela is delightful,' I protested. 'She's extremely beautiful and very kind. All her family have been most welcoming.'

'But it must be terribly strange for you?' She shook her head. 'Are you obliged to follow native customs? Is the palace clean? I believe they sit on the floor and eat with their fingers. Imagine that!'

'I came to India with the desire for adventure and new experiences,' I said. 'After all the sad events recently, I needed a complete change of scene.'

'Well,' said Mrs Clements, 'I should hazard a guess you have certainly found that.'

'It's very different from Hampshire but it didn't take me long to fall in love with the palace and my new family. Not everything is perfect.' I smiled. 'But for the first time in my life, I'm discovering who I am. I'd always been my mother's daughter until, for a short while, I was Charles' wife. Now I'm trying hard to forget sad Beatrice and become Bee again, the girl I left behind in India all those years ago.'

'My goodness!' Mrs Clements frowned. 'I hardly know what to say. Aren't most women perfectly happy to be somebody's daughter and then, if they're lucky, someone else's wife?'

'Please don't be offended. I always wanted a husband and family and I was never so happy as when I married Charles and then discovered I was to have his child.' A lump formed in my throat. 'But that has all gone now,' I said, my voice husky. 'And men want young brides, not women of my age. So I have to choose between being a grieving widow for the rest of my days or else doing my best to overcome my misery and find out what else I can do with my life.'

'I see,' said Mrs Clements. 'Have you thought what that something else will be?'

'I've had an idea,' I said, and explained to her what I planned.

'That's extremely ambitious,' she said, when I'd finished. 'But are you sure it won't be too much for you?'

'I can't let that stop me. So many people could be helped if the embroidery workshop is a success.' I handed her the peacock blue reticule. 'This is a small example of the kind of goods the workshop might produce.'

'It's delightful,' she said, examining the intricate embroidery. 'I'll certainly buy one of these when they are available.'

'You may keep it, if you like,' I said, 'but I wanted to ask you a special favour.'

'What kind of a favour?'

'You mentioned that your sister's husband owns a shop selling ladies' fancy goods. I wondered if you might be kind enough to give me his address? I wish to write to him and ask if he would consider stocking some of the items. You've already seen the rose-pink shawl Leela made for me so you know the quality of the work. If you felt able to endorse me, I shall be forever in your debt.'

Mrs Clements smiled. 'I would be delighted to recommend you. Perhaps you might be able to send my brother-in-law some samples?'

'Of course.' Enthusiasm for the project was bubbling up inside me again. 'And sketches and fabric swatches. We'll make items to order, too.'

We spent an interesting hour discussing my plans until a manservant announced that the palanquin awaited me.

'Do, please, come and visit me again, Mrs Sinclair,' said my hostess. She leaned towards me and spoke in an undertone. 'Mrs Ure is perfectly amiable but we have nothing in common.'

'Perhaps you would care to visit me at the Jahanara Mahal?'

'I'd have to ask my husband's permission. Would you introduce me to the ladies in the *zenana*? I cannot imagine how it would be to live imprisoned behind those fretwork screens.'

'The ladies don't consider themselves to be imprisoned and I'm sure they would enjoy your visit.'

I took my leave of Mrs Clements and climbed into the waiting palanquin. It was unbearably hot and stuffy behind the curtains but at least I was shielded from the intensity of the sun. I rested against the cushions, listening to the bearers' grunts as we jogged along and recalling the moment Harry had held me in his arms by the river. I wondered if he would have kissed me if Zephyr hadn't pushed his way between us. My heart began to race as I admitted to myself how very much I wished he had.

156

Chapter 19

Morning mist was curling up from the ground as I made my way through the garden just after dawn. The air was deliciously cool and the sky an opalescent dome high above. I eased my way behind the trellis, the dew soaking my shoulders as I brushed past the climbing passion flowers. The door to the outbuilding still hung crookedly from its hinges and creaked when I opened it a little further.

A rustling came from behind the door and I murmured, 'Swati, it's only me.'

A shape stirred in the shadows and then rose and came towards me.

I pressed a hand to my breast. 'You startled me, Jai!'

'Sorry, *aunty-ji*.'

'I've brought Swati a treat.' I held out some scraps of chicken I'd hidden in my handkerchief at supper the previous night.

Jai rewarded me with a wide smile and we hunkered down side by side to feed the dog. She fixed her gaze on the pieces of meat, every muscle in her body tensed as she took them delicately from my fingers. When she'd finished, her tail lashed and she looked up at me hopefully.

'No more for now,' I said, 'but I'll bring you something else later, if I can.'

'The puppies are growing,' said Jai. He stroked one of them under Swati's watchful eye.

'Jai,' I said, 'your father mentioned he'd asked you if you'd like to go camping with him. That sounds fun – just the sort of adventure I'd have loved when I was younger.'

'You?' He looked up at me, amused.

'I wasn't always as ancient as I appear to you now. I used to love to make camps in the garden and going fishing in the river. It surprised me you told your father you didn't want to go with him.'

He looked down at Swati, his expression set.

There was a smudge of dirt on his cheek and his resemblance to the Harry I'd known when I was young was uncanny. 'What I wondered,' I said, choosing my words with care, 'was if you refused because you were worried about leaving Swati and her puppies?'

'I don't want them to starve,' he mumbled.

'Would you trust me to look after them? I've been bringing Swati scraps every day, anyway. It would only take a little more effort to make sure she has fresh water and some company.'

He looked up at me, his brown eyes wide. 'Would you?'

'I'd like to.' I tickled Swati under her ear and she closed her eyes in bliss.

Jai let out a long sigh. 'I really wanted to go with *abbu-ji*,' he glanced at Swati, 'and he thought I didn't love him when I said I wouldn't.'

'I'm sure he never thought that,' I said firmly. 'Why don't you go and tell him you've changed your mind? I'll stay with Swati for a while.'

'Thank you, *aunty-ji*!' He wrapped his arms around my neck and squeezed me, his soft cheek pressed against mine for a second. And then he was off and the door squeaked shut behind him.

I patted the dog again. 'So, it's only you and me and the puppies for a while then, Swati.'

Her tail thumped the floor.

Later that morning I called to see Jahanara Begum. She sat on her throne, a handmaid behind her, wafting a peacock feather fan to stir the air.

'I visited Mrs Clements yesterday, my travelling companion on the journey to India,' I said. 'I remembered her brother-in-law owns a shop in London that sells ladies' fancy goods.'

'And you think he might sell the things the women will make?'

'I shall send him some samples and Mrs Clements has promised to let him know she vouches for the quality.'

'Excellent!' Jahanara Begum tapped her fingers on the arms of her throne. 'The difficulty is the length of time it will take for a letter to reach London and then the wait before you receive his reply.'

'I know,' I sighed. 'And, if he does agree to stock our goods, they still have to be made and shipped to London. If we're kept waiting for too long to receive payment, we'll all starve. So we must sell our goods here too.'

Jahanara Begum was silent for a while, her forehead creased while she considered this. 'I don't much care for the idea but there is always Parwar un-nisa Begum.'

'Your relative who visited us from the Nizam's *zenana*?'

'Just so. If I swallow my pride, perhaps you and Leela might visit her? If the Nizam's ladies could be persuaded to buy ... '

'Then other ladies of quality might follow?'

She nodded. 'You must act quickly, though. The monsoons will soon be here to cause more damage.'

'There's another difficulty,' I said. 'We shall need good-quality materials to make the first samples. I'm going to ask the ladies if they'll spare whatever they can from their wardrobes.'

'They must be persuaded to invest in their future but it's hard for them to understand since they have never suffered deprivation. Perhaps ... ' Jahanara Begum gestured to her handmaid and then murmured an instruction to her.

The girl pushed Jahanara Begum's throne forward, negotiating it carefully around the tiger-skin rug.

I rose from the footstool, unsure if I was dismissed.

Jahanara Begum called over her shoulder, 'Come with me.'

I followed as the servant pushed her mistress out of the room.

Lakshmi sat in a corner of the ante-room and hastened to her feet when she saw us. 'Is there something you need, Jahanara Begum?'

'Not at present.'

I glanced at Lakshmi, who sent me a questioning look. I shrugged slightly before following the Begum into a corridor.

We passed a number of closed doors until the handmaid opened the end one and wheeled her mistress inside.

The room was of a generous size, illuminated by a glazed roof light and *jali*-screened windows. A number of age-spotted mirrors in ornate frames were hung on the pink marble walls and a sumptuous Persian carpet lay on the floor.

'My dressing room,' said Jahanara Begum. She pointed to one of the carved chests arranged around the walls. 'See what you can find.'

I lifted the lid of the chest and wrinkled my nose at the pungent smell of camphor as I took out a beaded tunic of crimson silk.

There was a half-smile on Jahanara Begum's face as she laid it over her knees. 'There are some trousers to go with this and a veil of gold tissue. I wore these clothes the first time I danced for Asaf Jah.'

One by one I shook out folded saris, tunics and gathered trousers and laid them carefully on the floor until the carpet was smothered in pools of cobweb-fine muslin and shimmering silk in every shade of crimson, ochre, sapphire, violet, indigo and emerald.

'They're so lovely they take my breath away,' I murmured. I delved into the chest again and removed the last item, a wooden box.

Jahanara Begum held out her hands to take it from me. There

160

was a jingling sound as she withdrew anklets, bracelets and belts, all adorned with small gold bells. 'My dancing bells,' she said, wrapping a bracelet around her wrist and making it quiver so that the room rang with its high, clear sound. 'How these take me back to my youth!' She sighed heavily and bundled them back into the box. 'I'm a sentimental old woman and it is time to stop living in the past. If you think these are of use, take them, Bee.'

'You will always have your memories,' I said, 'but I promise you that these precious things will be treated with respect and made into exquisite items that will be loved by others.'

She nodded. 'I'm placing my trust in you.'

I bowed my head and nodded. 'There is one other thing,' I said.

The Begum waited.

'My brother was very scathing at my suggestion of the embroidery workshop. I'm afraid he might forbid Leela to take part.'

'I suppose he might.' She gave me a wry smile. 'Ralph is a good fellow at heart, though inclined to be self-important. He agreed to certain conditions when I allowed him to marry my great-granddaughter. I shall remind him of them.'

'Thank you, though I fear he will make no secret of his displeasure with me.'

'Do not allow him to divert you from this course.' She sighed heavily. 'I suppose now the palace servants must be told that I can no longer pay them.'

'At least you can offer some of the women another means of income.'

'And I shall not force any family to leave the palace if they are prepared to continue to work unpaid. I have a little money put aside so, for now, we can offer them one meal a day. Tell me what else you require.'

'A large space and your permission to arrange it in the most convenient way for the women to work comfortably.'

She inclined her head. 'Anything else?'

'Sewing essentials and embroidery thread to make the samples. I have a little money of my own and if Lakshmi will accompany me to the bazaar, I'll purchase what I can to allow the ladies to make a start.'

Jahanara Begum gave me a sharp look. 'You would spend your own money?'

'I fell in love with the Jahanara Mahal when I was a girl. I dreamed about it many times over the years, never imagining I would live here. The palace may be dilapidated but it still has the power to enchant.'

'Like the good bones of an ageing beauty?' Jahanara Begum's mouth curved in a rueful smile. 'Or a stiff old woman who was once a famously graceful dancer?'

'Or an old woman who still has a presence others will never achieve.' I reached for her hand. 'I may be a newcomer,' I said, 'but this is my home now and I will do whatever I can to save it.'

Her eyes were bright with tears. 'When I first met you, did I not say the Jahanara Mahal had been waiting for you?'

I smiled. 'And I believe I've been waiting most of my life to return to it.'

Two of Jahanara Begum's handmaids carried the chest of dancing clothes into the *zenana* sitting room and placed it in the middle of the floor, while the ladies watched with curiosity.

'Come and see what I have here!' I opened the trunk, pulled out a length of violet silk with a flourish and draped it around my shoulders.

The ladies rose from their cushions and surged towards me. Once the excited chatter had died down a little, I held up my hand for silence. 'Jahanara Begum has given us her dancing costumes. They have a great deal of sentimental value to her and I've promised we'll use them wisely to make our first samples.'

'It feels cruel to cut them up,' said Leela, holding up a sapphire blue tunic.

162

'I know,' I said, 'but it would be worse not to use this magnificent gift to do the very best we can to save the palace. Will you look at my sketchbook and help me to choose the most appealing selection of samples we can make?'

The discussion was intense but at the end of it we'd agreed who would make each item. Even the girls were judged capable of making embroidered handkerchiefs.

Afterwards, I returned to Jahanara Begum's quarters to find Lakshmi. She agreed to accompany me to the bazaar to purchase embroidery silks.

'I was astonished the Begum gave you her dancing costumes,' she said, as we walked out of the palace and into the scorching heat of the sun. 'They remind her of her past glories. I never imagined she would give them up.'

I paused at the foot of the palace steps to open my parasol. 'She's pinning all her hopes on this venture. I'm afraid it will need to be a success beyond my wildest dreams to solve all the financial difficulties.'

We walked along the terrace overlooking the river and stopped to watch the boats for a moment.

Lakshmi leaned her forearms on the wall and I glanced at her, wondering if she'd ever tell me about her feelings for Harry. Leela had thought at one time that Harry and Lakshmi would marry and I wanted to know if she still nursed hopes in that direction.

'You have surprised me, Bee,' she said.

'In what way?'

'I challenged you to find a means of breaking free from your unhappiness.' She gave me a sideways look. 'I didn't expect you to start such an ambitious project.'

'I've surprised myself,' I said. 'Perhaps it was because of your challenge. I was a wilful child but over the years since then my mother broke my spirit. Before that I remember my father telling me I could do anything I set my mind to.'

'My father told me the same thing,' said Lakshmi. She gazed at the distant city. 'Tell me about yours.'

We walked on and I slipped my arm through hers, pulling her to my side under the shade of the parasol. 'When I was small, he'd sit me on his shoulders and trot about the garden while I clung onto his hair, shrieking with a mixture of terror and excitement. He taught me to read and told me wonderful stories, saying he was really a king and I was his princess.'

'His princess?' Her fingers tightened on my forearm.

'Ridiculous, I know.' I sighed. 'But, despite his apparent affection for me, once Mother had taken me back to England, I never saw him again.' The echo of my childhood pain was clear in my voice.

'It still hurts you.' She spoke as if it was a fact, not a question.

'It was a long time ago,' I said. 'Today, I must find a range of embroidery silks at the best possible price and afterwards decide where to set up the workshop and find tables for cutting out the material. The floor might be dirty and the fabrics are delicate. And I need some lockable storage chests.'

'Leave that to me,' said Lakshmi.

Arm-in-arm, we ambled over the river bridge, discussing different options for a location for the workshop until we reached the crowded bazaar. A group of French soldiers jostled up behind us, so close that I smelled the garlic and tobacco on their breath. They called out to us, even being so bold as to tap us on the shoulder to make us take notice of them. Laughing and jabbering away in French, one of them suddenly plucked off the *dupatta* I wore over my head. There was a moment's respite from their insolent comments while they stared at my blonde hair.

Lakshmi whirled around, dagger already in her hand, and the soldier shrank back with a curse as she held it to his throat. His comrades jeered at him.

Snatching my *dupatta* from the insolent man's hands, I rearranged it over my head with as much dignity as possible.

Lakshmi stared at the soldiers, her dagger pointing threateningly at them, until they shrugged and turned away. 'Low-born pigs,' she muttered.

The incident shook me. I shouldn't have cared to meet them on my own.

'I'm going to teach you to haggle for the best prices,' said Lakshmi, as if nothing had happened, 'or you'll never be able to go shopping without me. Listen to what I say at the first stall and then you can try for yourself.'

Nearly two hours later we left the bazaar for the Jahanara Mahal with our arms full of bargains. We giggled together like schoolgirls while Lakshmi imitated the outrageous lies told to us by the stall-holders and I re-enacted my complete indifference to their claims of apparently sick mothers, starving children and impending homeless-ness if we didn't buy their goods at exorbitant prices.

I was beginning to appreciate the simple pleasures of female friendship. If I'd had even one good friend in Hampshire, perhaps I would never have come to India. 'I haven't enjoyed myself so much for as long as I can remember,' I said.

Lakshmi wiped away tears of laughter. 'No,' she said, her expression suddenly serious again. 'Neither have I.'

Chapter 20

During the following week the ladies made significant progress towards completing the first samples. I enjoyed sitting beside them in the *zenana* while working on an amethyst silk reticule, making suggestions for appropriate colours for the British market, engaging in their conversations and discovering more about them.

Samira Begum and Priya Begum embroidered a shawl together, each working on a different corner, while Leela and I sat nearby.

'I don't know what Great-grandmother said to my husband,' said Leela, 'but I'm surprised Ralph hasn't forbidden me from taking part. I imagined he would disapprove of me sewing to earn money.'

'Your father would not have approved,' said Samira Begum. 'Perhaps it is as well he is no longer with us to be perturbed by our plan.'

'Ralph was angry when I told him of it,' I said, 'but Jahanara Begum promised to speak to him. He's been avoiding me but he hasn't raised the subject again so perhaps he's becoming used to the idea.' I snipped off a loose thread of embroidery silk. 'He made me angry when he said women couldn't succeed in business. I sincerely hope we prove him wrong.'

'We must,' said Samira Begum. 'Otherwise what will become of us?'

'I've been thinking,' I said. 'The largest space in the palace is the Durbar Hall. It would be perfect for the women's workshop.'

'The Durbar Hall?' Priya Begum frowned. 'It was always used for the most important banquets and festivals when I was a girl.'

'Times change, *ammi*,' said Samira Begum, reaching out to pat her mother's hand. 'Everything is different now.'

I put the last stitch in the amethyst silk reticule and held it up to show them. 'We have a few completed samples now and Jahanara Begum will talk to the servants tomorrow.'

Priya Begum nodded. 'We shall watch from the ladies' balcony.'

'I'm going to see how the other samples are progressing.' I placed the finished reticule in the storage chest and stopped to have a few words with each of the ladies.

Bimla, despite her negative attitude to the idea of the workshop, had nearly finished embroidering tiny peacocks onto a beautiful piece of heavy silk that I intended to make into a lady's pelisse. The girls, giggling amongst themselves as they sewed, had made a small pile of handkerchiefs with different flowers worked in each corner. Indira, a frown of concentration on her rabbity face, was completing a diaphanous evening stole with borders of silver thread-work.

Delighted with the progress being made, I slipped out of the *zenana* sitting room and went to the palace kitchens, where I scrounged a piece of bread and a stale *dosa*.

A few minutes later, I opened the gate to the walled garden. From behind me came a shout and I turned to see Jai running towards me. I waited until he caught up with me.

'Hello, *aunty-ji*!' His wide smile was infectious.

'How was your camping expedition?'

'*Abbu-ji* and I had a most excellent time.' His eyes shone. 'We fished in the river, cooked our dinner over a campfire and slept under the stars.'

He chattered away, full of his adventures, as we made our way towards the derelict outbuilding.

Swati lifted her head when she saw us, her tail thumping so hard it stirred the dust into a cloud.

Jai fell to his knees and wrapped his arms around her, while she licked his cheek. 'How the puppies have grown!' he said.

I took the bread and the *dosa* from my pocket and fed them to Swati.

'Thank you for looking after them while I was away,' said Jai. 'I couldn't have left them on their own.'

'I've grown fond of them,' I said, ruffling his hair.

He grinned at me but then his smile suddenly disappeared.

'Jai!' said a man's voice behind me.

The boy leaped to his feet and I looked over his shoulder and was alarmed to see Harry looming above us, his face tight with anger.

'Didn't Sangita-Aunty tell you to get rid of that creature?'

Swati curled her lip at the angry tone of his voice and let out a deep and threatening growl.

'But Swati isn't in the palace,' stammered Jai.

I rose to my feet and stood beside him, praying the dog wouldn't attack Harry.

'It's still in the palace grounds, against Sangita-Aunty's express wishes. And you,' Harry looked directly at me, 'it's clear you have colluded with my son and encouraged him to disobey orders.'

'Swati is doing no harm here,' I said, being careful not to sound argumentative, even though my pulse had begun to race. 'It would have been cruel to let her suffer while she was whelping.'

'That isn't the point,' thundered Harry. 'Sangita, out of the kindness of her heart, has brought Jai up as if she were his own mother. He owes her enough respect to obey her commands.'

Jai's hand crept into mine. I couldn't fail him now. I squared up to Harry. 'Jai does owe Sangita love and respect,' I said, 'but, in my opinion, she is overly anxious about the perceived dangers of this particular dog.'

Harry's jaw clenched. 'That is not for you to decide ...'

I gave him a cold stare. 'Don't interrupt,' I said, sounding exactly like Mother. 'Swati is not infected by rabies or mange and we have taken the precaution of treating her with neem and eucalyptus oil to rid her of fleas. She has a gentle and friendly nature.' I held up my hand as Harry opened his mouth to speak. 'Furthermore, Jai has given me his solemn promise that Swati will leave the Jahanara Mahal once her puppies are weaned. I do agree with Sangita that we cannot have the palace overrun with packs of feral dogs.'

'You think to undermine my authority with my son?'

I glanced at Swati and was relieved to see she'd settled down and was occupied in cleaning one of her puppies. 'I think the friendship between a motherless boy and his dog is a very precious thing,' I said, 'especially if his father is so often away. If you remember, you, too, had a brown street dog that trotted along at your heels everywhere you went when you were a boy. Bandit was his name, I believe?'

Harry stared at me. 'You remember Bandit?'

'Of course I do. You loved that dog, just as Jai loves Swati.'

There was a long pause during which I refused to drop my gaze. Harry blinked. 'Jai, come with me!' he ordered.

Jai sent me a frightened glance and I let go of his hand. 'Go with your *abbu*,' I said. 'I'll stay with Swati.'

Harry left the outbuilding without another word and Jai trailed after him.

Heavy-hearted, I kneeled down beside Swati. The dog leaned against me, eyes closed as I fondled her ears.

The following morning, I used some more of my precious inheritance to send one of the servants into the city to purchase several large boxes of sweets. Then I went to see Hemanti.

'Welcome,' she said, ushering me into her small home behind the curtains.

I smiled at little Talin, asleep on a cushion.

'How are you keeping, Hemanti?' I whispered.

She placed a hand over her swelling stomach. 'Well,' she said, but I saw the lines of strain around her eyes.

'And Talin?'

'He cries for his father.'

'Your husband is still away seeking work?'

She nodded. 'I expected he would have returned by now. I am frightened that if he can't find employment, then he might sign up to be a soldier. What would happen to us if he died fighting the French?'

I glanced at her shelves and saw that the bowls of lentils and rice were almost empty. The employed servants ate from the palace kitchens but their families had to fend for themselves. 'I hope you have news of your husband soon,' I said. 'Hemanti, I wonder if you will help me?'

'If I can.'

'Jahanara Begum wants to speak to all the inhabitants of the palace in the Durbar Hall at noon. Would you ask those who live in this part of the palace to spread the word?'

Hemanti looked at me with a question in her eyes.

'You can say there will be sweets.'

Her face lit up. 'My brother works in the stables. I'll ask him to tell the gardeners.'

'Thank you. I'll see you in a while, then.'

I walked through the palace, letting everyone I saw know that they were to come to the Durbar Hall. Then I found the palace steward, Sangita's husband Gopal, in his cluttered office near the kitchens. His upright bearing and luxuriant black moustache made him a commanding figure. I introduced myself and asked him to pass on the message to the servants.

Once I'd completed my mission I called in to see Jahanara Begum. Her handmaid told me she was unwell but had expressed an urgent wish to see me.

The Begum was resting on a *charpai* and I was disturbed by the feverish light in her eyes and the beads of sweat on her brow.

'Is there something I can do for you?' I asked. 'You don't look well enough to meet the servants this afternoon.'

'I'm not,' she said. She appeared very frail, leaning back against her pillows.

'Shall I ask Gopal to postpone the meeting?'

'No! It is preying on my mind. The deed must be done. I will send for Gopal and ask him to break the news, but you must tell the women yourself about your plans.'

'Lakshmi says the servants will be angry.'

'Are you afraid?'

I hesitated. 'I would like to have her nearby, in case there's any disturbance.'

Jahanara Begum struggled to sit up and I adjusted the pillow behind her head. 'I should be the one to tell them.' She plucked fretfully at her shawl. 'I won't make the servants homeless for as long as I own the palace. They needn't leave if they can earn enough elsewhere to feed themselves. What use are all our efforts if the Jahanara Mahal becomes a ghost palace?' She clasped at my hand and then closed her eyes.

I wasn't sure if she was asleep. After a moment I gently pulled my fingers free. 'I shall come and tell you all about it later,' I whispered before I crept away.

Chapter 21

Later, with some trepidation, I made my way to the Durbar Hall, followed by Jyoti and three other handmaids from the *zenana*, each bearing aloft a platter of honeyed sweets.

Even before I reached the Durbar Hall, I heard the loud hum of conversation, pierced by children's cries and shouts. I paused a moment, drew myself up to my full height and pushed open the door.

Men squatted on the floor at one end of the room, while the women had gathered in the other with babies on their knees. A number of shrieking children chased each other. The sheer size of the assembly made me stop in the doorway. Although the doors to the garden were open, the atmosphere was hot and fetid, the air laden with the cloying odours of sweat and spices.

I spied Lakshmi standing at the side of the hall with Gopal, and went to join them.

'I'd no idea there were so many servants,' I whispered, placing the travelling bag I'd bought with me on the floor.

Lakshmi held a heavy steel-tipped staff in one hand. Her other rested on the pommel of her sword. A curved dagger hung prominently at her waist. 'We must be careful,' she murmured. 'There's a restlessness about them that I don't like and there have already been some raised voices. I suspect they have a notion of what is to come.'

'Do you expect any difficulties?' I whispered.

She shrugged. 'I am here to protect you.'

'Thank you.' My resolve wavered for a moment. I wasn't sure that she alone could save us if the servants turned into an angry mob. Then I saw Harry standing at the side of the hall, leaning against the wall with his arms folded. He was watching me with such a frown on his face that I could only assume he hadn't forgiven me for our argument.

Lakshmi banged her staff against the doorframe and Gopal held up his hand for silence.

Gradually, the crowd quietened. A child cried out and was hushed by her mother.

I caught sight of Hemanti and Talin. Sangita waved to me in a friendly fashion and I hazarded a guess that Harry couldn't yet have told her about my conspiracy with Jai to keep Swati secret from her. Lakshmi's grandmother, Usha, heavily veiled as before, sat beside Sangita.

Once there was silence, Gopal began to speak. 'Our beloved mistress Jahanara Begum is unwell,' he said, 'so she has instructed me to speak to you about an important matter. She has always taken care of her servants and your welfare remains close to her heart. Some of you even travelled in Jahanara Begum's entourage when she came to this palace fifty years ago.'

A shrunken old man held his hand up and I recognised him as the gatekeeper. 'I came with her then.'

'Unfortunately,' said Gopal, 'as a result of the theft of the fabled Rose of Golconda, the Begum has fallen on lean times.'

Many in the crowd nodded in understanding.

'The diamond was given to Jahanara Begum by her benefactor, with the intention of ensuring the continuing maintenance of the palace and all who served there. Since the diamond was stolen, the Begum has, one by one, sold her other jewels and personal possessions to cover these costs. Now, she has little left . . . '

Murmuring began amongst the gathering.

Gopal held up his hand to quieten them. 'The fact of the matter is that she is unable to continue to pay her servants after the end of this month.'

A roar went up from the assembly. Several of the men rose to their feet, shouting angry questions, and there was a chorus of accusing cries from the women.

I glanced at Lakshmi but she stood as straight as an obelisk, missing nothing as she surveyed the crowd.

'The Begum can't just turn us out in the streets!' A man with a heavy black beard waved his fist in the air.

An elderly woman pushed herself painfully to her feet. 'We've served her faithfully for years and this is how she repays us?' She began to weep. 'She promised there would always be a home for my family at the palace.'

'The Begum will not turn you out,' said Gopal, shouting over the hubbub. 'Those of you who wish to leave the palace to seek employment elsewhere are free to go. Alternatively, you may stay here, if you can earn enough outside the palace to feed yourselves. Furthermore, the Begum has asked this lady,' he looked at me, 'to speak to you about another way to earn your living.'

A vociferous discussion broke out amongst a group at the back of the hall. Then a dozen or so men, some of them with their wives by their side, pushed their way through the throng and left the hall.

Gopal turned to me. 'I have done as the Begum desired of me.' He looked at the unruly gathering and shrugged. 'I can do no more.'

Aghast, I watched him stride out of the hall. I had no idea how to calm the crowd and make them receptive enough to listen to my plans for a sewing workshop. I looked around for something to bang on the floor to draw everyone's attention and saw Harry unfold himself from half-reclining position. He caught my eye and I realised he was about to take control. Following our disagreement, I didn't wish to appear weak so I bellowed, 'Quiet!'

Angry faces turned towards me.

'Silence!' I yelled.

The noise abated a little and I snatched my opportunity. 'The fault does not lie with Jahanara Begum,' I shouted. 'You must blame the present painful situation on the thief who stole the Rose of Golconda.'

Usha let out a low wail and began to rock herself backwards and forwards. I watched as, still weeping, she stumbled her way out of the hall, supported by Sangita.

One of the men called out, 'Let the woman speak!'

I waited for a moment, noticing that Harry was working his way around the hall towards me. He exchanged a word or two with several of the men as he went.

Gradually the angry chatter died away.

'The Begum has been generous over the years,' I said. 'Almost all of you have extended family who now consider the palace their home, even though they may not be employed here.'

I glanced up at Harry as he reached my side.

'There are many artists, poets and musicians,' he said, his voice resonating around the Durbar Hall, 'who came to entertain the Begum's guests and have remained in the palace. Some of you here are honoured guests who, many years ago, were invited for a day, a week or a month and still continue to enjoy Jahanara Begum's hospitality. Some of you even have several generations of your own family living with you here now.'

I stepped forward, determined not to let Harry dominate proceedings. I raised my voice over the agitated talk. 'Jahanara Begum wishes you carefully to consider another option that may help some of you.'

I waited until there was a lull. 'The ladies of the *zenana* are setting up a workshop to produce high-quality, embroidered articles for sale.' I glanced up at the ladies' balcony and smiled, even though I could only see their shadowy outlines crowded together behind the screens.

'What use is that to us?' called out a man's voice.

I addressed him directly. 'It's of use to you because such a workshop may allow your wife to put food in your children's mouths.' I stared at him until he stopped muttering, and then faced the others. 'We require women of a hard-working disposition to assist with embroidery and plain sewing,' I said. 'We shall also need women to mind the children while their mothers sew and others to clean and work in the kitchens. There will be a meal provided every day and a roof over your head but, let me be clear, no salary until the finished goods are sold. Remuneration will then be on the basis of how many articles are finished to a satisfactory standard and sold.'

Hemanti waved to catch my attention. 'You say there is work for the women but what about our husbands?'

'The husbands of the women who work for us,' I said, 'may take paid employment out of the palace and return here at night. There will be no rent to pay.'

People began to talk volubly amongst themselves. Two men pushed and shoved each other and Lakshmi moved in to separate them, threatening them with her steel-tipped staff.

I didn't attempt to shout over the cacophony and started when Harry touched my elbow. 'I should tell them more about the workshop but . . . ' I shrugged at the sight of all the people milling around, gesticulating and talking at the tops of their voices.

'Wait awhile.'

Then I had another thought. I beckoned to the handmaids, standing in the doorway, and they threaded their way through the groups, offering the honey-soaked sweets sprinkled with chopped pistachios. Children, hands outstretched, clamoured to take the treats. A short while later many of the gathering had sat down again while they ate their sweet or licked their fingers.

Once the hubbub had quietened, I said, 'Tomorrow afternoon, here in the Durbar Hall, I shall talk to any of you women who are interested in working for the embroidery workshop. There will be sewing trials for suitable applicants.'

Opening up the travelling bag I'd brought with me, I took out the items the ladies and I had made. 'Here are some examples of the goods that will be produced in the workshop.' One by one, I held up the evening stole with the silver border, the amethyst reticule, the embroidered handkerchiefs and the shawl. 'Come closer if you have any questions.'

Most of the men and about a third of the women left the hall but, once the disturbance had settled, I was surrounded by the women who had remained. They stroked the fine material of the shawls, examined the handkerchiefs and laughed at the reticules. I was inundated with questions. One very persistent woman called Deepika had a beak of a nose and an imperious manner. She insisted on telling me at great length how she had learned to embroider from her mother, who had been an excellent needlewoman, and that I would think my prayers had been answered if I gave her work. Over her shoulder, I saw Harry watching me with a quizzical expression, a hint of humour lurking at the corners of his mouth. My spirits lifted, hoping that there was a chance for a reconciliation between us.

At last the women ran out of questions. 'Tonight,' I said, 'you may discuss this proposal with your husbands and decide if you would like to take part in the new venture. I hope I shall see some of you tomorrow.'

The women began to drift away, talking animatedly amongst themselves.

Harry, I noticed, had already left.

Chapter 22

The early-morning breeze was pleasantly cool in the garden and the long grass swished against my calves. Pushing my way behind the overgrown trellis, I froze when I saw a snake a few feet in front of me. After a moment or two it slithered away into the undergrowth and I let out my breath.

The door of the outbuilding was open and I heard the soft whines of Swati's puppies inside. What I hadn't expected, however, was to discover Harry crouched down with one of them in his hand.

'What are you doing?' I demanded.

He jumped. 'Oh, it's you! Don't sound so defensive, Bee. I'm not harming them.'

I glared at him. 'Put the puppy back.'

'So you don't want me to give this to Swati, then?' He held up a chunk of meat and a piece of bread.

I opened my mouth but was too surprised to speak.

He fed the meat to the dog, breaking the bread into pieces and murmuring soothing words all the while.

Once Swati had finished eating, I handed Harry the little muslin-wrapped parcel of scraps that I'd brought and he fed those to her, too.

As he bent over the dog I studied the back of his head, noticing his neat ears and the dark hair that curled onto the sun-browned skin of his neck. My fingers twitched slightly as I resisted the urge to reach out and touch his curls.

'She'll get as fat as *ghee* if we go on feeding her like this,' he said. 'Once the puppies are a little bigger, we should encourage her to go out and forage for food or she'll become too dependent on us.'

I nodded in agreement. 'What changed your mind about letting her stay for now?' I asked, still bewildered by his change of attitude.

Harry lifted one of the puppies onto his lap and stroked its head while Swati watched him with her ears pricked. 'You reminded me how much Bandit meant to me when I was a boy. Father didn't bother himself much with me, so my dog was my closest companion.'

My heart ached for that lonely little boy. 'Jai is happy,' I said. 'He's very fond of Sangita and he adores you.'

'I left the army to spend more time with him. Even though I still often have to be away, I'm determined to be the best father I can.' Gently, he returned the puppy to its mother. 'Jai told me you looked after Swati so he was free to come away with me.'

'It was easy to see how upset he was to miss such a treat but he's very loyal and wouldn't let Swati suffer. Besides, I'd seen how hurt you were after he refused your invitation.'

'Thank you.' Harry looked at the puppies again and wrinkled his forehead. 'All I have to do now is to deal with my conscience about defying Sangita.'

'Though I don't care for untruths, perhaps in this instance it's simply best to say nothing?' I said. 'I made an agreement with Jai that Swati would be returned outside the palace walls once the pups are able to fend for themselves.'

Harry nodded. 'I daresay there'll be some tears but he must learn to keep his word.' He stood up. 'As I wish to keep my word to you.'

'What do you mean?'

'I promised to take you for a ride in the countryside.'

I couldn't control the wide smile that spread over my face.

'Are you free to accompany me now?' he said.

'Yes, but not for too long. I have preparations to make for the women's sewing trials.'

I followed him out of the garden and we walked past the *pilkhana*. I heard the gentle thud of an arrow hitting its target even before we glimpsed Lakshmi at her archery practice.

Harry put a finger to his lips and shook his head but I was enjoying his company and had no mind to disturb her.

In the stable yard the *scyce* had already saddled Zephyr, who whickered when his master fed him a piece of *jaggery*.

I went to say hello to Mumtaz, whose head was poking over the stable door.

Harry opened the door of one of the other loose boxes and led out the prettiest little Arab bay mare. 'Her name is Breeze,' he said.

Breeze tossed her mane and looked at me with lively interest when I patted her neck. 'She's beautiful,' I said.

'She'll be perfect for both you and Sangita to ride whenever you have time. Dear old Mumtaz is really too small.'

My eyes widened. 'You'll let me ride her?'

Harry's dark eyes crinkled at the corners when he laughed. 'Of course, that's why I bought her.'

I wrapped my arms around the little mare, burying my face in her neck so that he wouldn't see how moved I was. 'Thank you,' I said, my voice muffled by her pretty mane.

'Let's get her saddled up, then.'

A short while later, the *scyce* assisted me into the saddle.

'How do you find her?' asked Harry.

'I'm higher up,' I said, 'and she's much narrower than Mumtaz.'

'We'll make a circuit around the *maidan* while you get the feel of her and then go into the countryside.'

After Mumtaz's phlegmatic character Breeze certainly appeared more energetic and her enthusiasm for being out and about on a beautiful morning was infectious.

Once we'd trotted around the *maidan* without mishap, Harry led us out of the palace grounds. We turned away from the river and the grand houses with their pleasure gardens and before long were riding side by side between paddy fields. After a while, the terrain began to rise and I saw the hilly outcrops I'd noticed from the palace towers.

'Are you all right?' asked Harry.

'Absolutely! Breeze seems to be enjoying herself, too.'

'There was something else I wanted to say to you.'

'Yes?'

'I want to apologise,' he said. 'I underestimated you. At the meeting there were moments when I thought you wouldn't be able to control the crowd.'

'I was afraid of that, too. What could Lakshmi have done on her own?'

'It was brave of you.'

'I'm not sure about that,' I said. 'I hoped to sweeten the medicine by offering a glimpse of hope to the women – to us all at the palace.'

Harry looked at me so intently the heat rose in my cheeks and I concentrated on guiding Breeze around a series of boulders half-hidden in the dry grass.

'Ralph cornered me a couple of times to tell me how hare-brained you must be even to consider such a scheme but, now, I'd put money on it that you're going to prove him wrong,' said Harry, a thoughtful expression on his face.

'In what way?'

'You have great determination and stand up for what you believe in. You certainly don't put up with any nonsense.' His lips twitched. 'I've experienced that for myself. What a shrew!'

I raised my eyebrows. 'That was unchivalrous of you, Mr Wyndham.'

His expression sobered immediately. 'I apologise.'

'Please don't feel you must,' I said with a half-smile. 'My mother and I were never close, but one thing I watched and learned from her was how to put the fear of God into servants and tradesmen and anyone else who presumed to take liberties.'

Harry threw back his head and laughed. 'I'll race you to the tree on top of that hill over there. So as not to disadvantage you, I'll give you a minute's head start.' He leaned over and slapped Breeze's rump.

She whinnied and then we were off. I crouched over between her ears and gripped her flanks with my thighs as the countryside flashed past. I'd never travelled so fast in all my life and when Harry raced past me just before we reached the top of the hill I was laughing like a Bedlamite.

'You're definitely no gentleman, Harry,' I called out, 'or you'd have let me win.'

He wheeled Zephyr around to face me. 'What, and risk you accusing me of not treating you like an equal? I wouldn't dare! I tell you what, though, Bee, it suits you to have the wind in your hair and roses in your cheeks. We must do this again.'

I glowed with pleasure as we led the horses down the hill towards the palace. I hadn't felt so happy for a long time.

Later that morning I was in the *zenana* with Leela, Samira Begum and Parvati, waiting for Lakshmi to accompany us to the Durbar Hall. Leela was so full of excitement about leaving the *zenana* for a while, she couldn't sit still.

Jyoti came and murmured to her. 'Your husband wishes to speak with you,' she said. 'He awaits you in your room. You too, *sahiba*,' she said to me.

My heart sank. I'd managed to avoid Ralph since we'd quarrelled.

Leela tucked her hand into the crook of my elbow and led me through the *zenana*. She opened the door to a spacious bedroom with a high ceiling. The bed was richly decorated with a purple bedspread embellished with gold.

'Where's Ralph?' I asked.

Leela draped her veil over her face before opening another door on the opposite side of the room.

My brother was sitting on the window seat in the corridor outside.

I'd often wondered how Ralph and Leela managed their marital arrangements in the *zenana*.

Unsmiling, he stood up to greet us. 'May I come to your room, Leela?'

He ignored me and I suspected that boded ill.

Once the door was closed, Leela let her veil slip down to her shoulders. She leaned forward and made her *namaste*. 'You are always welcome to my room, husband.'

'And, as my wife, you have always pleased me by your obedience,' he said, 'which is more than I can say for my sister.'

Leela said nothing but looked at him with a wary expression in her lovely eyes.

'What have I done to annoy you this time, Ralph?' I asked.

'It was my express wish, as you well know, Bee, that you forget all this nonsense about an embroidery workshop.'

'Jahanara Begum approves. More than that, she's pinned her hopes on the idea.'

'Don't you see, it's a scheme doomed to failure?' Ralph's eyes narrowed to slits in his plump face. 'Women, through no fault of their own, are incapable of making a success of a business.'

'So you say. Do you have any proof of that?' I kept my tone light and conversational but my fists were clenched behind my back.

'It's a known fact.'

'Only amongst men as narrow-minded as yourself.' I recalled Harry's encouraging words earlier that morning and smiled to myself.

Exasperated, Ralph ran his fingers through his hair. 'You never used to be so difficult, Bee. You're growing more and more like Mother.'

Anger seethed inside me as suddenly as an unwatched pan of milk reaching boiling point. 'At least I'm attempting to do something about the distressing situation here at the Jahanara Mahal. What steps are *you* taking to save our home, Ralph?'

His cheeks flooded beetroot red. 'If you insist on pursuing this madness, you can do it without the help of my wife.' He turned to Leela. 'Do you understand?'

'But . . . ' Her mouth trembled.

'Enough!' Ralph pinched the bridge of his nose. 'I'm already overwhelmed with work, assisting the Resident to ensure the French don't murder us all in our beds. I cannot allow myself to be troubled by this.' He sighed. 'Bee, you'd better run along to the Durbar Hall straight away. It's complete pandemonium there.'

'Pandemonium?'

'Lakshmi was trying to restore some kind of order but there are women servants everywhere. She told me you'd asked her to escort some of the ladies from the *zenana* to help you interview them. I'm certainly not exposing my wife to that.' He dropped a kiss on Leela's forehead. 'Be a good girl and I'll see you tonight when I return from the Residency.'

A moment later the door to the corridor closed behind him.

Leela's eyes were very bright and she blinked several times. 'I am sorry I cannot help you, Bee,' she said in a low voice.

'So am I but I haven't any intention of causing difficulties between a husband and wife.' I sighed. 'I'd better find out if Samira Begum and Parvati are ready to come with me.'

Lakshmi had arrived by the time we returned to the sitting room. 'We must hurry to the Durbar Hall now, Bee,' she said.

'Ralph said there are a great many women waiting?'

Lakshmi nodded. 'He told me Leela wouldn't be coming. I

believe it would be advisable for you to replace her with one or two of the other ladies.'

After a hasty discussion Veeda and Indira joined us.

Lakshmi went first, clearing the way of any men as we passed through the palace, followed by the ladies swathed in thick veils.

I brought up the rear of the procession, carrying my writing case, still angry with Ralph but also determined to prove him wrong.

Chapter 23

We heard the high-pitched chatter before we reached the Durbar Hall. I led the way inside, pushing a path through the throng until we reached one end of the hall.

Lakshmi banged the doors shut and the ladies from the *zenana* removed their heavy veils. The servant women turned towards us and I clapped my hands for attention.

'Thank you all for coming,' I said. 'Please be patient because it may take some time to speak to you all. I'd like you to make four groups and then wait to talk to the ladies. Please tell them if you have any expertise and experience in embroidery, or if you wish to work in the kitchens or mind the children. If the ladies decide you are suitable, then please come and speak to me.'

There was a great deal of laughter as the women jostled each other to form more or less orderly queues. Standing on the side-lines I watched carefully as the ladies of the *zenana* began to interview the palace women. The atmosphere was generally good-natured but some of those who were declined made angry protests and stormed out of the hall, slamming the doors behind them.

Sighing, I opened my writing case, took out a pen and an inkwell.

I titled four new pages in my notebook: Embroiderery, Plain Sewing, Kitchen/Domestic and Children. It wasn't long before the first successful applicants began to gather around me.

Several hours later I stretched my arms and flexed my back. I had pins and needles from sitting on the floor for so long and cramp in my hand from making so many entries in the notebook but all the women had been attended to. Many had been sent away disappointed but the most suitable were waiting to undertake a sewing trial.

Samira Begum and Veeda were yawning when I closed my writing case, while Indira and Parvati were quietly discussing the women they'd interviewed.

'I thought we would never be finished,' said Parvati.

Indira nodded. 'It surprised me how many of the women said they could sew.'

'As to that,' said Samira Begum, 'the proof will come when we see how well they do in the trials.'

Samira Begum and Parvati put on their veils and returned to the *zenana* with Lakshmi.

I called the twenty-five selected women back into the Durbar Hall to take their sewing tests.

'Please form a line here against the wall,' I said, 'and hold out your hands.'

There was a certain amount of giggling as the women shuffled into a row.

I walked along the row examining their outstretched palms. 'It's important you have clean hands all the time,' I said. 'We shall be working on expensive and delicate materials.' I picked out half a dozen of the women and sent them to wash their hands in the buckets of water Jyoti had brought to the hall earlier.

Afterwards, I divided them into two groups, those who would be demonstrating their embroidery skills and those taking a plain sewing test. Veeda laid out needles, thread and scissors for the women and I was pleased that Hemanti was one of those who had been selected.

'I want you each to take two of these,' I said. The ladies of the *zenana* and I had cut some old sheets into neat squares. 'Fold one square in half and sew me a seam down the long edge. Make your stitches small and neat, like the ones in this sample, and work as quickly as you can. When you've finished, Veeda will show you how to hem the second square to make a handkerchief.'

The women passed the sample around to see the standard required and Veeda sat with them to answer any questions.

I left them threading their needles and went to see the embroiderers, who were chatting to Indira while they waited. I gave each of them a handkerchief embroidered with a lotus flower in the corner and set them to copying the motif onto squares of fine muslin.

Most of the women worked quietly, occasionally pausing to look at the example or glancing at their neighbour's work. One or two of the younger ones whispered amongst themselves as they sewed and another kept tangling her thread into a knot and having to start again.

One by one, they completed the tasks and handed me their finished sample. Deepika, the bossy woman who had told me her mother was an embroiderer to an aristocratic family, had completed not only the lotus flower in one corner of her handkerchief but had also worked a rosebud in the others.

I wrote each of the women's names on a label and pinned it to their work, thanked them for taking part and promised to let them know soon which of them had been successful.

Lakshmi escorted us back to the *zenana*, where we enjoyed a cooling glass of lemon sherbet and began to examine the sewing tests.

*

A week later, I stood in the centre of the Durbar Hall. The morning sunlight flooded down from the domed roof light above, sparking flashes of ruby and gold fire from stones inlaid into the wall panels. There was nothing I could do about the deep fissures in the wall but the marble floor had been scrubbed until it shone and the ceiling and crystal chandeliers dusted free of cobwebs.

Just for a moment I imagined a snatch of music and the murmur of conversation during some long-ago banquet held here. How glorious the hall would have been then with low tables set with fine linen, gold dishes and sparkling glassware! The air would have been heady with the perfume of exotic flowers and fragrantly spiced platters of rich food.

The tables set out now, however, were far more rudimentary as they were fashioned from doors removed from empty rooms and fixed to trestles. Lakshmi had found four unused storage chests in various locations around the palace and these had been arranged at one end of the hall. Stout locks had been fitted to them and also to the large cupboard on the end wall.

I'd bought a basketful of scissors, thread and needles from the bazaar and, together with a pile of Jahanara Begum's costumes, began to set these out on the tables.

A shadow moved across the window and then I smiled as Harry came in from the garden. 'Nearly ready?' he asked.

'I think so.' I tucked a loose curl behind my ear. 'Jyoti is going to fetch drinking and hand-washing water. We've set up a nursery for the small children near the kitchens and another group of women are preparing *dhal* and *rotis* for the midday meal.'

Harry sauntered over to one of the tables and ran his hand over an emerald silk tunic. 'Is this one of the pieces Jahanara Begum gave to you?'

I nodded. 'It saddens me to cut them up but I hope we can make each one into something of even greater worth. Jahanara Begum was very slender so each garment is small but we'll cut carefully to make the maximum number of items from each one.'

'And what will you do with them, then?'

'I'll send a parcel of samples and sketches to a shop in Bond Street and to other shops in London and the larger cities, too. In the meantime, I must try to sell some of the goods here in Hyderabad.'

'Do you know anyone outside the palace who might buy them?'

I laid out a pair of gathered trousers made from silver gauze so that he didn't see the anxiety in my eyes. 'Not yet,' I said. He didn't respond, for which I was grateful, since I didn't have a better answer.

'I came to ask if you'd like to take a ride this evening. It will be cooler then.'

'I can't think of anything I'd like better.'

He gave me a smile that made me feel warm inside but then three women peered through the doorway.

I beckoned them in.

'I'll see you at the stables later on, then,' said Harry, raising a hand in farewell.

Very soon all the women had arrived and, once I'd welcomed them, I showed them the fine clothes we had to work with. 'We'll have to unpick the seams and lay the pieces flat before we can cut out the new patterns.'

I checked the cleanliness of the women's hands and set them to work. I wished I'd had one or two of the ladies from the *zenana* to assist me but it wouldn't do to upset their sensibilities by expecting them to work side by side with the lower-caste women.

The day flew by, fully occupied as I was answering questions and watching like a hawk to be sure none of the fabrics were spoiled. I had to keep a particular eye on one of the younger women, Kalpana, who disturbed the others with her incessant gossiping. Despite being so busy, a thrum of anticipation ran through my veins all day at the prospect of a ride into the countryside with Harry that evening.

Once the women had finished for the day, I returned to the *zenana* to see how the ladies had progressed.

'I have begun another shawl,' said Leela, defiance in her voice. 'I obeyed my husband by not coming to help you choose which women would have a place in the workshop but he cannot deny me the pleasant pastime of a little sewing.'

'I'm sad Ralph is so against the idea,' I said, 'but I shouldn't like to be responsible for any discord between you.' I rubbed my eyes. 'I'm going for a ride in the countryside to blow the cobwebs away before dark.'

Leela sighed. 'Sometimes, I envy you.'

Chapter 24

Harry was waiting for me in the stable yard with Zephyr and Breeze already saddled. I wore my russet riding clothes and had braided my hair, rather than wrapping it in a turban, since that looked more attractive. I was honest enough to admit to myself this was purely for Harry's benefit. He was dressed in a grubby turban again and tattered native trousers under a loose *kurta*. Clearly, he wasn't making any attempt to impress me.

Mumtaz looked at me over the stable door with her usual placid expression but the chestnut mare wasn't in her stable.

'Lakshmi must have ridden out with Aurora,' I said, as Harry helped me onto Breeze's back.

'She'd already gone when I arrived.'

We rode along the river bank towards the bridge. The late-afternoon shadows were lengthening as we crossed the Musi.

'We'll turn left down this way,' said Harry as we picked our way between sacred cows and carts, palanquins and bad-tempered camels.

The bazaar was still bustling. Pyramids of vegetables and sacks of rice and lentils narrowed the route. Garments hanging from a stall fluttered in the wind, making Breeze prance uncertainly from hoof to hoof. Street dogs roamed in packs and a woman balancing a tray on her head pulled at my ankle, entreating me to buy her fresh *chapattis*. Men cooked spicy *biryani* in open doorways and the greasy smoke from their fires made my eyes water.

Glancing into narrow side streets, I saw grand houses with latticed windows behind forbidding walls and high iron gates. Rats and street urchins skulked in the shadows, foraging in the gutters. I was relieved to be on horseback and safely above the teeming masses.

Then the city walls rose before us and we left the tumult behind as we clattered through one of the gates. Soon, we were riding over open ground and in a little while came to the ruins of an abandoned palace surrounded by the tumbledown walls of its pleasure gardens.

'I wonder if it disintegrated in the same earthquake that damaged the Jahanara Mahal,' I said, noting the sun-dried scrub growing between the flagstones of what had once been spacious rooms.

'It fell down long before that,' said Harry. 'I remember exploring it when I was a boy.'

The ground grew steeper and we climbed for some time until we stopped on a hillock from where we could survey the panorama of jumbled roofs and minarets of the walled city.

'The French have plans to build a grand memorial up here to General Raymond,' said Harry.

'Was it ever discovered why he died?' I asked.

He shook his head. 'It remains a mystery but they've replaced him with his deputy, Jean-Pierre Piron.'

'And does the Nizam hold Piron in the same regard as he did General Raymond?'

'It's too early to tell. Piron, however, is less sophisticated than Raymond and doesn't have his predecessor's charm.'

'I wonder then,' I said, 'if that might give Mr Kirkpatrick an opportunity to build upon his relationship with the Nizam and oust the French?'

'Kirkpatrick has already redoubled his efforts in that quarter.' Harry gave me a mischievous look, flicked the reins and spurred his horse into a trot. 'Come on!' he called over his shoulder, as Zephyr broke into a canter.

Breeze shot off before I was prepared, only too eager to race after them. Bouncing up and down, I clung on for dear life until I remembered Lakshmi telling me to meld with the horse. Relaxing, I soon slipped into the rhythm and enjoyed the feeling of the wind in my face.

Harry reined in after a while and we walked the horses side by side as we crested a ridge and began to descend on the other side.

'What's that?' I asked.

'The French army encampment.'

There were row upon row of tents, hundreds of them. As we drew closer, I saw men walking about between them. Wisps of smoke drifted on the evening air, carrying the aroma of roasting meat.

'It's a fearsome sight to see French soldiers in such vast numbers,' I said.

We descended the hill towards the river and, halfway down, passed a clump of trees.

'Don't look now,' said Harry, 'but that *sepoy* is one of the French scouts.'

Without turning my head, I glanced at a native sitting on the ground, his back against a tree trunk. His clothing was the same sandy colour as the parched grass and, if Harry hadn't pointed him out, I doubt I'd have seen him.

He watched as we trotted away but didn't accost us.

We gave the encampment a wide berth and it was as we turned to go along the river path that I looked back at the way we'd come and caught sight of a rider following in our footsteps. The horse came to a halt as we did and then turned and galloped, hell for leather, back up the hill.

'Harry,' I said, 'was that Lakshmi?'

He narrowed his eyes against the sun. The rider was momentarily silhouetted against the sky and then disappeared over the ridge. 'It can't have been,' he said with a slight frown. 'She's aware of the risks of riding alone so close to the French encampment. And so should you be.'

'I am,' I said. After the unsettling encounter with the French soldiers at the bazaar, I had no desire to be accosted by any of them again.

A week later Leela, Samira Begum and I took a warm bath scented with attar of roses. The handmaids massaged perfumed oils into our skin and hair in preparation for our visit to Parwar un-nisa Begum in the Nizam's *zenana*. Many of the servants had already left the palace but Jyoti and Jahanara Begum's two loyal handmaids had remained, unpaid, to look after us in the *zenana*.

Samira Begum lent me a snowy white tunic embellished with white embroidery. Made of gossamer-fine lawn, it had a myriad of tiny pleats falling from the yoke.

'We cannot be found wanting by Parwar un-nisa Begum or the Nizam's wives,' said Samira Begum. 'It is a matter of due respect.'

Jyoti slipped the tunic over my head and fastened the tiny pearl buttons down the front.

'We must arrive with ceremony for our visit to the Nizam's *zenana*,' said Samira Begum. 'The Nizam's ladies must assume our simple clothing and lack of jewels are to respect the memories of our dead husbands and not because we cannot afford better. We shall compensate by dressing our handmaids in the richest garments the ladies possess and adorning them with every single bracelet and ring to be found in the *zenana*. Leela may wear her wedding finery.'

Lakshmi and Sangita carried the chest of finished samples down to the *zenana* garden, where the palanquins awaited us. Jahanara Begum had requested Sangita accompany us dressed in her old uniform, complete with sword and jewelled dagger issued from the arms store.

Two large and, once, very fine palanquins had been brought out of storage in the *pilkhana* and given a thorough wash to remove the dust and cobwebs. Lakshmi had climbed up to fix new ostrich plumes on the roofs. The workshop women had made curtains from yellow chintz, purchased for a good price in the bazaar, and embellished them with gold brocade from one of Jahanara Begum's dance costumes.

Once we were ready, Samira Begum, Leela and I went down to the *zenana* garden, followed by the rest of the ladies, all a-twitter with excitement. We climbed into our palanquin and the handmaids and the chest of samples were installed in the other. Lakshmi and Sangita took up their positions to either side of us and we set off. The ladies waved their handkerchiefs in farewell but once we'd gone through the gated archway we closed the curtains against the stares of any passing men.

After a while, our pace slowed. Recognising the cries of the beggars and the reek of the river, I guessed we were crossing the bridge into the city. Sunshine on the yellow curtains filled our palanquin with golden light but the air soon became hot and stuffy.

Leela, exotically beautiful in scarlet and gold, leaned forward to twitch the curtain aside to peep out.

Her mother slapped her arm and pushed her back against the cushion. 'Do you want to ruin your reputation?' she hissed.

Downcast, Leela stared at her lap, twisting her gold bangles around her slender wrist.

A few minutes later Samira Begum sighed and reached out to squeeze her daughter's hand.

'Have you been to the Nizam's palace before, Samira Begum?' I asked.

'Many years ago, when life at the Jahanara Mahal was very different, my mother took me to visit the *zenana*. I met Bakshi Begum, the Nizam's First Wife.'

'Will we meet her today?' asked Leela.

'I doubt it. She is very important because she is the controller of the *zenana* disbursements.'

'Does the Nizam have many wives?' I asked.

She nodded. 'A great many. I also met Tinat un-Nissa Begum, the Nizam's Second Wife, risen from being Bakshi Begum's handmaid to the honour of the Nizam's bed. She is said to wield much influence over him. The relationship between these two most important wives was, and probably still is, very competitive. I was terrified of them both.'

The clatter and noise of the city lessened and then there was the sound of heavy gates slamming shut behind us. Our bearers' footsteps echoed as if we were in an enclosed space. Suddenly the palanquin tilted as we were carried up some steps, the bright sunlight dimmed, and we came to a halt.

I glanced at Leela, whose kohl-outlined eyes were bright with anticipation.

Sangita drew back the curtain and helped us to descend, while Lakshmi went to announce our arrival to the servants who had come running out of the palace.

We were in a vast quadrangle with raised single-storey buildings to all four sides, reached by stone steps. At the front of each building was a colonnade; our palanquins now rested in the shade of one of these.

The eunuch we had last seen accompanying Parwar un-nisa Begum to the Jahanara Mahal salaamed and motioned us to follow him inside. In the background, I heard a distant droning, as if we were near an orchard full of beehives. We left our shoes in a row upon the steps and our handmaids followed close behind, with Lakshmi and Sangita carrying the chest of samples between them at the rear of the procession. The humming sound increased as we walked across marble floors until we reached the heart of the Nizam's *zenana*.

Pausing at the threshold to a vast hall with an ornately painted

197

ceiling and gilded columns, my overwhelming impressions were of noise and the intensely sweet perfumes of tuberose, jasmine and orange blossom. The hall was crowded with women: sitting upon carpets, reclining against cushions, braiding each other's hair, nursing babies and amusing the small children that played by their feet.

The eunuch clicked his fingers at one of the handmaids and she threaded her way towards us between the seated women.

Three black-skinned women sang a melancholy song, barely audible over the busy chatter, the high-pitched voices of children at play and the twittering of birds in gilded cages.

There were two large groups of ladies discernible among the rest and at the centre of each, like a queen bee in her hive, sat a lady of mature years.

Samira Begum nudged me in the ribs and whispered, 'I see Bakshi Begum and Tinat un-Nissa Begum still each hold court among their sycophants.'

'The Nizam's wives?' I queried.

She nodded and then the handmaid led us to Parwar un-nisa Begum, who greeted us with every appearance of pleasure. A large ruby, suspended from a row of pearls, hung between her eyebrows, there were pearl drops in her ears and heavy gold bracelets from wrist to elbow. The scent of patchouli hung over her like a suffocating cloud. She bade us sit down beside her on a mound of luxurious velvet cushions.

'I wasn't sure if you would come,' she said. She introduced us to the seven or eight ladies reclining beside her but I was distracted by their magnificent jewels and promptly forgot their names.

Parwar un-nisa Begum glanced at the chest that Lakshmi and Sangita had placed nearby and laughed. 'Have you come to stay?'

Samira Begum smiled politely at the little joke. 'We have brought you a small present and also something that may be of interest to you.'

'A present?' Parwar un-nisa Begum beamed.

'The ladies of the Jahanara Mahal asked me to tell you how happy they were with the swing you sent them, which continues to give them the greatest pleasure. As a small and unworthy gesture they hope you may accept this paltry offering.' Samira Begum nodded to Jyoti, who lifted the lid of the chest and took out a parcel wrapped in muslin and tied with purple silk ribbons. She brought this to Parwar un-nisa Begum and laid it at her feet.

Parwar un-nisa Begum raised a finger to her own handmaid, who carefully opened the package to reveal a fringed shawl of violet silk, heavily embroidered with purple and gold thread.

Several of her ladies gasped and whispered amongst themselves, their bangles jingling.

The Begum was silent for a moment, then lifted the shawl and inspected the embroidery closely. 'I have many shawls,' she said, 'but none as fine as this.'

I gave a small sigh of relief as I watched her drape it around her shoulders. 'We are happy that you accept our gift,' I said.

'Where did you find it?' she asked.

'The ladies of the Jahanara Mahal made it especially for you,' said Leela.

'With their own hands?'

'Indeed,' said Leela.

Samira Begum glanced at me and then turned to Parwar un-nisa Begum again. 'As our greatly respected kinswoman, I hope I may speak openly with you?'

Parwar un-nisa Begum inclined her head. 'Of course.'

'It is with great sorrow,' said Samira Begum, 'that I must confess all is not well at the Jahanara Mahal.'

'Ah! I thought as much.' Parwar un-nisa Begum's expression was triumphant. 'It has been apparent to me for some years that the Jahanara Mahal is in decline. And when I hear that many of your servants are seeking work elsewhere ...'

'No shame is to be attributed to my respected grandmother,' said

Samira Begum in fierce tones, 'only to the thief who stole the Rose of Golconda from her many years ago.'

'I do not judge her,' said Parwar un-nisa Begum mildly, 'since the fault is not of her making.'

'The situation at the Jahanara Mahal has become so pressing, however,' I said, 'that the ladies of the *zenana* are taking matters into their own hands.'

'How intriguing!' said Parwar un-nisa Begum. 'But what can you do?'

'Embroidery,' said Samira Begum.

'How will that remedy the situation?'

I told her how we had come to the decision to start the workshop, how we were training the women of the palace and were already producing high-quality samples. 'Let me show you,' I said.

Jyoti handed me a white, quilted floor cloth from the chest and I spread it out at our feet. As I arranged the samples on the cloth, Parwar un-nisa Begum's ladies murmured and reached out to touch them. I'd brought a variety of embroidered slippers, handkerchiefs, gauzy *dupattas*, intricately beaded cushion covers, diaphanous veils and even half a dozen reticules.

'These are only some examples of our work,' I said. 'We will take commissions for whatever you wish in whatever colour you like best.'

Parwar un-nisa Begum pursed her lips as she looked at our wares. 'My kinswomen are so far fallen that they have become tradesmen and merchants?'

Samira Begum flushed and stared at her fingers clenched in her lap.

I stiffened my back and summoned up an expression of moral outrage. 'Certainly not!' I said. 'We are *craftswomen* and, as you have already said, our work is of the very highest standard. Why, a consignment is being shipped to England this very week for several of the most prestigious emporiums in London.' It wasn't the time to tell the whole truth and say the consignment was of samples only and being sent speculatively.

Parwar un-nisa Begum studied my face intently but I refused to drop my gaze until she looked away. Slowly, she reached out a beringed hand and caressed an embroidered cushion cover in sapphire with silver tassels.

I held my breath.

Her fingers moved to a lime green beaded reticule. Frowning, she picked it up. 'What is this?'

'It's a reticule – the very latest fashion in England,' I said. 'No woman of quality would dream of being seen out without one in polite circles. You can see it has a drawstring at the top and little treasures may be kept inside it, close to your person and free from prying eyes.' I glanced at some of the other groups of ladies, who had stopped chattering and were now watching us.

'I see.' Parwar un-nisa Begum opened the drawstring and peered inside. 'It's for secret things?'

'Any small item you wish to keep private.'

She laughed. Turning to her ladies, she asked them their opinion.

There was a chorus of replies and then they were reaching out to try on the slippers, to examine the beaded cushion covers and envelop themselves in the delicate veils. I hoped they wouldn't damage the samples in their enthusiasm.

Parwar un-nisa Begum unfolded a *dupatta* and shook it out, exclaiming over the way the embroidered border shimmered, but then a maid came to whisper in her ear. She dropped the *dupatta* and looked at me, her face grave. 'You have all been summoned to attend Bakshi Begum immediately,' she said. 'I do not advise you to delay.'

Samira's Begum's expression was fearful as we rose to do as we were told. 'Do you think the First Wife is angry because we have turned the Nizam's *zenana* into a bazaar?' she whispered.

'I imagine we're about to find out,' I said.

Chapter 25

In the late afternoon, I walked through the palace grounds, listening to the chirruping of the birds and enjoying the profusion of scented flowers. It made me sad to think that without any gardeners to tend to them they would soon become a jungle.

My heart lifted when I saw Harry was in the stable yard talking to the *syce*. He waved and I went to join them.

'You're dressed to ride,' he said.

'Will you accompany me?'

'I hoped you'd turn up,' he said. 'Breeze is champing at the bit.'

We waited, leaning on the yard wall, while the *syce* went off to saddle the horses.

'Samira Begum, Leela and I went to visit the Nizam's *zenana* this morning,' I said.

'A place of mysteries no man will ever see.'

'Except for the eunuch.'

Harry laughed. 'But he's hardly a man, is he?'

'We were summoned by the Nizam's First and Second Wife ...' Before I could say any more Ralph came running along the path with pounding footsteps. A peacock flapped noisily out of the way, emitting an ear-splitting screech.

'Bee!' he shouted, bursting through the gate into the yard. He mopped his overheated cheeks with a handkerchief. 'Leela said she saw you leaving the *zenana* in your riding clothes. I must speak to you immediately.'

'Catch your breath first, man,' said Harry.

Ralph took no notice of him and pushed his perspiring face at me. 'What's this tale about going to the Nizam's *zenana* this morning?'

'It's not a tale,' I said.

'So it's true! What on earth were you playing at?' He covered his eyes with his hand. 'Treating the Nizam's *zenana* like a common market stall, laying out your tat made from second-hand clothes of all things ...'

'The samples we showed them are of the finest quality,' I protested.

'God knows how I'm going to explain to the Resident that my sister bamboozled her way into the Nizam's palace, taking my wife with her, at a time of such delicate negotiations.' He closed his eyes as if in severe pain. 'Tinat un-Nissah Begum in particular, is haughty and tyrannical, greatly opposed to the British and with much influence over the Nizam.'

'I found her perfectly charming ...'

'All Kirkpatrick's efforts will have been in vain and it will cost me my position here if you've insulted the Nizam's ladies.'

'Have you quite finished?' I asked in icy tones.

Lakshmi walked across the yard towards us. Hearing the raised voices, she looked at me enquiringly but, before I could acknowledge her, Ralph had started to rant again.

'You must write a letter of abject apology to the Nizam's ladies, at once,' he said. 'Mark my words, we haven't heard the end of this. How *could* you do this to me, Bee?'

The whine in my brother's voice reminded me of when he'd been thwarted as a small child. 'Did you allow Leela to finish speaking,' I asked, 'or did you simply shout over her while she tried to explain?'

'Naturally, I hurried out immediately to catch you before you galloped off without a thought in your head for the damage you've caused.'

'If you'd taken the time to show some courtesy to your wife,' I said, 'you'd know that both Bakshi Begum and Tinat un-Nissa Begum were enchanted with the samples we showed them. I'm delighted to say we have received a substantial order, not only from the Nizam's wives but also from many of the ladies of his *zenana*.'

Ralph's face was a picture of warring emotions. His mouth opened and closed soundlessly several times.

Lakshmi snorted with sudden laughter. I caught sight of Harry, bent double and convulsed with mirth, and felt a bubble of laughter rising in my throat, too.

Eventually, the three of us wiped the tears of mirth from our eyes.

'I can't begin to see what you find so amusing,' complained Ralph, which set us off again.

Harry clapped him on the shoulder. 'I suggest you go and have another word with your wife and tell her how proud of her you are, for her part in achieving such a success with the Nizam's ladies,' he said. 'And perhaps you should apologise to your sister for making a hasty judgement?'

Ralph shook off Harry's hand and glowered at me. 'All I can say is that you'd better make sure you don't give the Nizam's ladies any cause whatsoever for complaint. If a *single* thing goes awry to compromise all the groundwork Kirkpatrick has undertaken with the Nizam, I shall hold you,' he prodded me in the chest with his forefinger, 'personally accountable. You'll be packed off back to Hampshire on the next ship.'

That threat wasn't so amusing and I no longer felt like laughing.

Harry took hold of Ralph's wrist and forced him to drop his hand. 'That's no way to treat your sister,' he said, all traces of laughter gone from his face.

Ralph winced and stepped back.

'I suggest you go and cool your heels elsewhere for a while.' There was a veiled threat in Harry's mildly spoken words.

Ralph gave me a look of loathing, barged his way through the yard gate and marched back towards the palace.

'You have made an enemy of your brother, Bee,' said Lakshmi. 'I came to warn you he was out for blood.'

'Thank you,' I said, still subdued by his threat and embarrassed by his manner. I was relieved to avoid having to comment further when the *syce* walked Zephyr and Breeze out of the stables.

Lakshmi patted Breeze's flank. 'I have a message for you, Bee, from my grandmother. She asked if you will call to see her in the morning?'

'Usha?' I was puzzled. 'Did she say why?'

Lakshmi shook her head. 'It surprised me. She rarely leaves the house or speaks to anyone other than family.'

'Come on then,' said Harry, offering me his linked hands to assist me onto Breeze's back. 'A ride in the country will take your mind off Ralph's bad humour.' He mounted Zephyr and rode towards the gate. Breeze and I followed. As we left the yard, I turned to wave to Lakshmi.

She was leaning over the wall with her chin propped on her hands, watching me, and didn't wave back. I wondered again if she was jealous of my growing friendship with Harry.

Before long we reached the open ground and he spurred Zephyr into a gallop. Breeze and I raced after them and then I didn't have the time or inclination to think about either Ralph or Lakshmi any more.

It was dusk when Harry and I returned to the stables. By the time we'd unsaddled the horses, the path through the grounds was lit only by the waning moon. The air was perfumed with the sweet scent of jasmine and the long grass rustled around our ankles. Suddenly I caught my breath and froze.

'What is it?' said Harry, his voice loud in the stillness.

I held a finger against my lips. 'Something moved over my foot,' I whispered. 'A snake or a rat perhaps.'

He pulled me back. 'Stay here!' He broke a small branch off a bush and slowly moved forwards along the path, sweeping the branch from side to side.

He returned a moment later and put his arm around my shoulders, holding me tightly to his side. 'Whatever it was, it's gone,' he said.

We moved on cautiously but I'd forgotten my fear and felt only the warmth of Harry's body against mine.

Soon, all too soon, we reached the palace. He let me go and, reluctantly, I took a step away from him.

The entrance was dimly lit by oil lamps but the marble halls and dim corridors stretched away into darkness.

He must have seen my apprehension because he picked up a lamp and reached for my hand. 'I'll escort you back to the *zenana*.' His boots clipped noisily across the floors, softly echoed by my sandals.

The wavering lamplight made the rooms and stairways that I now knew well by day seem strange again. Shadows loomed up unexpectedly. I jumped and gripped Harry's hand even tighter as a pale face stared at me out of the dark, only to discover it was my own reflection in an age-spotted mirror.

Harry appeared preoccupied and we walked without speaking. His fingers were lightly callused and rough against my palm and he smelled, not unpleasantly, of horses and dust. As we ascended the last staircase, the warm glow of lamplight greeted us in the ante-room to the *zenana*.

'Here we are,' he said, still holding my hand.

'Thank you for guiding me back.' I waited for him to release my hand but, instead, he twined his fingers through mine.

There was a long moment while we stood in silence, as if waiting for something. I held my breath, every nerve taut. My pulse began to gallop until I thought he must hear it.

Then he sighed gently and bent to kiss my cheek.

Awkwardly, I lifted my chin and our noses bumped together but then his full lips pressed against the corner of my mouth.

It was over in a second and he released my hand. 'Goodnight, Bee,' he murmured.

'Goodnight, Harry.'

And then he was gone, leaving me staring at the *zenana* curtain, attempting to compose myself before I stepped behind it.

Chapter 26

The following morning, at breakfast, Leela was prattling to the other ladies about the wonders of the Nizam's *zenana* while I relived the deliciously unsettling sensation of Harry's lips pressed against my mouth. Jyoti broke my reverie when she brought me a note from Mrs Clements. I unfolded it and read:

> *My dear Mrs Sinclair,*
>
> *I expect to travel with Mr Clements to Calcutta to meet Wellesley, the new Governor-General of India, in six weeks' time. There will be a great many balls and parties – what joy to have some entertainment after the retired life I lead here! I am delighted with the embroidered reticule that you made for me and wondered if I might commission your ladies to fashion two more, one in claret and another in emerald green with black beadwork? In addition, I require a cotton travelling dress with a wide border of embroidery to the hem, to disguise some of the dust. You know the style and colours I favour and I will leave it to your good taste as to the rest.*
>
> *Do let me know by return if this can be achieved in time, and*

*please do come and while away a lazy afternoon with me. I long
for a good gossip!*

I read the letter aloud to Leela.

'Will we have time to make them, in addition to the order from
the Nizam's *zenana*?' she asked.

'I don't want to turn any work away, even if I'm obliged to stay up
through the nights,' I said.

She nodded in agreement and I hastily penned a reply and sent it
off with Bhupal, who awaited my response.

I ate my last slice of mango before going, as requested, to visit
Usha, Lakshmi's grandmother.

Sangita opened the door to me but didn't give me her usual welcoming smile when she greeted me.

'Lakshmi said Usha asked me to visit her,' I said, stepping inside.

Sangita glanced over her shoulder. 'Something is worrying my
mother and I'm anxious,' she said in an undertone. 'I think you know
of her history and the terrible injuries she received all those years
ago when the Rose was stolen?'

I nodded.

'The physical difficulties are plain to see but the real damage is
in here.' She tapped her head with her finger. 'I wasn't born until
five years after she was injured but all the time I was growing up
she suffered from episodes of great distress. In more recent years I
thought she had improved but something has happened to change
that.'

'In what way?'

'I'm not sure.' Sangita rubbed her eyes, as if she was weary.
'Sometimes I hear her walking around during the night. At other
times she weeps for hours, just as she did when I was a child.'

'Have you asked what has upset her?'

'She won't speak of it.' Sangita twisted a corner of her *dupatta*
with restless fingers. 'Will you try to discover what is the matter?'

'She hardly knows me. I can't imagine she'll tell me her innermost thoughts.'

'Perhaps not.' Sangita sighed.

I followed her from the bright sitting room down a passage. There was no response when she knocked on her mother's door.

The reed blinds were lowered and the room shadowed. A *charpai* was pushed against one wall, the thin cotton bedspread folded neatly over the muslin sheets. Usha sat on the floor, her *dupatta* over her head so that her face was almost entirely covered.

I made my *namaste*.

She bowed her head in response. 'Close the door.'

I did as she asked, and heard Sangita's footsteps return along the passageway.

'Lakshmi said you wished to see me?'

'Lakshmi!' She sniffed.

I gave her an enquiring look, wondering what Lakshmi might have done to offend her, but she said no more. I waited, hands folded in my lap.

After a while, she said, 'So your visit to the Nizam's *zenana* bore fruit.'

'It was a much greater success than I dared to hope but we'll have to work quickly to complete such a large order.'

She nodded her head slowly. 'Bring me the basket from under the *charpai*.'

The contents of the basket were covered with a piece of calico and I watched with curiosity as Usha lifted out a large, folded piece of cream silk. She held it towards me.

Carefully, I spread it over my knees and saw it was an intricately embroidered panel about five feet square, edged with a border of crimson.

'It's the Jahanara Mahal!' I said. Beautifully worked in tiny satin stitches, the palace took pride of place in the centre of the panel, portrayed from the front and set within the Mughal gardens.

Fountains splashed in lotus-filled pools, roses scrambled over trellis-work and every minaret, balcony and window was shown in detail.

'It is the story of the palace,' said Usha. She pointed to embroidered vignettes, each about six inches square, running around all sides of the panel adjacent to the border. 'This one shows Muhammad Quli Qutb Shah, the founder of Hyderabad, building the palace as a fort two hundred years ago. Here, Marathi invaders are coming across the Musi in their boats and the next one shows the battle where the invaders are vanquished. This one is a tiger hunt and here the Mughal ruler of the time is out hunting with hawks.'

'It's so perfectly detailed,' I said.

'I have shown the successive owners of the palace and, here, the making of the pleasure gardens.' She leaned forward to look closely, oblivious when her *dupatta* fell aside and exposed the hideous scar down her cheek.

I forced myself to looked away, lest my pity for her disfigurement showed. 'And this scene must be Jahanara Begum's journey from Aurangabad to Hyderabad?' And there was Jahanara atop an elephant, dressed in her crimson dance costume with gold bells on her wrists and ankles. On her knee was the Rose of Golconda displayed upon a tasselled cushion like a cherry on a cake. The diamond glowed, pink rays of light radiating from it like leaping flames.

'That journey was a great adventure for me,' said Usha. 'I was the youngest member of the *zenana* guard at that time. I had never left Aurangabad before. All the guards had different jewels on their turban pins. Here I am, do you see, with my ruby pin?'

I peered at the scene and saw the female palace guards in their dark red tunics, mounted on black horses. One of guards was smaller than the others and had a red jewel on her turban.

Usha reached out to touch the embroidered elephants, the fine Arab horses, camels, the vast retinue of servants and the canopied bullock carts overflowing with chests of silver and jewels. Sighing, she said, 'So long ago.'

One by one, I studied the scenes of banquets and *nautch* dances in the Durbar Hall, tiger hunts, weddings and even funeral pyres. Then I frowned. 'What is this scene?'

She became very still and then shivered. 'That is Padma. You see the topaz on her turban? She is stealing the Rose of Golconda from Jahanara Begum's jewellery casket.' Usha spoke in a dull monotone. 'And here I am, watching her from behind a pillar. The pillar shakes as the earth beneath my feet trembles.' Her voice rose. 'The gods are angered by the theft.'

Unease prickled up and down my spine. 'Usha . . .'

She took no notice of me, caught up in the spell of the past. 'And here Padma is giving the Rose to her lover, Natesh.' She recited the story as if she had told it a thousand times before. 'I confront them and accuse Padma of stealing the precious diamond. Padma draws her dagger and attacks me. I defend myself and then Padma is lying on the ground in a pool of blood.' Slowly, she began rocking back and forth. 'I see Natesh is running away. I chase after him, calling him. He hacks at me with his sword. I can't believe he is attacking me. My face, my leg, my shoulder. I am blinded by blood running down my face. And the pain, the searing pain . . .'

'Please,' I said, anxious about her troubled state of mind, 'you mustn't upset yourself by telling me any more.'

'The pain in my thigh is like a thousand knives.' Her voice rose, full of anguish. 'It burns like a fire, devouring me. The ground is groaning and shaking again. The walls crack. I must stop Natesh!'

'Usha, that's enough!' I gripped her wrist and gave it a little shake. Abruptly, she became still.

'Usha?'

She drew a shuddering breath. 'The shame will haunt me all my days,' she whispered.

I looked at an embroidered scene portraying the earthquake damage at the rear of the palace but avoided drawing her attention to it in case it distressed her further. 'All that was so long ago,' I murmured.

'It is as yesterday to me. And the shame is still, and always will be, mine.'

'But *you* bear no shame!' I was astonished that she could think such a thing. 'You behaved with great courage in trying to prevent the theft.'

'It was my task to safeguard the precious Rose. Forty years later we feel its loss keenly. And it was my fault,' she whispered.

'You did everything you could,' I said. 'Your wounds are proof of your courage.'

She lifted a corner of the panel to show me. 'Here I am, lying on my *charpai* while my injuries heal. And here, Jahanara Begum is giving me water. She combed my hair and dressed my wounds with her own hands. And all the while the shame consumed me.' Tears rolled from Usha's chin and dripped onto the embroidery.

I was relieved that she appeared to have fully returned to the present. 'This scene shows a happier event. A wedding, I believe?' The heavily veiled bride and her groom sat on a raised platform under a canopy in the Durbar Hall. Rows and rows of guests looked on.

'Jahanara Begum released me from my duties as a guard and found me a husband – Dinesh. He was a good man. He never turned away from my damaged face and he gave me Sangita.'

'And here you are in this scene with both your children.'

'That's Nadeen, my eldest.' Smiling, she caressed the image of the smaller child. 'And my Sangita.'

I wondered why she didn't show the same favour to Lakshmi's mother, Nadeen. Studying the remaining scenes, I smiled at the most recent, depicting Leela and Ralph's wedding. There was space for several more scenes to run around the border. 'The rest of the panel isn't finished?'

She shook her head. 'Perhaps there will be babies again at the Jahanara Mahal. Or another wedding.' She lifted her head and looked at me through the narrow gap between the edges of her *dupatta*. 'Perhaps I shall work a picture of your embroidery workshop.'

I smiled. 'It would be an honour for the ladies of the *zenana*, and for the women of the palace, to be immortalised in this magnificent work.'

'I want to help fulfil the order for the Nizam's ladies,' said Usha. 'I must do my small part to make everything right.'

I was surprised and delighted by her offer. 'Your skill as a needle-woman will be a very great asset to the workshop.'

She bowed her head and I rose to take my leave.

Sangita waited for me in the hall. 'Did she say what has upset her?'

I shook my head. 'She showed me the beautiful embroidered panel of the Jahanara Mahal and recounted the story of the theft of the Rose. She became so agitated I couldn't press her.'

'*Maa-ji* still lives in the past, blaming herself for failing to prevent a wicked deed.' Sangita buried her face in her hands.

'Your mother has offered her considerable embroidery skills to assist the workshop. Maybe sewing will distract her from sad thoughts?'

'Perhaps,' said Sangita, sadly, 'though I fear nothing on this earth will ever cure her now.'

The fierce sun dazzled my eyes after the gloom of Usha's room. I arrived at the workshop at the same time as the women and set them to their tasks but I was still preoccupied by Usha's disturbing behaviour.

One of the women, Kalpana, gossiped and chattered all day until the sound of her strident voice grated on my nerves. I asked her to stop disturbing the other women. My patience snapped when she arrived, without apology, half an hour late after the midday break.

I held up the handkerchief she'd been hemming. 'Your stitches are too large and here,' I pointed, 'the thread is dirty and knotted.'

'That isn't my work. Someone else must have done that.' Her voice was surly.

214

'You know that's a wicked lie, Kalpana,' I said. 'You have proved to be unsuitable for this workshop and I must ask you to leave.'

Kalpana frowned, her bushy eyebrows almost meeting over her nose. 'Then pay me for the work I have done.' She took a step towards me and fixed me with a belligerent stare.

'You know I cannot pay you,' I said, standing my ground. 'Our agreement was that you would have a midday meal and no rent would be charged for your accommodation.'

Kalpana snatched the handkerchief from me and ground it under-foot. 'That's not what you said!'

'I said I *hoped* there would be money to be earned, after we have received payments for any goods sold. Now, pick up the handker-chief, please.'

She made no move to do so.

My clasped hands trembled but I could not tolerate Kalpana's attitude if I was to retain control of the other women. 'If I have to call the guard,' I said, summoning up Mother's tone of voice, 'she will escort you out of the palace and you will not be allowed back.'

Kalpana's expression was suddenly fearful.

'Jahanara Begum made her intentions clear. Although she cannot pay her servants, they will not be left homeless, so long as they con-tinue to carry out their duties.'

'I'm to go back to carrying water and sweeping floors?'

'The choice as to whether you leave or stay is yours,' I said, look-ing pointedly at the handkerchief on the floor.

After a long moment she picked it up and thrust it at me. Without another word, she left.

Slowly, I let out my breath.

The women had been watching, open mouthed, but now they bent their heads over their work.

Then there was silence, except for the creak of the *punkhas* stir-ring the stifling air overhead.

Chapter 27

As the weeks passed and the summer advanced, the heat grew increasingly oppressive. The sun smouldered relentlessly through the open windows of the Durbar Hall until it felt as hot as a tandoor oven. We opened the glazed panels in the roof light and the internal door to the palace to allow a flow of air. Blinds of split reeds hung at the casements and the women took it in turns to dampen them to cool the incoming breeze.

There had been a growing number of quarrels amongst the women and, although I imagined it was the high temperatures that had ignited them, something made me uneasy. I had to chastise several of them for shoddy work or poor timekeeping and then they would mutter amongst themselves, darting glances at me. The atmosphere became so hostile I dreaded going to the workshop.

My command of the language I'd learned as a child improved daily but the women often spoke too quickly for me. The people of Hyderabad and the Deccan plateau came from many different cultures and religious persuasions and, whilst most natives had a smattering of several languages, it wasn't always possible for me to follow their conversations.

When a fierce argument broke out between two of the women, Anjali and Radhika, it was perfectly possible, however, to ascertain from their covert glances that they were talking about me. By the time I'd risen from my cushion and gone to see what the trouble was about, several other women had joined in the altercation.

'Quiet!' I shouted.

Anjali and Radhika were pushing each other and then Anjali screamed when Radhika pulled her hair.

I attempted to separate them and received an elbow in the chest for my pains.

Deepika, solidly built, came to help. She hauled Radhika away and pushed her up against the wall.

Anjali, breathing heavily, rebraided her hair while sending malevolent glances at her opponent.

My heart racing, I clapped my hands for attention. 'Under no circumstances will I tolerate such behaviour in this workshop.'

Pravina started to speak but Deepika poked her firmly in the ribs and she subsided.

I stared at the women, one by one, hoping they wouldn't see how my hands trembled. I summoned up a vision of Mother reprimanding her servants and continued. 'Anjali and Radhika, you will leave the Durbar Hall immediately. If you wish to continue to work here, you will come and see me tomorrow morning with an apology. Is that understood?'

I fixed them with a fierce glare and, one after the other, they gave a small nod. 'Go then!'

The remaining women returned to their cushions, while I collected the two reticules that had been trodden underfoot. I brushed them down and was relieved to see that no real harm had been done.

'Listen to me!' I said.

Hemanti, now in her seventh month, looked up at me, wide-eyed and anxious.

'If you have a grievance,' I said, 'or some other difficulty, you

217

must speak to me about it. I shan't be angry. Is something disturbing you?' I studied their sullen faces, searching for answers, but learned nothing.

The women bent their heads over their work and I returned to mine.

When work finished, I counted all the scissors, needles and threads into the cupboard, as usual, and asked the women to hand in their sewing before they left.

Hemanti gave me the *dupatta* that she'd been hemming.

'I'm pleased with this. It's very neat, Hemanti,' I said.

She nodded and then glanced over my shoulder and her face broke into a wide smile.

Her husband, Manohar, stood in the garden doorway of the Durbar Hall with Talin in his arms. Manohar had failed to find work and returned to the palace where, without being asked, he had taken on the daily duty of carrying water from the well to the workshop, kitchen and nursery.

Talin held out his arms to his mother and she covered his face with kisses. I couldn't help watching this close-knit little family and, despite their worries for the future, I envied them.

After the women had left I locked the Durbar Hall. I visited the ladies in the *zenana* to see what progress they had made during the day, then, feeling restless, changed into my riding clothes and strolled through the grounds towards the stables. Heat still rose from the sun-baked ground and the grass was so dry it whispered as I passed by. Difficulties were crowding in upon me and I didn't know how to deal with them. And it wasn't only the uneasy atmosphere in the workshop and the worry about where the next project would come from that was nagging at me.

Perhaps I'd imagined it but I felt that awkwardness had arisen between Harry and myself ever since that goodnight kiss he'd given me. He'd gone away from the palace for a week or so afterwards, no doubt on Company business, whatever that might be. On his return, he was perfectly amiable but it seemed to me that he was a little distant. When we rode out together, he usually invited Lakshmi to accompany us and so we were rarely alone.

I was pondering this, wondering if I dared ask if I'd done something to offend him, when Jai jumped out from behind an oleander bush pretending he was a tiger and hoping to give me a fright.

'I've been playing with Swati's puppies,' he said, eyes shining as he fell into step beside me. 'They're growing so fast and like to pretend to fight with me.'

'Jai, you haven't forgotten your promise to set them free outside the palace walls, have you?' I said.

'But they aren't any trouble!' he protested.

'Not yet, but before long the puppies will have puppies of their own and then there'll be feral dogs everywhere.'

'But they'll be frightened, all alone.'

He looked up at me with an appeal in his brown eyes and I had to harden my heart. 'Why don't we go outside the palace grounds early one morning and I'll help you look for a new home for them? Swati must teach her puppies how to manage for themselves.'

The corners of his mouth turned down. 'I suppose so.'

We chatted about suitable places for Swati's new home until we reached the stable yard.

'There's my *abbu*!' said Jai, waving at Harry, who was saddling Zephyr in the stable yard.

Harry pinched his son's cheek, a smile in his dark eyes. 'And what kind of mischief have you been up to today, young man?'

'Nothing!' said Jai, indignantly.

I surmised Lakshmi must have gone for an evening ride since Aurora wasn't in her box and I hoped Harry and I might be able to exercise the horses alone for once.

The *syce* saddled Breeze and I stepped onto the mounting block.

'Do you want to come with us?' Harry asked Jai.

The boy nodded, a wide smile on his face, and I hadn't the heart to be disappointed at losing the opportunity of being alone with his father.

Harry lifted Jai onto Zephyr's back and climbed up behind him.

At Jai's request, we rode down beside the river. A cooling breeze sprang up as the sun began to sink. We saw egrets wading in the shallows, laughed at the antics of a troop of monkeys playing tag with their young and watched the boats, imagining improbable life stories for the men who sailed in them. There was a brazier by the end of the bridge and Harry bought us little bowls of deliciously fragrant *biryani*, which we ate sitting on the parapet while we watched the sunset.

I glanced up to find Harry watching me as I laughed at Jai's cheerful chatter. Our eyes met for a moment and he gave me a lazy smile, leaving me glowing. For an hour or two, I was able to pretend to myself that we were a family and that life could always be as happy and uncomplicated as at that moment.

It was almost dark when we returned to the Jahanara Mahal. The mournful cry of the call to prayer drifted over the water from the mosque and I discovered that my headache had completely gone.

The following morning Anjali and Radhika were waiting for me when I came to unlock the Durbar Hall.

'Will you tell me what you were quarrelling about yesterday?' I asked.

Anjali shuffled her feet and kept her gaze firmly fixed on the ground.

'She says you are working her too hard,' said Radhika.

'Everyone is working hard,' I said.

Anjali gave me a hard stare. 'But when will we be paid? I have children to feed and my husband cannot find work. Too many servants have gone into the city to look for work and now there are no places left.'

'That's why we provide a midday meal for you and your children,' I said. 'I know it's difficult but it's the best I can offer you at present. All the hours you work are written in my book and once we deliver the goods and receive payment, your share will be paid to you.'

'But I need to be paid now!'

I turned my palms up and shrugged. 'I don't have the money.'

'I want to come back to the workshop,' said Radhika. 'I said to Anjali yesterday that we have no other choice.'

'Then you may rejoin us, Radhika.' I turned to Anjali.

She pushed out her bottom lip. 'But everyone says ...'

'What does everyone say?' Despondency made me speak sharply.

'They say, how do we know you will pay us and will you be fair with us?'

I sighed. 'You will simply have to trust me.'

She hesitated and then shrugged.

It wasn't the apology I'd demanded but it seemed best to leave well enough alone.

It was another long, hot day but, although some of the women whispered and nudged each other and sent me sidelong glances, there were no more unpleasant scenes. I was relieved, however, when it was time for everyone to leave. Afterwards, I was about to lock the doors when I heard footsteps.

'Hello, Hemanti. Did you forget something?'

She shook her head. 'May I speak with you?' She glanced over her shoulder.

'Is something troubling you?'

'The women are talking about you.'

The thought made me uncomfortable but I'd already assumed something of the sort. 'Can you tell me what is being said?'

Hemanti bit at her thumbnail. 'Some say a woman cannot make a workshop successful and is no good at business. Especially as you are a *feringhi*. They say you treat them like bad children and will cheat them and make them work all day for nothing at the end. They say that you will beat them to make them work harder and then you will send them away from the palace.'

'I see.' I felt like crying but that wouldn't help matters. 'None of

221

that is true, Hemanti.' I forced myself to smile. 'Except, of course, that I am a *feringhi*.' A foreigner. Would I always be a foreigner to these women?

'I must go,' said Hemanti, 'before someone sees me with you.' She slipped out of the French doors into the garden.

I buried my face in my hands. I'd left Hampshire imagining I'd start a happier life in Hyderabad but, despite my very best intentions, it wasn't turning out like that.

A cough came from behind me and Harry stepped through the doorway. 'I'm afraid I was eavesdropping,' he said.

'Then you know why I'm in despair. Can't these women see how hard I'm trying to help them? They think that somehow, by witchcraft perhaps, I can summon up the money to pay them.'

'They're frightened for the future, that's all.'

'Why do they think I'll cheat them?' I blinked back tears of self-pity. 'They're so ungrateful!'

'Perhaps you're not dealing with this in the right way?'

Harry was so calm in the face of my indignation and distress that it only served to irritate me. 'How should I deal with them, then, if you're so clever?'

He sighed. 'These are simple women but they don't like it when you, a *feringhi*, shout at them as if you are a schoolmarm and they are naughty children.'

'Then they shouldn't behave like naughty children! Why, one of the women even told me a bare-faced lie.' I clenched my fists at the memory. 'When I complained about the poor standard of her work, she said someone else had done it.'

'The British hold the truth in such high esteem,' Harry said, in soothing tones, 'but, to an Indian, truth is fluid. They believe a lie avoids unpleasantness. If you were an inexperienced junior officer in the army, I'd advise you to get to know your men better, to share a drink with them and tell them a joke. And always to lead them into the line of fire.'

'Well, that's really helpful to me, isn't it?' I said, sarcasm dripping from every word.

He clicked his tongue in sudden exasperation. 'Do you know what I think, Bee Marchant . . .'

'Sinclair,' I interrupted.

He took a step towards me. 'I'm trying to help but you're not listening. Right now, you sound like your mother. As a boy I used to sit on the other side of the garden fence, listening to her railing at the servants. On and on it went. I used to pity you. And now you're turning into her.'

I gasped and tears sprang to my eyes. 'That's a low blow, Harry Wyndham. And my mother was right: your manners are no better than a savage's.'

'A savage?' He strode towards me, eyes glittering like jet, and gripped me by the shoulders. 'I'll show you *savage*!'

He pressed his lips to mine so hard that my head tipped back.

Shocked, my mouth opened under his kiss.

Wrapping an arm like an iron bar around my waist, he pulled me against him, holding my head so firmly with his other hand that I couldn't turn away.

I discovered I didn't want to turn my face away. My knees began to crumple and I slid my arms around his neck to prevent myself from slipping to the ground.

At last, he released me and I stood trembling before him, my eyes downcast with shame.

His breathing was fast and uneven. He wiped his face with his palm. 'I apologise, *Mrs Sinclair*, for my atrocious manners.' Turning on his heel, he strode from the room.

Heart pounding, I knew I should ask Ralph to horsewhip Harry Wyndham immediately. Touching my bruised mouth, I fancied I could still feel the burning imprint of his kiss on my lips.

Chapter 28

Once I'd recovered my outward, if not my inner, composure, I left the Durbar Hall. The late-afternoon sun was still swelteringly hot and the air humid. Flies buzzed annoyingly around my head and kept settling on my face. I brushed them away with an irritated wave of my hand. My thoughts were in chaos. Harry's stubble had grazed my cheek and my mouth throbbed. I didn't know how I could ever look him in the eye again after what had passed between us. And yet, I was sure there had been passion as well as anger in his kiss. No one had ever kissed me like that before and I had no idea how to make sense of my turbulent emotions.

'Bee!'

I looked up to see Lakshmi on the path ahead.

'Do you want to ride out with me?' she said. 'Don't worry, you don't have to see Harry. He's just galloped off on Zephyr as fast as if invading Marathis were after his blood.'

'Why should I worry about Harry?'

Lakshmi slipped her arm through mine. 'I saw you with him earlier.'

I came to an abrupt halt. 'When?'

'Through the open door of the Durbar Hall. I saw him force himself upon you. I'd have come to your assistance but then he let you go.'

'We had an argument,' I said. It wasn't only the heat of the sun that made my cheeks burn.

'I guessed that. Why?'

Sighing heavily, I said, 'The women in the workshop resent me. They're as bad as Ralph in thinking I can't make the business succeed because I'm not only a woman, but also a foreigner.'

'Could they be right?' She was silent for a moment then continued. 'I apologise, Bee, but how can selling a few pretty things pay enough to keep all these women? And as for saving the palace ... '

'Each item is a small work of art and will command a high price.' There was a tremor of uncertainty in my voice. 'And don't you see? I must at least *try* to make it work.'

She looked doubtful. 'Am I to blame for this? I challenged you to find something to do with your life.'

'And I have.'

'But you could have chosen simply to embroider yourself a beautiful shawl instead of this foolish project of saving the palace and providing employment for everyone who lives here. You are disappointed in your brother and sad because in reality the palace of your childhood dreams is semi-derelict.' She shook her head. 'It would perhaps have been better for you if you had never come here.'

I pictured Alice's smug face and imagined her lording it over me in the house that should have been mine. 'It was impossible for me to stay there,' I said.

Lakshmi shrugged. 'And now you have fallen into Harry Wyndham's snare.'

'Of course I haven't.' A sudden breeze lifted my *dupatta* and blew it across my face.

'Don't sound so angry, Bee! You are not the first to make that mistake. I have seen the way you look at him.' She shook her head. 'But, as your friend, I tell you this: he will never marry you.'

'I'm not looking for a husband!' I protested. But was that really true?

'Harry loved Noor and will always revere her memory. No other woman will ever take her place.'

She appeared so downcast I could only assume that Harry had made the intensity of his feelings for his wife clear to Lakshmi in the past. It made me uncomfortable to think she might have been that close to him once. 'I don't want to think about Harry,' I said. 'I'd like to come for a ride with you but I must change and visit the ladies in the *zenana* first.'

The ladies restored my spirits somewhat, since the embroidery for almost all the items they'd been working on was finished. The girls, full of shy giggles, showed me their handkerchiefs and I told them how pleased I was to see their skills growing.

'Another two days' work will be needed for this shawl for the Nizam's First Wife,' said Samira Begum, 'but since it will be fringed, no hemming in the workshop will be necessary.'

I draped the shawl of saffron silk over my forearm and examined the twining stems, sinuous leaves and glorious flowers depicted in satin stitch. A myriad of colours shaded each flower so that it appeared almost real. 'This is beautiful,' I said.

Priya Begum smiled. 'I am proud to know our work will grace Bakshi Begum's shoulders.'

'I hope it will bring great pleasure to her,' said Samira Begum.

'I don't doubt it,' I said, 'and in a few days I shall deliver it to her.'

Later, as Lakshmi and I trotted up the parched hillside behind the palace I was unable to stop myself reliving over and over again the argument with Harry, ending in that fierce kiss. I'd hated him for overpowering me by sheer force but at the same time there had been something so wild and untamed about him that I'd thrilled to it. I burned with shame at the thought but I admitted to myself I wanted him to kiss me again. But how different it would be if only he'd kiss me with tenderness ...

'Shall we gallop?' called Lakshmi.

I nodded and we thundered up the hill. Lakshmi, as competitive as ever, soon spurred Aurora ahead. I didn't want to race her and allowed my thoughts to stray to what Harry had said. He'd made me angry but might there be a grain of truth in his taunt? I'd have to make more effort to understand the workshop women.

A sudden gust of wind buffeted my clothes. Although the sun still shone brightly, the sky had turned a strange purplish colour. The air was suffocatingly close.

Lakshmi waited for me on the brow of the hill, dark clouds billowing behind her.

I rode up the slope and reined in beside her.

'You are not concentrating on your riding, Bee,' said Lakshmi. 'Sit up straight and take proper control of Breeze or she'll misbehave.' She sighed. 'Are you *still* thinking about Harry?'

I turned away from the intensity of her gaze to look down at the Musi, curving like a silver snake in the valley below. Then the sun went behind a cloud and a hot breeze tugged at my hair.

Lakshmi lifted her head to sniff the air. 'The rains are coming.'

As she uttered the words, a fat drop of water spattered against my cheek.

'The first shower of the monsoon season! We'd better hurry back, if we're to avoid a soaking.' She dug her heels into Aurora's flanks and bolted off down the hill.

Within seconds, the rain began to fall steadily, releasing the hot, musky scent of the earth. I followed Lakshmi more sedately, nervous that Breeze's hooves might slip on the wet boulders half-hidden by the scorched grass. But then the heavens opened, the rain hissing down in torrents and swirling into pools on the iron-hard ground.

This rain was nothing at all like the polite Hampshire drizzle I was used to. After only a few moments, I was soaked through my clothes right down to my skin. The hillside was engulfed in opaque mist and I galloped after Lakshmi, shaking water out of my eyes.

She slowed, turning in the saddle to beckon me on with a sweep of her arm and then raced off again.

Afraid of losing her in the mist, I hurtled after her as she careened down the hill. My jaw was clenched and my eyes narrowed to slits against the teeming rain as I crouched over Breeze's neck.

'Come on!' yelled Lakshmi.

Aurora was on a large granite outcrop only three lengths in front of me when Lakshmi abruptly turned her to the left.

Too late to do the same, Breeze continued straight on and, unexpectedly, launched herself upwards. I gasped as we flew through the air and then landed with such a thump that I bit my tongue. The mare stumbled and I slipped sideways off the saddle.

The ground came spinning towards me and slammed against my abdomen with the force of a runaway bullock cart. My scream was cut short as all the air was expelled from my lungs. Stunned, I felt as if an elephant was standing on my chest. Then I was fighting for breath and losing. Spread-eagled on the sodden ground, sheer terror overwhelmed me. I clutched my throat, certain I was going to die.

A lifetime later, the spasm released and, little by little, I breathed again. I struggled to sit up, the pain like a dagger between my ribs. I rested my chin on my knees until my pulse steadied. Breeze was nearby, head down and grazing, oblivious to the torrential rain.

Lakshmi looked down at me from Aurora's back. It was only for a second or two but shock appeared to make time slow down. She slid from the saddle and fell to her knees beside me.

'Bee! Are you hurt?'

'I ... I'm not sure.' Rain drummed down on my head. I was shaking and everything ached but, apart from the deep grazes on the heels of my hands and a cut to my knee, nothing seemed to be broken.

'I was frightened,' she said. 'For a moment I thought ...' She shook her head. 'Let me help you up.'

My muscles and sinews protested as I forced myself to stand, my legs trembling. My turban had fallen off and my sodden hair clung to my shoulders.

'The gods smiled on you today,' she said, pointing to where I'd fallen.

Galloping down the hillside, I hadn't noticed that the granite outcrop, from which Breeze had jumped, concealed a steep drop on the other side. There was a deep fissure about six feet wide in the ground below. I stared at it and felt sick. 'Breeze might have broken her legs,' I said.

'And you might have slipped into the bowels of the earth and disappeared for ever. It's old earthquake damage.'

'But you often ride up here,' I said. 'You must have known it was there?'

'The rain made it hard to see. I didn't know where we were until the very last moment,' she said, 'and then it was too late to warn you. I thought you'd follow me.'

I trembled at what might have been.

'It's said you are not a true horseman,' said Lakshmi, 'until you've been thrown and then climbed straight back into the saddle.'

I swallowed and took a stumbling step towards Breeze. 'Then I'd better prove the truth of that.'

Lakshmi had to give me a leg-up but a few minutes later I was mounted again.

In silence, we walked the horses through the pelting rain back to the palace.

The ladies were alarmed when I limped into the *zenana* and they saw my clothing was plastered with mud. Samira Begum insisted on

229

sending for warm water and the ladies followed me to the bathroom, murmuring expressions of sympathy.

Jyoti stripped off my filthy clothes and exclaimed in horror at the cuts and bruises that already blossomed from shoulder to shin as she sponged me free from mud.

I stepped into the bath and sighed in relief as I lowered myself into the warm, jasmine-scented water.

Several of the ladies joined me and I found their subdued chatter soothing.

Jyoti washed the mud from my hair. I closed my eyes as she gently massaged coconut oil into my scalp. Half asleep, it seemed to me I was a child again and Madhu was beside me.

The following morning, I awoke to discover I'd overstretched every muscle and tendon in my body and that my bruises were startling shades of indigo and purple. The prospect of the women sniggering at me because I'd fallen off a horse made a day in the workshop unappealing. I hobbled down the *zenana* corridor and ducked through the crimson curtain.

I halted when I saw Harry in the ante-room. I let the curtain fall behind me, wishing he hadn't seen me.

Grim-faced, he said, 'A word, Mrs Sinclair?'

I was taken aback that he addressed me so formally.

'The way I behaved last night was unpardonable,' he said. 'I apologise unreservedly.'

There was a long silence while I floundered for the right words.

'I see that you do not wish to accept my apology,' he said, 'and I can't blame you for that. Perhaps it would be best if I simply removed myself from your presence?'

He turned to leave and before I could stop myself I caught hold of his sleeve. 'Wait!'

'Yes?'

'I was distressed by your accusations yesterday, it's true, but

230

now I have carefully considered what you said,' I gabbled, 'and I shall attempt to find a better way to work with the women in the workshop.'

'I see,' he said. 'I'm pleased to hear that but I wasn't apologising for my comments, since they were nothing but the truth.'

Really, the man was insufferable!

'No, it was the ...' He looked at a point somewhere over my shoulder. 'It was my action I regret. I promise that will never happen again.'

'Oh.' I stared at my feet. That wasn't what I wanted at all. 'I'd prefer it if you didn't call me Mrs Sinclair,' I said. 'And, since we both live here at the Jahanara Mahal, it would be unfortunate if there were a disagreeable atmosphere between us, don't you think?'

'That's generous of you.'

'Perhaps we could set it all aside and continue as before?' I wondered if he heard the note of hope in my voice.

Harry gave me a small bow, as formal as if we were in a Hampshire drawing room. 'As you wish. Now, if you will excuse me?'

'Yes, of course.'

He hurried away and I sighed with disappointment as his footsteps receded down the stairs. Once it was quiet, I limped on my way to the workshop to face the women.

It rained for most of the day, hammering on the roof of the Durbar Hall. The women weren't as difficult as I'd expected, perhaps because the downpour had lifted some of the stifling heat. There was some subdued chatter as various items were completed and given to me to store in the chest. I was pleased to finish the travelling dress and reticules for Mrs Clements, too. When I closed up the Durbar Hall at the end of the day, my spirits were somewhat restored.

Even though the rain had ceased by then, there was no question of forcing my aching body to go for a ride that evening but I had another idea. The ladies in the *zenana* had made good progress, too, so I collected their finished articles and carried them back to the Durbar Hall.

I laid clean sheets on the floor in the centre of the hall and arranged the shawls, *dupattas*, reticules, bodices and handkerchiefs to show them off to their best advantage. Together they made a magnificent sight. I walked around the edges of the display and my heart nearly burst with pride. The evening sun through the skylight cast a golden glow over the gloriously embroidered shimmering silks and rich satins, filmy gauzes, soft velvets and fine lawn. The brilliant colours sang and the sight cheered my heart. I hoped that, when I showed the women in the morning, they couldn't fail to share my pride in their achievements. Perhaps that might go some way to healing the breach between us.

It was then I decided to see if Ralph would come to look at the fruits of our labours. I hurried though the palace as fast as my aches and bruises would allow and knocked on the door to his quarters.

He looked at me warily. 'Is something wrong?'

He must have only recently returned from the Residency since he was still wearing his European clothing. 'Nothing is wrong,' I said, 'but I want to show you something.'

'I'm about to change.'

'Can it wait? I want you to see while there's still good light.'

He sighed. 'Is it really important?'

'It is. Come on.' I linked my arm through his, ignoring his surprise, and pulled him away with me.

We arrived at the Durbar Hall and I unlocked the door. 'Close your eyes, Ralph!'

'I'm no longer a child, Bee.'

'Indulge me,' I said and led him inside. 'Now open them.'

The sun still shone, illuminating the dazzling array of goods, and I watched Ralph's face carefully.

Silently, he walked all the way around the display, bending to examine a silver tissue *dupatta* more closely and then to pick up a purple velvet reticule and peer at the peacock silk lining inside. He replaced it carefully and then turned to me. 'I had no idea, Bee,' he said. 'These are exquisite and more than fit for the Nizam's wives.'

'I'm so pleased you approve of them.'

He put his arm around my shoulders. 'It's not been easy, learning to know each other again after all these years, has it? I'm sorry if I said some unkind things. I'm working so hard to build a career here at the Residency but it's an uphill struggle. The truth is, I'm not as quick-witted as I'd like to be. It makes my nerves jangle.'

His gloomy expression made him look like the little brother I remembered. Now he'd let down his guard, it seemed to me that perhaps his arrogance was a mask for his insecurities. 'I've been a thorn in your side too, haven't I?' I said. 'I don't mean to be.'

'I know. And I haven't forgotten what a difficult time you've had. You're my only blood relative and I don't want you to go back to Hampshire.'

'I want to make my home here.' I glanced at the cracks in the Durbar Hall walls. 'If it doesn't fall down around our ears.'

Ralph nodded. 'I'll go and make my peace with Leela. She doesn't complain but I know I made her unhappy when I told her she couldn't be a part of your embroidery scheme.'

Locking the doors carefully, I returned to the *zenana* with a spring in my step.

Chapter 29

During the night it rained. It made a noise unlike any downpour I'd ever heard in England. It hammered down in sheets in the courtyard outside my bedroom. Lightning forked across the sky and great cracks of thunder made me jump. I peered out from behind the casement and, each time lightning flashed through the darkness, glimpsed water swirling in the gullies outside. The air was cooler and I felt invigorated again, sure that the downpour heralded better times.

At last, I returned to bed. Soothed by the pounding beat of the rain on the roof, I fell into a dreamless sleep.

In the morning, Leela came to speak to me as I was leaving the *zenana*. 'How are your bruises today?'

'Still very tender.'

'Ralph told me you have stopped quarrelling.'

'He was very impressed by the beautiful things we've made and apologised for thinking we couldn't do it.'

She smiled. 'I'm happy for that.'

'Today there are only a few items to finish in the workshop. Then we'll pack them carefully, ready for delivery.'

'The ladies will enjoy a holiday and a chance to rest their eyes,' said Leela. 'But where will the next order come from, Bee?'

I was worried about that, too. 'That's tomorrow's task and I'm already late to open up the workshop.'

Hurrying through the palace grounds to the Durbar Hall, I found myself anticipating the women's pleasure at the display of their work. The sun was hot again and the sodden ground steamed as the rain evaporated. Mist shrouded everything. The rain had battered the long grass but dewdrops hung from the trees and bejewelled the flowers.

The women were already gathered outside the Durbar Hall and I gave them a cheerful smile as I unlocked the doors and waved them in ahead of me. Then someone at the front of the crowd shrieked. Another woman let out a long, high-pitched cry, followed by another and then another. The sound of such distress made me go cold.

'What is it?' I pushed my way between the keening women, suddenly gripped by an unnameable panic, and came to an abrupt halt. Then I let out a moan and ran forward, falling onto my knees.

Every item of the precious display was sodden, the dyes of the jewel-bright silks bleeding into each other and staining the white sheet beneath, the devastation cruelly illuminated by the light from the glazed roof dome above.

The floor was flooded and my trousers were soaked where I knelt but none of that mattered. I snatched up item after item with shaking fingers, hoping to find even one that wasn't ruined but each was waterlogged, staining my fingers with a rainbow of dye.

Stunned, I buried my face in my hands, giving in to my despair, while all around me the women wept and beat their chests.

I felt a hand on my shoulder and looked up to see Hemanti's tear-stained face.

'Look!' she said, pointing upwards.

The rain had not, as I'd supposed, entered through a new leak in the roof. Every single glazed panel in the roof light was wide open.

The women were so distressed I sent them home. My own despair had given way to blinding anger and I strode out of the Durbar Hall, slamming the doors behind me. I didn't lock them since there was no longer anything of value left inside.

Lakshmi was in the ante-room to Jahanara Begum's sitting room, talking to her mistress's handmaid.

'I'd like to see Jahanara Begum,' I said, too incandescent with rage for the usual pleasantries.

The girl gave me an anxious glance and motioned me to follow her.

'Lakshmi, come with me,' I said. 'This concerns you.'

'Me?' She remained still, studying my face. I grabbed her sleeve and she allowed me to pull her along behind me.

Jahanara Begum sat on her gold and crimson throne under the baleful gaze of the tigerskin rug.

I bent to touch her foot and pay my usual respects.

'What troubles you, *beti*?' Her dark eyes studied me intently.

I took a breath to regain my calm. 'Last night we finished making the goods for the Nizam's ladies. I laid them out in the Durbar Hall in a magnificent display. Even Ralph was impressed. I wanted the women to see the finished articles all together before they were delivered.'

'Is there some difficulty?'

'There has been a catastrophe.' I shook my head. 'No, not a catastrophe, a criminal act. Lakshmi, as the palace guard, must find the perpetrator.'

Jahanara Begum's fingers clenched around the gilded tigers' heads on her throne. 'Tell me!'

'During the night, while a violent storm raged, someone entered the Durbar Hall and opened all the windows around the roof light. The rain flooded the floor and soaked the display. Every one of the embroidered goods is ruined.'

Jahanara Begum hid her eyes with her hand. 'Who would do such a thing?'

'I don't know ... it's such a spiteful act,' I said, my voice wavering. 'The women have worked so hard. Who could possibly wish to deprive them of the opportunity to earn their living?'

'Bee,' said Lakshmi, 'did you forget to close the windows last night when you left?'

'Of course not,' I snapped.

'The weather has been so hot ...'

'No, Lakshmi! I closed them. I always open them straight after I unlock the doors in the morning and then close them again once the women leave at the end of the day.'

'Bee, did the women see you close them?'

I frowned, remembering. 'I don't think so. The long rods make a screeching noise when I wind them round to screw the windows shut. Sometimes the women have questions at the end of the day so I wait to close the windows until after they've gone.'

'Did you lock the Durbar Hall?' asked Lakshmi.

'Ralph will vouch for that,' I said triumphantly. 'I took him to see the display of goods when he arrived back from the Residency. He was with me when I locked up.'

'But will he also confirm that the roof windows were shut then?'

'I'm sure he will. The air was stifling again by the time I returned to the Durbar Hall with him.'

'My difficulty,' said Lakshmi, 'in understanding what has happened is that in all my time at the palace I have only been aware of one set of keys for the Durbar Hall, one key for the garden doors and one key for the internal doors to the palace.'

'That is true,' said Jahanara Begum. 'The spare keys were mislaid many years ago.'

'So,' persisted Lakshmi, 'you hold the only set of keys for the Durbar Hall, Bee. I don't see how it would have been possible for anyone, other than yourself, to gain access to the hall to open the windows.'

I stared at her. 'But I'm sure I closed them.'

237

She shrugged and glanced at Jahanara Begum, who watched us through narrowed eyes.

'I closed the windows,' I repeated.

Neither of them spoke but Lakshmi sent me a pitying glance.

Unable to bear the way they looked at me, I hurried from the room.

Shock that Lakshmi and Jahanara Begum blamed me for the disaster made me numb. I ran out of the palace, heedless of my painful muscles and bruised ribs, only knowing that I had to put some distance between us. Without conscious thought my footsteps took me down to the river path, just as they used to when Mother had accused me of some childish misdemeanour.

The sun scorched my face and the humidity nearly suffocated me. At last I couldn't run any more. All I wanted was somewhere cool to hide. My halting steps led me past the country houses of the rich and then I came to a pavilion. It had been built onto the boundary wall of a garden, projecting like the prow of a ship, raised up to take advantage of the river view. The front section was supported on columns, almost concealed by bushes, and I bent double and crept underneath.

The shady space had been sheltered from the previous night's downpour and the ground was dry. I sat down and wrapped my arms around my knees while I relived what Lakshmi had said. I *had* closed the skylight windows. I was absolutely sure of it. Wasn't I?

Later, I uncurled myself from the ground and sat up, wincing at my painful muscles. I must have slept for hours, exhausted by the day's distressing events. I peered out through the bushes and saw the leaden sky with dismay. The birds had stopped singing and thunderous clouds were rolling in fast. I'd have to hurry if I were to reach the palace before the monsoon broke. Although I had no desire for my return to be greeted by accusing faces, I had nowhere else to go.

I'd covered only a few yards when the clouds burst. Water swirled along the path as if it were the bed of a stream and I had no choice but to slip and squelch through ankle-deep mud. I didn't hear the pounding hoof beats until the horse was nearly upon me and I jumped out of the way as fast as I could, stumbling into a bush that jabbed my temple with a sharp twig.

The horse slowed and the rider jumped to the ground, landing in a puddle with a splash.

'Damnation!' Harry wiped spatters of mud from his face. 'Where the hell have you been, Bee? People are out looking for you.'

I untangled myself from the sodden bush. 'Who is looking for me?'

'Lakshmi is riding out over the hillside, your brother is quizzing stallholders in the bazaar and the servants are running all over the palace searching every room.'

'But why?'

'Because Jahanara Begum is worried about you. Now get up onto Zephyr before we all drown in this damnable rain, you troublesome female!'

'Troublesome?' I said, my voice full of indignation. 'I haven't done anything.'

'Come here!'

I gasped at the pain in my bruised ribs as he picked me up and tossed me onto the saddle before hoisting himself up behind me.

'Jahanara Begum was convinced you'd thrown yourself in the Musi,' he said.

'But I can't swim.'

'The Begum's point exactly.' He clamped his arms around my waist and picked up the reins. Turning Zephyr around, he set off at a smart trot back the way he'd come.

The rain pounded on my head and ran down in rivulets inside my saturated clothing. I leaned back against Harry, taking a little comfort from the sensation of his arms around me and his warm and muscular chest against my back. I might as well enjoy it while I could because it wasn't likely to happen again.

All too soon, we arrived back at the palace stables, where Lakshmi waited for us.

Harry dismounted, grasped me around the waist with both hands and swung me down to the ground.

I grimaced as his hands squeezed my bruised ribs.

'I apologise if my touch offends you,' he said, his mouth set in a forbidding line.

'It's not that ...'

Lakshmi ran up to hug me before I could explain. 'You're safe! We were so frightened for you.' She turned to Harry. 'Where did you find her?'

'Down by the river, some distance beyond the Residency.'

'The river!' She brushed a dripping lock of hair off my cheek. 'I would never have forgiven myself if something I or Jahanara Begum had said drove you to drown yourself.'

'I didn't try to drown myself!'

'I know you wanted to help by starting the embroidery workshop,' she said, 'and it was only a terrible mistake that you forgot to close the windows in the Durbar Hall ...'

I disentangled myself from her arms. 'But I *didn't* leave the windows open!'

Lakshmi shrugged and glanced at Harry.

'I see no further purpose in standing here in the pouring rain debating the matter,' he said. 'The horses must be rubbed down.' He looked at me. 'And you had better go and change, too.'

There was nothing more to be said and I splashed my way back to the palace in a temper.

Chapter 30

After I'd changed into dry clothes, it took a great deal of courage for me to address the ladies in the *zenana*. They had already heard from Lakshmi, of course, that all their hard work had been for nothing and I had no doubt she'd also told them the catastrophe was my fault.

'I don't know by what means an unknown person was able to find their way into the Durbar Hall or why they should act in such a malicious way,' I said. 'But I wish to make it clear that I did *not* leave the windows open.'

'I believe you, Bee,' said Leela. 'You are always a careful person.'

'Thank you, Leela.' I smiled at her, so grateful for her belief in me. 'If the fault had been mine, I would have admitted it. The question is, who would be so cruel and to what purpose?'

The ladies murmured and looked at each other.

'And for now, we can continue to pull our hair in despair over our loss,' I said, 'or we can start again. If you decide this is what you wish to do, then I shall speak to the women to see if they will also agree to continue. I'll leave you now to discuss this amongst yourselves without any fear of me persuading you into a course of action that makes you unhappy. In the morning, I will accept your decision without question.'

I left the *zenana* and went to see Usha, since I didn't know if anyone had informed her of the disaster.

She wept when I told her everything had been ruined and I could only watch helplessly as she rocked back and forth, blotting her eyes with her *dupatta*.

Then she gripped my wrist and looked up at me, heedless that her scarred face was no longer hidden. 'We must start again,' she said. 'I will work all day and every night if necessary but we *cannot* fail to save the palace.'

'Everyone living here needs our venture to be a success,' I said. 'I cannot imagine who would want to destroy everything we made but, whoever it was, they must have a set of keys for the Durbar Hall.'

Usha became still. 'There is only one set of keys.'

'I know. It was hanging up in my bedroom all night. No one could have stolen the keys away from me and later returned them without my knowledge.'

'The second set of keys was lost many years ago,' she said. 'I was still a member of the palace guard then. We searched for them for many days. You must take great care, Bee. Bad blood will out.'

'Bad blood?'

But she had retreated within herself again, her *dupatta* hiding her face as she muttered inaudibly.

I said goodnight and left to confront my next painful task.

Ralph opened his door to my knock. His face was drawn and tired. 'I was so worried, Bee. I searched all through the bazaar and around the city for you and was so relieved when I heard Harry had found you.'

I'd expected him to rage at me and his reaction to the disaster was disconcerting. I followed him into his quarters and was surprised to see a table and chairs, covered with maps and papers, in his sitting room.

He smiled slightly. 'I'm still sufficiently anglicised to prefer to sit at a table when I'm writing or working on documents, which is most evenings.'

'I imagined you'd be furiously angry with me because the goods for the Nizam's *zenana* have been ruined.'

'I'm too dispirited about the continuing negotiations to expend my energy in fury any longer. What's done, is done, Bee, but I confess I'm fearful of his reaction. If he believes his wives have been insulted, he'll use that as proof that the British are untrustworthy. In that case, we don't stand a chance of ousting the French and we'll all be back in England before we know it.' He rubbed his eyes. 'God knows what Leela would think of that.'

'I'm trying to find a way to save the situation,' I said. 'The order was finished early. I'd allowed plenty of time because I had no means of knowing then how long would be needed. I'm hoping to persuade the ladies to begin again and, in this case, the completed order will only be a week or two late.'

'I'll leave it to you to do the best you can, Bee. The British foothold here may depend upon it.'

The weight of that responsibility wearied me. 'Ralph, who would deliberately set out to cause this damage? Lakshmi is convinced it's my fault. Will you confirm to everyone that the windows were closed when we were in the Durbar Hall last night?'

'I have no recollection of whether they were or not,' he said. 'Now, if you'll excuse me, I must finish this paperwork.'

My only chance of proving I was not culpable disappeared with his dismissal. I returned to my room and spent a lonely evening wondering what to do next.

The following morning, I was dismayed to see half a dozen buckets set out in the *zenana* to catch rainwater dripping through the ceiling and wondered how many other roof leaks there were in the Jahanara Mahal. I joined the ladies for a breakfast of fruit and mint tea. I had little appetite and picked at a few pieces of mango and papaya while I waited for them to tell me their decision.

Samira Begum rinsed her fingers and dried them on her napkin. 'Bee, we talked until late last night and decided in the end that it makes no difference who opened the windows in the Durbar Hall; the result was the same, whether it was an accident or an act of malice.'

I would have been happier if the ladies all firmly believed it hadn't been my fault but I had no choice but to accept their comments. 'And how shall we proceed?' I asked.

'We do not care to sit here in our *zenana* waiting and wondering if the palace must be sold,' said Samira Begum. She held up the saffron silk shawl. 'We still have this, out of harm's way, for the Nizam's First Wife.'

'Our embroidery may not be enough to save the Jahanara Mahal,' said Leela, 'but we will make every effort. Meanwhile, it will keep our minds and fingers usefully employed.'

'Then I shall discuss it with the workshop women to see if they wish to continue.'

I visited Hemanti and asked her to invite the women to meet me at noon. Then I steeled myself to return to the Durbar Hall.

I collected up the damaged items, my heart aching at the destruction of such beautiful work, and set them in a sodden heap. At least I had stored Mrs Clements' travelling dress and reticules in the chest and they were undamaged. I mopped the floor, but, however hard I scrubbed, I couldn't remove a lingering crimson stain from the white marble.

When the sun was at its zenith, the women began to drift into the Durbar Hall. Once they were all seated on the floor, I stepped forward to speak to them.

'We cannot change what has happened,' I said, 'but we can use this as an opportunity to take stock. Although we produce high-quality work, not everything has been a success.' I studied the rows of sullen faces. 'I want more than anything for the workshop to be successful, for all our sakes, but I wonder now if I went about it the wrong way.'

Several of the women shifted position and exchanged sidelong looks.

'Since I am a woman, a newcomer to the palace *and* a foreigner, some of you were aggrieved when I told you what to do. There has been discord between us and it's time to find a better way of working together.'

'What are you suggesting?' called out Deepika.

'We all have our strengths and our weaknesses. Perhaps one of my weaknesses is that, with the best of intentions, I took too much responsibility upon myself.'

Several of the women nodded their agreement.

'But,' I continued, 'we *must* find a way to save the palace and to provide a means of earning a living. Are we still in agreement that an embroidery and sewing workshop is the best way of achieving this?' I looked around, searching their expressions for either support or hostility as they fell into a lively discussion between themselves.

After a while Deepika, who appeared to have nominated herself as spokeswoman, stood up. The others fell silent. 'At present, we do not have a better idea.'

I nodded. 'Then I have a suggestion as to how we may work in harmony in the future.'

'Tell us,' said Deepika.

'I propose I will no longer stand above you as an overseer. You, I and the ladies of the *zenana* will all have an equal say in the way the workshop is run. We should discuss how work will be procured, who is best suited to making each article and how much should be charged for it. You will decide for yourselves how much you can be paid and if everyone is to be paid the same amount or if this will depend upon an individual's skill and speed of working. The results of these decisions will be known to all. Everyone's voice will be heard and you will vote to make any changes.'

There was total silence for a few moments and then a sudden hubbub as they all began to speak at once.

'We will decide for ourselves how much we earn?' called out one of the women.

'You would all have to agree on that,' I replied, 'taking into account the expense of buying new materials. You would also vote to decide who is best suited to each particular role in the workshop and who should be in control.'

The murmuring began again until Deepika waved her hands at the gathering and there was quiet. 'We need to think about this strange idea.'

'Of course,' I said, 'but in the meantime, we must decide what to do about the order for the Nizam's *zenana*. Are we going to make new goods to replace the damaged ones? I dare to hope a prestigious order such as this will bring us new enquiries.'

Deepika glanced at the women and most of them nodded.

I smiled in relief, hoping that the news would help to mollify Ralph. 'At least the saffron silk shawl for Bakshi Begum has escaped damage,' I told them.

'But what about the rest?' said Hemanti.

'There is still some fabric remaining from Jahanara Begum's costumes,' I said. 'And I was looking at the spoiled articles and wondering if some might be saved by washing out the stains or cutting around the embroidered section and making a smaller item from it. Perhaps those that are lightly stained might even be dyed a darker colour?'

Anjali stood up. 'My brother is a *dhobi*. He has many men and women working for him and washes the clothes of the rich men in the city. I will ask him for advice.'

'That's an excellent idea, Anjali.' She looked pleased with

herself and sat down again. 'Why don't you all look at the damaged items and see if you can suggest ways any of them can be saved or altered?'

An hour later I left the women. From the good-humoured comments they made as I waved goodbye, I was hopeful that we'd find a better way of working together in the future.

Chapter 31

Over the next fortnight the women in the workshop spent many hours discussing how it might be managed. I sat on the sidelines, relieved it was no longer my sole responsibility, and then relayed the main points of the discussions to the ladies in the *zenana* for their suggestions. There were some arguments and a few tears but everyone voted on each decision until all were reasonably happy. Several women were chosen to manage different projects. My role was to liaise between the workshop and the *zenana* and to find new business. All the while the women talked, their fingers flew as they cut, stitched and embroidered to reproduce the water-damaged items.

One morning, with Jahanara Begum's consent, I borrowed the palanquin and went to the Residency to deliver Mrs Clements' order. She was pleased to see me and I forgot my troubles as I listened to her lavish praise for her new travelling gown and reticules.

'There is really so little to buy of a fashionable nature for a European woman here in Hyderabad,' she said, 'but I knew you would bring me just what I like.'

'I made the pattern from one of my gowns,' I said, 'but allowed a little more fullness in the bodice for you. And the green embroidery suits your complexion.'

Mrs Clements held the dress to her face and preened at her reflection in the mirror. 'I wish now that I'd asked you to embroider me a new ball gown, too, since I shall be attending so many receptions in Calcutta. Everyone wants to meet the new Governor-General. He's adamant that we must hurry up and trounce the French, then shoo them out of India before it's too late.'

'My brother tells me that the Nizam is still reluctant to join forces with the British.'

Mrs Clements sighed heavily. 'Mr Clements talks of nothing else.'

I enjoyed a cup of tea with my hostess and, as I left, was pleased to receive payment for her goods.

On leaving the Residency bungalows, I instructed the bearers to convey me to the bazaar. Remembering my earlier unpleasant experience there with French soldiers, I asked one of the men to accompany me.

I came to an arrangement with Faisal Mahmoud, the stallholder from whom I'd previously bought dress fabrics. He would sell the workshop's embroidered slippers, purses and other small items, keeping a percentage from every item sold. I negotiated for various silks, gauzes, velvets and muslins, including offcuts that were too small to be of much use to his other customers, though at the end of the lengthy process I suspected he'd done better out of the deal than I.

After Faisal had wrapped my purchases, he pulled from under the counter some ravishing peridot-coloured silk. 'I will make you a special price,' he said, 'because it matches your eyes.'

I fingered the green silk and was gripped by a longing to possess it. Soon I would be out of mourning for Charles and it wasn't hard to persuade myself I'd need clothes appropriate to my new life.

*

Later, I saw Jai, together with half a dozen other children, mountaineering over the fallen masonry at the rear of the palace. He came running to see me.

'There's something I want to show you,' I said. 'Will you ask Sangita if you may come for a walk with me along the river path?'

'What is it?' His face was bright with curiosity.

'It's a surprise.'

He raced off, his skinny legs pumping up and down, and a sudden pang of loss for my baby son gripped me again. The raw agony of grief over his death had dissipated but it still lay in wait to lacerate me all over again when I least expected it.

I sat on a block of stone while I waited, listening to the children playing and wondering where they would go if the palace had to be sold. For myself, the prospect of living in a Residency bungalow in close confinement with Ralph was not a happy one. Returning to England, however, would be far worse.

My despondent musings were interrupted when I heard Jai's running footsteps returning.

'I can come with you!' he called.

I saw then that Harry was following close behind the boy. I hadn't seen him since he'd found me along the river path battling through the driving rain. He'd been very brusque with me when we'd parted.

'Jai tells me you're going to the river,' he said. 'May I join you?'

We set off with the boy chattering away about the game he'd been playing with his friends, relieving me of the necessity of making conversation. Harry wore a dust-coloured turban that, together with his worn native clothing, made him blend into the landscape. I wondered again about his covert duties for the Company.

The over-ripe reek of mud reached us even before we saw the river.

'It's always like this before the monsoons raise the water level,' said Harry, wrinkling his nose at the stench.

250

Jai ran off along the path ahead of us as we stepped under the welcome shade of some overhanging trees.

'I wanted to show Jai ...'

'Where are you taking ...'

'I'm sorry, I interrupted you,' I said.

'Not at all.' Harry sighed. 'Look, this is awkward but I believe I may have been a little curt with you when I saw you last. I ought to explain that I wasn't angry with you.'

'That's exactly how it appeared to me.'

'That wasn't it at all. Bee, I know how hard you and the other women have worked to make the embroidery workshop a success. When I heard what had happened, I knew you'd be utterly devastated. And then Jahanara Begum was terribly worried for you. Her panic was infectious.'

'You thought I might harm myself?'

He held back a thorny stem, allowing me to pass without scratching myself. 'After all that happened to you before you left England, I wondered if the disaster in the workshop might be the final straw.' He turned to look at me, his expression troubled. 'I was afraid for you.'

I was surprised and touched. 'Even when I lost my baby last year, so soon after my husband's death, I never contemplated such a terrible act.'

'I'm greatly relieved to hear it. I do understand, though, how dark a place the world can be when you lose a spouse.'

Lakshmi had spoken nothing but the truth then, when she told me about his deep and enduring love for Noor. Then there was no more time to talk of sad things because Jai came racing back to us.

'It's too hot to run, Jai,' I said.

'I want to see the secret! Is it far?'

I shook my head. 'We need to go around the next bend in the river.'

'I'll make sure there are no snakes or tigers in the way.' He hurried on again, swishing at the long grass with a stick.

251

'May I ask where you're taking us?' asked Harry.

I shook my head. 'You'll have to wait, like Jai.'

'When you smile at me like that,' he said, in teasing tones, 'you look exactly like the mischievous eight-year-old Bee I remember.'

It was impossible not to smile again. 'We did have some fun, didn't we?'

'If only we'd found the Rose of Golconda then, we wouldn't be in such a precarious situation at the Jahanara Mahal today.' He sighed. 'I can't tell you how many hours I spent looking for it.'

The river curved and Jai came to walk between us. 'Are we nearly there?'

'Do you see that pavilion on top of the garden wall over there?' I said. 'It looks like the prow of a ship overlooking the river.'

Jai frowned. 'Is that the secret?'

'Wait and see!'

The next section of the path had been left in a quagmire by the rain and I saw where Zephyr's hooves had churned it up when Harry found me. I glanced in dismay at my sandals.

'Stay here, Jai,' said Harry.

I gasped as he scooped me up into his arms.

'I apologise,' he said, setting me down again in a hurry. 'I had no intention of being over-familiar.'

'No, it's not that and you don't have to keep apologising,' I said, my arms still around his neck. 'I had a painful fall the other day when I was riding Breeze. I'm black with bruises and my ribs are very tender. I should be grateful, however, if you would carry me over the mud.'

'Bruised ribs?' said Harry. 'Is that why you made such a face when I lifted you onto Zephyr the other evening? It wasn't because you thought I was forcing myself upon you?'

'Not at all.'

'In that case ...' He lifted me into his arms again as carefully as if I were made of spun glass and began to negotiate his way through the mud. 'How did you fall?'

'Lakshmi and I were out on the hillside when we were caught in the monsoon. When she galloped for home, Breeze and I raced after her. I couldn't see properly because of the teeming rain.' My head rested on Harry's shoulder and I noticed the dark stubble on his jaw. Our close proximity and his faint scent of sandalwood made me forget what I was saying.

'Go on,' he said.

I forced myself to look away. 'Lakshmi beckoned us on and then, just as we reached the top of a rocky incline, Aurora veered off to one side. The ground fell away sharply from the crest of the peak but it was too late for Breeze to follow. She leaped high in the air and came down hard on the other side several feet below.'

Harry drew in his breath sharply.

'I fell and was badly winded. When I came to my senses again my first thought was for Breeze but I saw straightaway that she was all right.'

'She might have killed you both.'

'Or broken her legs. There was a deep crack about six feet wide at the bottom of the incline. Earthquake damage, Lakshmi said.'

'I know where that was.' He shook his head in disbelief. 'What was Lakshmi doing taking you there?'

'The rain was torrential. We couldn't see anything clearly.'

'*Abbu*!' shouted Jai.

We had crossed the mire but Harry still held me in his arms. 'You can put me down now,' I said, flustered.

He set me carefully on the grass but his arms remained around me. Our faces were so close I hardly dared to breathe.

'*Abbu*!' shouted Jai again.

'I'm coming, Jai!' called Harry.

Reluctantly, I loosed my hold around his neck and watched him plod back through the mud to fetch Jai. When they returned, I held out my hand to the boy. 'Come!'

I led him to the tangled bushes at the base of the garden pavilion and pulled aside some of the undergrowth. 'Go inside,' I said, 'and tell me if you agree that this is a perfect new home for Swati and her puppies.'

Jai's eyes widened and then he scrambled underneath the pavilion.

Harry gave me a searching look and bent double to follow his son.

A few minutes later they both emerged. 'What do you think?' I asked.

Jai ran to me and wrapped his arms around my waist. 'Thank you, thank you, *aunty-ji*! It's the very best home for Swati.'

I hugged him back and bent to kiss his silky hair. 'As soon as I saw it, I knew it would be just right,' I said. 'It's well hidden and the river is nearby for drinking water. We'll find some dry grass to make her a lovely soft bed.'

'And there are big houses nearby,' said Jai, his eyes shining. 'Swati can go and sit outside the kitchen doors. The servants will be sure to feed her because she's so beautiful.'

I caught Harry's eye and tried not to laugh. 'Beauty is in the eye of the beholder,' I said solemnly.

Harry snorted and turned away.

'How will we bring the puppies here?' asked Jai. 'They're too young to walk this far.'

'I have an idea about that,' I said. 'Leave it with me.'

'Have you noticed the sky?' said Harry. Great black clouds were gathering above.

'It's going to rain again!'

Harry hoisted Jai into his shoulders and carried him back over the mire.

Then it was my turn.

'That was very well done, Bee,' Harry murmured in my ear as he lifted me up. 'I've been dreading having to upset him by insisting Swati and the pups are sent away.'

'It's a shame he isn't able to keep one of the puppies,' I said. 'It would make him so happy.'

'Sangita would never allow it.' Harry's face was only inches from mine. 'You really care about Jai, don't you?'

'How could I not?' I studied the curve of his full mouth and longed to touch a finger to his lips but by then we had crossed the quagmire and he put me down.

'We'd better hurry!' said Jai, looking at the darkening clouds chasing across the sky.

Harry loped off after his son and I hurried along behind. After a few minutes, Harry stopped and held out his hand to me.

The first drops of rain spotted my upturned face and then, hand-in-hand and laughing, the three of us ran back to the Jahanara Mahal.

Later on, I was rubbing my hair dry by the open window, watching lightning fork across the sky. There was a tap on my bedroom door. I opened it. Lakshmi stood outside.

'May I speak to you?'

Reluctantly, I stepped aside and she followed me in.

'Be careful of the bucket,' I said. Rainwater dripped through the ceiling and plopped into the bucket with a sound as regular as a metronome.

'Bee, I know you are angry with me.'

'Yes, I am. You are in charge of security here and I expected you to make at least *some* effort to discover who might have damaged the goods for the Nizam, not accuse me outright of neglecting to keep them safe.'

She sighed. 'I cannot believe people unknown let themselves into the Durbar Hall, with keys that vanished forty years ago, in order to open the windows with malicious intent.'

'All I know is that I didn't leave them open.' I started at a sudden boom of thunder overhead.

'But Ralph cannot confirm that,' she said. 'I asked him. You must try to see it from my point of view, Bee. It is not in the interests of anyone in the palace for your embroidery workshop to fail. It was a terrible mistake but no one is angry with you.' She held out her hand to me. 'Please, let us be friends again.'

I stared at her hand. I was sure I'd locked the windows. But what if I *had* forgotten? It was something I did every day. Might I, just perhaps, have remembered closing them the day before? The truth was, I couldn't be absolutely sure.

'Bee?'

Slowly, I reached out to take her hand.

She smiled and then hugged me. 'It made me unhappy to think I might have lost your friendship,' she said. 'You are so different from the ladies in the *zenana*, who have little idea of life outside. But you and I are alike in many ways, I think.'

'Perhaps,' I said. 'I certainly don't want us to be enemies.'

'What happened cannot be changed, Bee, but we can put it behind us and begin again.'

She was right, of course. It did no good to look back.

Chapter 32

By the end of August, it was still fiercely hot and humid. The monsoon rains evaporated in steaming clouds whenever the sun reappeared. Black fungus blighted the inside walls of the palace. Everything smelled dank and mouldy and I was annoyed to discover that mildew had spotted my clothing. The rain and the heat kept us indoors a great deal but the time was used profitably to recreate the items for the Nizam's *zenana*. Our eyes became strained from working late into the night by lamplight and our fingers were sore with pin-pricks.

There had been changes in the way the workshop was run and I had to admit that they were an improvement. The women appeared more settled and, now they had control, no one complained about not having been paid.

Twice, Harry went away for a few days, and each time he and Zephyr arrived back at the Jahanara Mahal mud-spattered and filthy. He was evasive about where he'd been and I soon learned not to jest or even comment upon his disappearances.

It was the anniversary of Charles' death when Leela and I were able, at last, to wrap the items for the Nizam's *zenana* in fine muslin.

We were full of excitement as we placed the parcels into a silk-lined chest, layered with dried rose petals and sweet-scented herbs.

'We have achieved much,' said Priya Begum, as the chest, tied with fluttering scarlet ribbons and gold braid, was loaded into one of the palanquins with Deepika and Anjali.

Leela and I travelled in the other palanquin, watching the ladies wave us off as we were carried out of the *zenana* garden. We closed the yellow curtains for the remainder of the journey.

Leela kept her eyes downcast, making no attempt at conversation.

After a while, I touched her wrist. 'Are you unwell?' I asked.

'My stomach is churning,' she said. 'I worry what will happen if the Nizam's ladies do not pay us today.'

'I know,' I admitted. 'We can only politely request payment. We cannot risk causing a diplomatic incident by pressing the Nizam's wives further and perhaps causing offence.'

Leela leaned back against the cushions, eyes closed, until we arrived at the Chowmahalla Palace. A short while later, the Nizam's ladies greeted us with delighted cries.

Deepika's and Anjali's eyes shone with excitement and awe as they took in their luxurious surroundings while they distributed the goods.

Then we were summoned to approach Bakshi Begum.

We paid her the appropriate respects and Leela laid the saffron-coloured shawl on a silk cushion at her feet.

The Nizam's First Wife remained silent for a whole minute while she fixed us with a flinty stare. 'I have been waiting too long for this,' she said, at last.

I swallowed, wondering if she would refuse to accept it and mentally berating myself for not thinking to deliver the shawl in advance.

'Explain yourself!' she said.

Haltingly, I told her the truth about the monsoon damage and how we'd worked late every night to replace the goods.

She continued to stare at us, stony-faced, and then dismissed us from her presence with a wave of her hand.

Humiliated, we returned to sit with Parwar un-nisa Begum.

'The Nizam's First Wife is angry,' she said.

I told her how the order had been damaged by the monsoon. 'I should have brought her shawl earlier and explained that the other items would be late.'

'You made a mistake in not sending Bakshi Begum a gift,' said Parwar un-nisa Begum,' she said. 'Now, you may expect the payment to be late, too. If she pays at all.'

Aghast, I glanced at Leela, who was close to tears.

Parwar un-nisa Begum shrugged. 'Still, the rest of the ladies are happy with their goods and none of them have complained about late delivery. It's unfortunate for you that Bakshi Begum controls the purse strings.'

Later, we left the *zenana*, clasping a long list of items required for a further order.

'What are we going to do?' asked Leela, once the palanquin curtains were closed. Her brown eyes were anxious.

'I don't see how we can refuse to fulfil this new order,' I said. 'It's an honour to receive it, especially after Bakshi Begum was angry with us, but we can't buy the new materials without first receiving payment.'

'Ralph is going to be so angry,' said Leela.

We passed the remainder of the journey to the palace in troubled silence.

Leela returned to the *zenana* and I asked the bearers to wait for me with one of the palanquins at the back of the palace while I went with Deepika and Anjali to the workshop. It was my difficult task to tell the women that we hadn't as yet received payment. There were several wails of dismay and the news that we had another order did little to allay their fears.

Their unhappy voices were still ringing in my ears when I left them to meet Jai and Harry by the garden pavilion, as previously arranged.

'Ready?' I asked.

'As long as the little devils haven't escaped again,' said Harry, a mischievous glint in his eye as he glanced fondly at his son.

'They're not devils, *abbu*!' Jai's expression was outraged.

'In any case, I can't waste any time,' said Harry. 'I have a meeting with the Resident this afternoon.'

We made our way to the old outbuilding. As we walked, I told him what had happened at the Nizam's *zenana*.

'Don't look so unhappy, Bee,' he said. 'Bakshi Begum's well known for finding ways to demonstrate her power. Perhaps she'll relent once she's made her point.'

I could only hope he was right.

Swati was inside the outbuilding, nosing at a deep-sided wooden box. The puppies inside whined and growled as they played. Harry covered the box with a cloth and hoisted it into his arms.

Jai tied a piece of rope around Swati's neck and we set off to the waiting palanquin.

Swati and I climbed inside and Harry placed the box of puppies by my feet.

'Was ever a dog so spoiled?' he said. 'Yellow chintz curtains, no less!'

'Jahanara Begum was most understanding about lending us the palanquin,' I said. 'I explained that Swati mustn't see where we are going or she'd only bring the puppies back.'

The bearers lifted up the palanquin and jogged away with Harry and Jai running alongside.

We arrived at the little sanctuary beside the river where, earlier in the day, Jai had collected a mound of dried grass for Swati's bed. Harry placed the puppies onto this while their mother had a good sniff all around. Very soon the puppies, tails wagging, were exploring their new home too.

'I begged these from the kitchens,' said Harry, opening a cloth folded around some bread and other scraps.

'I don't want to leave them,' said Jai, his chin trembling.

'We had an agreement,' said Harry gently. 'Swati will look after them but they must learn to fend for themselves now.'

'Jai, there is one other thing,' I said. 'Jahanara Begum tells me that there's a terrible rat problem in the yard behind the kitchens. She asked me to keep my eye open for a bold puppy that could be trained to be the Jahanara Mahal's official rat controller. Might you be able to find a suitable one somewhere?'

Harry and Jai both stared at me.

'A puppy?' said Jai. 'One of Swati's puppies?'

'I suppose that might do,' I said, 'if it's fierce enough. It'll have to live in the stables, though.'

Jai pounced on one of the puppies. 'This one! He's very bold and he'll be an excellent ratter.'

'If you're sure . . .'

'Yes, yes, *aunty-ji*, I'm very sure!' Tears of joy ran down his cheeks and he buried his face in the puppy's neck.

'In that case, Harry, don't you think the perfect name for such a bold and fearless puppy would be Bandit?'

Harry gave a shout of laughter and encircled both Jai and me in his arms with the puppy between us.

Later, I was walking in the grounds, taking the early-evening air and fretting about how I could encourage Bakshi Begum to pay us, when I ran into Harry again, this time in company with my brother.

Ralph greeted me, radiating good cheer, and I guessed Harry hadn't told him that Bakshi Begum was annoyed. He'd find out soon enough.

'We've just returned from the Residency,' he said. 'Will you join us for dinner? We've asked Lakshmi, too. We shall tell you some interesting news we heard today.'

'I'd like that.'

Harry gave me one of his dazzling smiles and I returned to my room to change, putting Bakshi Begum out of my mind and refusing to allow her to spoil the evening. It seemed appropriate, since it was my first day out of mourning, that I dress for dinner in the trousers and *kameez* I'd made from the soft green silk I'd bought from Faisal Mahmoud.

I shivered slightly as I drew on the trousers and the lustrous silk caressed my skin. While I stood rebraiding my hair beside the bedroom window, I watched the sun set and thought about poor Charles. We'd been married such a short time and it saddened me that, already, his kind face was fading from my memory.

Lakshmi knocked on my door and I put away my sad thoughts and invited her in. She wore her outfit of lime green and gold again, the colours picking out the flecks of green in her eyes. The amber glass bangles I'd bought her in the bazaar clinked on her wrists.

'You have cast off your widow's clothing?' she asked.

'Today is my first day out of mourning.' I lifted up my arm to look at the shimmering silk of my sleeve. 'It feels strange to be wearing anything so luxurious.'

'We are both wearing green tonight.' She pulled me to the damp-mottled mirror on the wall and rested her head against mine as we studied our reflection.

'It suits us,' I said, 'even though our colouring is so different.'

'We look like sisters.'

'Only in a very dim light.' I smiled at her comment. 'And you're much younger than I am.' I peered into the mirror again, noticing that Faisal Mahmoud was right: the green of my eyes was intensified by the peridot colour. It pleased me that I looked well, despite being beyond the first bloom of youth. 'Shall we go?'

'Wait, you have no jewellery!' Lakshmi slipped two of the bangles off her arm. 'Wear these tonight.'

They were still warm from her skin as I slid them over my wrist

262

and a sudden sense of occasion made me anticipate the evening with pleasure.

We hurried through the darkening palace, our sandals tapping on the marble floors and our bangles jingling. In the ante-chamber to the dining room, the carved timber doors, twice the height of a man, stood ajar. They were no longer flanked by menservants in white tunics and red turbans.

At our entry Harry and Ralph rose from their cushions around the low table. The dining room was illuminated by the flickering light of a many-branched chandelier, vividly bringing to life the painted murals of turbaned nobles mounted on gaily caparisoned elephants as they embarked on a tiger hunt.

Harry's eyes widened as he saw me, causing me no little satisfaction. 'How very lovely you look tonight, Bee,' he murmured, taking my hand and leading me to one of the floor cushions.

I sat down cross-legged, noting that Harry, too, had taken trouble to dress for dinner. He looked stunningly handsome in pristine white trousers with an embroidered tunic of cream and gold.

'You're out of mourning, Bee!' said Ralph. 'Is it truly a year since your husband passed on?'

I nodded, unable to speak for a sudden memory of poor Charles' frightened face in his last days. Harry brushed my wrist in a gesture of sympathy.

Lakshmi was watching us closely but then Ralph escorted her to a place opposite me at the table. 'There are no menservants to usher us into the dining room tonight,' she said.

'The usual footmen have been fortunate enough to join the East India Company's army as *sepoys*,' said Ralph.

An elderly manservant entered, carrying a tray of dishes. His bearing was upright and his moustache silver but his gnarled hands trembled as he distributed the platters amongst us.

The spicy aromas made me hungry, especially when I noticed some particularly appetising onion fritters. I smiled to myself, remembering the first time I'd had dinner in this room six months before, when I hadn't known how to manage without a knife and fork.

'Leela wasn't feeling well and had fallen asleep when I called to see her this evening,' said Ralph, 'so I couldn't ask her about your visit to the Nizam's *zenana* today, Bee.'

My spirits sank. 'Poor Leela!' I said, delaying the moment I'd have to tell him we'd angered Bakshi Begum. 'She looked tired this morning.'

'And?' said Ralph.

'The ladies were so delighted with their purchases,' I said, 'that we left with another substantial order.'

Harry caught my eye.

Ralph let out a sigh of relief. 'Well done, Bee. I've been so concerned it might not go well and there would be political repercussions.'

'We reused what we could from the items damaged by the rain, although very little could be saved. The remainder of the order was faster to make this time because the women are more experienced now. There was one small problem, though.'

Ralph looked up sharply from his dinner plate. 'What was that?'

'Bakshi Begum hasn't paid us,' I said.

'For God's sake, don't hound her for settlement!' said Ralph.

I opened my mouth to confess she was already displeased with us but Harry frowned and shook his head. 'And is there less unrest in the workshop than before?' he asked before I could say more.

I nodded. 'I took your advice and discussed with the women better ways for them to have their say.' His approving smile flustered me almost as much as his gaze. 'They were unsure at first but now they've voted for their own group leaders.'

'Voted? The women?' said Ralph, eyebrows raised. 'Whatever next!'

I straightened my back to do battle with him but Harry pressed his knee against mine in warning. I subsided, taking pleasure in his nearness, since he made no effort to move away. And it would be a pity to start another argument with my brother.

Lakshmi suppressed a yawn and changed the subject. 'What is this interesting news that you bring from the Residency today?'

'Admiral Nelson has won a great victory for the British,' said Ralph, reaching across the table to take another sweetmeat, glistening with honey and almonds. 'He engaged with the French fleet in Aboukir Bay at the mouth of the Nile.'

'By the end of the night,' Harry told me, 'the British sustained losses of nine hundred men. The French, however, lost ten times as many.'

'It must have been a terrible sight,' I said, imagining the screams of the wounded men.

Lakshmi pushed her plate away as if the thought sickened her, too. 'That is a considerable setback for the French. Napoleon's army will be stranded in Egypt, won't it?'

'Exactly!' said Ralph. 'Now the British have control of the Mediterranean again, the French would find it hard to establish a permanent presence in Egypt.'

'Why would they want to?' I asked.

'They intended to use Egypt as a staging post for their army while they fought the British for control of India,' said Harry. 'They planned on strengthening their expeditionary forces by combining with the army of Tipu Sultan. Without the Egyptian trade route being open to us, the British couldn't supply and augment their own troops.'

'I hadn't appreciated how battles fought so far away might affect us here,' I said.

'Believe me,' said Ralph, grim-faced, 'if we'd lost the battle for the Nile, we'd have been in dire straits.'

'Now, of course,' said Harry, 'it's possible the Nizam may align himself with the British after all, since the French are in a much less advantageous position than before.' His hand brushed mine as he passed me one of the dishes and a shiver danced down my spine, despite the warmth of the room.

'The French still have much greater forces than the British in Hyderabad,' said Lakshmi.

Ralph spooned a generous helping of rice onto his plate. 'That's true, but since General Raymond died the Nizam has lost confidence in the French. Not that it is anything you and Bee need worry about.'

I opened my mouth to say that, of course, it concerned us, too, but my brother had turned his attention to Harry.

The men continued to discuss the situation and all the while I bathed in the warmth of the light in Harry's eyes each time he looked at me. His glances made my skin tingle and I was unable to concentrate on the conversation. Instead I studied his hands, noting his long fingers, olive skin and a crescent-shaped scar across one thumb.

Gradually, I fell silent as the others talked of *sepoys* and mercenary regiments, pincer movements and pre-emptive strikes. Lakshmi, due no doubt to her military training, appeared to take a great deal more interest than I did and Harry took trouble to explain the situation to her.

I didn't want to leave the party but I was tired after working late over my embroidery for so many nights and my head began to nod. When Ralph called for brandy, I rose and said goodnight.

'Let me escort you back to the *zenana*,' said Harry, and my heart leaped at the prospect.

Lakshmi smiled. 'Please, Harry, stay and enjoy your brandy.' She linked her arm through mine. 'I must go to bed, too, if I am to rise early to practise my sword skills. Bee and I will go together.'

Disappointed but also relieved, I glanced back over my shoulder as we left the room and met Harry's lingering gaze. I wondered if he could read the regret in my eyes.

Chapter 33

Despite my fatigue, I was hot and my mind remained too active for me to sleep. Harry's gaze had followed me all evening and, even with my limited experience of the ways of men, it wasn't difficult to tell he was taking a particular interest in me. And I, oh, yes, I was most definitely interested in him.

I tossed and turned under the mosquito net, feeling unbearably confined. Finally I left my room and tiptoed out of the *zenana*. There was enough moonlight for me not to need a lamp and it was dream-like and calming to wander through the deserted halls and shadowy rooms of the palace. It seemed a long time ago that I'd been frightened, walking alone in the dark.

The old watchman, huddled asleep on a blanket in the hall, barely stirred as I let myself out. I walked down to the terrace and leaned on the wall to look at the river, the dark waters swollen with the monsoon rains and reflecting back the silvery moonlight. Windows glowed amber in the city on the opposite bank and the sound of distant drumming drifted on the breeze.

Still wide awake, I meandered through the grounds. I peered into Breeze's box as I passed the stables and her head came up when I whispered her name. The straw rustled as she shifted her weight, releasing a comforting waft of warm horseflesh. Mumtaz and Ralph's chestnut gelding were asleep and Zephyr whickered. Closing the gate to the stable yard behind me, I entered the walled garden.

Inside the pavilion, I sat on the *charpai*, clasping my hands around my knees and watched the bats swooping after mosquitoes while I daydreamed about Harry. It didn't matter that I wasn't a girl any more or that my mother wouldn't have approved of his manners or that his work was shrouded in secrecy, all I knew was that when I was with him there was a tiny, glowing coal of happiness and excitement within me that grew brighter every day.

The perfumed air was soft on my face and the velvet sky so full of stars I felt entirely insignificant. An owl hooted and then a ghostly white shape flickered across the periphery of my vision. I froze and stared into the darkness but nothing else stirred. I returned to my imaginary world where Harry looked at me adoringly as he carried me in his strong arms and laid me with infinite care upon a grassy bank and then ...

A footfall on the gravel path made me freeze and a figure moved stealthily towards me.

'Bee?' came a whisper. 'Is it you?'

I started, one hand to my breast.

And then Harry was standing before me in the shadows.

The air seemed to shimmer between us and a fierce heat raced up my neck and seared my cheeks. I remained motionless, struck dumb with yearning but afraid my feverish longings were written on my face.

He took a step closer, too close for politeness, and his breath fanned my forehead. Slowly, he lifted my unresisting hand and pressed my palm to his chest. His sandalwood-perfumed skin felt warm and firm through the thin cotton, and the rapid pounding of his heart echoed my own.

Reaching behind me, he pulled the ribbon from my plait and loosened my hair so that it fell in silky waves around my shoulders. Bending over me, he dropped soft kisses on my eyelids, my cheeks, my throat, while I stood as still as if I were carved from marble.

His hand dropped to the curve of my breast and then paused.

Instead of pushing him away, as any decent woman would have done, I swayed towards him, clutching his shirt, the clean masculine smell of him filling every breath I took.

He lifted my chin with his forefinger so that I had to look at him. His eyes glimmered in the moonlight as he studied my face.

I made the tiniest movement towards him; an unspoken permission granted.

He kissed my mouth, tenderly at first and then with growing passion.

We sank down onto the *charpai* and I was undone; a fever was upon me and all constraint unleashed. Shivering, I ran my hands down his naked back, hesitating as my fingertips encountered a series of ridged scars and wondering how he had come by them.

I let him kiss me and touch me wherever he and I desired, pressing myself shamelessly against him. When he entered me I clung to him and wrapped my thighs around his waist while an unendurable, aching longing blossomed at the core of me, pulsating like white heat until it exploded in a shower of stars and I ceased to be.

I awoke to misty grey light and the echoing calls and liquid birdsong of the dawn chorus. My cheek rested on a damp and mildew-scented cushion and my hip was pushed into the sagging webbing of the *charpai*. A striped squirrel sat on the pavilion's top step, watching me with bright and inquisitive eyes. I lay still, gradually recalling the extraordinary events of the previous night.

A smile curved my lips. My encounter with Harry had been so unimaginably different from my marital duties. Charles had pressed dry lips to mine and, when he could no longer ignore his need, lifted my nightdress. I used to lie quietly while he made love to me, quickly and apologetically, when I would have responded with passion if he'd shown any himself. Afterwards, he would pat me and say, 'Thank you, my dear,' as if I'd brought him a cup of tea, and then retreat to his side of the bed.

No, indeed, love-making with Harry hadn't been remotely like that. Still flushed with the languour of our passion, I reached a hand behind me. Suddenly apprehensive, I turned over.

Harry had gone.

A pink rosebud lay on the pillow beside mine but there was no trace of warmth on the faded cotton. After what had happened between us, I was dismayed that he'd left me without a word.

Throwing off the thin sheet, I remembered I was naked. The musky odour of our love-making still clung to my skin. I snatched up my crumpled clothing from the tiled floor and scrambled into it, anxious to return to the *zenana* before I was missed.

Then my pulse began to race at the dawning of a humiliating thought. Perhaps I'd mistaken his intentions. If that were so, I had only myself to blame for behaving like a wanton. For a few sublime hours I'd convinced myself he loved me but, in the cold light of dawn, I wondered what man would resist a woman who clung to him and encouraged him to ... I buried my face in my hands.

The squirrel chattered at me, flicked its tail and scampered away.

I gathered up the pink rose from the pillow and left the pavilion. Hurrying along the path, I peeped around the garden door to satisfy myself that there was no one to see me. I'd almost reached the stables when I was discomfited to find Lakshmi walking towards me, leading Aurora. Her gait faltered for a moment and then she waved.

Unable to avoid her, I brazened it out by waving back. 'You must have risen extremely early,' I said, 'it's barely light.'

'You know I like to ride out before the heat of the day.' She looked me up and down and raised an eyebrow on seeing the rose in my

270

hand. 'And you, Bee? What are you doing all alone out here, even before the sun has risen?'

My hair was still tumbled around my shoulders and I hastily began to plait it. 'It was so sultry last night that I couldn't sleep. I walked in the gardens and sat in the pavilion. I must have dozed off.' I gave a self-conscious laugh. 'The next thing I knew, it was morning.'

'You shouldn't go out alone in the garden at night.' She paused, almost as if waiting for me to tell her that I hadn't been alone. 'If you want to sleep outside,' she continued, 'the ladies sometimes drag their beds out into the *zenana* garden in hot weather. No harm will come to you behind those high walls, but out here . . . ' She glanced around at the neglected grounds. 'Out here, you never know if you might meet some wild creature or a manservant with bad intentions.'

'I expect you're right,' I said.

'At the very least, I expect the mosquitoes will have feasted upon your tender English skin.' It sounded as if that would please her.

It began to rain again as I walked with her to the stables.

'Zephyr isn't here,' said Lakshmi, with a slight frown. 'I thought Harry . . . ' She hesitated. 'He must have ridden out very early, too.'

'Yes, he must have,' I said, with a bland smile.

Standing by the window in the *zenana* sitting room, I watched the torrents of rain battering down the flowers in the garden below. Reliving the touch of Harry's fingers running down my naked back the previous night, I jumped when Jyoti touched my shoulder.

'*Sahiba*, you have a visitor,' she said.

My daydream shattered, I saw Mrs Clements standing behind her.

'Thank you, Jyoti,' I said.

'My dear,' Mrs Clements whispered, eyeing my gathered trousers askance, 'I'd no idea you had gone *completely* native.' She gave an uncertain glance at the ladies sitting on their cushions while they worked on their embroidery tasks.

'Not completely,' I said, drawing her over to the window seat. I knew the very idea of sitting on the floor would be abhorrent to her, especially since there were several puddles of water that had missed the buckets positioned to catch leaks.

'I hope you'll forgive me for calling upon you without notice,' she said, 'but I bring what I believe you will think is good news.'

'How interesting!'

'My little jaunt to Calcutta was most enjoyable and the travelling dress and the reticules you made for me attracted a great deal of attention. In fact,' her expression could only be described as smug, 'I bring you a number of requests for similar merchandise.' She took a folded paper from her reticule and handed it to me.

I read with gratification the neatly written list of customers' names and the items they required. 'This is really very kind of you, Mrs Clements.'

'I'm pleased to be of help. We British must stick together. Of course ... ' She glanced at the ladies sitting on their cushions and draped in their bright, and sometimes almost transparent, clothing and then back at my trousers.

I decided to rescue her from her awkwardness. 'Tell me about Calcutta. Were there as many receptions and balls as you expected?'

'I hardly slept a wink while we were there, so taken up was I with making new friends and becoming reunited with old ones.' She smiled happily. 'And I met Richard Wellesley, the new Governor-General.'

'What did you think of him?'

'An interesting man whose heart is set on purging the French from India. He's utterly of the opinion that only a strong British presence can control corruption and tyranny in the Indian states.'

'Do you agree with him?' I asked.

'Mr Clements is firmly of the opinion that this is the way forward.'

I noted she made no reference to her own opinion. 'But is that for the protection of the Indian people or to further the expansion of trade for Britain?'

272

'That's the beauty of the scheme,' said Mrs Clements earnestly. 'It's for both. We shall all prosper under a co-ordinated regime.' She leaned forward and whispered, 'The natives are incapable of organising the slightest thing without an immense amount of noise and fuss and they simply don't have our standards.'

I bent my head to hide my blushes. If she knew about the standard of my behaviour the previous night, she'd be appalled. 'Perhaps I might have agreed with you once,' I said, 'but the women in the embroidery workshop are organising the work themselves now and proving most successful. Why, we received a second order from the Nizam's ladies, since they were so pleased with the first.'

'Well, I'm delighted to hear that, though I can't help thinking you would do better to find yourself another husband and live amongst your own sort, rather than working your fingers to the bone and living amongst . . . ' She glanced at the ladies again. 'Strangers.'

Tight-lipped, I said, 'In fact, most of these ladies *are* my family, now. Would you like to meet them?'

Mrs Clements gathered up her reticule with indecent haste. 'Another time, my dear.'

I walked with her to her palanquin waiting outside and waved her off into the downpour, wondering if she was right. Perhaps I had turned native. Certainly I'd find it difficult to return to the narrow-minded world of genteel society in a Hampshire village but I was still, however, a *feringhi* in India. The truth was, I no longer quite fitted in anywhere. Strangely, as a widow living in the largely enclosed world of the Jahanara Mahal, I had more freedom than I'd experienced since I was a child growing up in one of the Residency bungalows.

Including, of course, the freedom to humiliate myself by allowing Harry Wyndham to make passionate love to me without any ties of matrimony.

Chapter 34

I was restless and apprehensive, knowing I wouldn't be able to settle until I'd seen him again. Perhaps he'd kiss me and tell me he loved me but I had to accept the possibility he'd simply amused himself with me for one enchanted night and had no intention of making an honest woman of me. Mortified by this bitter thought, I hoped to take my mind off my troubles by returning to the workshop.

I initiated a discussion with the women about what to do with the second order from the Nizam's *zenana*, since we still awaited payment from Bakshi Begum.

'If we make what we can with the materials we have,' said Deepika, 'perhaps we will be able to sell the items elsewhere, if necessary.'

'Perhaps we should make Bakshi Begum a present?' I said.

After much discussion, it was decided to give the Nizam's wife a silk handkerchief case embroidered with twining roses and honeysuckle and a dozen monogrammed handkerchiefs.

We gasped as a piercing shriek came from the adjacent hall, followed by a resounding crash and several screams. The door burst open and an elderly man entered, waving his arms and shouting in a dialect I didn't understand. Alarmed, I followed the women as they rushed past him.

Inside the living quarters, the air was thickly clouded with plaster dust. Coughing, we cupped our hands over our noses. An extensive section of the decorative ceiling had thudded to the floor, followed by a still-gushing torrent of water. Women wailed at the sight of their flattened possessions.

Later, after buckets had been fetched and the task of shovelling the sodden plaster outside had begun, I slipped away and splashed through the waterlogged grounds to the stables.

There was still no sign of either Zephyr or Harry.

As I hurried disconsolately back across the yard, Jai appeared in the doorway of one of the outbuildings.

'*Aunty-ji*! Come and see Bandit's new home.'

The puppy lay curled up in a wooden crate lined with a sack. 'Is he settling in?' I asked.

'He was crying last night so I slept beside him.'

It sent chills down my spine to hear that he had been wandering the grounds the previous night. I'd never have forgiven myself if Jai had discovered me, naked and in his father's arms. 'Didn't Sangita mind that you spent the night here?'

Jai shuffled his feet in the dust. 'It was Bandit's first night without Swati and I knew he'd be frightened.'

'Sangita would have been frantic if she'd discovered you weren't in your bed. Will you promise never to do that again, unless you have her permission?'

Jai's face fell. 'She'll never allow me to sleep with Bandit.'

'Still,' I said, 'he had you with him for his first night.'

I hesitated then but couldn't resist asking. 'Zephyr has been out all day. Is your father coming home soon?'

Jai shook his head as he returned Bandit to his box. 'Yesterday he told me he was going away for a few days.'

'A few days?' I said, dismayed. 'Where has he gone?'

'Somewhere secret, I expect. He always tells me it's best for me not to know.'

'I see.' A flare of hope blazed in my breast. Perhaps Harry wasn't avoiding me after all, though, until he returned, I'd be left wondering. I sighed and bent down to stroke the puppy. There was a thunderous roaring sound outside, as if a hundred sacks of coal were being tipped into the coal hole all at once.

And then there was an expectant silence that seemed to stretch forever before the screams began.

Jai and I looked at each other and ran.

Another section of the palace wall had collapsed into a vast pile of rubble. The palace looked like a dolls' house with one side open. Babies were yelling and women wailing. An elderly woman whimpered on her *charpai*, her sleeping alcove open to the elements. Overturned braziers hissed and steamed in the lashing rain.

'Oh, Jai!' I said, gripping his hand.

People came running from all parts of the palace. Lightning flashed and we saw Sangita racing towards the wreckage. She stopped dead when she saw her foster son and clutched a hand to her heart.

Jai pulled his hand free from mine and ran into her waiting arms.

I watched for a moment but then, no longer wanted, slipped away.

In the aftermath of the structural collapse, Jahanara Begum gave instructions that the servants should move to safer quarters in another part of the palace.

Several new cracks, however, had opened up in the building and those already in the Durbar Hall had grown even wider. Parallel fissures had opened up in the floor between the storage cupboard and the external wall, as if a pathway three feet wide had dropped by several inches. Other than some cuts and grazes, no one had been seriously hurt and the general opinion was that it might all have been far worse. The inhabitants of the Jahanara Mahal dusted themselves down and continued with their lives.

The new order from the Nizam's ladies, together with the one from Mrs Clements, kept me fully occupied. We completed and sent the present for Bakshi Begum. I liaised between the *zenana* and the workshop and took stock of remaining materials and embroidery silks. It was a relief to be busy but it didn't prevent me from fretting about Harry's return and what we would say to each other then.

One afternoon, the rain ceased and I visited the bazaar, taking Jai with me. He trotted along beside me, carrying my basket and making me smile as he chattered about Bandit's latest demonstration of supreme intelligence.

We steered a wide berth around a group of French soldiers buying sweetmeats and visited Faisal Mahmoud's stall.

He greeted me with a grin. 'I have sold your embroidered slippers, purses and handkerchiefs,' he said. 'Bring me more and I may risk taking a selection of *dupattas* with beaded or embroidered borders, too.'

'There is no risk at all for you!' I commented tartly.

Once our business was concluded, Jai and I followed a deliciously savoury aroma drifting on the breeze. It led us to a brazier at the edge of the bazaar and I bought us each a scoop of *biryani* on a freshly cooked *chapatti*.

We left the hustle of the bazaar behind and hunkered down to eat it beside the river near the bridge.

'What are you laughing at, *aunty-ji*?' asked Jai, his eyes full of lively curiosity.

I finished my mouthful of biryani, the spices tingling on my lips. 'I was thinking how shocked my friend Mrs Clements would be, if she could see me now.'

'Shocked?'

277

'English ladies don't sit on the floor or eat with their fingers.'

His expression was puzzled. 'But why not?'

'A very good question.' I was about to embark on an educational discourse on cultural differences when I saw I'd already lost Jai's attention and he was peering over my shoulder.

'Father!'

I started and looked behind me, dropping rice into my lap. Harry and Zephyr were trotting onto the bridge in the direction of the Jahanara Mahal.

Jai called out but Harry was already swallowed up by the throng teeming over the bridge.

'Eat your *biryani*, Jai, and then we'll hurry back.' Filled with trepidation, my heartbeat began to skip as I contemplated the forthcoming meeting. My appetite entirely deserted me.

Jai stood up, his cheeks bulging. 'I've finished, *aunty-ji*.'

I threw my remaining scraps into the river and the ducks descended on them with a great deal of wing-flapping and raucous quacking. Jai pulled me by the hand and we pushed our way through the crowd.

Sometime later, we arrived at the Jahanara Mahal and hurried in the direction of the stables. I had no idea what I would say to Harry, and could only be relieved that Jai's presence would forestall any awkwardness.

As we approached the stable yard, I saw that Lakshmi and Harry were involved in an earnest conversation. We were too far away to hear what was being said but he must have asked her a question because she shook her head decisively. He turned but she pulled him back and then touched his cheek as she spoke again.

That familiar gesture made me halt. Was there still something between them? I watched as Harry pulled off his turban and ran his fingers through his hair.

Jai ran to his father. '*Abbu*! I am here, *abbu*!'

The grim expression on Harry's face was replaced by a smile. He caught Jai up and set him on his shoulders.

I walked towards them with lagging steps.

Jai was telling his father all about the monsoon washing away the palace wall and our visit to the bazaar and how we'd just missed him.

I waited until there was a momentary pause in this excited prattle. 'Welcome back, Harry,' I said.

Unsmiling, he nodded at me.

Despair gripped me. It was immediately apparent that this was not to be a joyful lovers' reunion. Holding the shopping basket in front of me like a shield, I stood mutely in front of him.

Lakshmi filled the awkward pause in our conversation. 'Did you have a successful visit to the bazaar, Bee?'

'Yes. Thank you.'

'I would have come with you,' she said, 'we had such fun last time, didn't we?' She took my arm. 'Let us walk to the *zenana* together and you can show me what you have bought.'

'I'll see you later, *aunty-ji*!' called Jai.

I waved, glad Lakshmi had given me an excuse to escape. She drew me away and I glanced back through a mist of tears to see Harry watching me, stony-faced. I made an animated show of gossiping with Lakshmi, manufacturing an excuse to laugh and hide my wretchedness.

Once the stables were out of sight, my shoulders sagged and I became silent.

'Bee?' Lakshmi turned to me, her expression full of compassion. 'Harry asked me, as your friend, to speak to you.'

'He did?'

'He wondered ... ' She sighed. 'This is so difficult. He has placed me in a most uncomfortable position.'

'What is it, Lakshmi?' My voice sounded flat.

'I told him he is a coward not to speak to you directly,' the words tumbled out of her, 'but he said he had no desire to discuss it with you and I thought it would be worse for you if you waited and hoped, while all the time ... '

'All the time, what?'

'He told me something happened between you in the garden the other night. When I saw you with your hair loose the other morning, I did wonder. I hope you know, after all the sad events last year, that I want only happiness for you now?' She caught my hands between hers. 'It hurts me to tell you but Harry thinks you have misinterpreted his feelings for you.'

The blood rose to my face, scalding my cheeks.

She touched my cheek, just as she'd touched Harry's. 'Bee, I'm so sorry but I did warn you. He will never love any woman other than his dead wife.'

I gave a brittle laugh. 'It was fun to amuse myself by flirting with him,' I said, my heart breaking, 'but I'm astonished he might have thought I was serious.' I squeezed her hand, hoping she wouldn't feel how mine shook. 'You're a true friend to take it upon yourself to alert me but really, there was no need.'

She looked at me doubtfully. 'You are certain?'

'Absolutely! Harry is a good-looking rascal, but as for losing my heart to him ... nothing could be further from the truth. After all, he's hardly the type of man I should wish to marry!' But, even as I said those Judas words, I knew that was exactly, in my heart of hearts, what I had hoped for.

Chapter 35

I moved through the next few days like an automaton, hollow-eyed from lack of sleep. At night I walked the floor, scolding myself for my stupidity in believing Harry might have loved me. I wasn't at all sure I'd convinced Lakshmi of my lack of feelings for him, either.

It seemed an impossible task to rise from my bed each morning but experience had taught me that the anguish would not lift until I allowed the daily routine to distract me. Accordingly, I summoned up all my willpower and one morning went to visit Usha.

I found her embroidering a new scene on the wall hanging of the Jahanara Mahal.

'I wondered when you would come,' she said. 'I finished the last shawl two days ago.'

'We've been busy with the new order for the Nizam's ladies,' I said, 'but I've brought you the pattern pieces of some velvet slippers to embroider.'

She snipped a thread and began to fold up the wall hanging.

'May I see?' I asked. I studied the new scene. 'Oh!' I said, upset. The vignette showed the Durbar Hall with water gushing through the windows onto the goods arrayed below. 'It's beautifully embroidered,' I said, not wishing to cause offence, 'but I don't like to be reminded of such an unhappy event.'

Usha shrugged. 'Many unhappy events in the history of the Jahanara Mahal are displayed here, but what is important is the truth. There must be no more lies.'

'Lies?' I asked.

She snatched the panel from me and bundled it away. 'Show me what you have brought for me to work on this time.'

A little while later I left but even the prospect of sitting with the chattering women in the workshop while I was in such a melancholy frame of mind exhausted me. I took a walk through the palace grounds, hoping to clear my head, but the happy sounds of children at play as I passed the nursery only increased my misery.

Returning to the *zenana*, I retreated to the window seat to work on a cushion cover. I was threading my needle when Leela came to sit beside me.

'Bee, I have something to tell you,' she said. Her expression was full of apprehension.

'What has happened?' I asked in alarm.

'I hope you will think it happy news but . . . ' She looked down at her fingers, nervously twisting the bangles on her wrist.

I knew immediately. 'Happy news, Leela?'

She nodded, eyes downcast. 'I am expecting a baby.'

'But that's wonderful!' I hugged her, so that she wouldn't see how my chin quivered. 'I'm delighted for you and Ralph.' And I was, though my heart still ached for my own loss.

'Truly?' She smiled shyly. 'I thought it might upset you after . . . '

'How could I not be delighted?' I asked. 'I shall look forward to holding my new niece or nephew in my arms in a few months.'

'I hope it is a boy,' she said. 'All husbands want a boy, don't they?'

I maintained a bright face as we talked about the new baby. After

Leela had gone to see her mother, I stared at my embroidery for a long time without making a single stitch.

In the evening I called on Ralph after he returned from the Residency. When he opened the door to my knock, he'd already changed out of his formal clothing.

'I came to congratulate you, little brother,' I said. 'Leela told me that she's increasing.'

Ralph's ears turned pink and he couldn't contain a wide smile. 'It's marvellous, isn't it? I'm going to see her in a minute or two, in case there's any little thing I can bring her.' Frowning, he said, 'Did you have strange fancies, Bee when you were expecting?'

I shook my head. 'I've heard that some women crave chalk or coal but the best thing you can do for her is to let her know she is loved, despite her changing figure, and to understand that she might be nauseous or very tired at times.'

'I see. Thank you, Bee.'

He caught my hand as I turned to leave. 'I haven't forgotten it's only a year since you lost your own babe and this news must be upsetting for you. I'm sorry.'

His concern for me was so genuine that I was overcome with renewed affection for him. 'It is sad for me but that doesn't alter my great happiness for you.'

He hugged me. 'That isn't my only good news,' he said. 'I'm bursting to tell someone though I'm trusting you to keep this under your hat.'

I nodded.

'James Kirkpatrick's hard work has paid off at last,' he said.

'In what way?'

'The Nizam has signed a treaty with the East India Company.' Ralph appeared to swell with pride as he said the words. 'Kirkpatrick has made excellent progress in persuading Old Nizzy to ditch the French following their defeat at Aboukir Bay. The terms of the treaty are such that we shall provide six thousand troops to protect him, *providing* he dismisses the French from his territory.'

'And what is the advantage to us?'

'Forty-two thousand pounds a year.' Ralph smiled complacently as my jaw dropped. 'And, of course, the British will gain a much stronger foothold in India.'

'I see now why your negotiations were so important,' I said.

'Enough of politics! My wife will be waiting for me. Shall I escort you to the *zenana*?'

I shook my head. 'I intend to take the air before I retire.'

Dusk was falling. In the distance, I heard the mournful howls of jackals. Almost without thinking, my footsteps led me through the gathering darkness into the gardens and I found myself in the pavilion again.

I sat on the *charpai*, hugging one of the cushions to my breast. Closing my eyes, I caught my breath as I smelled a hint of Harry's sandalwood mingling with the mildew. A mere breath of wind stirred my hair as I clutched the cushion and the pavilion echoed with the whispering sighs and murmurs of our love-making.

The following morning, I was breakfasting with the ladies when the eunuch from the Nizam's *zenana* arrived. He presented Samira Begum with a leather bag, stating that it had been sent by Her Esteemed Highness Bakshi Begum. After he'd left, Samira loosened the drawstring and tipped a large pile of gold coins into her lap.

The ladies laughed and clapped their hands and I experienced a profound sense of relief.

'Bakshi Begum must have been pleased with the handkerchiefs we sent her,' said Leela.

I hastened to the Durbar Hall to tell the women we had received payment. Their rousing cheer threatened to make another wall of the palace collapse.

Deepika, who had been voted workshop manager, clapped her hands and the women, including those who worked in the kitchens and nursery, crowded around. 'After all your hard work, now you will be paid,' she said.

I sat on my cushion and laid the coins out before me. Holding up my notebook, I said, 'A careful record has been made of all the hours each of you have worked. You've already voted as to how the money should be divided. The ladies' share of the earnings will be handed to Priya Begum, who controls the *zenana* expenses.'

'As we agreed, different rates will be paid according to the kind of work and level of skill achieved,' said Deepika. 'A certain sum has been kept back to buy more materials for the next order, and a percentage of everyone's earnings will be deducted for the palace repair fund.'

It gave me immense pleasure to see the women's smiling faces as we handed them their wages.

'We'll finish early today,' I said, once everyone had been paid, 'but tomorrow we must be here bright and early.'

Hemanti, her new baby daughter in her arms, came to speak to me before she left. 'I want to thank you,' she said, 'for starting this workshop. I don't know what we would have done if there had been no work.'

I could hardly take my eyes off her baby and stroked the downy little head. 'She's so beautiful,' I murmured.

Hemanti nodded. 'Manohar and I are truly blessed.'

I watched her walk away, my empty arms aching.

Hard work was my salvation over the following weeks. The second order for the Nizam's ladies was completed and delivered and by the end of it I was exhausted. To add to my troubles, I had a recurring stomach complaint, common enough in India but I guessed it was exacerbated by my unhappiness. Despite this, the collection of items for Mrs Clements' acquaintances was finished, packed and then taken away to be delivered to Calcutta by two of the menservants. In addition, I embroidered a waistcoat for Ralph. It delighted me that my brother and I had become friends again and I wanted to acknowledge that with a special present.

Provided it wasn't raining, I fell into the habit of riding out with Lakshmi in the cool of the evenings. As usual, she called for me at the *zenana* one evening so we could walk to the stables together.

'I want to call in on Ralph,' I said. 'I've finished his waistcoat.' I held it up to show her.

Lakshmi fingered the dark red cotton embroidered with cream, black and scarlet. 'It's striking and most beautifully made.' She sighed. 'I never managed to sew neatly. Grandmother tried to teach me but we always became angry with each other.'

'I could teach you, if you like, but you have other skills, Lakshmi,' I said. 'We can't all be good at everything.'

She gave me a strange look. 'But sometimes people imagine we should be.'

Ralph was delighted with his waistcoat and invited us into his quarters.

I stepped through the doorway and halted in sudden alarm.

Harry was sitting at the table with a map and paperwork spread out before him. He half rose to his feet when he saw me and then subsided again.

It wasn't only the burning shame I'd endured because I'd behaved like a wanton and he'd tossed me aside that distressed me. No, it was worse than that. As soon as I saw him I knew I still wanted him and would do it all over again.

'Good evening, Harry,' I said. I couldn't look directly at him and forced a smile onto my lips. He'd avoided me over the past few weeks, too, for which I was thankful. Once or twice I'd seen him in the distance and that had been enough to agitate me for the remainder of the day and then to disturb my dreams.

'Good evening,' he said, and turned to Lakshmi. 'Going riding?'

Mortified by his indifference to me, I clenched my fists and wondered how soon I could escape without making Ralph curious.

'Bee and I often ride out together in the evenings,' said Lakshmi, watching me.

It occurred to me with a jolt that Harry might object to my continuing to ride Breeze since our friendship had ended. It was painful to address it but I didn't want to ride his horse again without his express permission.

'Sangita rarely has time to ride Breeze,' I said. 'Is it acceptable to you if I continue to exercise her?'

'That was my intention,' he said curtly.

Lakshmi bent to look at the map laid out over the table. 'What's going on here?' she asked, pointing to several pins pushed into it.

'Six thousand men, along with a train of artillery, are travelling the hundred and fifty miles up from Guntur to join the two Company battalions already stationed in Hyderabad.' Ralph laughed. 'And we'll see how the French like that!' He picked up a piece of *jaggery* from a bowl on the table and popped it in his mouth.

Harry frowned. 'Perhaps it would be better not to discuss such matters openly, Ralph?'

'My sister is discreet.'

'Don't concern yourself, Harry,' said Lakshmi. 'The news of the secret treaty with the Nizam is already being whispered about in the bazaars.'

'Are we expecting a battle?' I asked.

'That won't be necessary,' said Harry, 'if only the Nizam will give the French their marching orders.'

Ralph shook his head and sighed. 'Kirkpatrick's concerned. It's been weeks since the Nizam signed the treaty. He intends to arrange for two English-officered battalions of mercenaries to station themselves beside the Residency, just in case the French decide to attack before the new troops arrive.'

'A largely unmanageable group of criminals, deserters and

ruffians,' said Harry. 'Nonetheless, they'll fight on behalf of the British. Unless, of course,' he gave a wry smile, 'the French make them a better offer.'

It made me uneasy that matters might come to a head in Hyderabad before we had sufficient troops to protect us. 'How long will it be before the soldiers arrive from Guntor?'

'Another week or two,' said Ralph. 'By the middle of October at the latest.'

Lakshmi looked out of the window at the sky. 'We should go, Bee, or it will be too late for our ride.'

Ralph kissed my cheek. 'Thank you for my handsome waistcoat, Bee. I appreciate the time and effort you took to make it.'

'Goodnight, Harry,' I said.

He nodded and his gaze burned into me as Lakshmi and I left. I glanced over Ralph's shoulder as we said goodnight and Harry was still watching me, his dark eyes unfathomable.

'I hope you aren't still making yourself unhappy over Harry?' said Lakshmi as we walked to the stables.

'Of course not!' I lied.

Chapter 36

Some days later I was in the Durbar Hall with the women when we received a visitor from the Chowmahalla Palace. Without warning, the door from the garden was flung open and Lakshmi stood there, out of breath. 'The Nizam's emissary, Suleiman Medhi Khan, is on his way to speak to you, Bee. I came as fast as I could to warn you.'

The women erupted into excited chatter.

I hurried to the door and was aghast to see that three elephants, four camels and twenty or so men on horseback were already making their way towards the Durbar Hall.

The first of the elephants came to a stop before the open door and a magnificently dressed man with a black beard and moustache descended from the *howdah*. He had the gold mouthpiece of a hookah pipe clamped between his thin lips and was followed by a servant carrying the hookah vase. The remainder of his entourage crowded around him.

Stepping forward, I bowed low and made my *namaste*. 'We are honoured by your visit,' I said, my thoughts in turmoil. Had this emissary been sent to complain about the order delivered to the Nizam's ladies?

'You are Beatrice Sinclair?' The hookah pipe remained firmly between his clenched teeth as he spoke. He eyed the fallen masonry but made no comment.

'I am.' I couldn't prevent myself from staring at the large diamond and pearl aigrette in his turban, which was extravagantly topped by feathers.

Suleiman Medhi Khan lifted a languid hand and servants carrying cushions, bolsters, trunks and decorated floor cloths bustled into the Durbar Hall.

I whispered to Lakshmi to ask if she could arrange some kind of refreshments.

Dumbfounded, I trailed after Suleiman Medhi Khan as he followed his servants. I hoped they wouldn't trip over the rifts in the floor.

Within moments, the servants had laid out the floor cloths, bolsters and cushions and our uninvited guest had made himself comfortable with his finely pleated and full-skirted tunic carefully arranged around him.

The women had retreated to the other end of the hall, where they whispered amongst themselves and peered out from behind their *dupattas* at the deputation.

Suleiman Medhi Khan indicated that I should sit on the small cushion placed at his feet.

'To what do we owe this honour?' I asked.

Slowly, he looked around the Durbar Hall, his gaze pausing at the deep fissures in the wall and floor and then the neatly folded piles of fabric and half-finished embroidered items before turning back to me. He sucked on his hookah pipe and the bubbling of the water within the vase was surprisingly loud in the silence that had fallen over his entourage.

Blowing out a slow stream of honey-perfumed smoke, he stared at me with eyes as calculating as a snake's. 'Her Esteemed Highness,' he said, 'Bakshi Begum, honoured you by wearing a shawl embroidered

290

by this workshop in the presence of her husband, his Supreme Eminence, Nawab Mir Nizam Ali Khan.'

'How gratifying!' I said.

Suleiman Medhi Khan nodded and drew on his hookah again.

Half a dozen servants sidled in with trays of mint tea and a platter of *halwa*, which they passed amongst our guests.

I caught sight of Lakshmi in the doorway. She nodded her head at the refreshments and shrugged as if to say that was the best that could be done at such short notice.

I decided to take the initiative. 'May I enquire if his Exalted Highness approved of our work?'

'You will be delighted to hear that he was moved to grant you the privilege of supplying new decorative caparisons for his elephants.'

'For his elephants!' I remembered my manners. 'That is indeed a very great privilege,' I said, my heart sinking. 'The quality of the embroidery we do here is undeniable but ... ' I hesitated.

I detected a tiny gleam of amusement in Suleiman Medhi Khan's eye as he said, 'Perhaps you have not had the opportunity before to produce such a specialised piece of work?'

'Unfortunately not.' I pasted a confident smile on my face. 'However, perhaps you might allow us to borrow a sample? I am sure then we will be able to make what you require.'

Suleiman Medhi Khan raised his finger and two of the servants lifted up the chest they had brought, placed it on the ground before me and opened the lid.

A vast piece of blue-and-scarlet-embroidered velvet was folded up inside. I spread it out as well as I could and saw immediately that the caparison was sun-faded and fraying in places and the opulent gold embroidery was tattered. Nevertheless, it had once been spectacular.

'I am instructed to inform you that only your best work and materials will be acceptable,' said Suleiman Medhi Khan. 'The caparisons will be used in processions to demonstrate His Exalted Highness' magnificence. The colours are to be in panels of predominantly scarlet and gold with tassels of dark blue, but you are at liberty to design richly embroidered motifs of your own choice. You will present the first caparison to me for inspection and approval.'

I bit my lip. Such a piece would be extremely expensive to produce, both in terms of time and for the high cost of gold thread and velvet. I doubted we had sufficient funds to purchase what we needed.

Suleiman Medhi Khan sighed. 'I have anticipated what you might perceive to be another obstacle in fulfilling His Exalted Highness' command.'

His manservant stepped forward to hand me a heavy leather bag.

I opened it and gasped. I'd never before seen so many gold coins in one place.

'This is an advance of half the payment for the first caparison,' said Suleiman Medhi Khan.

All that gold for half the work! 'How many caparisons will be required?' I stuttered.

'His Eminence has twenty elephants. Twenty-five such items should be sufficient at present.' He blew a stream of smoke in my general direction. 'And then, of course, there are the camels.'

'Of course,' I said faintly, 'we mustn't forget the camels.'

Jahanara Begum rested on a *charpai* in her mirrored sitting room, appearing tiny and frail against the great bank of pillows. 'When you first arrived here, I knew it in my bones!' she said. 'Since the theft of the Rose of Golconda, the Jahanara Mahal has been waiting for you to come and save us.'

'I'm not sure about that,' I demurred. 'There's an enormous amount of work to be done but the payment is extremely generous. Even allowing for the cost of metal wire for the gold work, there will be an excellent profit. And if Suleiman Medhi Khan is happy with the first sample and there are twenty-four more to be made . . .'

'Not forgetting the camels,' said Jahanara Begum, laughter lurking at the corners of her mouth.

I smiled. 'A camel is such an awkward shape to fit. I wonder how many the Nizam owns?'

'Many more than the number of elephants. And then there are his horses ...'

'Perhaps the livery of his servants, too?' I paused. Even the thought of all that work made me feel more exhausted than usual.

'Is there enough in that purse to make some repairs to the palace after the women have been paid?'

'Even if there isn't enough to mend the roof, we can spare the funds to pay some of the menservants to clear the rubble from the back of the palace.'

Jahanara Begum nodded. 'The Nizam's elephants will be the saving of us, *beti*,' she said, 'and if we can provide paid work for the remaining men, I will sleep again at night.'

Deepika accompanied me to the bazaar, where we bought the best quality velvet from Faisal Mahmoud for the caparisons. We charged him with finding a good supplier for the reels of fine gold embroidery wire we needed. I was relieved to have Deepika at my side to negotiate a commission for Faisal that wasn't too exorbitant.

The workshop women were enthusiastic about the new enterprise and full of excitement that, by working together, we might save the palace.

'Who knows where it will end?' Hemanti said to me, her eyes shining. 'Once the nobles of Hyderabad hear of our work for the Nizam, they will all want to buy our embroidery.' She bent low to touch my feet. 'We could not have done this without you.'

It gave me such pleasure to see the women's confidence blossom as they discussed how best to organise themselves into efficient working parties, but even more to feel that I was finally becoming accepted.

'If we are to finish the caparisons in good time we must take on more women for the plain sewing,' said Deepika. 'The current needlewomen who show aptitude may then be trained to become embroiderers.'

'I have a list of women I had to turn away after the initial sewing trials,' I said. 'Many of them will be perfectly suitable.' I glanced around the Durbar Hall at the women bent over swathes of scarlet velvet. 'We'll need more space, too.'

Deepika laughed. 'That is not a difficulty at the Jahanara Mahal.'

'I never imagined that this workshop might grow from making a few reticules and embroidered slippers to something so much greater,' I said.

'None of us did,' said Deepika. She puffed up her chest. 'Perhaps we women hold hidden possibilities a man cannot dream of?'

We designed the caparisons so that they could be embroidered in manageable sections and then laid out on vast tables to be stitched together. I knew better now than to insult the ladies of the *zenana* by suggesting that they should train the workshop women in embroidery skills. Instead, we gave them the most complicated designs to work while Deepika and I, the most accomplished embroiderers in the workshop, set up training sessions for those women who had the aptitude and desire to learn.

At the end of each day, even though I had the satisfaction of seeing the women's skills growing as the first caparison began to take shape, my eyes were gritty with fatigue. All the time I was sewing, my thoughts ran over and over the shameless way I had allowed, no, encouraged, Harry to behave, and how he had then cast me aside. And yet, I still loved him.

The following day I went into the once-grand room adjacent to the Durbar Hall. It was badly water-stained and the windows were cracked and broken but I thought it might be possible to repair it sufficiently to extend our working space. Since he had always been so willing to help us out in the workshop, I sought out Hemanti's husband, Manohar.

I found him squatting on the ground outside his quarters with a group of other men.

'May I speak with you for a moment?' I said.

He jumped up with alacrity and followed me to stand a little distance away from the others.

'Jahanara Begum wishes to make the back of the palace safe,' I said. 'I wondered if you and a few of the other men would like some paid work, stacking all the masonry carefully and propping up the openings to the servants' old quarters with strong timbers? The windows in the room on the other side of the Durbar Hall need to be repaired too, along with repairs to a roof leak. Then the boundary walls to the grounds must be made secure from intruders.'

'French soldiers?' asked Manohar.

'Exactly. It makes me uncomfortable to think that they might simply walk in.'

He nodded. 'The men and I shall keep watch most particularly.'

'That would give us all peace of mind, Manohar. There's enough money to pay a dozen men but I'd like you to recommend which ones will do a good day's work.' I told him how much we could pay each man.

His eyes lit up. 'Definitely I shall be most happy to do this for you, *sahiba*. We shall be ready to start work straightaway.'

'Thank you, Manohar.' Relieved that the first small step had been taken to repair the palace, I went to visit Usha.

Jai was sitting on the doorstep and jumped up to greet me. 'Sangita has made some *halva*,' he said. 'Would you like to try it?'

Sangita called out a welcome and we exchanged pleasantries for a while. When I'd finished my *halva*, I put the dish aside. 'I've brought more work for Usha,' I said.

'She is in her room as usual.'

I found her embroidering the wall hanging of the Jahanara Mahal but she folded it away without showing me the new scene.

'It is excellent news that the workshop has such prestigious work for the Nizam,' she said, her voice far more animated than usual.

'Isn't it marvellous?' I said. 'I've brought a caparison panel for you to work on. Gold work is required but I know that will present no difficulty to a skilled needlewoman such as yourself. Here's a drawing to show the pattern but you are free to make small changes if you wish.'

'Gold work and velvet! This will be expensive.' She examined the fine gold wire and silk thread that I handed to her.

'The Nizam is paying us well so we can afford the best materials and still have enough to make some repairs.'

'Repairs? What kind of repairs?' Absent-mindedly, she wound the gold wire around her finger as we spoke.

Her voice was so sharp that I looked at her in surprise. 'I'm afraid for the children playing on the fallen stonework, in case they hurt themselves. The men are going to stack the stone and secure the boundary walls until we can afford to rebuild the back of the palace properly.'

'Only that?'

'Eventually we will be able to buy materials to mend the roof.' I saw that she'd wound the gold wire so tightly around her finger that the tip had grown dark. 'Usha! You'll hurt yourself.'

She drew a breath and looked at me with unfocused eyes. Blinking, she unwound the wire.

'You have everything you need for this panel?'

Slowly, she nodded.

'Then I shall take my leave of you but you can always ask Jai to find me if you want to send me a message.'

Since she didn't answer, I went to say goodbye to Sangita.

Chapter 37

Mrs Clements sent her manservant, Bhupal, with a note for me, requesting I call on her at once.

I have important news. To that end, I have sent a palanquin to fetch you.

It appeared that Mrs Clements had no wish to suffer the awkwardness of visiting me in the *zenana* again. Asking Bhupal to make the palanquin wait, I changed into my dove grey dress to avoid offending her delicate sensibilities.

'My dear Mrs Sinclair!' Her cheeks bore hectic spots of colour and a strand of frizzy red hair had escaped from her cap. She clasped my hands and drew me into the sitting room. 'I hardly know where to begin, it's all so sudden. I know, tea!' She clapped her hands for Bhupal again and despatched him to the kitchen.

'You seem flustered,' I said. 'I believe you have some important news?'

'Indeed I have! The Residency is all at sixes and sevens but Mr Clements slipped out to inform me of recent events.'

'Which are?' I prompted.

'Oh, yes! I do believe I shall soon be returning to England.'

'But why?'

'We've received the dreadful news that Napoleon Bonaparte has landed in Egypt.' She fanned her overheated face.

'I thought Admiral Nelson had crushed him at Aboukir Bay?'

'He did but Napoleon has rallied and captured both Alexandria and Cairo. He intends to re-establish the old route through Suez, abandoning the longer route to India by the Cape of Good Hope. So, you see, his troops will be able to reach us far more quickly.'

This was devastating news indeed.

'A message Napoleon sent from Cairo to Tipu Sultan was intercepted by our spies,' said Mrs Clements. 'He wrote to say he has an innumerable and invincible army and fully intends to release Tipu from *the iron yoke of England*. The nerve of the man!'

'I suppose the question is,' I said, 'now that the Nizam knows about Napoleon's successes, will he break the new treaty? Perhaps he won't dismiss the French forces after all.'

'All I know is that Mr Clements thinks it safer for me to return home. There's our son to think of. I cannot bear to contemplate what might happen to him if full-scale fighting with the French breaks out in Hyderabad.'

'Our battalions will be here soon from Guntor . . .'

'Three days' march away, apparently, but they will be as nothing against the might of the French forces. Why, they already have fourteen thousand men here!' She gave a shuddering sigh. 'So I wondered if you wished to return to England with me? We were good companions on our outward journey.'

'Return?' I pictured the green fields and peaceful villages of Hampshire, safely out of Napoleon's reach. And, of course, Alice in possession of what had once been my home. I shook my head. 'There's nothing there for me.'

'If you're caught up in a war here,' said Mrs Clements sharply, 'there may be nothing for you anywhere.'

'Perhaps not but I prefer to take my chances with my family.'

'Family? Well, there's your brother, I suppose.' She went to her writing desk and pulled out a letter. 'Don't say I didn't warn you but if you're determined to be obstinate and remain in the line of fire, perhaps this will keep you occupied. My brother has received your samples and responded to my letter. He wishes you to supply him with this order for his shop.'

I took the letter from her and my heart swelled as I read the long list of articles required. 'Thank you so much, Mrs Clements. I'm delighted to tell you that the workshop also recently received a large and prestigious order from the Nizam and we're in the process of enlarging our workspace and employing additional workers. We'll complete these items for your brother as soon as possible.'

'All I can say,' sighed Mrs Clements, 'is that I hope, if you are rash enough to remain here, the trade routes to England still exist after Napoleon has finished with Hyderabad.'

Three days later, in a state of high excitement, Jai came running to find me in the workshop.

'Bandit has done it, *aunty-ji*! He's killed his first rat. Isn't he clever?'

'Undoubtedly an astonishingly intelligent dog.'

'Look! It's enormous.' Jai unwrapped the bundle he carried and held the dead rat out towards me. 'Will you show it to Jahanara Begum?'

'Perhaps, as an old lady, she might be squeamish.' The sight of the rat's yellow teeth and bloodstained throat certainly made me queasy. 'I'll tell her all about it but would you be kind enough to bury it before it begins to smell?'

'I'll throw it over the palace walls, *aunty-ji*. The jackals will finish it off tonight.'

'Very good.' I pressed my fingers to my mouth as my stomach threatened to rebel. 'I have to visit the bazaar, Jai. Would you like to come with me?'

A short while later we set off together to visit Faisal Mahmoud, who had procured more embroidery silks and gold and silver brocade for the workshop. The sky was heavy and I hoped it wouldn't rain again before we returned to the palace. As we crossed the narrow bridge over the Musi, we leaned over the wall to look at the river churning under the bridge. The fast-flowing torrent had been heavily swollen by the recent rains and tree branches, dead cats and other detritus swirled by.

The bazaar was as hectic as ever. We pushed our way amongst the throng but today the beehive hum of voices gave me a headache and the ripe smells of overcrowded humanity, animal dung and sweet frangipani sickened me.

Jai stopped and cocked his head. 'What's that?' he said.

From outside the city walls came a fast-paced, regular noise, growing increasingly louder. Thump, thump. Thump, thump, it went, on alternate higher and then lower notes. Over the rhythm came a hoarse shout and then the sound of a drum thudding in time.

'Soldiers!' I said. 'It must be the battalions from Guntur.'

We weren't the only ones who'd heard them. I snatched Jai's hand and gripped my basket as we were swept along by the eager crowd. Pressed closely amongst the horde in the narrow streets, I had to make an effort not to panic. Eventually we surged out of the eastern gate of the walled city.

And then we saw them. The soldiers passed by in a relentless stream, never breaking stride, stopping for nobody. Their marching steps thundered through the air, ricocheting off the city walls until the sound was so deafening it vibrated inside my skull, my heart banging in time with the drumbeats. I was filled with profound relief that they had arrived at last.

Jai and I flattened ourselves against the ancient stone and watched until the very last soldier and buffalo-drawn gun carriage had passed, followed by ragged children and a pack of barking pariah dogs.

'Come on!' yelled Jai. His hand slipped from mine as he ran after them.

Rain spotted my face as I called out to him but he was caught up in the feverish excitement and darted on ahead. Afraid I'd lose him, I had no choice but to follow.

By the time we reached the Musi, close to the French cantonments, it was raining heavily. The soldiers began to ford the river, leading the buffaloes and manhandling the heavy artillery behind them. There was a great deal of shouting and disturbance as the cannons became bogged down in what were normally muddy shallows but were now deep and swirling waters.

We watched for a while. Once the downpour was too heavy to allow us to see what was happening, we turned and hurried back to the Jahanara Mahal.

A week later, after a long day in the workshop, Leela came to greet me when I returned to the *zenana*.

'Ralph came home early,' she said. 'He wants you to attend a reception tonight at the Residency. It is to welcome Captain John Malcolm, James Kirkpatrick's new assistant.'

My heart sank. I'd hoped to retire early and attending a reception was the last thing I wanted to do. 'I've nothing suitable to wear,' I protested.

'The dove grey dress you wore the other day is most graceful,' said Leela. 'It would look very fine with your pink shawl.'

I sighed. 'The dress isn't an evening gown but the shawl you made is so beautiful it makes even the plainest garment look elegant.'

'Will you allow me to arrange your hair? There are pink roses in the garden and I shall find you some jewels.'

Once I'd washed and put on the dress and shawl, I was content to sit while Leela twisted my hair into an elaborate chignon, nestled pink rosebuds amongst my curls and dabbed attar of roses behind my ears.

Samira Begum clasped a necklace of pearls around my neck and Bimla slid her bracelets of rose gold over my wrist. Jasmin lent me a handkerchief she'd embroidered with roses and led me into the sitting room. The fuss and attention when the ladies admired my appearance revived me.

'Do not forget to take notice of every little thing tonight,' said Leela. 'You must be the eyes and ears of our *zenana*.'

It warmed my heart to have such female friends for the first time in my life but I was sad that a life in purdah denied Leela the opportunity of a pleasurable outing with her husband.

Priya Begum turned me around. 'You had become one of us but, just for tonight, you are a perfect English lady again.'

I flushed with delight at her comment and was filled with love for them all.

It had rained all week and Ralph arranged for the palanquin to wait by the main doors of the palace so we wouldn't get soaked. Plump and pomaded in his evening dress, he handed me inside. We kept the palanquin's curtains closed to avoid being spattered by mud.

'Listen to that damned rain hammering on the roof!' he said. 'The Musi is in full spate. When the remainder of our battalions arrived last night, it was impossible for them to bring their artillery safely across the river. They had to stay on the other bank.'

'On the French side? Will the French attack them?'

Ralph shrugged. 'It's astonishing that hasn't happened already. The wretched Nizam still hasn't issued orders to them to disarm. It feels as if the whole of Hyderabad is holding its breath, waiting.'

The palanquin lurched to a halt outside the Residency's domed pavilion and Ralph led me inside. The pavilion served as the state dining room and a number of men stood about inside with glasses in their hands.

Ralph fetched us glasses of wine and introduced me to several of the Residency staff. I saw Mr and Mrs Clements talking to Mrs Ure, the doctor's wife, on the other side of the room but, before I could speak to them, James Kirkpatrick joined us.

'Mrs Sinclair! How delightful to see you. I do hope you haven't been too distressed by the present uneasy military situation?'

'Naturally, the uncertainty makes us all anxious,' I said.

'My sister has remained admirably calm in the circumstances,' said Ralph.

'I assure you, Mrs Sinclair,' said Kirkpatrick, 'everything is being done to chivvy the Nizam into ordering the French to lay down their arms.'

'I'm sure that it is.'

'Meanwhile, I'm delighted to hear from your brother that you've found favour with the Nizam and his wives.'

'The workshop is thriving. We've received a prestigious commission to make the state caparisons for the Nizam's elephants and a second order for his *zenana*.'

'Impressive!'

'My sister has herself embroidered a fine waistcoat for me, too,' said Ralph.

Kirkpatrick smiled. 'Then, when the current difficulties are resolved, I shall know where to come when I require one for myself.' He glanced over my shoulder. 'Will you excuse me? Captain Malcolm has arrived.'

'Ralph, tell me about Captain Malcolm,' I murmured as the Resident walked away. 'He's Kirkpatrick's new assistant, I understand?'

'Malcolm is Scottish,' said Ralph succinctly, 'and a great supporter of Wellesley.'

Out of the corner of my eye I saw a lean figure approaching us through the gathering. I froze when I recognised Harry.

'Good evening,' he said. He was attired in immaculate evening dress and appeared perfectly at home at a Residency reception.

I forced my lips into a smile but his handsome looks and the shaming memory of his rejection had struck me dumb again.

Ralph clapped him on the shoulder. 'I thought you might return too late to join us tonight, Harry.'

'I've been watching the troops struggling to ford the river,' he said. 'It's going to be impossible to get the artillery across until the waters subside.'

'Jai and I were there when the first battalions crossed,' I said. 'It was difficult enough before all the rain that followed.'

Harry looked at me and, discomfited, I dropped my gaze.

'My son spends a lot of time with you, doesn't he?'

'We enjoy each other's company. On that afternoon,' I said, endeavouring to maintain light conversation, 'Jai came to tell me Bandit had killed his first rat. I can confirm it was enormous and bore the signs of being most savagely attacked. Jai had the corpse all wrapped up in a cloth, hoping I'd present it to Jahanara Begum to prove Bandit was earning his keep.'

Harry laughed. 'And you managed not to have a fit of the vapours?'

'Certainly not!' I said.

Ralph was craning his neck to look at the Resident and Captain Malcolm. 'I can't help wondering,' he said, 'if Malcolm has been sent by Wellesley to make sure Kirkpatrick doesn't deviate from his new Forward Policy.'

'Forward Policy?' I asked.

'Wellesley's intention is to annex as much of India as possible for the British government,' said Harry, all traces of laughter gone from his eyes. 'He aims to increase Britain's dominion over the continent at every possible opportunity.'

I was shocked. 'But that makes him no better than Napoleon!'

'I can only cling to the hope that Britain will take a more benign approach than France does. At least Kirkpatrick prefers to work with the locals, rather than simply to subjugate them.'

Mrs Clements bustled towards us, elegantly dressed in emerald silk trimmed with several yards of black lace. She carried the reticule embellished with jet beads that I'd made for her to take to Calcutta.

Once the usual pleasantries had been made, she laid her fingers on my wrist. 'It's all arranged,' she said. 'I am to leave for England tomorrow. I implore you once again, my dear, won't you come home with me?'

Harry, in the process of lifting his glass to his lips, started and spilled a few drops of wine.

'Go home?' said Ralph, frowning at me. 'This is your home now.'

'I have no intention of returning,' I said, 'but I thank you for your kind invitation, Mrs Clements.'

'I beg you to reconsider,' she urged. 'It's not safe for you here. Mark my words, there will be fighting. At least remove yourself to somewhere less dangerous. It's difficult enough that there are so few European women in Hyderabad but, if the enemy prevails, heaven knows what it will be like with thousands of French soldiers rampaging through the city, filled with bloodlust.' She gave me a pointed stare. 'Or *worse*.'

'I have my brother to protect me,' I said.

'Absolutely!' said Ralph, throwing back his shoulders in a vain attempt to appear fearless and intrepid.

Harry coughed to suppress a chuckle but couldn't hide the gleam of amusement in his eyes.

Poor portly Ralph was so unlike Harry. I remembered then, running my fingers down Harry's naked back, stroking the firm skin and taut muscles. He caught me looking at him and, perhaps, read the yearning in my face, because his expression became serious again. I couldn't look away and, to my shame, felt tears start to my eyes.

Mrs Clements sighed heavily. 'If nothing I can say will make you change your mind, Mrs Sinclair, then I'm sorry for it.'

I blinked rapidly and smiled at her. 'I appreciate your kindness, Mrs Clements, and wish you a safe journey.'

After she'd returned to her husband, Ralph patted my hand. 'I hope she hasn't rattled you, Bee?'

'I was already rattled,' I said, 'but I can't leave India, not when, at last, I've returned to the place where my heart belongs.'

Harry stared at me, a slight frown creasing his brow.

Chapter 38

I was in the workshop, supervising the sewing together of the finished panels of the first of the elephant caparisons, when the Nizam's emissary, Suleiman Medhi Khan, called again. This time he had brought only half a dozen horsemen with him and there was no question of his servants bringing in piles of floor cushions for his comfort.

I made my salaam to him and invited him into the Durbar Hall.

'My visit will be brief,' he said, teeth still clenched around the mouthpiece of his customary hookah. 'His Supreme Eminence is removing his court to the Fort of Golconda this very morning and my presence is required. Since it is not yet known how long the court will remain there, I shall take this opportunity to inspect the work completed so far.'

'We've made good progress,' I said. 'In fact, if you would care to accompany me to the sewing table, you will see that we are stitching together the embroidered panels. The gold and sapphire tassels are already being sewn to some of them.'

The women working on the caparison retreated to the other end of the hall.

Suleiman Medhi Khan walked slowly around the sewing table in complete silence, only bending over now and again to scrutinise some detail.

The rich tones of the gold-work border glinted in the sun from the roof light above and the fabulously intricate embroidery worked on the scarlet and sapphire velvet made me proud to be involved in such a commission.

Suleiman Medhi Khan's utter silence, except for the bubbling of his hookah, began to make me anxious and I glanced at the women, huddled together and watching us covertly.

Finally, the Nizam's emissary straightened up and waved a hand languidly to indicate I might approach him.

I stood before him, remembering to keep my gaze downcast and my expression demure. He blew out a cloyingly sweet stream of smoke from his hookah and I had to resist waving it away.

'It is satisfactory,' he said. 'You will therefore continue to produce the additional twenty-four caparisons.'

'We are delighted you find our work acceptable,' I said, my pulse dancing a little jig.

Suleiman Medhi Khan nodded to one of the servants, who came forward with another leather bag of gold coins. 'Each month I will call to inspect the work, take away any finished items and bring you another purse.'

I took the heavy bag of gold from the servant. 'We are honoured by your visit, Suleiman Medhi Khan,' I said, making a low salaam. I hadn't expected to be paid so promptly but now I held in my trembling hands the means to make some significant repairs to the Jahanara Mahal.

He gave me a thin smile. 'In return, the Nawab Mir Nizam Ali Khan's elephants will be honoured by the high quality of your work.' He gathered his entourage and left the Durbar Hall in a swirl of tobacco-scented smoke.

*

After I finished work for the day I went to find Manohar. I was pleased to discover that, despite the intermittent heavy rain, he and his men had made significant progress. Now that we'd received payment from the Nizam's emissary, I was able to instruct them to continue.

In the *zenana*, the ladies were putting away their embroidery when I told them the good news of Suleiman Medhi Khan's unexpected visit.

'So, as long as he continues to approve the caparisons, we have work enough to last for two years?' said Samira Begum, her face illuminated by her smile.

I sagged back against the wall, rubbing my tired eyes. 'Our hard work has proved worth the effort. The workshop is a success and I'm sure we'll receive new orders once the wealthy families of Hyderabad know we have been trusted by the Nizam. Now we can pay the women again and begin to make the palace safe.'

'All of this in only a few months,' said Priya Begum, dabbing her eyes with her *dupatta*. 'My mother is right: the Jahanara Mahal was waiting for you, Bee Sinclair.'

I hoped she didn't see the sadness behind my smile. It was rewarding to have brought the workshop into being but it would never compensate me for not having a husband and child of my own. 'The workshop women are relieved to be earning enough to feed their families but their greatest pleasure today was that many of their husbands will now also be employed. The Nizam has been generous.'

Priya Begum sighed. 'But he has retreated to Golconda?'

'He must believe the situation between the French and the British in Hyderabad is dangerous,' said Leela. 'My husband does not sleep at night for worrying.'

Jyoti brought us mint tea and a platter of fruit and sweetmeats and we set aside talk of the worrying prospect of two armies poised for battle on our doorstep.

Sipping my tea, I listened to the ladies' inconsequential gossip, happy to take my rest in pleasant company after a busy day. I overheard Parvati Begum murmuring to Bimla that her daughter Esha had become a woman.

'I had prepared her so she wasn't frightened by the appearance of blood,' Parvati Begum said, 'but I can no longer ignore the fact that Esha is fourteen. She must have a suitable husband very soon.'

Parvati's voice faded away, drowned by a rushing sound in my ears. Despite the evening warmth, I shivered, suddenly overcome by a deathly chill. Black spots began to dance around the edges of my vision. I put my tea glass down with a clatter on the marble floor.

'Bee?' Leela's face loomed into view. 'Are you all right?'

My lips were numb. 'I feel faint,' I mumbled.

'Put your head between your knees.'

I shut my eyes and buried my face between my knees, trying to control my panicky breathing.

Leela rested her hand on the back of my neck until the fit had passed.

'Are you unwell?' she asked, chafing my hands.

'Only overtired,' I whispered, 'and then there's the worry about what will happen if the French attack.'

Samira Begum and Parvati had come to see what was happening.

'Go to bed,' said Samira Begum, 'and rest tomorrow. You have been working too hard.'

Leela stroked the hair off my face, her bracelets tinkling. 'I will send Jyoti to rub your head with scented oils until you sleep.'

The ladies fluttered around me, patting and comforting me and promising to bring me herbal tea and medicine. There was a lump in my throat as they accompanied me to my room, drew off my shoes and laid me on the bed. They closed the shutters against the low rays of the evening sun and left Jyoti to massage my scalp. After a while, I feigned sleep and she tiptoed away.

Tears seeped from my eyes. The ladies had shown me such kindness and concern, so much more than my mother ever had, but I was going to bring dishonour on them all. It hadn't occurred to me, until I heard Parvati mention that Esha had begun her courses, that I had missed mine. I'd been so preoccupied and unhappy after Harry rejected me that I hadn't considered the possible consequence of what had happened between us.

A perfumed garden, a sky studded with stars and a heart full of misplaced love had seduced me into a bewitching night of passion. And now, as surely as the darkness follows the light, what in other circumstances would have been a wondrous event, was going to bring about my shame and condemnation.

It rained heavily again that night and I barely slept, calculating over and over the days since the last time I had bled, but my courses were always regular and I was sure there was no mistake. It was obvious to me now that my exhaustion and nausea were brought about by pregnancy. And I wanted this baby, Harry's child, so very much. To know that he didn't want me struck a pain in my heart, as sharp as any dagger.

In the morning the downpour had ceased. I could only wish that my own fears had evaporated as quickly as the rain. I returned to the workshop and moved through the day in a daze, embroidering, answering questions and inspecting finished work, while all the time I tried to ignore my rising panic. It was impossible to imagine how I might remain at the Jahanara Mahal but I had nowhere else to go. I felt like a mouse in a maze and could detect no means of escape.

My wandering thoughts were disrupted when Manohar came into the workshop, his *dhoti* and face dirt-streaked, and asked to speak to me.

'We have moved the fallen stones away from the palace,' he said, 'but there is something I must show you. Please, memsahib, will you come with me?'

Outside, the men leaned on their shovels, talking animatedly amongst themselves. The tumbled blocks of stone were stacked in neat piles ready to be used in rebuilding the rear wall. The damaged balconies that had been hanging drunkenly from the first floor had been taken down and the yawning gaps in the wall supported with timber props.

'You've made a neat job of making it safe,' I said.

'We repaired the gap in the wall around the palace,' Manohar said, 'but ...' He shrugged. 'This morning it has been knocked down again.'

'But who would have done that?'

He rubbed his nose. 'Some people say it will anger the gods if we rebuild what they knocked down.'

I sighed. I knew better now than to antagonise him by saying that was nonsense. 'What was it you wished to show me, Manohar?'

'Do you see here?' We stood about ten feet away from the exterior wall of the Durbar Hall and he pointed to an area of earth that had recently been hidden beneath the tumbled masonry.

A ditch, about a yard wide and a foot or two deep, ran from one end of the Durbar Hall, growing shallower as it disappeared into the overgrown shrubbery. 'What is it?' I asked. 'A gulley to take the rainwater away from the foundations?'

Manohar's eyes gleamed with excitement. 'There is a story in the village that in our great-grandfathers' day, there was an ancient hidden passage leading from the Durbar Hall out onto the hillside. Those were dangerous times and it was a secret escape for the nobles and warriors in case marauding war parties attacked the fort.'

'You think this ditch might mark the course of a secret underground passage?'

He shrugged his agreement.

'If that is so, it appears it has partly fallen in.'

Manohar nodded. 'The monsoon rainwater pooled on the palace

roof then seeped down through the walls and a servants' passage that has been closed for years. It must have flowed out under the floors.'

'And you think it went down into the secret passage?'

'There is still water flowing out over the hillside,' he said.

I studied the ditch. 'If the water has washed away the roof supports of the tunnel then it might be dangerous.'

'Perhaps the men and I should dig into part of the ditch to see? We can fill in the tunnel with earth and rubble again later to make it safe.'

'That's an excellent idea, Manohar.' I frowned while I thought. 'I've not seen anything inside the Durbar Hall to indicate a secret passage but I shall examine the walls carefully. Please carry on here.'

He shouted at the men, beckoning them towards him.

I returned to the Durbar Hall but decided not to disrupt the women's concentration with talk of a secret passage. They would find out soon enough.

At the end of the day, after the others had gone home, I walked around the walls, running my finger over the panelling and the inlaid semi-precious stones, searching for a hidden door. I smiled sadly to myself, remembering a similar but long-ago search made by three children looking for the lost Rose of Golconda. As before, there was no sign of what I sought.

I collected a newly cut panel of scarlet velvet for the next caparison, embroidery silks, gold wire and mirrored sequins, and put them into my basket before setting off to see Usha.

Jai was playing chase in the courtyard with his foster brothers and sisters when I arrived. He ran up to me and grabbed my hand, breathless with excitement. '*Aunty-ji*, did you hear?'

I looked down at his shining face and my heart turned over with a sharp pang of longing. I had grown so fond of this little boy, Harry's son, and wished he were my own. If I were forced to leave the palace in shame, he would never know he had a sibling. It hurt me that I'd lose Jai, too.

He shook my hand. '*Aunty-ji?*'

'I'm sorry. Did I hear what?'

'The men have found a secret passage under the ground!'

'We aren't sure yet if it's a tunnel,' I said.

'It is! I know it is. And I'm sure that's where the Rose of Golconda is hidden. My father has told me all about the Rose.'

'I'm sure he has,' I said. 'I remember looking for it with him when I was only your age.'

'This time, we'll find it.'

There was such confidence in his tone that I almost believed it.

Sangita invited me inside. 'I'm worried about my mother,' she said in an undertone. 'Something has upset her but she won't tell me what it is.'

'I've brought her more work,' I said. 'Shall I take it away again?'

She shook her head. 'Embroidery gives her less time to brood. She won't hurt you but her behaviour is a little strange.'

I went into Usha's room. The Jahanara Mahal wall-hanging was draped over her knees. When I sat beside her she hastily folded it so I couldn't make out the details.

'I'd love to see how you have progressed with it,' I said.

She shook her head. 'Not yet.'

I lifted the scarlet velvet out of my basket. 'I've brought you another panel. This one is to have mirrored sequins sewn around the edge.' I held out the gold wire, the embroidery silks and a scaled sketch of the design, but she didn't take them from me. Nonplussed, I placed them on her *charpai*.

She stared as if she wasn't really seeing me then started to clean her fingernails with a needle. 'Jai said the servants are digging in the ground, searching for a tunnel.'

'Some of the earth has sunk at the back of the palace, underneath where the wall tumbled down in the monsoon,' I said. 'The men are going to see if it's an underground passage that has collapsed. If so, they'll make it safe.'

She scraped at her nails. 'Why must they meddle?' Her voice was harsh. 'Tell them to take care not to anger the gods!' She stabbed the needle into her finger and a drop of bright blood fell onto her wall hanging.

It alarmed me when she began to rock backwards and forwards, muttering to herself and rubbing at the blood spot.

'Usha?' I leaned closer to try and hear what she was saying. It was no use; she'd retreated somewhere inside herself again so I stood up to leave.

She snatched at my wrist with a claw-like hand, making me start. Her eyes were clouded and she no longer looked sane.

'What is hidden,' she whispered hoarsely, 'must stay hidden or the curse will fall upon us.'

Shivering at the sudden reappearance of her deranged state of mind, I closed the door behind me and hurried away.

Chapter 39

The following evening, Lakshmi came to the *zenana*. 'The rain has cleared. It's a beautiful evening for a ride,' she said.

I wondered if horse riding might be dangerous for a woman in my condition. I was bone-weary from lying awake worrying about the future and knew that, sooner or later, I must tell Harry what had happened. I dreaded his reaction to what was bound to be unwelcome news.

'You're so pale and tense,' said Lakshmi. 'A ride will take our minds off any impending battles.'

I found the prospect of feeling the wind in my hair again appealing. The intense heat had gone out of the day and the evening was lit by the dusty glow of the sunset as we walked towards the stables. Digging had commenced outside the Durbar Hall and Lakshmi and I peered down into the ditch.

'It does look as if it's an underground passage, doesn't it?' she said. 'You can see the rotten timbers that were used to shore up the sides and the roof. I'd heard rumours that a passage existed but no one knew where it was.'

When we reached the stable yard, my heart began to pound at the sight of Harry tending to Zephyr.

He nodded at us as he ran his hands down the horse's foreleg and then lifted it to inspect the hoof.

'A stone?' asked Lakshmi.

'I removed it yesterday and wanted to be sure it'd healed.' He straightened up and mounted Zephyr. 'I'm sure I don't need to warn you both to stay on this side of the river if you're going to ride? The French will have scouts all over the place in the current circumstances.'

'It seems to be a stalemate,' said Lakshmi.

'James Kirkpatrick went to Golconda last night to give the Nizam an ultimatum,' said Harry. 'If he hesitates any longer before dismissing the French, Kirkpatrick will have no other option but to attack.'

'Why don't you ride with us?' asked Lakshmi.

'Not tonight,' said Harry, looking down from Zephyr's back.

His gaze sought mine and I wondered if he saw the naked longing in my eyes or the warmth flooding my face. Somehow, soon, I would have to summon the courage to tell him about the baby.

He frowned slightly and said, 'I have something else to do this evening.' Wheeling Zephyr around, he trotted smartly out of the yard.

After he'd disappeared, I noticed Lakshmi was watching me intently.

'Harry is right,' she said. 'We must stay on this side of the river.' Her mouth curved in a smile. 'Who knows what fate might befall us if we met a wicked Frenchman?'

'I suspect a wicked Frenchman would be more than a little surprised if he attempted to take any liberties with *you*, Lakshmi. You'd see him off in no time, probably without his ears.'

Lakshmi laughed as if I'd said something frightfully amusing. The evening sun struck blue fire from her sapphire turban pin. She linked her arm through mine as we went to fetch the horses.

*

317

The following day passed quietly enough. I spent some time with Hemanti and a small group of the women, teaching them how to embroider simple motifs onto handkerchiefs. It was a joy to see their delight as their skills increased, bringing them a chance of higher remuneration.

Afterwards, I worked on my own embroidery, while mentally rehearsing how to tell Harry of his impending fatherhood. If he was prepared to support me, I could travel to another city and pretend to be recently widowed. Or perhaps I'd tell Ralph I was returning to England on the pretext of seeking further business for the workshop. Once the child was born, I'd return to the Jahanara Mahal and say I'd adopted it. The fabrication was thin but I might be able to brazen it out.

That evening, I declined to ride with Lakshmi and, instead, took a walk through the grounds. Surrounded by the sweet perfume of frangipani and roses, I attempted to find calm in the sound of trickling water in the rills and fountains.

The sun was setting in a blaze of misty gold when Ralph, returning from the Residency, found me in the courtyard garden sitting on the edge of the fountain pool. He plumped down beside me with a weary sigh.

'Difficult day?' I asked, as one of the peacocks came and pecked the ground by our feet.

He massaged his temples. 'The tension at the Residency is palpable.'

'Harry said Kirkpatrick has given the Nizam a deadline.' I batted away a persistent mosquito that whined around my face.

'We've still heard nothing from His Highness so Kirkpatrick has arranged for the *sepoys* to start a mutiny behind the French lines early tomorrow morning.'

'Why?' I trailed my fingers in the pool, watching the goldfish flip their tails as they swam away.

'We hope the resulting chaos will disrupt any resistance when our men attack the French forces.'

'But they have so many more men than we do.'

'I know.' My brother chewed at a corner of his moustache. 'Sixteen thousand against our force of less than a third of that.'

It was a frightening thought.

'Kirkpatrick is sending his spy to the French cantonments tonight to find out the mood of their men. He'll cut the bullock traces, too. Then the French won't be able to move their artillery, which will even up our chances.'

'Spy?' I snatched my fingers out of the pool and shook water off them. 'Don't tell me it's Harry who is going into that lion's den? It'll be dangerous.' I heard the edge of panic creeping into my voice. 'What if he's caught? They'd kill him!'

Ralph glanced at me and then away again. 'What makes you think he is a spy?'

'Ralph! I may, in your opinion, be a mere woman but I'm not entirely deficient in my wits. I know Harry was in the army and is frequently away on unspecified reconnaissance missions. He told me himself his mother was French and he's fluent in that language, as well as various Indian dialects, all of which would allow him to slip undetected into the enemy camp.'

'I'm not at liberty to comment on such matters.' Ralph pursed his mouth.

'Do you have any idea how pompous you sound? When is he going to the French camp?'

My brother sighed heavily. 'Since you already know so much, I can tell you he left the Residency just before I did. He wanted to say goodbye to Jai before he went tonight. But for God's sake, don't go blabbing about it to anyone else.'

I reared to my feet. The peacock squawked, rattled its tail feathers and flew up to the top of the trellis. 'So he might still be here?'

Ralph laughed mirthlessly. 'You're not thinking of trying to stop him? In any case, he'll be back before dawn.'

I hurried away without answering him.

'Bee? Bee, for goodness' sake!'

Ignoring his plaintive cry, I broke into a trot. The stables ... Harry would take Zephyr. Or would that make him too conspicuous? My steps faltered and I changed direction. Jai would know if his father had already left.

The sun was sinking fast now and Harry would want to be sitting around the campfire, sharing his supper with the French soldiers and listening to their talk before they turned in. If they guessed he was a spy, they'd kill him.

My footsteps pattered over the granite flagstones as I dashed across the central courtyard and swung myself around the first pillar of the colonnade leading to Sangita's apartment.

As I hurtled around the corner, I cannoned into Harry, who was hurrying in the opposite direction. He grunted and dropped the parcel he was carrying.

He seized me by my shoulders and held me away from him. 'Where are you going in such a hurry?'

My breath was coming in short gasps and I had a stitch. 'I thought I might be too late...'

'Too late for what?'

I drew in another breath and wrenched myself free from his grip. 'So I was right!' I bent to pick up the clothing that had spilled out of the parcel he'd dropped. A French soldier's coat and hat.

'Give me those!' He snatched them from me.

'Harry, you can't go there tonight! They'll kill you if they know what you intend to do.'

He studied me, his face suddenly devoid of expression.

'The whole situation is like a tinderbox.' I laid a hand on his wrist. 'They'll be extra nervous now and on the lookout for spies and infiltrators. Think what will happen to Jai if they catch you in the act of cutting the buffalo traces,' I pleaded.

His lips twitched, in anger or distress, I wasn't sure which. 'Ralph tipped you off, I suppose?'

'I guessed it; he denied it.'

'I shall have something to say to him later.' I shrank back as Harry leaned closer, menace in his eyes. 'You would be ill advised to mention this to anyone. Anyone at all. '

'Of *course* I shan't. I have no intention of placing you in additional danger, but I *beg* you not to go.'

'I must do my duty.' He stared at me, brow furrowed. 'Why should you care what happens to me?'

'Because . . .' He was so close that I could see the stubble on his jaw and smell the faint odour of perspiration on the coat he carried. My courage failed me; this was not the time to tell him about the baby and he didn't want to know how much I loved him. I sighed at the hopelessness of it all. Nothing I could say would change his mind about doing what he had to do. 'Think of Jai,' I murmured, lowering my gaze so that he wouldn't see my despair.

'I never stop thinking of my son,' said Harry, his voice hoarse. He pushed past me and then turned back. 'If you really want to help . . .'

'I do.'

'Then, if anything should happen to me, be a friend to Jai.'

'I am. I will remain so, but, *please*, be careful.'

And then he pulled me towards him and kissed me, hard, on the lips. Before I could react, he'd released me and was sprinting across the courtyard, leaving me trembling.

I watched him go, wondering if his kiss was simply the act of a man who knew he might die tonight or if, perhaps, he might care for me after all.

My turbulent thoughts made it impossible for me to sleep. Finally, I rose from my bed and went outside into the night air, cooler now that October was on its way out. I paced back and forth, picturing what Harry might be doing and inventing ever more fanciful plans as to how I might keep my baby and still stay at the palace.

There was some moonlight and I meandered my way to the

stables to discover that Zephyr's box was empty. Harry must have taken him after all. I waited for a while, sitting on the mounting block in the yard and hoping he'd completed his mission and would return at any moment.

Then I heard a horse whicker outside the yard and a man's answering murmur. Joy and relief welled up in me and I ran along the path to meet him.

But it wasn't Harry.

'Whatever are you doing out here at one in the morning, Bee?' called Ralph. 'You half frightened me to death, looming out of the darkness like a ghost!'

I swallowed my disappointment. 'I might ask the same of you.'

He slid down from the saddle to walk beside me. 'Still, I'm pleased you're here. I have excellent news.'

I started as a figure detached itself from the shadows and ran towards us.

'What's happening, Ralph?' It was Lakshmi. 'I heard comings and goings earlier this evening and then saw you riding into the palace just now. I thought I ought to investigate.'

'Nothing to worry about, Lakshmi,' he said, 'in fact, quite the reverse. A messenger from the Residency came to fetch me as I was preparing for bed.' His voice was full of exultation. 'At ten o'clock tonight, the Nizam finally issued orders to the French *corps* stating he's dismissed their leaders.'

Lakshmi gasped.

'So the deadlock is over?' I said.

'Piron acted immediately,' said Ralph. 'He sent two of his officers to the Residency to confirm he'd surrender tomorrow. Captain Malcolm will go to the French cantonments in the morning to supervise the collection of their arms.'

'It's really over?' said Lakshmi. 'The French have so many men, I didn't think it was possible.'

'There were times when I believed that, too.' Ralph led his grey mare into the stable yard. 'But now, all I want is my bed. It will be a busy day tomorrow.'

I waited until Lakshmi had disappeared into the night. 'Ralph, what about Harry? Is he safe?'

'He'll find out what's happened soon enough and return in his own good time.'

'As long as none of the French soldiers discover what he was doing.'

My brother sighed. 'Harry's perfectly able to take care of himself. You worry too much, Bee. I know you have feelings for him . . .'

I took a hasty step backwards.

'Don't look so surprised! It's perfectly obvious you still care for your childhood sweetheart.'

'He was never that!'

Ralph shrugged. 'I'm going to bed. I advise you to do the same.'

I left him without another word and returned inside.

After sitting on my bed for some time, I knew I wouldn't sleep. I crept out of the *zenana* and wandered through the whispering corridors and vast shadowy rooms of the palace. Moonlight filtered through the fretwork window screens and there was no sound except for the distant howl of jackals. I might as well have been a ghost. At last, too tired to walk any more, I curled up on a window seat in one of the upstairs rooms from where I could keep watch on the stables.

Later a movement outside disturbed my reverie and I peered through the screen into the moonlit yard. A figure was leading out a horse. I leaned forward for a better view. Once they reached the rough grass before the newly opened gap in the perimeter wall, the rider mounted. Frowning, I watched Lakshmi and Aurora disappear from view.

Chapter 40

Muzzy-headed with exhaustion after only an hour's scattered sleep, I rose the following morning and returned to the stables. Aurora was back in the yard but Zephyr was still missing. Reluctantly, I went to the workshop.

It was difficult to concentrate on my embroidery, wondering all the while if the surrender of French arms had taken place and Harry would soon return. I couldn't help worrying that he might have been caught before the French agreed to surrender. I became distracted while teaching the women how to decorate a border with a simple double running stitch and, in the end, I went to the stables again. Zephyr's stall remained empty.

At midday I went to the *zenana* for my midday meal. Leela sat at the centre of a group of ladies and beckoned me to join them. 'My husband has sent news,' she said. 'Events have not gone to plan.'

My stomach somersaulted unpleasantly. Had something happened to Harry? 'What is it?' I said sharply.

Leela's eyes widened in surprise at my tone. 'Captain Malcolm arrived at the French camp this morning to collect the weapons and was seized by a group of *sepoys*. Mr Kirkpatrick was unable to prevent the mutiny from spreading as fast as cholera. By now the *sepoys* have captured Piron, too.'

'So any hope of a peaceful surrender is lost?' My mind flew immediately to Harry, trapped within the French camp.

'There is certain to be bloodshed,' said Bimla with relish.

'Nothing to do now but to wait,' said Samira Begum.

Time passed painfully slowly while I waited and worried. Later, I went to see what progress Manohar and his men had made.

Several yards of the tunnel had been exposed, starting from the shrubbery and working back towards the Durbar Hall. A gang of children, Jai amongst them, squatted on their haunches to watch the men as they worked.

'It is without doubt an underground passage,' Manohar told me, leaning on his spade. 'We must dig down to find unstable places, then fill with them with rubble so they cannot collapse any further.'

Jai ran up to me, his cheeks streaked with dirt. 'Soon the whole tunnel will be opened,' he said. 'Perhaps then we shall find the diamond.' His face looked strained.

'Don't be disappointed,' I said. 'There's no good reason why it might have been hidden there.'

'But we have searched everywhere else and it's the only place left! If we find it, perhaps my father will come home.' There was a desperation in his voice that tore my heartstrings but I could not lie to him.

'Jai, I'm worried about your father, too,' I said, 'but I know he loves you above all else and will come home the instant he's able to.'

He nodded, his eyes huge and solemn.

'I wonder . . . ' I said. 'Jai, come with me.'

He trotted along beside me as I returned to the Durbar Hall.

'The tunnel leads towards the end wall of the workshop,' I said. 'There's a big cupboard there. Perhaps the opening to the tunnel is hidden inside?'

Jai gave me his lovely smile and slipped his hand in mine.

We removed the piles of folded material and crates of finished articles stacked inside the cupboard and then we could see that the rear wall was made of wooden match-boarding.

'I'd have expected it to be plastered,' I said.

Jai rapped his knuckles on the boarding. It sounded hollow. Feverishly, he ran his fingers around the edges.

'Look!' I said. There were some large knotholes in the timber. I squinted through one of them into the blackness beyond, then poked my finger into it. As I removed my finger, the panel moved slightly.

I looked at Jai and he nodded. It didn't take us long to discover that a full-length panel two feet wide could be lifted up and away. A dark void was exposed, with a rotting wooden ladder leading downwards.

Jai's whole body trembled with excitement. 'I'll go down.'

I snatched hold of his collar as he placed his foot on the first rung of the ladder. 'No, you won't, it's far too dangerous! You can ask Manohar to bring a light.'

A short while later Manohar and Jai returned. Manohar carried an oil lamp and gingerly descended the ladder, brushing away swathes of sticky cobwebs as he went. Once he reached the bottom he disappeared.

'Can you see anything?' called Jai.

Manohar reappeared. 'It is without doubt a tunnel but it has collapsed after a few feet. It is impossible to enter.' He climbed up the ladder again.

Jai heaved a sigh of disappointment. 'I'm going to watch the men digging up the tunnel from the outside again. I must be there when they find the diamond.'

At the end of the day there was still no sign of Harry and I called on Ralph in his quarters.

'Is there any news of poor Captain Malcolm?' I asked.

He shook his head. 'The Resident is waiting to see if the *sepoys* can be persuaded to release him. Kirkpatrick isn't banking on that being successful, though, and is preparing to take a hard line with them.'

'What can he do?'

'Frighten them into laying down their arms. Those of our men and artillery still trapped by the flooding on the other side of the Musi will surround the French cantonments under cover of darkness tonight. Orders are to site the gun carriages on the ridge above the French lines. And then, on this side of the Musi, the rest of the British force will position their guns about four hundred yards behind Piron's camp.'

'Won't they be too far away?'

'The guns have an excellent range from the opposite bank and will be aimed directly at the French magazine.'

I couldn't let myself think what might happen to Harry if he was trapped in the French camp and the magazine exploded.

Ralph patted me awkwardly on my shoulder. 'Chin up, Bee. Harry's been in many a tight place and has always wriggled out of it before.'

His kindness took me by surprise and I nodded, unable to speak in case I broke down.

'If I have news, I'll send a messenger,' he said. 'Don't be surprised if you hear gunfire.'

At dawn the following morning I ascended the tower at the front of the palace. My legs ached as I climbed the steep stone stairs and I stopped at each of the arrow slits, which allowed me glimpses of the city and the river.

At last I reached the top, emerging onto the floor of the tower room. Sun glinted on the mirrored mosaics of the domed roof. Once it had been beautiful but now it was water-stained and festooned with cobwebs. I went to open the rickety door to the balcony and my foot caught the bottom of an ancient ladder leaning against the wall. It fell, showering me with dust.

On the balcony, the wind plucked at my hair as I glanced down at the craggy hillside. Goats scrambled over the inhospitable granite outcrops below, grazing on the thicket of thorn bushes. I shaded my eyes against the rising sun to stare out along the Musi. Without a telescope, it was impossible to see if the British artillery had been positioned to surround the French camp on the opposite bank.

At least, I reflected as I descended the stairs again, there had been no cannon fire as yet. I'd be sure to hear that wherever I was in the Jahanara Mahal. I could only hope that Kirkpatrick's tactics succeeded and the *sepoys* would be intimidated into laying down their arms without bloodshed.

I returned to the *zenana*, where the atmosphere was subdued, and breakfasted with the ladies.

'I'm so worried, Bee,' said Leela, nervously winding the end of her plait round and around her finger. 'Ralph received a messenger from the Residency during the night, ordering him to attend with all haste. What if there is fighting and the British don't win? Will Ralph and I have to leave Hyderabad? And you, too?'

'Ralph's sure to return as soon as he can,' I said, knowing my words were of little comfort. My own anxious thoughts were for Harry. Not knowing where he was or if he was hurt or in danger was torment to me. And then there was the way he'd kissed me as he left to go on his mission. I touched a finger to my lips, half hoping to feel the firm imprint of his mouth again. I was still stunned by his cruel rejection of me after that magical night in the pavilion and his parting kiss had rendered me utterly confused. Sighing, I determined not to think about it any more but to make myself useful in the workshop.

We were all working quietly when Hemanti whispered that Jai was trying to attract my attention. I looked up and saw him hovering in the doorway. He held a large bundle in his arms, wrapped in calico, and I stepped outside to speak to him.

'Is there news of your father?' I asked.

His expression was troubled as he shook his head. He held out the bundle to me. '*Usha-ji* asked me to bring this to you.'

I pulled back a corner of the calico and saw that it contained Usha's wall-hanging. 'Did she send a message?'

He shrugged. 'She said you would know why she'd sent it.' He shuffled his feet and said, 'Sometimes *Usha-ji* frightens me. She says strange things.'

'Did she say something strange about this?'

'Well . . .' He wrinkled his nose. 'She said to tell you to "beware bad blood". It sounds frightening, doesn't it?'

'That was strange but I shall like to see how she has progressed with her wall-hanging.'

A yell came from one of the men digging the underground passage outside.

'They've found something!' said Jai.

We peered out of the doorway at the labourers, shouting and gesticulating as they crowded around a man standing waist-deep in the trench.

'The diamond!' said Jai, running towards the men.

Smiling at his wishful thinking, I deposited the wall-hanging in the workshop and hurried after him. Drawn by the commotion, the women followed us, full of excited conjecture.

Manohar, spade still in his hand, ran to me. 'Come at once, memsahib!'

He cleared a path between the growing crowd by the simple means of swinging his spade from side to side and clouting anyone who remained in his way.

A moment later, I found myself at the edge of the trench.

Manohar jabbed his spade towards a bundle of rags half buried in the ground. 'Look!'

I peered into the trench and caught my breath. Nestled within the rags, the ivory dome and hollow eyes of a skull grinned up at me.

One of the women let out a loud wail.

Feeling slightly sick, I made an effort not to recoil and said, 'I wonder how long it's been here?'

Manohar shrugged.

I bent down to take a closer look. 'There's something there in the rags, just above the eye sockets ...'

He hesitated then probed the rags, an expression of distaste or fear on his face, and extracted a curved turban pin.

I took it from him and rubbed it with my fingers to reveal the glint of gold, green enamel and tiny diamonds. 'This must be valuable. I shall show it to Jahanara Begum and ask if she recognises it.'

Manohar used a broom to sweep aside the soil and a moment later it was clear that it wasn't only a turbaned skull that had been buried in the earth. A whole skeleton lay before us, wearing the remains of a tunic wrapped by a cummerbund decorated with gold braid.

And protruding from the skeleton's chest, was the jewelled hilt of a dagger.

A dagger I recognised.

Jahanara Begum took the dagger and the turban pin from me and stared at them in silence. She dropped them in her lap. Her eyelids fluttered and she clutched at her breast.

I hurried forward to support her, alarmed I might have given her too great a shock to bear.

Her handmaid brought medicinal drops and fanned her with peacock feathers.

'Are you still faint?' I asked, gently chafing her fingers.

Her eyes remained closed. 'It was the shock,' she whispered. 'I never expected to see this dagger again. Or the turban pin.'

'I thought at first the dagger was Lakshmi's,' I said, 'but it can't be. It's exactly like hers but this one must have been buried for years.'

Jahanara Begum shook her head. 'It isn't the same. My benefactor provided me with six members of his harem guard. Each had their own dagger, all with different jewels matched to their turban pins, which bore a single stone. Lakshmi's dagger is decorated with sapphires, but this one has rubies. It belonged to Usha.'

'Usha!'

'But this,' Jahanara Begun hid her face in her hands, 'this curved turban pin, is one I gave to my steward Natesh. It has to be his body that has been found. I don't understand . . . '

'Natesh?' I struggled to remember where I'd heard the name before. 'Wasn't he the man who stole the Rose of Golconda?'

'And also the secret lover of Padma, one of my guards. Usha said she saw Natesh kiss Padma when she handed him the stolen diamond. She confronted them. There was a fight and Usha stabbed Padma. Usha told me Natesh snatched her dagger to stop her from killing Padma but, when he realised she was dying anyway, he ran off, taking the diamond and the dagger with him. Usha chased after him and he attacked her with his sword, slicing open her face and slashing her thigh before he escaped.'

'He didn't escape, though, did he?' I said. 'So who stabbed him with Usha's dagger?'

Jahanara Begum bowed her head, running her fingers along the rusty edge of the blade.

I reached out to still her hand, frightened she'd cut herself.

She heaved a deep sigh. 'I must think! Will you tell Lakshmi to bring Usha to me?'

Gently, I took the dagger from her and laid it on the floor by her feet. 'I'll go now.'

But then Jahanara Begum suddenly sat bolt upright. 'The Rose of Golconda! Could it still be on Natesh's body or did someone take it from him? *Beti*, go at once and search the skeleton!'

Chapter 41

When I arrived outside the Durbar Hall, Lakshmi was already beside the trench dispersing the crowd that had gathered. I took her aside and hastily told her what had passed between Jahanara Begum and myself.

Under our direction, Manohar and his men lifted the skeleton onto a blanket and covered it from sight. Lakshmi and I stood guard beside it while we watched the men sieve the earth that had surrounded the body for the past forty years. We didn't say what we were looking for but kept a careful watch over every sieveful of soil, picking through the stones before they were deposited in a heap.

Jai crept up to me and his hand slipped into mine. 'Are you looking for the diamond?' he whispered.

'I expect Natesh's killer ran off with it,' I murmured, 'but we must be sure.'

'I wish my father were here,' he said wistfully. 'He promised he'd come back soon. Do you think he might have been hurt?'

His woebegone expression pulled on my heartstrings and I hugged him tightly for a moment. 'There's no gunfire,' I said, to reassure myself as much as him. 'Hopefully, your father will return soon.'

Once the earth from Natesh's last resting place had been sifted, Lakshmi directed the men to carry the skeleton to the old elephant stables.

Jai trailed behind us and looked so unhappy when I tried to send him away that I allowed him to accompany us, provided he stood at a distance from the skeleton. I didn't want him to have bad dreams.

Lakshmi and I peeled back the blanket and picked carefully through the skeleton's rotting tunic and trousers, searching for any place the diamond might have been concealed. We removed the cummerbund and what was left of the turban, smoothing flat the pleats and folds of fabric.

Lakshmi sighed. 'It's not here, is it?'

I looked with distaste at the earth lodged under my fingernails and hoped it wasn't mixed with blood. 'Someone must have stabbed Natesh and run away with the diamond. What I don't understand is how his body came to be in the tunnel. I thought it had been forgotten about for years?'

'Since Natesh was the steward,' said Lakshmi, 'he had access to every part of the palace, except the *zenana*. Perhaps he discovered it and kept his knowledge quiet, thinking it might be useful one day. His body must have been buried when the passage collapsed during the second earth tremor.'

I shuddered. 'I wonder if he was actually dead or only injured, then. Jahanara Begum's curse certainly exacted its revenge on him,' I said. 'We'd better fetch Usha. Perhaps she can shed some light on what happened. Maybe Natesh had another accomplice.'

Jai held my hand tightly as Lakshmi and I hurried to see Usha. It upset me to see him so anxious.

Sangita opened the door and Lakshmi told her what had happened.

'Go and talk to her, by all means,' said Sangita. 'I hope you find her more rational than I did this morning. She made me shiver, prophesying evil walking amongst us and muttering about shame and atonement and how the price always has to be paid.'

'She lives in a world of fear none of us can see,' said Lakshmi.

Sangita took Jai's hand. 'Come with me. I shall cut up some jack-fruit for you.'

Lakshmi led me to Usha's room and tapped on the door. There was no response so we went in.

Usha lay on her *charpai*. Her veil was thrown back to reveal her damaged face contorted into a rictus of agony. Her foam-flecked lips were blue and there was a pool of vomit on the floor.

Lakshmi glanced at me, her face frozen with shock. She touched her fingers to the side of Usha's neck. 'She's gone,' she whispered.

My hand was shaking when I bent to pick up a small, empty bottle from the floor. I sniffed it and grimaced at the strong scent of bitter almonds. 'Poison.' I handed the bottle to Lakshmi.

Her eyes welled with tears. 'My grandmother never loved me and now she never will.'

I reached for her hand. 'Lakshmi, her mind was disturbed . . . '

Her eyes flashed with anger. 'When I first came to the palace, she turned her back on me. I was little more than a child and it wasn't my fault my mother ran away with my father. I am *not* my mother and the sin was not mine.'

'Of course not,' I said, in soothing tones.

Her chin quivered. 'I thought, in time, she'd learn to love me, but now it's too late.'

'She was a confused old lady with troubled thoughts.' I looked at Usha's body again. 'But what made her take poison? And why now?' I hesitated. 'Lakshmi, could *she* have killed Natesh?'

Lakshmi stared at me, shaking her head. 'If she'd stolen the Rose, why was she still living here? Surely, she'd have run away, sold the diamond and lived a life of luxury?'

'Perhaps she was too ashamed?'

Lakshmi glanced around the small room, as spare as a nun's cell.

In a sudden frenzy, she pulled out boxes and baskets from under the *charpai* and scattered the contents. She flung back the lid of the chest, delved inside and raked through Usha's possessions. Ripping apart the cotton lining of the chest, she inspected it closely before rolling over the body to search beneath the bed linen.

'Lakshmi, don't!' I said.

She sighed heavily and then closed her grandmother's eyelids with her thumb and forefinger. 'Will you leave now, Bee? This is a family matter. I wish to break the news to my aunt.'

'I'll keep the children occupied in the garden.'

Later, Lakshmi came to find us. 'Children, will you go to your mother? She has some sad news to tell you. Be kind to her!'

Jai ran up to me and gripped my hand. 'Is it about my father?'

'No, it isn't,' I said, and saw the tension drain out of his skinny frame.

Sangita's children ran off, their little faces apprehensive.

'We'd better go and tell Jahanara Begum,' I said.

As soon as she saw us, without Usha, she guessed. She wrapped her arms about her and turned her face away while we related what had happened.

Later, after we'd left her in the care of her handmaid, Lakshmi returned to comfort Sangita.

I collected the package containing Usha's wall hanging from the workshop and went to the *zenana* to break the sad news.

'Once, Usha was such a lively girl,' said Priya Begum, 'hardly like a guard at all, although she was very strong and an excellent horsewoman.'

Priya Begum and Samira Begun were old enough to remember Usha but the younger ladies barely knew her since she'd led a secluded life after she'd received her dreadful injuries. All, however, knew the story of her bravery in preventing the traitor Padma from running away with the Rose of Golconda.

While the ladies were reminiscing, Leela whispered to me.

'There was a message,' she said. 'Ralph asked me to tell you Captain Malcolm and General Piron were released late last night. Some of the *sepoys* had once been under Malcolm's command and didn't want to be involved in kidnapping him.'

'There was no bloodshed?' Leela shook her head and I sighed in relief.

'When the remaining *sepoys* woke up to find themselves surrounded,' she said, 'they agreed to surrender. The British cavalry rode in and took possession of their magazine and artillery.'

God willing, Harry was safe! After all that had happened, fatigue overwhelmed me and I retreated to my room to rest.

I reclined on the bed and unfolded Usha's wall hanging, I marvelled again at her tiny stitches and ability to embroider such detailed vignettes. It saddened me that her mind had been turned to the edge of madness by her tragic past and that such exquisite talent was now lost. I ran my finger over the scenes, tracing the story of the palace from the first stone laid, through wars and successive owners and then Jahanara Begum's arrival with her entourage.

I came to the embroidered picture of the dreadful day when Usha had peeped out from behind a pillar to see Padma stealing the Rose of Golconda. All around, the palace shook in the earthquake and pieces of stone fell to the ground.

And then something caught my attention. I leaned closer to look. My pulse began to race. Usha had made two tiny alterations since I last saw the vignette and they changed everything. Still reeling, I noticed something else. A new scene had been inserted after the one depicting Jahanara Begum nursing Usha back to health. It told quite a different story from the one everyone had believed for forty years.

I sat still, listening to the blood pounding in my ears, while I assimilated these revelations, wondering if they could really be true.

There was only one way to find out. I hurried from the room, sprinting towards Sangita's apartment.

Jai was outside playing with little Candra.

'Jai,' I said breathlessly, 'is Lakshmi here?'

He shook his head. 'She went to the stables.'

I turned on my heel and dashed across the courtyard.

Lakshmi was tying panniers to Aurora's saddle when I reached the yard. 'Are you going somewhere?' I asked.

Her mouth was pressed in a thin line as she tightened the girth. 'I can't stay here. My grandmother has disgraced our family by killing herself.'

'But you can't go!' I was dismayed. 'The palace is your home. Besides, I'd miss you.'

She glanced at me, stony-faced. 'Usha made so many comments about atonement that I've begun to think she may have been involved in the theft of the diamond. I don't know how or where it is now ...'

'But I do.'

Her fingers became still and she turned slowly to look at me. 'You know where the Rose is?' She frowned. 'How can *you* know anything about it?'

'I have reason to believe Usha killed Natesh and stole the diamond from his body.'

'Then she has been cursed by it ever since!'

'Lakshmi, if we were to find the Rose and restore it to Jahanara Begum, you would be feted, not reviled.'

She stared at me curiously. 'You would let me take credit for finding it?'

'Why not? And I know where to look.'

'What fairy tale are you telling me now?' She lifted her foot into the stirrup.

'I'm not! Usha's wall hanging shows us what really happened.' I caught hold of her sleeve. 'When she originally sewed the story of the theft, Usha reversed the colour of the jewels in the turban pins. Now that scene shows Padma watching while Usha stole the Rose. And there's a new picture showing where she hid it.' I held out my hand. 'Come! We'll search together.'

337

Lakshmi studied my face intently, her expression tense. 'By all the gods, Bee, if you are right this changes everything.'

Our footsteps skittered over the marble floors as we ran through the palace, racing along the corridors and taking stairs two at a time. At last we came to the tower.

We were out of breath by the time we emerged into the room at the top. The sun's glare through the glazed doors had heated the little room into an oven. I dragged open the balcony doors to admit a welcome breeze.

'Where is the diamond, Bee?' said Lakshmi. Her gaze raked the walls, searching for hiding places.

'The wall-hanging shows Usha climbing a ladder.'

The worm-eaten ladder leaned drunkenly against the wall and Lakshmi tested the strength of one of the rungs by thumping it with her fist. It disintegrated into dust.

I glanced up at the mirror-lined dome above. 'You're stronger than me. Can you lift me up?'

She gripped me around my knees and thrust me into the air.

I reached up, as high as I could, my fingers scrabbling to catch hold of the sill running around the base of the dome. Then I slid my palm from side to side, sweeping around the ledge.

'The wall hanging showed Usha taking the diamond out of her dagger sheath and placing it on here,' I said.

'But how could she have climbed up?' said Lakshmi. 'Her injuries were too severe. She must have hidden it here after she recovered and, meanwhile, kept the Rose secreted in her dagger sheath?'

'Perhaps she made up the story about Padma when she realised she was too badly injured to escape.' I grimaced in disgust as spiders' webs, dead insects and the dust of decades fell onto my upturned face as I fumbled along the ledge. 'Move me a bit further round, will you?'

Lakshmi took a few steps and I continued to search.

'What I don't understand,' I said, 'is why Usha didn't run away with the Rose once she'd recovered.'

'She often muttered about atonement,' said Lakshmi. 'Perhaps Natesh was a false lover and used her to steal the Rose because she had access to the *zenana*? If she realised he was going to abandon her and run off with the diamond, she'd have been angry enough to kill him.'

'She killed two people for that diamond. Perhaps, later, she regretted it.' Desperately, I stretched out my fingers. 'It's not here.' I sighed, deeply disappointed. 'I was so sure ...'

'So she tricked us with her wall-hanging!' Lakshmi's voice was full of bitterness.

And then I touched something with the tip of my finger. I reached higher, every muscle straining. A shiver of excitement ran through my whole body. 'I think I've got it!' I said, my voice shaking.

I slithered down. Lakshmi held me as close to her as if we were lovers, and her face was radiant with hope and expectation.

Slowly, I uncurled my fist.

The fabulous Rose of Golconda, as large as a pigeon's egg, glittered on my palm.

Lakshmi pressed her fingers to her mouth, her eyes full of shock. 'All these years,' she murmured, 'and it was here all the time.'

Chapter 42

The breeze stole through the balcony doors and fanned my hot cheeks as we stood and gazed at the Rose.

'Only think what good this will do,' I whispered, in thrall to the pink fire glinting and flashing from the stone as it lay on my hand in the sunlight. Joy and relief bubbled up in my breast. 'Jahanara's troubles are over and the palace can be repaired straight away. Imagine how many lives the Rose will change for the better.'

'It will invest its owner with great power and provide them with a life of undreamed of luxury.'

Lakshmi's words broke the enchantment of the diamond. There was something wrong about the reverential tone of her voice. I lifted my gaze to her face and was dumbfounded by the avaricious gleam in her eyes.

She stared back at me with the calculating intensity of a tiger with prey in its sights.

'Lakshmi?' I said uneasily.

'The Rose is going to give me the life I've always wanted,' she said.

Stunned, I saw her extend her hand to snatch the diamond from me.

I didn't stop to think. I snapped my fingers shut over it. Leaping backwards out of the doors onto the balcony, I held the Rose out over the balustrade. 'Stay there,' I said, 'or I'll drop it! You'd never find it in the thicket below.'

'Give it to me!'

'Never!' A tremor of disbelief at her treachery rippled through my body, leaving me cold and shaking. 'How could you even think of taking it for yourself?'

Lakshmi kicked the balcony door and it rebounded against the wall. The glass cracked and fell to the floor in shards. 'What does it matter to you?' she hissed. 'You've made a success of your wretched workshop so the old woman doesn't need the diamond any more. You *owe* me a chance of happiness!'

'I owe you?' I was bewildered.

'You ruined my childhood . . .'

'You're as mad as your grandmother,' I said. 'I'd never met you before I came to the Jahanara Mahal.'

She laughed but there was no humour in the sound. 'You didn't need to be in India to ruin my life. In fact, not being here only made you all the more precious in the eyes of our father. All he ever talked about was his perfect little daughter, who had been snatched away from him and taken to England. I've hated the apparently flawless, sickeningly beautiful and astonishingly clever Bee, for as long as I can remember. It was almost a disappointment when I met you and you weren't like that at all.'

'Our father?' A shiver of unease ran down my back. 'What are you talking about?'

'Why do you think that harpy of a mother of yours left India? I'll tell you why. She discovered her husband had set up house with his Indian *bibi* and that they had a child. Me.' Her mouth quivered and for a moment I thought she might cry.

'We're . . . sisters?' I said. I shook my head. 'I don't believe you. Besides, my father didn't care about me at all once I'd left India.'

341

'He never stopped talking about you.' Lakshmi's face contorted as she suppressed tears. 'He was seduced by my mother but he never really noticed me.'

All at once, Mother's terrible anger began to make sense. That anger had burned within her for as long as I could remember, while she poured her vitriol on all those around her. In the end, it had consumed her.

'I thought you might have guessed,' Lakshmi told me.

'How could I?' But then I recalled dressing for dinner and Lakshmi drawing me to the mirror and saying we looked like sisters. 'So that's why Mother hated everything about India,' I said. 'Your mother stole my father away from us. *You* stole my father away from me.' Resentment burned inside me, against Father and his mistress and Lakshmi.

'He used to write to you,' my half-sister said, 'letters so full of love that each one was a knife in my heart. He even made me help him choose birthday presents for you.' Her lip curled. 'And you cared so little for him you never wrote back.'

'But I did write! I had no letters or presents from him, and for years I cried myself to sleep thinking of him.' Bright, hot anger coursed through my veins. Of course, now I understood; Mother must have destroyed our correspondence.

Lakshmi's eyes glittered. 'I've spent my life trying to be better than you. It was a shock when my English half-brother came to the palace and married Leela, but dim-witted Ralph matters little to me. It was always *you*, his golden-haired girl, our father adored. I shall no longer allow you to stand in my way.' She unsheathed her dagger. 'Give me the diamond!'

Mutely, I shook my head.

She looked at me with loathing in her face. 'You should have left the palace after I tried to frighten you away.'

I stared at the dagger, my mouth suddenly dry. 'What do you mean?'

'Do you remember losing yourself on your second night here? You heard me following you and took fright.' She laughed. 'You slept on the cold floor that night! I hoped it would make you leave. And then there was the matter of the monsoon rains flooding the Durbar Hall.'

'So it was you who opened the windows?' Of course it was. I could see it now. 'You destroyed the fruits of our hard work simply to satisfy your own selfish desire to see me brought down?' My voice rose in anger and sorrow. 'How could you, Lakshmi?' The wooden balustrade wasn't high enough to support my wrist and my arm ached as I held the Rose out over the void.

She gave a tight little smile. 'When I was looking for storage chests for the workshop, I discovered the lost keys to the Durbar Hall in an old trunk. It was almost too easy to convince everyone you'd forgotten to close the windows.'

She'd even made me question myself. Anger flared and in that moment I hated her.

'And then there was the time we rode out during the first monsoon rain,' she said. 'The gods were with you that day when Breeze jumped clear of the crevasse.'

The casual way she spoke of it made me shiver. 'Your jealousy was so great you planned to lead me to my death?'

She shrugged. 'On the spur of the moment. I don't like to be thwarted. And then there's Harry.'

I wouldn't give her the satisfaction of asking what she meant. The muscles in my outstretched arm trembled and I shifted my stance a little.

'I saw you together in the pavilion,' she said.

I swallowed back the bile that rose in my throat. That she should have been there at such a private and precious time, *watching* ...

'Once,' she said, 'I wanted him for myself. But even though I befriended Jai, Harry still, oh, so politely, turned me down. And then you came along and I had to watch him falling in love with you.'

343

She sighed. 'Still, now I have Jean-Philippe. He is going to take me to Paris.'

I was outraged. 'A Frenchman?'

'I like to be on the winning side. And I played my part by passing on snippets of information.'

'You spied for the French?' I shook my head in disgust. 'I would have valued you as a sister but now I can't bear to think the same blood runs in our veins.'

'Neither can I.' Her mouth twisted. 'Still, Jean-Philippe and his men will find the Jahanara Mahal makes a good strongpoint on this side of the Musi from which to suppress the British. And they will be able to walk straight in through the broken-down perimeter.' She laughed. 'All I had to do was murmur superstitious nonsense in the ears of the servants and the wall came down again.'

'Perhaps you don't know that the French have already lost?' I said. 'I doubt your Jean-Philippe will be in any position to carry you off to Paris now.'

Quick as a flash, she sliced her dagger through the air only a hair's breadth away from my face. 'Well, I shan't need him any more. I'll have the diamond.' Scowling, she said, 'You can't stay like that for much longer. Soon, your arm will tire and then I'll have you.'

Seeing the expression of hatred on her face, I didn't doubt her. I fought back flutters of panic, determined she wouldn't see my fear.

'It irked me when you succeeded with Harry where I'd failed,' she said, 'but I put a stop to that! I told him, oh, so sympathetically, that you'd asked me to say you'd changed your mind about him, once you'd discovered he was half the man your husband had been. A man's self-worth in the bedroom is so fragile, isn't it?'

No wonder Harry had backed away from me so fast. 'You are despicable,' I told her, through gritted teeth. 'My father, *our* father, would have been bitterly disappointed in you.'

'Don't you dare say that!' She lunged towards me.

'Stop!' I opened my hand, exposing the diamond. 'One more move and I'll let it fall.'

'You won't!'

'Yes, I will.' I lifted my chin. 'It's of far less importance to me than it is to you. If I'm going to die, I'll make sure you won't have the diamond. Remember, Lakshmi, anyone who steals the Rose is cursed.' I smiled defiantly. 'Somehow, it *will* poison your life. Look at what happened to Natesh and your grandmother. Both were destroyed by their greed for the Rose.'

'Be silent!' There was fear in her voice.

We remained motionless, at a deadlock, but my arm was numb and my fingers tingling.

'The saddest thing,' I said, 'is that, if you'd told me before, I would have been so proud to take you into my heart as a beloved sister. The times spent riding and visiting the bazaar together, laughing over the experiences we shared, were special to me.'

'I don't believe you!' Just for a heartbeat, a flicker of regret passed across her face.

And then came a soft footfall on the stairs.

Lakshmi whirled around as Jai emerged from the stairway.

My stomach clenched sharply with fear and love for him.

'I've been listening to you, Lakshmi,' he said. 'You mustn't hurt Bee or take the Rose.'

'Jai, run!' I yelled.

Lakshmi launched herself at him and pinned him to the ground. He squealed and wriggled as she dragged him to his feet and, when he tried to pull free, slapped him.

I let out a yelp of distress. 'Let him go!' I was desperate to help him but the only weapon I held against Lakshmi was my control of the diamond.

Ignoring me, she imprisoned Jai against her chest and lifted him onto the balcony, just out of my reach. She leaned him backwards over the balustrade.

I squeezed my eyes shut, still holding the diamond out over the rocky ground so far below. Taking a calming breath, I said, 'Don't make it worse for yourself. Let Jai go, Lakshmi, and I'll never speak of this. He's only a child.'

'Give me the diamond, then.'

Jai shrieked, 'You shan't have it!' He flailed his arms and lashed out with his feet, kicking her shins.

'You little devil!'

I gasped when I saw her dagger pressed against the tender skin of his neck. 'Stop!' I screamed.

'Only if you give me the diamond.'

'Don't give it to her, *aunty-ji*!' Jai's feet swung about in the air, desperately seeking the ground as she forced him backwards.

Birds of prey circled the tower, as if they were waiting for him to fall.

Nauseous with dread, I calculated whether I could snatch Jai before Lakshmi could cut his throat or push him to his death. But if she did that she'd have nothing left to bargain with.

Lakshmi cursed under her breath and pricked the point of her dagger into his neck.

Terror-stricken, he screamed as blood welled up and stained the blade.

Nothing mattered any more except relieving his fear. I pulled my arm up over my head and flung the diamond down the stairwell. I heard it bounce off the stone steps. 'Damn you forever, Lakshmi!' I yelled. 'May the diamond heap curses upon you and your descendants until the very end of time!'

She gasped and gave me a frightened look. Then she let Jai go and raced after the diamond.

I threw myself forward and grabbed him as he teetered on the balustrade. He flung his arms around me and wrapped his legs about my waist. I carried him away from the balcony and we clung to each other, huddled on the floor of the tower room, waiting for Lakshmi to come back and kill us. I buried my face in Jai's neck, rocking him and whispering soothing words while his skinny frame was wracked by sobs.

A great bellow of rage came from the stairwell, followed by a screech.

Then Lakshmi and Harry burst into the tower room. Blood trickled from Harry's right shoulder and I gasped when Lakshmi raised her dagger to strike him again.

He was too fast for her and grabbed her wrist, his dagger striking upwards, but she twisted away, wrenching herself free from his grip. It was then that I saw a glimmer of pink fire in her left hand as she shoved the Rose into her dagger sheath.

I could hardly bear to watch as Harry and Lakshmi circled each other for what felt like a lifetime, their blades flashing in the sunlight as they dodged and feinted, their shoes scuffing up the dust on the floor.

Jai still clung to me, his whole body shuddering.

Harry dodged a vicious thrust, sidestepping out of Lakshmi's reach, but blood had already soaked the front of his tunic and he was breathing heavily. He switched the dagger to his left hand, lunging at Lakshmi and slitting open her sleeve.

She yelled and whirled around, her dagger held high as she bore down on him.

I kicked out my leg and caught her shin. She fell headlong through the door to the balcony but was up and on her feet by the time Harry launched himself at her.

She deflected his blade, and he grunted as she sliced his forearm. His dagger clattered to the floor. Shouting in triumph, she kicked it over the edge of the balcony.

Whimpering, I buried Jai's face in my shoulder and held him tight. I couldn't allow him to see his beloved father die.

Harry staggered but then he had Lakshmi in his arms, holding her so close her movements were hampered. Her blade was inches away from his face and he gripped her wrist as she struggled to gouge out his eye. Harry's breath came in shallow gasps. The balcony floor was slippery with blood.

Fumbling behind the shattered door, I snatched up the largest shard of glass. Jai was still wrapped around my waist, clinging like a limpet, but I heaved myself to my feet.

'Let him go, Lakshmi!' I shouted.

'He's nearly finished,' she panted. 'And then it's your turn.'

A shriek of rage burst up from inside me and I sprang at her, raking the dagger of broken glass down her arm.

Her eyes opened wide in shocked surprise.

A red mist blurred my vision and I raised the shard to slash her throat.

Shoving Harry away from her in a convulsive movement, she threw herself backwards out of my reach. There was a crash of splintering timber.

And then she wasn't there.

Chapter 43

Harry lurched against me and we steadied each other. A section of the balustrade had gone.

Covering Jai's eyes, I leaned forward to look over the edge.

Lakshmi's broken body lay spread-eagled on the rock far below.

My teeth started to chatter and shockwaves of icy shudders overtook my body. 'My sister,' I whispered.

White-faced, Harry glanced at me and then enfolded us both in his arms. He tried to prise his son's fingers free from my neck but Jai only gripped me all the harder.

'Jai,' said Harry, 'you're safe.'

The boy lifted his tear-stained face at the sound of his father's voice. Still clinging to me, he threw one of his arms around Harry's neck. The three of us remained entwined together until we had all stopped sobbing.

At last, Jai heaved a deep breath. 'I'm sorry, *abbu*, but we lost the Rose.'

Harry, his jaw still trembling, kissed his son's forehead. 'It doesn't matter. You are more precious to me than any diamond could ever be.'

I made to free myself from the tangle of limbs, intending to leave Harry and his son to share their private moment.

'Don't go!' said Jai as he clutched my hand.

I gave Harry a questioning glance.

He caressed my cheek with his forefinger. 'Stay with us,' he whispered. 'Please. I can't bear it without you.'

Hope swelled in my heart. I captured his hand, pressing it to my face. 'You don't have to,' I whispered back.

'I'm all right now,' said Jai a few moments later. He wiped his tear-stained face on his shirt.

'We'd better dress our wounds,' said Harry, plucking at his blood-stained tunic. He examined the cut on Jai's neck and ruffled his hair. 'Thankfully, it's not deep.'

'And all the bravest soldiers have a scar or two,' I said.

Harry lifted my hand and inspected the throbbing gashes across my palm and fingers where I'd gripped the shard of glass. 'I'm afraid you won't be doing any embroidery for a while, my darling.'

'We must tell Sangita about Lakshmi,' said Jai.

'And I'll tell you both how I found the Rose of Golconda,' I said.

A little while later, we found Sangita making garlands of flowers to drape over Usha's bier. She saw the blood on our clothing and rose to her feet in alarm. Already shocked and grieving over her mother's suicide, the news of Lakshmi's treachery was too much for her. 'Gopal and the men are gathering wood to make my mother's funeral pyre down by the river,' she said; 'and now this!' She covered her face with her *dupatta* and wept.

I comforted her until the storm of weeping calmed.

She rallied then, bringing a basin of water, bandages and some healing powder for our wounds.

'As I returned to the palace from the French cantonment,' said Harry, 'I was walking through the grounds when I heard Jai scream. I thought my heart would stop when I saw Lakshmi holding him over the edge of the balcony.'

350

I remembered how my own heart had pounded at the sight.

'I raced through the palace and up the tower stairs,' he said. 'I could hardly believe what I was seeing when Lakshmi snatched up the diamond from the step, right before my eyes. She stabbed me, but I wasn't going to let anything stop me from reaching you or Jai.'

Euphoria thrummed in my veins. Despite what Lakshmi had said to him, he'd still loved me, even when he thought I'd cast him aside.

Jai tugged at his father's sleeve. 'Lakshmi said she was going to Paris with a Frenchman.'

Harry rubbed his face with his palms. 'So she admitted it.'

'She's been passing him information,' I said.

'I know.'

I looked at him in amazement. 'How?'

'She frequently went out riding in the night and took too much interest in military matters.'

'Why didn't you say anything?' I couldn't believe he was taking the news so calmly. 'Ralph kept telling her the army's plans.'

'Your brother,' said Harry, 'isn't as simple as he looks. I suspected her of spying for the French, so we fed her false information, guessing she'd pass it on. Anything else we discussed with her was already common knowledge.'

Jai's head began to nod.

'He's exhausted,' said Sangita, stroking the hair off his brow. 'Let me put him to bed and watch him. You must bring Lakshmi's body to me, Harry, and then speak with Jahanara Begum.'

He kissed his son then turned to me. 'Later,' he whispered, pressing his lips to my bandaged hand. And then he was gone.

Jahanara Begum gripped the arms of her tiger throne, chin raised to brace herself against despair. The wall-hanging lay across her knees, telling her for the first time the true story of Usha's heinous deception.

Harry and I sat on footstools before her.

'So, yet again, the Rose of Golconda is stolen from me,' she said, 'and this time by that traitor's granddaughter. I should have known Padma would never betray me. She lost her life defending what was rightfully mine and for all these years I have maligned her, deceived by Usha's lies.'

'According to the scenes Usha embroidered, she suffered and was betrayed, too,' I said. 'Natesh, the man she loved, seduced her to gain access to the diamond and then he destroyed her beauty and her health. In her way, she tried to atone. She worked so hard to embroider beautiful things to raise money to save the palace.'

Jahanara Begum shook her head. 'You are more charitable than I, *beti*. She watched as the palace fell into disrepair and the servants went hungry when she could have stopped it by returning the diamond.'

'Perhaps she couldn't face either the shame or having to leave the palace?' said Harry.

Jahanara Begum sighed. 'I should have grasped there was something false about Usha's story when I nursed her after the theft. I discovered she was pregnant. She was so ashamed and wept, telling me she had been seduced by one of the servants, who had then left the palace.'

I couldn't look at her, knowing that I, too, was carrying an illegitimate child.

'After all Usha had suffered,' she continued, 'in, as I thought, trying to protect the diamond for me, I saved her from dishonour by finding her a husband and paying him to accept the child. Nadeen, Lakshmi's mother, must have been Natesh's child.'

Nadeen, my father's mistress and the cause of so much misery. Had Natesh's 'bad blood' that flowed in Lakshmi's veins led her to behave so wickedly? Or was that caused by our father's failure to make provision for her?

'When Manohar and I recovered Lakshmi's body,' said Harry, 'the Rose wasn't in her dagger sheath. We searched the hillside but it's an impossible task amongst the thorn trees.'

'Perhaps, one day, someone will find the Rose in a dish of goat stew,' I said, gloomily.

Harry smiled sadly. 'I suspect generations of small boys to come will continue to comb the hillside, looking for the diamond.'

'And who knows? Perhaps, one day, they will find it,' said Jahanara Begum. She reached out to take my hands. 'Meanwhile, your workshop, *beti*, has brought the security to the palace that we'd hoped for from the Rose. Didn't I say the Jahanara Mahal was waiting for you to come and bring her back to life?' She smiled, her dark eyes glittering. 'From now on, you shall be my Rose of the Jahanara Mahal.'

'The Rose of the Jahanara Mahal,' said Harry. 'I like that.'

'Life is more important than any diamond,' said Jahanara Begum, giving Harry a sly glance. 'I daresay you will wish to demonstrate your gratitude to Bee for saving your son?'

He looked at me with such love in his eyes that it was hard not to throw myself into his arms. 'There is a great deal for us to discuss,' he said gravely.

'Indeed there is,' said Jahanara Begum. She gave me a penetrating look. 'And I suggest you waste no time.'

There was a hint of a question in her eyes that made me blush. Could she have guessed my secret? I covered my confusion by gathering up Usha's wall-hanging. 'No matter what has happened,' I said, 'this is a treasure and I propose to hang it in the Durbar Hall.'

'As you wish,' said Jahanara Begum. 'Now, go, both of you, with my blessing.'

Harry grasped my hand as we left Jahanara Begum's quarters. He didn't speak as he marched me purposefully through the grounds of the palace.

'Where are we going?' I asked.

'To do something I should have done several weeks ago!' He strode on until we reached the garden. Harry pushed open the door and then we were off again until we came to the pavilion. He pulled me up the steps and, once we were inside, turned me to face him, gripping me by my shoulders.

'What is it?' I asked, disturbed by his grim expression.

'Tell me the truth.' His dark gaze bored into me. 'Did you ask Lakshmi to tell me that you found me an unsatisfactory lover?'

'Certainly not!' I said. 'Nothing could be further from the truth.'

Some of the tension in his jaw relaxed. 'I was too hurt to discuss it with you but the more I thought about it, the more false it seemed. And then, each time I saw you, there was such a wounded look in your eyes but I didn't know why.'

'How I wish you had asked me!' I said. I intended to ask my own burning question. 'Did you ask Lakshmi to tell me that you're still so in love with Noor you could never love again?'

'No, I didn't. And it isn't true, which should be patently obvious to you.' He released his grip on my shoulders. 'And now we've dealt with that,' he cupped my face gently in his hands, 'we shall start again.' He bent down to kiss my lips as gently as a feather.

There was a singing in my ears and I reached out for him, pressing myself against him, the heat of his body searing through my clothing. And then his arms were around me and he kissed me with a fierce concentration that left me breathless and weak with longing.

He released me, his chest rising and falling as he steadied his breath. 'I think we'd better stop,' he said, 'at least until we have one last thing straight. Bee, my beautiful … Bee, my Rose of the Jahanara Mahal … I've cared for you since you were a skinny little girl with dirty knees …'

'I like that,' I said indignantly, 'you were always far grubbier than I!'

'Don't interrupt! Can't you tell I'm trying to propose to you?'

'Are you?' My pulse was skipping so fast I could hardly breathe. 'Then haven't you forgotten something?'

'What?' His dismayed expression was almost comical.

I leaned forward and whispered in his ear.

354

'Well, of course I love you, you infuriating woman!' He kissed my forehead, my cheeks, the tip of my nose. And then looked deep into my eyes. 'I love you with all my heart, Bee, and I want to marry you, if you'll have me.'

'Before I say yes and tell you how much I love you too, there's one other thing,' I said, a sudden surge of anxiety making me nervous again. I sank down onto the *charpai*, my knees suddenly unable to hold me up.

He sat beside me and nuzzled my neck. 'Are you worried about Jai?' he said. 'He's a good boy . . . '

'I love Jai already and would be proud to be his stepmother.' I shook my head. 'The thing is, if I marry you, by early next summer we will be a family of four.'

Harry became very still and I froze for a long, heart-stopping moment, wondering if my news had changed everything. And then I saw the joy dawning in his eyes.

He gave a shout of laughter and pulled me into his arms. 'So that was what the old witch meant by wasting no time! We must be married straight away.' He kissed me again, so tenderly this time that tears of happiness weren't far away.

We sat entwined for a long while, quietly sharing our innermost thoughts and making plans for our future at the Jahanara Mahal.

Later, I picked up Usha's wall-hanging and spread it out over my knees, showing Harry the story of the palace from its earliest days as a fort and then as a luxurious palace when Jahanara Begum and her retinue first arrived. I traced the palace's story through treachery and betrayal and then into decline.

'One day,' I said, as we sat hand in hand and watched the great orange sun begin to set, 'now that the workshop is going to be successful, I hope to be embroidering a scene at the end of the story, depicting the Jahanara Mahal's restoration to its former beauty.'

And there were still spaces, as Usha had said, for new scenes to celebrate weddings and the birth of babies.

Historical Note

I visited India ten years ago and have never forgotten the impact it made upon me. As Mrs Clements observes, it is an assault on the senses and, when I look at the photographs I took then, I can immediately smell cinnamon, jasmine and drains, and hear the intense clamour of the streets, though there are more cars these days than camels.

And the colours! Even the poorest women wore deeply saturated hues of fuchsia, scarlet and saffron. One of my abiding images is of being driven through the countryside, in a landscape of red dust and scrubby grass, and seeing a woman dressed in scarlet swaying gracefully as she carried a water pot on her head. There was no visible habitation nearby and I still wonder where she was going.

Then there were the vast palaces and forts. I found their decaying grandeur impossibly romantic and often dreamed of walking through them alone, listening to the whispers of all those who had lived there in times long ago. It was this that inspired me to write *The Palace of Lost Dreams*.

The book is set mostly in 1798 when the British East India Company had been in India for two hundred years. In the beginning female dependants were usually left at home, and it surprised me to discover that many British men enthusiastically adopted the cultured Indian ways, both Moslem and Hindu, and regularly married local women. These marriages were usually happy and the resulting Anglo-Indian children mixed freely in both societies. The boys were frequently sent to England to be schooled and later returned to join the East India Company army. It wasn't until 1791 that an order was issued preventing those with an Indian parent from owning land or being employed by the Company. Since these children were thus deprived of the opportunity to earn a living, if their skin was sufficiently fair, they were sometimes sent 'home' and absorbed into English society.

At the end of the eighteenth century the British government began an intensive effort to work with the East India Company, who already had armies in place, to snatch power and control over India as a whole. From a modern-day perspective, the means used to achieve this takeover were shocking.

In 1797 the two once-great powers in India, Mysore and the Marathas, had declined in strength and it was a good time for Britain to stake its claim. The Marquis of Wellesley, elder brother of the Duke of Wellington, arrived in India in 1798 to take up his new post as Governor-General at a time when Britain was locked in a global struggle for supremacy with France.

Since Napoleon had also set his sights set on India, Wellesley had to move quickly. To achieve his aims, he set up a system of Subsidiary Alliances, which signed away an Indian state's independence and right of self-defence. The alliance system was advantageous to the British since they could now maintain a large army at the cost of the states themselves. The first Subsidiary Treaty was signed between Wellesley and the Nizam of Hyderabad on 1 September 1798.

The military events outlined in *The Palace of Lost Dreams* in October 1798 are factual. The British Resident, James Kirkpatrick, did send a spy to arrange a mutiny behind French lines on the morning of 21 October and to cut the bullock traces, to prevent the French moving their artillery. My hero, Harry Wyndham, as that spy, is of course fictional.

At dawn on 22 October, the French army awoke to find themselves surrounded. Kirkpatrick promised the mutineers their back pay and future employment in one of the mercenary corps if they began to lay down their arms in the next fifteen minutes. These terms were accepted and within a few hours the largest French force in India was disarmed by the British, who had only a third of their number, without any casualties or a single shot being fired. This turning point, combined with Admiral Nelson's sinking of the French fleet in Aboukir Bay, effectively ruined Napoleon's dreams of India becoming a French colony.

Glossary

abbu –	daddy
abbu-ji –	father (the suffix *ji* denotes respect, as in *Sangita-ji* and *aunty-ji*)
ammi –	mother
ayah –	maid or nursemaid
beti –	daughter, used in the sense of 'dear'
chapatti –	unleavened flatbread
charpai –	bedstead with a woven mattress
dadi-ma –	grandmother
dupatta –	veil or long scarf
feringhi –	foreigner
ghee –	clarified butter
halwa –	a sweet desert made from semolina, grains and nuts
howdah –	a seat for riding on the back of an elephant
idlis –	small cakes or pancakes made from fermented rice batter
jaggery –	a sweet confection made of boiled raw cane sugar
jalebi –	a sweet cake shaped in a spiral and soaked in sugar syrup

maa-ji –	mother
maidan –	soldiers' drill yard
masala dosa –	a crisp pancake with a spicy potato filling
namaste –	a respectful form of greeting
pilkhana –	elephant stables
punkah –	a framed cloth ceiling fan operated by ropes
purdah –	curtain (Persian): the custom of screening women from men behind a curtain
rani –	queen
sahiba –	a respectful term of address for a lady
syce –	a groom

Italy, 1819. Emilia Barton and her mother Sarah live a nomadic existence, travelling from town to town as itinerant dressmakers to escape their past. When they settle in the idyllic coastal town of Pesaro, Emilia desperately hopes that, this time, they have found a permanent home. But when Sarah is brutally attacked by an unknown assailant, a deathbed confession turns Emilia's world upside down.

Seeking refuge as a dressmaker in the eccentric household of Princess Caroline of Brunswick, Emilia experiences her first taste of love with the charming Alessandro. But her troubling history gnaws away at her. Might she, a humble dressmaker's daughter, have a more aristocratic past than she could have imagined?

Caught up in a web of treachery and deceit, Emilia is determined to discover who she really is – even if she risks losing everything . . .

Available now from Piatkus